KT-473-387

Praise for the novels of Anne O'Brien

"An engaging romance with well-developed and fetching characters.
An enjoyable, heart-wrenching read."
—*Booklist*

"O'Brien has excellent control over the historical material
and a rich sense of characterization, making for a
fascinating and surprisingly female-focused look at
one of the most turbulent periods of English history."
—*Publishers Weekly*

"Better than Philippa Gregory."
—*The Bookseller (UK)*

"Anne O'Brien is fast becoming one of Britain's most popular
and talented writers of medieval novels. Her in-depth knowledge
and silky skills with the pen help to bring the past to life and put the
focus firmly on some of history's most fascinating characters."
—Pam Norfolk, *Lancashire Evening Post*

"Anne O'Brien is definitely an author to watch
for historical fiction fans."
—*One More Page…*

The FORBIDDEN QUEEN

ANNE O'BRIEN

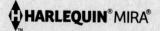 HARLEQUIN® MIRA®

If you purchased this book without a cover you should be aware that this book is stolen property. It was reported as "unsold and destroyed" to the publisher, and neither the author nor the publisher has received any payment for this "stripped book."

Recycling programs
for this product may
not exist in your area.

ISBN-13: 978-0-7783-1431-8

THE FORBIDDEN QUEEN

Copyright © 2013 by Anne O'Brien

All rights reserved. Except for use in any review, the reproduction or utilization of this work in whole or in part in any form by any electronic, mechanical or other means, now known or hereafter invented, including xerography, photocopying and recording, or in any information storage or retrieval system, is forbidden without the written permission of the publisher, Harlequin MIRA, 225 Duncan Mill Road, Don Mills, Ontario M3B 3K9, Canada.

This is a work of fiction. Names, characters, places and incidents are either the product of the author's imagination or are used fictitiously, and any resemblance to actual persons, living or dead, business establishments, events or locales is entirely coincidental.

® and TM are trademarks of Harlequin Enterprises Limited or its corporate affiliates. Trademarks indicated with ® are registered in the United States Patent and Trademark Office, the Canadian Trade Marks Office and in other countries.

For questions and comments about the quality of this book, please contact us at CustomerService@Harlequin.com.

Printed in U.S.A.

To George, as ever, whose knowledge of English medieval history is improving in leaps and bounds.

Genealogy of Owen Maredudd ap Tudor

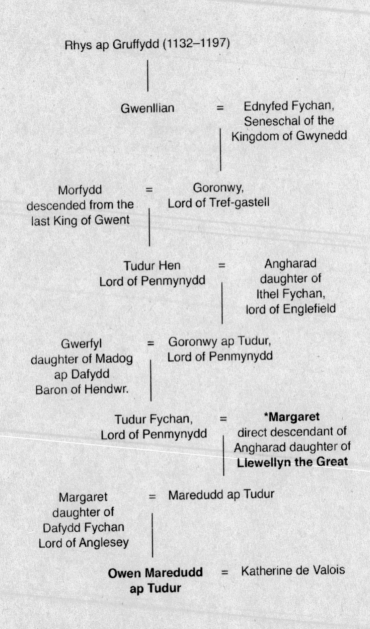

Rhys ap Gruffydd (1132–1197)

Gwenllian   =   Ednyfed Fychan, Seneschal of the Kingdom of Gwynedd

Morfydd descended from the last King of Gwent   =   Goronwy, Lord of Tref-gastell

Tudur Hen Lord of Penmynydd   =   Angharad daughter of Ithel Fychan, lord of Englefield

Gwerfyl daughter of Madog ap Dafydd Baron of Hendwr.   =   Goronwy ap Tudur, Lord of Penmynydd

Tudur Fychan, Lord of Penmynydd   =   ***Margaret** direct descendant of Angharad daughter of **Liewellyn the Great**

Margaret daughter of Dafydd Fychan Lord of Anglesey   =   Maredudd ap Tudur

Owen Maredudd ap Tudur   =   Katherine de Valois

*Margaret's sister **Ellen** was the mother of **Owain Glyn Dŵr**

The Descendants of Katherine de Valois and Owen Tudor and the Start of the Tudor Dynasty.

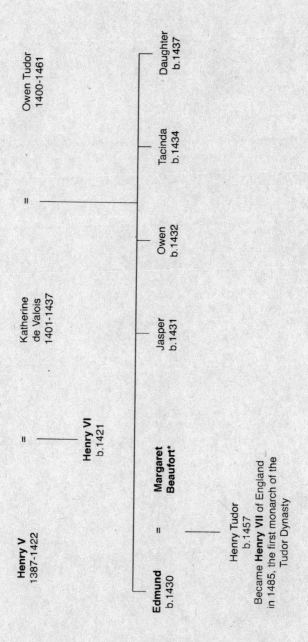

Henry V
1387-1422

=

Katherine
de Valois
1401-1437

=

Owen Tudor
1400-1461

Henry VI
b.1421

Jasper
b.1431

Owen
b.1432

Tacinda
b.1434

Daughter
b.1437

Edmund
b.1430

=

**Margaret
Beaufort***

Henry Tudor
b.1457

Became **Henry VII** of England
in 1485, the first monarch of the
Tudor Dynasty

*See below for Margaret Beaufort royal blood line.

The Descendants of John, Duke of Lancaster (John of Gaunt)

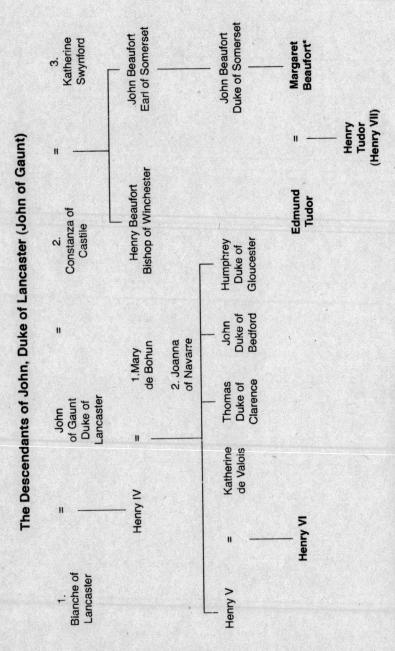

*Margaret Beaufort's royal Beaufort blood line
gave Henry Tudor his claim to the English throne

The
FORBIDDEN
QUEEN

'You have witchcraft in your lips, Kate.'

King Henry to Katherine: Shakespeare's Henry V

'[a woman] unable to curb fully her carnal passions'

Contemporary comment on Katherine de Valois: J. A. Giles,
ed., Incerti scriptoris chronicon Angliae de regnis trium regum
Lancastrensium (1848)

1

IT WAS IN the *Hôtel de St Pol* in Paris, where I was born, that I chased my sister through the rooms of the palace, shrieking like some demented creature in torment. Michelle ran, agile as a hare pursued by a pack of hounds, and because of her advantage of years I was not catching her. She leapt up the great staircase and along a deserted gallery into an antechamber, where she tried to slam the door against me. There was no one to witness our clamorous, unedifying rampage.

I flung back the heavy door so that it crashed against the wall. My breath was short, my side clenched with pain, but my belly was so empty that I would not surrender. I pounded in my sister's wake, triumphant when I heard Michelle whimpering in distress as her feet slid and she cannoned into the corner of a vast oak press set against the wall. From there she lurched into yet another audience chamber, and I howled with imminent victory. There was no way out from that carved and gilded room. I had her. Or, more importantly, I would have what she gripped in her hand.

And there she was, standing at bay, eyes blazing, teeth bared. 'Share it!' I demanded.

When, despite her laboured breathing, she stuffed a piece of bread into her mouth, I sprang at her, and we fell to the floor to roll in a tangle of foul skirts, unwashed legs and greasy, unbraided hair. Teeth and nails were applied indiscriminately, sharp elbows coming into play until, ploughing my fist into Michelle's belly with all my five-year-old weight, I snatched the prize from her. A stale crust and a charred bone of some unidentifiable animal that she had filched from the kitchens when the cook's back was turned. Scrambling up, I backed away, cramming the hard bread into my mouth, sinking my teeth into the flesh on the bone, my belly rumbling. I turned from the fury in her face to flee back the way we had come.

'What's this?'

Despite the mild query, it was a voice of authority who spoke. I pulled up short because my way was barred, yet I would still have fled except that Michelle had crept to my side. In our terrible preoccupation we had not heard the approach, and my heart was hammering so loudly in my ears that I was all but deafened. And there, beating against my temples, was the little pressure, the little flutter of pain, that often afflicted me when I was perturbed.

'Stop that!'

The mildness had vanished, and I stood quietly at last, curt-seying without grace so that I smeared my skirts even more with grease and crumbs. There was no governess to busy her-self about our manners or our education. There was never any money in our household to pay for such luxuries.

'Well?' The King, our father, lifted agitated eyes to the ser-vant who accompanied him.

'Your daughters, Sire,' the man replied promptly, barely respectful.

'Really?' The King blinked at us. Then smiled brightly. 'Come here,' he said, at the same time as he drew a jewelled knife from his belt.

We flinched, our eyes on the blade, where the light slid with evil intent as the King slashed indiscriminately at the space before him. Our father was known to lash out at those nearest to him when the mood was on him, and we were not encouraged even when the servant removed the knife from our father's hand—no cleaner than mine—and tucked the weapon into his own belt. Our father's eyes were alight with a strange, knowing gleam. Unperturbed when I shrank away, he stretched out his hand to lift a lank curl of my hair from where it clung against my neck in matted hanks, like the fleece of a sheep after a long winter. His fingers tightened and I tensed all my muscles, waiting for the pain when he forgot his strength.

'Which one are you?' he asked, gently enough.

'Katherine, Sire.'

'Yes, you would be. You are very small.' He quirked a brow. 'And you?'

'Michelle, Sire.'

'Why are you not at your lessons?'

I slid a glance at Michelle, who simply hung her head. There had been no one to teach us anything for at least a month.

'Well?' A familiar harshness again coloured his demand. 'Cat got your tongue?'

'*Madame*, our governess, has gone away,' I ventured.

'Has she? Who dressed you this morning? No, don't bother to answer that.' The fire in his eyes dimmed as he swung round to address the servant. 'Why are they like this? Little better than animals?'

'There is no one, Sire.'

'Why not? Do they not have their own household? Where are their servants?'

'They too have gone, Sire. They have not been paid for many weeks now.'

The King bent his stare on me. The rapid blinking was unnerving but his question was both lucid and clear. 'What are you hiding behind your back, Katherine?' And when I showed him, he seized my hand and growled, 'When did you last eat—apart from that?'

'Yesterday, Sire.' It was Michelle who answered. Words were beyond me in my fright.

'And you stole the bread and meat? Be silent, both of you!' the King roared before we had even begun to make our excuses, and we were silenced. 'Before God! You're no better than gutter urchins from the Paris stews! I should have you whipped.'

I sidled up to Michelle and clutched at her skirts, almost faint in my terror. Would our father truly beat us for our sin? I let the bread and meat fall to the floor as the trembling in my limbs became uncontrollable. I was never a brave child.

'Where is their mother?' he demanded. The servant shook his head. 'Wait here!'

The King marched from the room, leaving the three of us an uneasy trio. What if he never came back? What if he forgot about us? Yet, indeed, it might be to our advantage if he did. I glanced at Michelle. Should we escape while we had the chance? She shook her head, and so we remained, listening to his footsteps fading into the distance. A little silence fell, broken only by my feet scuffing the floor and Michelle sniffing. The servant sighed heavily. And then in the distance footsteps returned. Our father strode back through the door, bringing a gust of wild, unfettered energy as he circled his arms like the sails of a windmill.

I whimpered.

'Here!' He thrust a goblet, heavy with gold and the glimmer of precious stones, into the servant's hand. 'Sell it!' the King snarled with a show of uneven, discoloured teeth. 'Pay a servant to tend to them. They need food and garments, fitting for my daughters.' He stared down at us for a brief moment, puzzlement in his face, before marching once more from the room.

We were duly fed. I don't recall if we were given new clothes.

So that is what I remember, the most vivid memory of my childhood. The cold, the hunger, the deprivation and neglect. The constant fear. The stark misery, product of the heedlessness of those who were set to care for us. Were Valois princesses allowed to suffer from misery? We were. We wallowed in it. For a little time matters improved for us, but how long could the coin raised by the sale of one gold cup last? Within a matter of weeks the coin had slipped into the hands of the servants and we were as starving and filthy as before as we roamed the palace like lost souls, bellies clapped hard against spines.

Who were we, Michelle and I? Was it accepted that Valois princesses should be raised in such squalor? Even though we were daughters of King Charles and Queen Isabeau, there was no one to plead our cause. Michelle and I were part of a vast family, of six brothers and five sisters, offspring of that most puissant King Charles VI of France and his even more powerful wife, Queen Isabeau of Bavaria.

Vastly fruitful in their marriage, the King and Queen were now estranged beyond repair. We, the younger children, trapped between them, became the victims of their hatred. My brothers were all dead, except for baby Charles, my sisters wed or had taken the veil, and Michelle and I were left to survive the shocking detachment of both parents.

Why should they care so little?

That was easy to understand as we grew older. The King our father suffered from an indisposition, increasing in virulence, that robbed him of his wits. He swung from incomprehension to lucidity, from violence to grinning insouciance, with terrifying regularity. In his worst moments he detested the Queen, hurling abuse and blows indiscriminately. As a wife who shared his bed and his Court, he had cast her off entirely. Some whispered that he had every right.

What scandal reached our ears, with its burden of sin and depravity.

For our mother, robbed of a husband who could be guaranteed to know her name, kept a separate court from our father, where she entertained a procession of lascivious amours. I might be young but the gossip was ribald and indiscreet, the innuendo clear enough to be within my understanding. I might lack a pair of shoes that were not worn through, but the Queen spent money with a lavish hand on her clothes and her courtiers, enjoying a life full of affairs of passion that horrified the courts of Europe.

A woman of outrageous physical need, it was said that she lured an endless stream of handsome, well-born men to warm her sheets. Even, it was whispered, my own father's young brother, Louis of Orléans—until he was done to death by assassins under the orders of John the Fearless, my father's Burgundian cousin. My own little brother Charles, the Dauphin since his brothers' deaths, it was whispered, might not be my father's son.

These were my parents, I their daughter Katherine. What an inheritance for a young girl to shoulder. Madness on one side, wanton lewdness on the other. The lurid rumours filled my young mind. Would I become like Charles and Isabeau? Would I inherit my parents' natures, as I had inherited my mother's fair hair?

'Will I be mad and wicked too?' I whispered to Michelle, naïve and afraid, appalled at the prospect that I would be pointed at, sneered over, ridiculed. I could not bear that.

'I don't see why you should,' she pointed out with good common sense. 'Our sister Marie was born pious—and smug about it. Why else would a woman take the veil? *I* have no intention of running amok or stripping to my shift for every man I see. Why do you think *you* should be tainted with our family shortcomings?'

This comforted me a little, until hunger and neglect forced me once more to acknowledge that my life, my hopes and fears, had no meaning for anyone. Isabeau's reputation might paint her a woman of heat and passion, but none of it ever over-lapped into maternal warmth. With the King enclosed in his chambers, and the Queen engaged in her own pursuits, Mi-chelle and I survived as best we might, like the animals that the King had called us.

Until without warning our mother, Queen Isabeau, de-scended. It was not a happy reunion.

'Holy Mother of God!'

My mother the Queen took one look at us. Even she, after her initial outburst, was silenced. Keeping her distance from the lice and squalor, she issued orders in a tone that brooked no disobedience. We were swept up, as if we ourselves were despised vermin, bundled into cloaks as filthy as we were and packed into a litter. The Queen, understandably, travelled sep-arately and luxuriously in an eye-catching palanquin, whilst Michelle and I huddled in our hard carriage, cold and fright-ened, shivering with fear like a pair of terrified mice since no one had bothered to tell us of our destination. In this manner we, the two youngest of the Valois princesses, were delivered to the convent at Poissy.

'These are the last of my two daughters. I leave them with you. They have sore need of discipline,' the Queen announced on arrival.

It was after dark and the sisters were preparing to attend Compline, so there was no welcome for a child. I was fright-ened into silence. The figures in their white tunics and scap-ulars were ghostly, the Dominican black veils and cloaks threatening to my mind. My sister, smug and pious Marie, might already have taken her vows and be one of these shadowy beings but, so much older than I, I did not know her.

'This is Michelle,' the Queen continued. 'Her marriage is arranged to Philip of Burgundy. Do what you can with her.'

I clutched Michelle's hand, my fears multiplying at the thought of being alone with these magpie-clad creatures in so cold and bleak a place. How could I survive here, alone, when Michelle left to marry? My great-aunt, Marie of Bourbon, Prioress of Poissy, eyed us with chilly hauteur, much like one of my father's raptors.

'They are filthy.' Supercilious, fastidious, her pale eyes flitted over us, disapproving. 'And this one?'

'This is Katherine. She is five years or thereabouts.' Isabeau did not even know my age. 'All I ask is that she be clean and well mannered. Suitable for a bride. There must be some high-blooded prince who will look favourably on her in return for a Valois alliance.'

The Prioress looked at me as if it might be a task beyond her abilities. 'We will do our best for her too,' she announced. 'Does she read? Write?'

'Not that I am aware.'

'She must be taught.'

'Is it necessary? Such skills are irrelevant for her future role, and I doubt she has the mental capacity to learn. Look at her.' The Queen was cruel in her contempt as I snivelled in terror, wiping my face on my sleeve. 'She will be wed for her blood, not for her ability to wield a pen.'

'You would have her remain ignorant?'

'I would not have her made a pedant. As long as she can catch a prince's eye and grace his bed, someone will take her.'

They talked over my head, but I understood the tone of it and cringed from the shame that I knew I must feel. And then, the arrangements at an end, Isabeau looked at me directly for the first time.

'Learn obedience and humility, Katherine. Be a credit to your name. You will be whipped if you choose to run wild here.'

I looked at the floor.

'If you are sullen, who will wed you, Valois or not? No husband wants a sullen wife. And without a husband you will remain here and take the veil with your sister Marie.'

Those were her final words. She left without touching me. I was not sullen, but how could I explain? I dreaded a life I did not know or understand.

I was taken to a cell with Michelle. I could not complain, for we were not separated and it was suitably if sparsely furnished. Were we not princesses? I was given instructions to lie down, not to speak but to go to sleep, to rise the next morning at the bell for Lauds before dawn. My life at Poissy would begin.

And so it did. I lacked for nothing materially in those years. I was scrubbed and fed and given a modicum of instruction, I attended the services and learned to sing the responses. I learned obedience and humility, but no confidence such as blessed Michelle. All in all, it was a life of mind-numbing monotony as the years passed, coupled with anxiety over the strange prince who would one day take me if I proved to be pretty enough and humble enough. It was a cold existence.

'They have need of discipline,' the Queen had said.

And that was what we got. No love. No affection. Great-Aunt Marie's rule was uncompromising, so that living at Poissy for me was like being encased in a stone tomb.

'Which sins have you committed this week, Katherine?' the Prioress asked, as she did every week.

'I broke the Greater Silence, Mother.'

'On one night?'

'Every night, Mother,' I admitted, eyes on the hem of her fine habit.

'And why did you do that?'

'To speak to Michelle, Mother.'

Michelle was my strength and my comfort. My solace. I needed her in the dark hours when the rats pattered over the floor and the shadows encroached. I needed to hear her voice and hold tight to her hand. If I had no confidence as a child, I had no courage either.

The Prioress's white veil shivered with awful indifference to my plight. 'Have you made confession?'

'Yes, Mother.'

'You will spend two hours on your knees before the altar. You will learn the value of the Greater Silence and you will keep the rules. If you persist, Katherine, I will put you in a cell of your own, away from your sister.'

I shuddered, my mind full of the horror of that threatened isolation. I made my penance, my knees sore and my anguish great as I knelt in the silent, dark-shadowed church, but I learned a hard lesson. I never broke the rule again, the fear of separation from Michelle a far greater deterrent than any whipping. My mind did not have the strength to encompass such shattering loneliness. So I did not speak, but I wept silently against Michelle's robust shoulder, until I learned that tears were of no value. There was no escape for us from the dank walls and rigid rules of Poissy.

'You will not speak,' the Prioress admonished. 'Neither do I wish to hear you weeping. Give thanks to God for His goodness in giving you this roof over your head and food in your mouth.'

The silent threat was all too apparent. I wept no more.

Thus was the tenor of my young days as I grew into adolescence, becoming no more poised or self-reliant as the years of my life crawled past. I learned to control my emotions, my features and every word I uttered, in fear that I might give offence. I had no map or chart to guide me in what love, or even affection, might mean. How to measure it, how to respond to it.

How could a child, who had never tasted the warmth of her mother's arms or the casual affection of a father, or even the studied care of a governess, understand the power, the delights of love given freely and unconditionally? I did not know love in all its intricacies.

All that was made plain to me in those years was that to keep my feet on a narrow path and obey the dictates of those in authority over me earned me recognition and, very occasionally, praise.

'I hear that you have learned to play the lute with some minor skill,' the Prioress observed.

'Yes, Mother.' I flushed with pleasure.

'That is good.' She eyed my heated cheeks. 'But pride is a sin. You will say three Aves and a Paternoster before Vespers.'

If I tried hard enough to follow the rules, to live as good a life as the Prioress expected, would I not become a creature worthy of love? Perhaps my father the King would recognise me and lavish affection on me. Perhaps the Queen would grow to love me and smile on me. Perhaps someone would rescue me from Poissy so that I might live as a Valois princess should live, to my immature mind, wrapped around with luxury, with silk robes and a soft bed.

I could never control my dreams of a better future. My heart remained a useless, tender thing, yearning for love, even when my childish dreams of rescue came to naught. For no one came to release me from my convent cell. No viable husband appeared on my horizon, however obedient I might be.

I did not see the Queen again for more years than I could count.

Then, when I was nearing my fifteenth year, Isabeau, our unpredictable and absent mother, found her way back to Poissy. I was summoned to her presence, where I went, drawing on all my hard-learned composure. I no longer had Michelle, now wed to our Burgundian cousin, to stand at my side, and regretted it.

'You have grown, Katherine,' she observed. 'In the circumstances I suppose I must open my coffers for some new garments for you.'

Her gaze travelled over me, from the coarse cloth that strained over my developing body down to the well-worn leather on my feet. Voluptuously plump, her own extravagant curves clothed in silk and damask, the Queen's mouth tightened at the prospect of spending money on any project not for her own pleasure. But then, startling me, she smiled, stepped close and took my chin in her hand, to lift my face to the weak light struggling through the high window slit in the nuns' parlour.

I tried to bear her firm grip and close scrutiny with an inner calm I did not possess. I found that I was holding my breath. Certainly I dared not raise my eyes to her face.

'How old are you now?' she mused. 'Fourteen? Fifteen? Almost a woman grown.' Now I risked a glance. Isabeau had pursed her lips, eyes, always speculative, taking assessment of my features, as her fingers combed through a lock of hair that had strayed from my coif. 'Your features are pure Valois. Not bad on the whole. There is elegance about you I would not have expected.' She smiled a little. 'The colour of your hair is mine—spun gold—and perhaps your nature too will be mine. Should I pity you or commend you?' Her eyes sharpened. 'Yes, it is time that you were wed. And I have a husband in mind for you, if I can catch him and hold him tight. What do you think of that?'

A husband. My eyes widened, a little weight of anticipation settling in my belly like a cup of warm ale on a frosty morning, but since it was entirely a surprise, I could not say what I thought about it. I had expected it, prayed for it to happen one day, but now that the moment had come...

'Do you ever have anything to say, Katherine?' Isabeau asked caustically.

This I considered unfair, since she had had no occasion to ask my opinion on any matter since the day she had delivered me to Poissy. Not that I would dare to give it.

'I would like to be wed,' I managed, as a dutiful daughter must.

'But will you make a good wife? You should be perfect for my purposes. You're pretty enough, your blood is Valois, you're well formed and there's nothing to suggest that you will not be fertile,' she mused as my cheeks flushed. 'It is unfortunate, of course, that he has refused you once.'

'Who has refused me, *maman*?'

'That blood-drenched butcher Henry.'

I blinked, all attention. All shock.

'Henry of England,' Isabeau retorted, as if I were ignorant rather than astonished. 'Your dowry wasn't good enough, high enough, rich enough, for his august consideration.'

This robbed me of all responses. The weight in my chest became a flutter of nerves. I had been offered to the King of England, my dowry negotiated and my hand rejected. All without my knowing.

'The question is, can we change his mind?' She released me

with a snap of her fingers as if she might magic some solution from the cold room.

I was free to step back, away. And did so, but found the words to ask, 'Does he still consider me, if he has refused me once?'

'He wants France,' Isabeau responded willingly enough, as if pleased to have an audience, but the sneer in her voice put me in my place. 'It wasn't enough for him to drain our lifeblood at Agincourt. He wants France for himself and his heirs, by some ancient line of descent from his long-dead Valois ancestress Isabella, who wed an English king.' She turned her stare back on me. 'He offered to wed you but only on condition that you came with two million gold crowns sewn into your shift as your dower. *Two million.*'

So much. My breath slammed into my throat. I could not imagine so many gold coins.

'Am I worth so much, *maman*?' It was beyond belief to me.

'No. Of course you are not. We offered six hundred thousand crowns, and told the English King he was lucky to get as much, considering the state of our finances. So he demanded eight hundred thousand, and a trousseau, but no less. And that was the end of that. We haven't got it, and the King is too witless to be able to don his own hose, much less debate a treaty.'

'So he does not want me.' My hopes, once soaring, now dipped like a summer swallow. 'I will not be Queen of England.'

'You might if we are able to remind him of your existence. So how do we remind your prince, *ma petite*?' Her endearment might be tender but her tone was brittle mockery as she grasped my shoulders and forced me to face her. 'Do we trail you onto a battlefield, so that he might catch a glimpse of your qualities as his sword cuts a vicious path through our French subjects? Or do we exhibit you at a siege, where he can peruse a possible bride on his right while he starves our people to death on his left?' She released me abruptly.

'Sometimes I see no way forward with such a man. But I must be persuasive. We need him. We need him in an alliance with Valois against those who would reduce France to civil war. And perhaps I see a way. We could send him a portrait, so that he can see your prized Valois features for himself, before his eye begins to stray elsewhere.' Isabeau tapped a foot as her gaze once more rested thoughtfully on my face.

Her words sank deep into my mind. If Henry of England looked elsewhere for a bride, what would become of me? The enclosing walls of Poissy loomed higher and colder. Marriage to even a hostile suitor, a man who had spilled French blood without compunction on the battlefield at Agincourt, would have something to recommend it, especially if he were a King and rich. And so I was brave—or desperate—enough to take hold of Isabeau's trailing gilt-embroidered sleeve.

'It would please me to wed Henry of England,' I heard myself say. Even I heard the desperation in my voice. 'If you could remind him of my existence.' I swallowed hard as I saw the disdain for my naïvety in Isabeau's eyes. And without thinking I asked the question that leapt into my mind. A young girl's question. 'Is he young?' And then another. 'Is he good to look at?'

Isabeau shook my hand from her sleeve and walked towards the door, her skirts making a brisk hush of displeasure against the bare boards, so that I regretted my failure to guard my words.

'Foolish questions. You are too importunate, Katherine. No man will wish to wed a woman who steps beyond what is seemly. The King of England will want a quiet, biddable girl.' Her lips stretched from elegant *moue* to implacable line as she considered. 'But perhaps I will send a portrait, and perhaps the outlay for a competent artist will prove worth the spending.' Her lips smiled but her eyes acquired a gleam, like a fisherman planning to outwit a pike that had run him ragged for far too long.

'Perhaps all is not lost and we can still shackle Henry to our side. You might still be the keystone in our alliance, *ma petite* Katherine. Yes.' She smiled, a little more warmly. 'I will arrange it.'

And she did, whilst thoughts of marriage filled my mind.

Why did I want this marriage so very badly? It was more than wealth and rank. Far more. All I knew was that this marriage would be the opening of a door into another world: a world that could not be worse than the one in which I had lived out my childhood.

In truth, I yearned for affection, for love. Why should I not find it with King Henry of England? I cared not if he was as ugly as the devil or the despoiler of our noble French aristocracy on the battlefield. I would be a wife, and Queen of England, and that must be a blessing. Perhaps he would grow to like me, and I to like him.

'Don't give him another thought, Kat,' Michelle remarked on a visit to me—for she did not forget me in her new role of Duchess of Burgundy. 'You've neither seen him nor spoken with him, and he's twice your age. He only asked for you after he asked for our sister Isabella. And then Jeanne. And even Marie.' Michelle ticked the names of our sisters off on her fingers with cynical precision. 'How did *I* manage to escape? Perhaps he did not realise I existed. And now I am no longer available.' Her face was stern with her warning.

'Face it, Kat. Any daughter of France would do for him. It is not a matter of love, but of vainglory. Rejected by Isabella and Jeanne and Marie, conceit will not allow him to be slighted again. That's the only reason he persists—and you are the only princess left.'

There was no arguing against that, but still I clutched at a golden future.

'He'll forget all about you as soon as another candidate is paraded before him.' Michelle completed her destruction. 'He'll not see you, will he, shut away in this place? And even if he did, you're not a desirable object. If we can't offer a dowry closer to the two million gold crowns he demanded, he'll see you as little better than a beggar and reject you out of hand—again. You'll have Isabeau shrieking at you before long that you are of no value to her.'

I sighed, but continued to hug my long-cherished hopes close in the dark hours, where they began as a bright beacon on a hilltop, but gradually dwindled to a weakly flickering candle flame as the weeks passed and there was no news. Forlornly I considered my situation. Isabeau would be angry because I had failed to catch Henry's interest. Even worse—far, far worse to my mind—was the thought that Henry did not want me. It seemed that the convent doors were preparing to slam shut, to close me in for ever.

To my relief Isabeau did not descend on Poissy to vent her fury, but the portrait did. I saw it, because Michelle brought it to me, before it was swathed in soft leather to protect it from weather and sea water on its journey, and was truly appalled. The artist was either lacking in talent or had been paid too little. The long Valois features were there right enough, and not beyond liking, for my oval face was not uncomely, my neck had a certain poise. But my lovely hair was completely bundled up and obscured by a headdress with padded rolls over deep crispinettes, the whole structure made complete with a short muslin veil that neither flattered nor seductively con-

cealed. As for my skin, always pale, it had been given more
than a touch of the sallow. My lips were a thin slash of paint
and my brows barely visible.

Michelle gasped.

'Is it so bad?' I asked uncertainly, knowing that it was.

'Yes. Look at it!' She stalked to the window embrasure and
held up the offending article. 'That ill-talented dabbler in
paint has made you look as old as our mother. Why couldn't
he make you young and virginal and appealing?'

I looked at it through Michelle's eyes rather than my own
hopeful ones. 'I look like an old hag, don't I?' My silent plea
to the Virgin was impassioned.

*Holy Mother. If Henry of England does not like my face, may he
at least see the value of my Valois blood.*

And how did my erstwhile suitor receive my portrait? I
never knew, but I was informed by the Prioress that my days
at Poissy were numbered.

'You will leave within the month.' Great-Aunt Marie's manner was no more accommodating than on the first day that I
had stepped over the threshold. But I no longer cared. That
new life was approaching fast.

'Yes, Mother.'

'King Henry has made a vow to wed you.'

'I am honoured, Mother.' My voice trembled as I shook
with a new emotion.

'It is a political alliance. You must play your part to chain
Henry to Valois interests.'

'Yes, Mother.' One day soon I would wear fur-edged sleeves
far richer than those of Great-Aunt Marie.

'I trust that you will take to your marriage the attributes
you have learned here at Poissy. You training here will be the
bedrock on which to build your role as Queen of England.'

'Yes, Mother.'

Bedrock. Role. Chaining Henry to Valois interests. It meant nothing to me. I could barely contain my thoughts, or the smile that threatened to destroy the solemnity of the occasion. I would be a bride. I would be Henry's wife. My heart throbbed with joy and I hugged Michelle when next I could.

'He wants me! Henry wants me!'

She eyed me dispassionately. 'You are such a child, Katherine! If you're expecting a love match, it will not happen.' Her voice surprised me with its harshness, even when, at the distress she must have seen on my face, her eyes softened. 'We do not deal in love, Katherine. We marry for duty.'

Duty. A cold, bleak word. Much like indifference. Foolish as it might be, I was looking for love in my marriage, but I would not display my vulnerability, even to Michelle.

'I understand,' I replied solemnly, repeating the Prioress's bleak words. 'Henry will wed me to make a political alliance.'

And in truth doubts had begun to grow, for there had been no gifts, no recognition of King Henry's new-kindled desire for me as his wife, not even on the feast of St Valentine when a man might be expected to recall the name of the woman he intended to wed. There were even rumours that he was still looking to the royal families of Burgundy and Aragon, where there were marriageable girls on offer. How could that be? I think I flounced in sullen misery. My Burgundy cousins, the daughters of Duke John, were inarguably plain, and surely the Aragon girls could not be as valuable as I to the English King's plans to take Europe under his thrall.

I offered a fervent rosary of Aves and Paternosters that the portrait had been more flattering than I recalled to fix me in his mind, and that he would make his choice before I became too old and wizened to be anyone's bride. Before I became too old to covet sleeves edged with finest sables.

★ ★ ★

'Is the English King young? Is he good to look at?' I had asked the Queen.

Now I knew.

King Henry took my breath. I saw him before he saw me. King Henry the Fifth of England, in all his glory. There he stood, alone in the very centre of the elaborate pavilion, quite separate from the two English lords who conversed in low voices off to one side. Oblivious to them, and to us—the French party—hands fisted on his hips and head thrown back, Henry's eyes were fixed on some distant place in his mind, or perhaps on the spider weaving its web into one of the corners between pole and canvas. He remained motionless, even though I suspected that he knew we had arrived.

For his own reasons, he made no effort to either acknowledge us or to impress us with his graciousness. Even his garments and jewels, heavy with symbolism, were worn with a cold insouciance. Why would he need to impress us? We were the supplicants after all, he the victor.

But what a presence he had. Even the magnificent pavilion with its cloth of gold and bright banners was dwarfed by the sheer magnetism of the man. His was the dominant personality: the rest of us, English and French alike, need not have been there. I was filled with awe. And a bright hope. I had anticipated this meeting for three years. I was eighteen years old when I finally met the man I would wed, if all things went to plan, in that splendid canvas-hung space on the banks of the Seine at Meulan.

On one side of me stood Queen Isabeau, resplendent in velvet and fur, accompanied by a sleek and powerful leopard, a hunting cat and not altogether trustworthy, held on a tight rein by a nervous page. King Henry might not see the need to impress, but Queen Isabeau did.

On my left was my second cousin, John, Duke of Burgundy, thus buttressing me with royal power and approval. Duke John was sweating heavily in his formal clothing with its Burgundian hatchings.

My father, who should have led the exchange of offers, was not present, having been deemed mad today, attacking with tooth and nail the body servants who had attempted to clothe him for this occasion. They had given up and my mother had taken command of the proceedings, leaving my father locked in a room at Duke John's headquarters in Pontoise.

Finally, behind us, filling the entrance to the pavilion, was the necessary pack of soldiers and servants clad in Valois colours to give us some semblance of regal authority, the vividly blue tabards imprinted with enough silver fleurs-de-lys to make my head swim. We needed every ounce of authority we could fashion out of defeat and lure this English king into some manner of agreement before we were entirely overrun by English forces.

And I? I was the tender morsel to bait the trap.

We must have made a noise—perhaps it was the leopard that hissed softly in its throat—or perhaps King Henry simply felt the curiosity of my gaze, for he abandoned the spider to its own devices, turned his head and stared back. His gaze was cool, his face unresponsive to the fact that every eye was on him, his spine as rigid as a pikestaff. And then there was the scar. I had not known about the scar that marked the hollow between nose and cheek. But it was not this that took my eye. It was the quality of his stare, and I felt my blood beat beneath my skin as he made no gesture to respond to our arrival. His appraisal of me was unflatteringly brief, before moving smoothly on to Duke John and Isabeau.

Well, if he would not look at me, I would look at him. I knew he was thirty-two years of age because my mother had so informed me. Much older than I, but he carried the years well. He was tall—taller than I, which I noted with some degree of satisfaction—tall enough to handle the infamous Welsh longbow with ease, a man who would not feel a need to be resentful of a woman who could cast him in the shade. He was fair skinned with a straight blade of a nose.

Surprisingly to me, his physique was slender rather than muscular—I had expected a more robust man for so famous a soldier—but I decided there might be hidden strength in the tapering fingers that were clenched around his sword belt. Did he not have a reputation for knightly skills and personal bravery? And also for exceptional manners, but not at this moment, for the hazel gaze, as bright as a tourmaline, returned and fixed once more on my face. He did not make me feel welcome to this meeting of high diplomacy where my future would be decided. He was assessing me as he might have assessed the merits of a mare for sale.

In that moment it seemed to me that his appraisal and manner were quite as careless of my person and my predicament as Great-Aunt Marie's.

A little frisson of awareness touched my nape. This was a man with a high reputation, a man who could grind us into dust if he so desired. I must play my part and make an impression as a princess of Valois, even though a breath of fear flirted along the skin of my forearms like summer lightning.

Willing courage into my bones, I locked my eyes with his even as my knees trembled at my presumption, until Duke John cleared his throat, like an order given to commence battle. The two English lords abandoned their deliberations, while Henry turned full face—and Isabeau stiffened at my side. I wondered why, noting the direction of her interest, and that her finely plucked brows had drawn down into the closest she would dare come to a diplomatic scowl.

I followed her stare, curious, and understood. My mother was rigid with fury, not because of the ostentatious wealth of the rubies, as large as pigeon's eggs in the chain resting on King Henry's breast and the opulence of the trio of similar stones, blinding in the sun, which he wore on the fingers of his right hand. Not even because of the golden lions of England that sprang from two of the quarters on his heavily embroidered thigh-length tunic, although they were heraldically threatening enough. It was the fleurs-de-lys of France, silver on blue, a mirror image of our own livery, that occupied the two counterposed quarters on Henry's impressive chest, shouting to all the world that this man claimed our French Crown as confidently as he claimed his own. He had claimed it before we had even taken our seats to discuss the delicate matter. I had been wrong. He was without doubt here to make an impression after all, but not to win friends, only to ensure that he cowed us into submission before a word had been exchanged.

As I heard Isabeau's sharp inhalation and saw the barely disguised disdain in her face, I understood that this negotiation might still come to nought. I might still not reach the altar as a bride.

Holy Virgin, let him want me enough to accept a compromise. Let him want me enough to accept my mother's concessions. Make my mother compliant enough to offer concessions.

The two English lords were approaching.

'The Duke of Bedford,' Duke John muttered sourly out of the corner of his mouth. 'The King's brother. The other's the Earl of Warwick—another bloody puissant lord.'

But at least they granted us that belated welcome, speaking in French for our comfort and my unspoken gratitude, for my English was not good beyond commonplace greetings.

Lord John, Duke of Bedford, brother to the magnificent Henry, bowed and introduced us to Henry of England.

'*La reine Isabeau de France. Et sa fille, Mademoiselle Katherine.*'

And the Earl of Warwick gestured us forward, his hand hard on the collar of a wolfhound that had taken fierce exception to the presence of the leopard.

'*Bienvenue, monsieur, mes dames…*' continued Lord John. '*Votre présence parmi nous est un honneur.*'

A flurry of bowing and curtseying.

'*Bienvenue, Mademoiselle Katherine,*' Lord John encouraged me, smiling with a friendly gleam in his eye, and I found myself smiling back. So this was the Duke of Bedford, whose reputation was almost as formidable as King Henry's. I liked his fair face and amiable features. I liked it that he had taken the trouble to speak to me and put me at my ease, as much as it was possible, even though my heart continued to gallop.

His brother, the King, took no such trouble. King Henry still did not move, except for a furrow growing between his well-marked brows. So he was frowning at us, and his voice, clear and clipped, cut through the formal greetings.

'We did not expect you to arrive quite yet.'

And he spoke in English. The frown, I decided, was not for me but for his brother's kindness. This haughty King intended to speak in English, forcing us to struggle in a language in which not one of us was able to converse equably. He looked us over, chin raised in chilly superiority, while my mother, glorious with a gold crown and jewelled fingers, stiffened even further under the scrutiny. Could my heart beat any harder, without stopping altogether? This was going from bad to worse, and King Henry had yet to exchange one word with me.

'We understood that you wished to begin negotiations immediately,' Isabeau replied curtly, in French.

'Is the King not present with you?' Henry demanded, in English.

'His Majesty is indisposed and rests at Pontoise,' Isabeau responded, in French. 'His Grace of Burgundy and I will conduct negotiations in His Majesty's name.'

'It is my wish to communicate with His French Majesty.' Henry, in English.

I sighed softly, overwhelmed by despair at the impasse. Was King Henry truly so insufferably arrogant?

The King waited with a shuttered expression. Warwick shuffled, his hand still firmly on the hound's collar, Bedford studied the floor at his feet, neither one of them venturing into French again. It could not have been made clearer to us that the English King's word was law. And there we stood, silence stretching out between Henry and Isabeau, until, in the interest of diplomacy, Duke John jettisoned his pride and translated the whole into Latin.

Finally, drawing me forward into his direct line of sight, he added, 'We wish to present to you, Your Majesty, the lady Katherine.'

And I stepped willingly enough, glowing with female pride, for they had truly slain the fatted calf for me. I had no need to feel shamed by my appearance on that day. I was the one bargaining point we Valois had, and Duke John—not my mother, of course—had decided that I was worth some outlay. More coin than I had ever imagined in my life, the vast sum of three thousand florins, had been spent on my appearance. I prayed I would be worth it as I breathed shallowly, my palm damp with nerves within my cousin's heavy clasp.

And so, splendid in my fur-edged sleeves at last, I made my first curtsey to Henry of England.

I had a price to pay for my moment of glory. It was all very well to dress me as if I were already Queen of England, but in a hot tent on a sultry day in May, I was as heated as if I were labouring in the royal kitchens.

The heart-shaped headdress that confined all my hair sat heavily on my brow like a boiled pudding, the short veiling clinging damply to my neck. The folds of the houppelande, quite beautiful and as blue as the Virgin's robe, furred and embroidered and belted beneath my breast with a jewelled girdle, were so heavy that trickles of sweat ran down my spine. But I braced myself against the discomfort.

I suppose I looked well enough, a true princess, as I lifted my skirts a little way with my free hand to exhibit the pleated under-tunic of cloth of gold. All very fine—except that it was all outward show. My linen shift was old and darned and rough against my naked flesh. My shoes let in the damp from the dew-laden grass. The florins had not run to new shoes or undergarments, but the King would not notice that beneath my magnificently trailing skirts and jewelled bodice.

King Henry took in my glory, sleeves and all, in one comprehensive, dismissive glance.

'We are gratified,' he said, but still in English. 'We have long wished to meet the princess of France, of whom we have heard so much.' And he bowed to me with impeccable grace, his hand on his heart.

'*Monseigneur.*' Now that I was face to face with him, almost within touching distance of those snarling leopards on his tunic, any initial courage fled. I sank into a second low curtsey, because he seemed to expect it of me, my eyes, cravenly, on the floor until I felt a stir of air, heard a foot fall, and the soft boots that he wore came into my vision. His hand was stretched down to me.

'My lady. You must stand.'

It was gently said, yet undeniably a command. I placed my hand in his and he drew me to my feet. Leaning a little, in formal recognition, he lightly kissed me on one cheek and then the other. And then on my mouth with the softest pressure of his own. My heart fluttered. Blushing from throat to hair-line, I felt the blood run hot under my skin as his lips brushed against me and his battle-rough palms were firm against mine. All I could think was: King Henry has kissed me in greeting. I stared at him, no words coming to those lips he had just saluted.

'The rumours of your beauty do not lie, Lady.' He led me a little distance away from our audience, his voice warming as he did so. 'Now I can see for myself the value of the gift that the House of Valois would make to me.'

This was undoubtedly a compliment, but his face was so stern. Did Englishmen not smile? I struggled with the English, embarrassingly tongue-tied, searching for a suitable reply.

'Do you speak English?' he asked, when I failed.

'Only a little, *Monseigneur*,' I managed, with what I must presume was an appalling accent. 'But I will learn more.'

'Of course you will,' he affirmed. 'It is imperative that you do.'

'I swear I will practise every day,' I replied, unnerved by the seriousness of his response.

But Henry's interest had moved from my lack of linguistic skill as his eyes fell from my face to the bodice of my gown where a gold-mounted sapphire was pinned at my neckline.

'What is it, my lord?' I asked anxiously: the frown was back.

'The brooch.'

'Yes, my lord? It is a gift from Duke John, to honour the occasion.'

'Where is the gift I sent you?' he demanded.

I shook my head in incomprehension. Seeing it, Henry condescended to address me in fluent court Latin. 'I thought you might have worn the brooch, *Mademoiselle*.' A rank chill drew all colour from his tone.

'Which b-brooch, my lord?' I stammered.

'I sent you a brooch as a token of my regard. A lozenge with a fleur-de-lys set in gold with rubies and amethysts.'

'I did not receive it, my lord.'

The frown deepened. 'It was a costly item. A hundred thousand ecus, as I recall.'

What could I say? 'I do not have it, my lord. Perhaps it was lost.'

'As you say. Perhaps it fell into the hands of my enemies. I expect it graces the war coffers of the Dauphinists, your brother's misguided supporters who would fight against me.'

'So I expect, my lord.'

It was a strangely unsettling conversation, leaving me with the thought that it was the value of the lost gift that concerned him more than the failure of it to reach me and give me pleasure. The English King was obviously displeased. I risked a glance, wondering what he would say next, but the matter of jewellery had been abandoned.

'I have been waiting for you all my life, Katherine. It is my intention to wed you,' he announced with cool and precise diction. 'You will be my wife.'

He did not ask if I would be willing. We both knew I would follow the dictates of my family. But still I responded from my heart.

'Yes, my lord. And I would wish it too.'

And as he raised my hand to his lips, in a neat gesture of respect, Henry smiled at me at last, a smile such as a man might use towards the woman he had an admiration for, a woman he might hold in some affection. A woman, I thought, whom he might actually come to love. The austere planes of his face softened, his eyes gentled. In that moment his simple acceptance of me overwhelmed me and I sank into admiration for this beautiful man. I returned his smile, my cheeks still flaming with colour.

'Katherine,' he murmured. His English pronunciation made of it a caress.

'Yes, my lord?'

He is not harsh, I thought, seduced by the power of his proximity, the allure of his direct gaze, he is not cold. He is handsome and potent and he wants me as his wife. I was, I decided, sliding into love with him, so easily, and when Henry kissed my cheek again, and then the palm of my right hand, my heart leapt with joy, imagining the picture we must present to our noble onlookers, the King of England treating me, the youngest of the Valois daughters, with such gallantry.

'I must send you another jewel,' he said.

'And I will take great care of it,' I replied.

A sudden outburst of animal temper thrust between us, and we turned to where the Valois leopard bared its fangs at the English hound that now lunged, barking furiously, drowning out any stilted conversation between their owners. I flinched away, but Henry abandoned me and strode forward.

'Take them out!' he snapped, his curt English harsh with irritation. 'Who in their right minds would bring a hunting cat to a formal negotiating table? That is the end of proceedings for today. We will begin tomorrow at dawn, with no distractions of any nature.'

Whether we fully understood or not, the meaning was clear. Henry bowed with magnificent condescension and strode from the pavilion, followed by Warwick and the recalcitrant hound. But my lord of Bedford stayed behind and walked towards me.

'There is nothing to fear, my lady,' he said softly in French.

I did not know whether he meant from the animals or from his brother.

'Thank you, my lord.' I said. And I meant it. His assurance was a soothing gesture after Henry's abrupt departure.

Thus my wooing at Meulan left me in a muddle of heaving emotion. Here was a man who did not dislike me, who would make me Queen of England. Could he perhaps come to love me? Only time would tell. If I was to be the prize to draw Henry back to the negotiating table, then so be it. It pleased me well enough.

I touched my fingertips to my lips where he had kissed me.

Could I love a man I had met only once in my life? It appeared that I could, if admiration and a trembling of the heart signified love. He had cast an enchantment over me, simply by smiling at me and calling me by my name. The scar of some old wound did nothing to mar his beauty. To me, he was everything I had dreamed of.

A Queen of England must be able to speak the language of her husband's subjects. Had not Henry commanded me to learn? I applied myself to conversation with one of my father's household who had more than a few basic words to string together, encouraged by the thought that perhaps it would win some commendation from my betrothed. Perhaps he would smile at me again.

'Good morning, my lord. I hope you are in health.' Or I might ask him: 'Do you hunt today, my lord? I would wish to accompany you.' Or even: 'Do you admire this new gown that I am wearing? I think it is very fine.' My adeptness at politics was less sure, but I could ask: 'Do we welcome the French ambassador to our Court today? Will there be a celebratory feast?' When my clumsy Gallic tongue had difficulties with celebratory, my impatient tutor, a young lad of fewer years than my own, suggested festive, which I could manage. I even became proficient in the crucial phrase: 'I will be honoured, Majesty, to accept your hand in marriage.'

'He will take you,' Isabeau declaimed with clenched jaw. 'I will not let this alliance escape.' Black anger shook her. Now removed from Poissy and based in Paris, back in the *Hôtel de St Pol*, I kept out of her way.

And then, miraculously, out of nowhere:

'It is decided. Your dower will be without rival. He'll take you.'

A golden cloud of conviction hovered over the Queen's brow. She even touched my cheek with what could have been a caress. I watched her warily from where I sat on my bed. All I could recall was that our previous dower offer had fallen far short of matching the English King's demand, so why should Isabeau's new planning be any better? We had even less money at our disposal since Henry controlled all trade routes in the north of France, so that our royal coffers rattled in emptiness.

'Why will Henry take me?' I asked.

'I've made him an offer that he would be a fool to refuse. And he is no fool.' And when I looked justifiably baffled, Isabeau's glance slid to mine with sly satisfaction. 'He will take you because when he does, he will get the Crown of France as well.' Pausing, to make an impression—and succeeding—she added, '*That* will be the dower carried by your royal blood, *ma petite*. Not a coffer full of gold coin but the Crown of France. How can he argue against that?'

I was stunned, as if the Crown of France had dropped from the ceiling to land at my feet. This was mine, to take with me as a dower to my husband? My new silk-lined bodice—Isabeau was spending some money on me at last—suddenly felt too tight. The mirror I had been holding fell from my hand, fortunately onto the trailing hem of the blue damask to save it from harm. Could Isabeau actually do this? As I retrieved my mirror, my hands trembled with the enormity of what she had done.

'Will my father allow it?' I gasped.

'Your father will have nothing to say in the matter. How should he? He hasn't the wits to string two words together.'

So she had taken the decision on her own authority. 'You will disinherit my brother Charles?'

'Without compunction.' Her strong hands closed on my shoulders, and with only the barest hesitation she kissed me lightly, unexpectedly, on each cheek. 'You carry all our hopes, Katherine. He will not refuse you now. How could he, when you hold his heart's desire in your pretty hands? He wants the French Crown—and this is how he can get it without spilling one more drop of blood, English or French. He will smile all the length of the aisle to the high altar where you will stand with him and exchange your vows.' Her smile grew.

'You will present yourself in the audience chamber within the hour, and there we will discuss exactly how you will conduct yourself when you meet with Henry of England. Nothing—absolutely *nothing*, Katherine—must be allowed to stand in the way of this alliance. You will be the perfect bride.'

Her conviction as she strode from the room was a magnificent thing. And so was the implied threat, so that I subsided into an inelegant heap on my bed, careless of any damage to the fine cloth. All my tentative delight in this marriage drained away as her words struck home. Of course he would accept me, and not for my face and virginal hair, my becoming gown or because I could say 'Good morrow, my lord!' in English. He would accept me if I were in my dotage with a face as creased as a walnut.

What had Isabeau said? Henry would be a fool to refuse me, and he was no fool. Who would refuse a Valois princess who came with the whole extent of her country as her dower? For the first time in my life I felt compassion for Charles, who would be heir no longer.

I thought, sardonically, that I must start my English lessons again.

My lord, I am honoured that you will stoop to wed me, so unworthy as I am. But I do bring with me an inestimable gift.

Hopeless!

As I informed Michelle, who came to commiserate. 'Henry will not care whether I can speak with him or not. I could be the ugliest of old crones, and he would accept me. He would wed me if he found me on my deathbed.'

Michelle hugged me. 'He won't want an ugly old crone, Kat. He needs a young wife to carry a son for him.' She pushed a ring, its dark stone encased in gold, glowing with untold powers, onto the forefinger on my right hand. 'Wear this, a beryl to guard against melancholy and poison. And remember me when you are Queen of England, for who's to say that we will meet again?'

And that was no comfort to me at all.

Within the week I received a gift from my betrothed, which this time found its way into my hands: a formal portrait of the King of England in an intricately worked gilded frame, set around with enamelling and precious stones. I studied it, allowing the soft wrappings to fall to the floor.

'Now, why do you suppose he has sent me this?' I asked Michelle.

'To impress you?'

'He doesn't have to.'

'To remind you how imperious he is?'

'I have not forgotten that.'

I held the painting at arm's length, perplexed. I knew what he looked like, so why reacquaint me with it? He had no need to win my hand or my admiration. I would do as I was told.

So why this little masterpiece of artistry? With it came a folded piece of manuscript.

'Read it for me,' I said, as Michelle's learning was a good few steps above mine. All I had ever absorbed at Poissy had been the ability to pluck a semblance of a tune from the strings of a lute.

'"*To the Princess Katherine. In expectation of our imminent marriage,*"' Michelle read. 'It is signed by Henry too.'

A nice thought. I carried it to the light to inspect it further. It was a fine representation of Henry in profile, and one I could endorse, as I had seen much of Henry's profile at our only meeting: a high brow; a straight nose; a dark, level gaze. The artist had caught the heavy eyelids and the well-marked winging brows. He had captured the firm lips, a little full, leaving the viewer with the impression of an iron will, but with a hint of passion too perhaps. And the wealth. The importance.

The portrait left no stone unturned to announce the man's superiority. A gold collar, rings and jewelled chain, the glimpse of a paned sleeve in figured damask. It was impressive.

I touched the painted surface with my fingertip, wishing not for the first time that he smiled more readily. But, then, neither had I in my portrait. I smiled at his painted features, encouraged by what I had just noticed.

'Well? What do you think?' Michelle asked, tilting her head to see what had made me smile.

'I think he is a man who knows his own mind. He is very proud.' And I held the portrait up for her to see more clearly. The artist had left out the scar on his face. And was that very bad? It made him appear very human to me. Perhaps he had sent the little painting because he simply wanted to acknowledge me as his new wife, giving me ownership of a very personal likeness. If so, it hinted at a depth of kindness beneath the austere exterior. I hoped that Isabeau was wrong. I hoped that I meant something more to King Henry than a means to a political end, a living and breathing title deed to the Kingdom of France. 'I like him,' I said simply.

'And I think that you must grow up quickly, Kat. Or you might get hurt.'

I did not listen. There was no room for any emotion in my heart but joy.

2

I MADE IT to the altar at last in spite of all obstacles. Henry Plantagenet waited there for me, regally magnificent.

'My lady Katherine.' He welcomed me with a chivalric bow. 'I rejoice. You are even more beautiful than my memory recalled. Your new English subjects will honour my choice of bride.'

His words were formal, but I could not doubt the admiration in his gaze. Clothed in a cloth-of-gold bodice, I allowed myself to feel beautiful, my body transformed by Isabeau's tirewomen into a royal offering fit for a King. I was scoured from head to toe, my hair washed and brushed until it drifted like a fall of pure silk. My brows plucked, my nails pared, my skin cleansed with tincture of cowslip to remove any hint of a freckle, I was polished and burnished until I glowed like a silver plate for Henry's delectation. Beneath a translucent veil my hair spread over my shoulders, as brightly gold as the cloth beneath, proclaiming my virginity to God and the high blood of England and France.

Thus arrayed, I stood before the altar in the Church of St John in Troyes, my hand enclosed in that of Henry of England. His clasp was firm, his expression grimly austere as we faced the bishop, but perhaps he was simply preoccupied with the solemnity of the occasion.

Intense cold rose up from the floor and descended from the roof beams and I shivered with it. Henry's hand around mine too was cold, and I was trembling so hard that I thought the whole congregation must see it, my veil shivering before my eyes like sycamore flowers in a stiff breeze. Oh, I had no fear of his rejection at this eleventh hour. When Henry had been required to place on the bishop's missal the customary sum of thirteen pence, in symbolic payment from the groom for his bride, my eyes had widened as a stream of gold coins had slid from his hand. Thirteen gold nobles, so vast a sum. But, then, perhaps thirteen gold nobles was a small price to pay for the Kingdom of France.

Another shiver shook me from head to foot.

'There's no need to tremble,' he whispered as the bishop took a breath. 'There's nothing to fear.'

'No,' I whispered back, glancing up, grateful for the reassurance, pleased that he was smiling down at me. How considerate he was of my apprehension. Of course he would understand that a young girl raised in a convent would be overawed.

The bishop beamed at us. Turning to Henry, the phrases rolled around us.

'*Vis accípere Katherine, hic praeséntem in tuam legítimam uxórem juxta ritum sanctae matris Ecclésiae?*'

'*Volo.*'

There was not one moment of hesitation; neither was there any lover-like glance in acknowledgement of our union. Staring straight ahead as if sighting an enemy army approaching over a hill, hand still gripping mine, Henry made his response so firmly that it echoed up into the vaulting above our heads, to return a thousand times.

'*Volo, volo, volo.*'

It rippled along my arms, down the length of my spine.

Henry was as proud as a raptor, an eagle, his response a statement of ownership, of both me and of his new inheritance.

I swallowed against the rock that had become lodged in my throat. My mouth was so dry that I feared I would be hopelessly silent when my moment came, and my mind would not stay still, but danced like a butterfly on newly dried wings over the disconcerting facets of my marriage.

The royal Valois crown was my dowry. Henry would become the heir of France. The right to rule France would pass to our offspring—Henry's and mine—in perpetuity as the legitimate successors. I had been handed to him on a golden salver with the whole Kingdom of France in my lap for him to snatch up. My Valois blood was worth a king's ransom to him.

The butterfly alighting for a brief moment, I glanced across at Henry. Even he, a past master as he was at the art of cold negotiation, could not govern his features enough to hide the glitter of victory as he took the vow.

The bishop, who was staring encouragingly at me, coughed. Had he been addressing me? I forced myself to concentrate. Within the half-hour I would be Henry's wife.

'*Vis accípere Henry, hic praeséntem in tuum legítimum marítum juxta ritum sanctae matris Ecclésiae?*'

I ran my tongue over my dry lips.

'*Volo.*'

It was clear, not ringing as Henry's response but clear enough. I had not shamed myself or the decision that had been made in my name. Many of the French nobility would wish that it had never come to pass. When my mother had offered me and the French Crown in the same sentence, there had been a sharp inhalation from the Valois court. But to save face, to dilute the shame of deposing the reigning King, my father was to wear the crown for the rest of his natural life. A sop to some, but a poor one.

The bishop's voice, ringing in triumph, recalled me once more to the culmination of that hard bargaining.

'*Ego conjúngo vos in matrimónium. In nomine Patris, et Fílii, et Spíritus Sancti.* Amen.'

All done. Henry and I were legally bound. As the musicians and singers, lavishly paid for and brought all the way from England by Henry, began a paean of praise, and we turned to face the congregation, the clouds without grew darker, and rain began to beat against the great west window.

I shivered, denying that it was a presentiment of things to come, as, perhaps in impatience to get the business finished, Henry's hand held mine even tighter and I slid a glance beneath my veil. Not an eagle, I decided, but a lion, one of his own leopards that sprang on his breast. He positively glowed, as well he might. This was a triumph as great as Agincourt, and I was the prize, the spoils of war, giving Henry all he had hoped for.

There would still be war of course. My brother Charles, the Dauphin, and his supporters would never bend the knee. Did my new husband realise that? I was sure he did, but for now Henry, head held high, looked as if he were King of all the world. And in that moment realisation came to me. I, the much-desired bride, was not the centrepiece of this bright tapestry. Henry was the focus of attention, the cynosure for all present, and so it would always be in our marriage.

'You're trembling again,' Henry said quietly.

The nerves in my belly tensed, leapt. I had not expected him to speak to me as he led me down the aisle to the great west door; his eye was still quartering the congregation, as if searching out weaknesses on a battlefield.

'No,' I denied. I stiffened my muscles, holding my breath— but to no avail. 'Yes,' I amended. He would know that I was lying anyway.

'Are you afraid?' he asked.

'No,' I lied again.

'No need. This will soon be over.'

This increased my fear tenfold, for then I would be alone with him. 'I'm just cold,' I said.

And at that moment a break in the clouds allowed a shaft of pure gold to strike through the window to our right as if a blessing from God. It engulfed him in fire, glittering over the jewelled chain that lay on his breast. The leopards flexed their golden muscles as he breathed and his dark hair shone with the brilliance of a stallion's coat. The light glimmering along the folds of my veil were of nothing in comparison.

He was magnificent, and I found that I was clinging to his hand with a grip like that of a knight upon his sword. Henry, reading the apprehension in my face and in my grip on him, smiled, all the severity vanishing.

'A cup of wine will warm you.' The hard contours of his face softened. 'It is done at last,' he said, and raised my fingers to his mouth. 'You are my wife, Katherine, and my Queen, and I honour you. It is God's will that we be together.' And there in the centre of the church with every eye on us, he kissed my mouth with his. 'You have made me the happiest man in the world.'

My trembling heart promptly melted in the heat of flame, and I could feel the blood beating through me, to my finger-tips, to the arches of my feet. Surprising me, a little bubble of joy grew in my belly, stirred into life by no more than a salute to my hand and lips from the man at my side, and I felt happy and beautiful and desired.

Beguiled by the idea that I was Henry's wife and he had honoured me before all, I smiled on the massed ranks as we passed them, confidence surging within me. I would never feel unworthy or unwanted or neglected again, for Henry had rescued me and given me a place in his life and in his kingdom.

We waited at the point where, the arches soaring above us, the chancel crossed into the nave of the church. Behind us the procession of English and Valois notables took its time in beginning to form, allowing us a few words.

'England waits to greet her new Queen,' Henry said, nodding towards a face he recognised to his left.

'I hope to see England soon,' I replied, relieved that my voice was quite calm with no hint of the sudden dread that gripped me that I would have to live in England, a country I knew nothing of, with people who were strangers to me. My overwhelming happiness had been short-lived indeed.

'You will enjoy the welcome I have prepared for you. You will be fêted from one end of the country to the other.'

Turned back from the crowd to me, his face was illuminated by his smile. Handsome in feature, power rested on his shoulders as easily as a summer-weight silk cloak. But what did he see in me? What would he wish to see in me? With what I hoped was intuition, I lifted my chin with all the pride and dignity of a Queen of England, and smiled back.

'Thank you, my lord,' I replied. And in the light of his obvious pleasure, a newborn certainty that Henry would care for me and protect me from my inexplicable anxieties, prompted me to add, 'And thank you for the gift, sir. I value it. It was very kind...'

My words dried up as his brows twitched. 'I sent no gift, Lady.'

'But yes.' Had not the note with it made the fact explicit? 'You sent the portrait.' But I saw the lack of comprehension, the hint of censure in the flat stare, and realised that I had made a mistake. Pride and dignity fled. I instantly floundered into an incomprehensible reply, making matters worse, furious

with myself, despairing of my inability to hold tight to confident tranquillity as Michelle would have done.

'Forgive me. Perhaps I was mistaken,' I managed, flushing
to the roots of my hair. I prayed, my thoughts scrambling, that
Isabeau was not close enough to hear me exhibit my desperate lack of sophistication.

'I expect my brother Bedford sent it,' Henry remarked.

'Y-yes,' I stammered. 'I expect that was so.' I dropped into
clumsy silence as our procession shuffled in impatience to
move. His brother. Of course. I remembered John of Bedford's
kindness at our first meeting. Henry had seen no need to give
me such a symbol of his esteem. I swallowed hard against the
hurt that it meant so little to him, but chided myself. I was too
easily hurt. I must grow up quickly, as Michelle had warned.
It was not Henry's fault that my happiness was so transient a
thing. It was mine.

Perhaps sensing the turbulence in me, Henry patted my
hand as if I were a child, before looking back over his shoulder
to address those who pressed close behind. His three brothers,
Bedford, Gloucester and Clarence. His uncle, Bishop Henry
of Winchester. And he grinned.

'Are you ready? My dear wife is near frozen to death. Her
health is my prime concern. If you intend to stay in my good
books, you'll walk sprightly now.' His grin encompassed me
too. 'Lend her your cloak, John. You can manage without.'

Lord John obeyed with a laugh, and I found myself wrapped
around in heavy folds of velvet. Henry himself fastened the
furred collar close against my neck.

'There. I should have thought of it. It becomes you better
than it does my brother.'

My dear wife. His fingers were brisk and clever, his kiss between my brows light, and still I shivered, but now with pleasure at the depth of his consideration. I was wed to Henry of

England. I had a family. For the first time in my life I belonged to someone who put my happiness before anything else, and his touch heated my skin.

Was this love? I was certain that it must be, as my heart was swamped with unnamed longings. I looked up at my new husband as we paced slowly towards the now open door, to discover that Henry was still looking at me, coolly assessing his new possession, until his beautiful mouth curved in a renewed smile and his eyes gleamed with the candles' reflected light. His grip was sure, resonating with authority: I knew he wanted me and would not let me go, and I was glad of it.

I was truly dazzled. My hopes for this marriage were beyond any woman's dreams. And it was God's will—had Henry not said so? All would be well. I knew it.

'Well, all in all, it could be worse. Or could it?' A sly chuckle followed.

I was sitting in the place of honour for my wedding banquet.

'She's young.'

'But *Valois*.'

'She's handsome enough.'

'If you like pale and insipid.'

'I'm surprised Henry does. I thought a more robust wife would bring him to heel at last.'

I flushed uncomfortably. Whatever I was, I was not a robust wife. The burgeoning confidence that had stiffened my spine at my wedding was draining away like floodwater into a winter sluice. Do they not say that eavesdroppers never hear any good of themselves? How true. Unfortunately, my understanding of English had improved sufficiently for me to grasp the gist of the conversation between the little huddle of three English ladies.

Blue-blooded and arrogant, they had accompanied the English court to my marriage, and now as my bridal feast drew to its close, when I knew that I must stand to make a dignified exit beneath the prurient gaze of the feasting masses, they had moved to sit together and gossip, as women will. They were not wilfully cruel, I decided. I supposed they thought I would not understand.

'Do you suppose she's inherited the Valois…problems?'

'There are so many.'

'*Madness*, forsooth. Have you seen her father? No wonder they shut him away.' The owner of that voice was a rosy-cheeked brunette with decided opinions, and none to my advantage.

I glanced at Henry, to sense his reaction, but he was deep in some discussion with his brothers Bedford and Clarence to his right that necessitated the manoeuvring of knives and platters on the table.

'And treachery…'

'Extravagance…'

'Adultery…'

The eyes turned as one to Isabeau, who was leaning to attract some man's attention, and the voices dropped to a whisper, but not enough for me to be deaf to their judgements.

'She likes young men, the younger the better. Nought but a whore. And an interfering bitch when it comes to politics.'

'We must hope there's nothing of her mother in her.' The brunette's eyes flicked back to me. I stared stolidly before me, concentrating on the crumbs on the table as if they held some message. 'Madness would be better than uncontrollable lust.' A soft laugh drove the blade into my unsuspecting flesh.

The heads were together again. 'It's always a problem if the bride is foreign and of a managing disposition. She'll want to introduce French ways. Pursue French policies.' There was an inhalation of scandalised breath. 'Will she expect us to speak French with her?'

'Will she seduce our young courtiers, do you suppose, climbing into their beds when the King is away?'

By this time I was horror-struck. Was this what the English thought of me, before the knot was barely tied? A dabbling French whore? And would I be expected to take these women as my damsels? Would I have no choice in the matter?

'She doesn't have much to say for herself. Barely two words.'

They are cruel, a voice whispered in my head. *They don't like you. They mean to hurt you.*

I knew it to be true. They had already damned me, dismissed me as inadequate for my new role. I tried to close my ears but a little interlude of quietness fell, while the minstrels quaffed ale and the musicians tucked into any passing platter they could waylay.

'She doesn't look like a managing woman. More a timid mouse.'

Resentment surged beneath my black and gold bodice. This should have been a moment of spectacular satisfaction for me, a celebratory feast. The Mayor of Paris had sent Henry wagons full to the brim with barrels of wine in grateful thanks that he had not razed their city walls to the ground. My mother's lips might twist at their treacherous pandering as she drank the fine vintage, but the quality was beyond compare.

Above my head the banners of English leopards and Valois fleurs-de-lys hung heavy in the hot air. I should have been exultant. At my side sat the most powerful man in Europe, and to my mind the most handsome, so how could I be so foolish as to allow these English women to destroy my pleasure? The clear voices continued in inexhaustible complaint.

'She looks cold.'

'Do you suppose our Henry can thaw her?'

'He'll need to. He'll expect a son before the year is out.'

'But can he be sure that any child is his?'

I grew even colder, isolated on a little island in the midst
of a sea of conversation that did not include me, any reply I
might have sought to make frozen in my mouth. Momentarily
I felt the urge to stretch out a hand to touch Henry's sleeve,
for him to come and rescue me from this unkindness, and I
almost did, but Henry was tearing a flat round of bread, placing the pieces at right angles to each other to represent—well,
I wasn't sure what.

'There's trouble brewing here,' he pointed out. 'And here.'

'It's not insoluble,' Clarence stated. 'If we can take the town
of Sens.'

More warfare. Dismay was a hard knot in my belly. I drew
my hand back.

'Sens—that's the fortress that's the key to this.' Henry nodded. 'We can't postpone it. Their defiance will only encourage others.'

'There's still time to celebrate your wedding, Hal.' And I
discovered that Henry's brother, Lord John, was smiling at
me. 'You have a young bride to entertain.'

'Of course.' Henry turned his head, his eyes alight, his face
animated, his smile quick and warm when he saw I had been
listening. 'But my wife will understand. I need to be at Sens.
You do understand, don't you, Katherine?'

'Yes, my lord.' I wasn't sure what it was that he hoped I
would understand, but it seemed to be the answer he required
from me, for he began once more to reorganise the items on
the table.

'And after Sens has capitulated…'

I sighed and kept my eyes lowered to the gold plate before
me. Where had *that* come from? I wondered. Any gold plate
we had had been sold or pawned—or was in Isabeau's personal

treasury. So probably it was English, brought for this occasion so that they could impress us with their magnanimity. Perhaps I would always eat from gold platters. I was Queen of England now.

A whisper hissed, an unmistakable undercurrent, breaking once again into my thoughts. 'She'll not keep our Henry's interest. Look at him! He's already talking warfare and he hasn't yet got her into bed!'

'Not exactly smitten, is he?'

I tried not to be wounded by the gurgle of laughter.

'He'll want a woman with red blood in her veins, not milk and water. Someone lively and seductive. She looks like a prinked and painted doll.'

Lively? Seductive?

Of course I was not lively! Did they expect me to run amok? As for seductive—if that meant to use my female arts to attract a man, I did not know how to, and dared not try. What did these women expect of me when every possible rule for my good behaviour had been drilled into me by my mother after the failure of that first attempt to make a marriage at Melun? Nothing must jeopardise this negotiation at Troyes. Nothing! My conversation and my deportment must be perfect. I had been so buried under instruction that I had become rigid with fear of Isabeau's revenge if Henry should reject me.

But of course these haughty English women did not know. How would they? And neither did Henry—for I would never admit it to him. I could not bear to see the condemnation in his face that I should be so weak and malleable.

I could feel my mother's eye on me even as she sat along the table and conversed with someone I could not see. Dry-mouthed, I lifted the cup to my lips, but it was empty except for the dregs. I replaced it, awkward with nerves under her stare, so that the gold-stemmed goblet fell on its side and rolled a little, the remnants of the wine staining the white cloth, before it fell to the floor with a thud of metal against wood.

I held my breath at my lack of grace, praying that no one had noticed. A hopeless prayer: it seemed that every guest in the room had noticed that the new French wife was so gauche that she must drop her jewelled cup on the floor in the middle of her wedding feast.

Isabeau frowned. Bedford looked away. Michelle raised her brows. Gloucester inhaled sharply. An almost inaudible ripple of laughter from the ladies informed me that they had noted my lapse of good manners and added it to my list of faults. I clasped my hands tightly in my lap, not even attempting to rescue the vessel. If only the floor beneath my feet would open up and swallow me and the cup from view.

And then my heart sank, for Henry forsook his planning. Stretching down, without expression, he picked up the gleaming object, tossed it and caught it in one hand and placed it before me once more. And that drew everyone's attention, even if they had missed my inelegance in the first place.

'Shall I pour you more wine, Katherine?' Henry asked.

I dared not look at him—or at anyone. 'Thank you, sir.'

I had no intention of drinking it. That way would be madness, drinking to oblivion, to hide the speculative attention, but it was easier to agree than refuse. I had learned that people were far happier when I agreed.

He looked at me quizzically. 'Are you content?'

'Yes, my lord.' I even smiled, a curve of my lips that I hoped would fool everyone.

'This interminable feast will soon be over.'

'Yes, my lord. I expect it will.'

'You will become used to such occasions.'

'Yes.'

I opened my mouth to say something more flattering, but

he had turned away—and I caught my mother's eye again. Like that of a snake: flatly cold and lethally vicious. Her earlier instructions rushed over me in a black wave, delivered in her curt, clear voice as if she were sitting at my side, even drowning out the female gossips.

Don't speak unless you have something to say, or are spoken to.

Smile, but don't laugh loudly. Don't show your teeth.

Eat and drink delicately, and not too much. A man does not wish to see a woman scooping up every scrap and crumb on her plate, or licking her fingers.

I would not, even though my starving childhood had given me a respect for the food on my plate.

Modesty is a virtue. Don't express strong opinions or argue. Men don't like a woman to argue with them.

Don't be critical of the English.

Don't flirt or ogle the minstrels.

I did not know how to flirt.

If this marriage does not come to fruition because he takes a dislike to you, I'll send you back to Poissy. You can take the veil under the rule of your sister. I will wash my hands of you.

'I suppose she is still a virgin. Can she possibly still be a virgin—from that debauched French court?' The brunette's whisper reached me like an arrow to my heart.

Pray God this feast came to an end soon.

Henry bowed me from the dais with gratifying chivalry, kissing my fingers, and handed me back into the care of my mother for the final time. Wrapped around in my own anxieties, I noted that the trio of English women rose too: they were indeed to be part of my new household.

And so I was escorted ceremonially to my bedchamber, with much waspish chivvying at how any lack of experience would soon be put to rights, but my mother silenced any more silliness when she promptly closed the door, without any word of apology, on their startled faces. Outside the door they twittered their displeasure. Inside I flinched at the prospect of another homily. I could not escape it, so must withstand whatever advice she saw fit to administer. Soon I would be my own woman. Soon I would be Henry's wife in more than name and God's blessing. Soon I would be beyond my mother's control and Henry would not be unkind to me.

As an unexpected little flicker of expectancy in my future at Henry's side nudged at my heart, I stood while the gold and ermine was removed, my shoes and my stockings stripped off, until I was clad in nothing but my linen shift. And then I sat as instructed so that Guille, my personal serving woman, could unpin and comb my hair into virginal purity. Isabeau stood before me, hands folded.

'You know what to expect.'

Did I? I was lamentably lacking in knowledge of that nature. My mother had resembled a clam, Michelle shyly reticent of her experiences with Philip, and I had had no loving nurse to ensure that I knew what to expect. I had quailed at asking Guille for such intimate details.

'Or did the black crows at Poissy keep you in ignorance of what occurs between a man and a woman?'

Well, of course they had. The black crows considered anything pertaining to their bodies beneath their black robes to be a sin. My knowledge was of a very general nature, gleaned from how animals might comport themselves. I would not admit it to my mother. She would think it my fault.

'I know what happens,' I said baldly.

'Excellent!' She was clearly delighted that the burden of instruction would not fall on her as she moved to the cups and flagon set out on the coffer, poured the deep red liquid and held one of the cups out to me. 'Drink this. It will strengthen your resolve. Rumour says that he is experienced, as he would be at his age, of course. He was a wild youth with strong appetites—he led a notorious life of lust and debauchery, so one hears, until he abandoned his dissolute companions.'

'Oh.' Obediently I took a sip, then handed the cup to Guille. I did not want it.

'You will not be unwilling or foolishly naïve, Katherine.'

Would he dislike me if I made my ignorance obvious? That tender new shoot of optimism withered and died.

'What must I not do that is naïve, *Madame*?' I forced myself to ask.

'You will not flinch from him. You will not be unmaidenly. You will not show unseemly appetites.'

Unmaidenly? Unseemly appetites? I was no wiser. Flinching from him seemed to be something I would very readily do. Will he hurt me? I wanted to ask, but rejected so naïve a question. I imagined she would say yes because it would please her.

'Don't sit there like a lump of carved stone! Do you understand me, Katherine?'

'Yes.'

'That is good. All he wants from you is a son—more than one for the security of the succession. If you prove fertile, if you breed easily, and there's no reason that you shouldn't since I did, then he'll be quick to leave you alone.' She frowned, deciding to say more.

'They say that since his father's death and gaining the English Crown, he has been abstemious. He is not driven by the demands of the body. He'll not expect you to act the whore. Unless his years of chastity have fired his passions, of course.' She frowned down at her hands, clasped before her. 'It may be so. One never knows with men.'

My inner terrors leapt to a new level. How could I possi-

bly play the whore? And if even my mother was uncertain…
'What does one not know about men?' I managed.

'Whether they have the appetite of the beast between the sheets.'

I swallowed. 'Is it always…unpleasant?'

'In my experience, yes.'

'Oh… Did Gaston have the appetite of a beast?' I asked, re-membering a particular flamboyant young courtier ensconced in the *Hôtel de St Pol* before I engaged my mind, and instantly regretted it. *'Pardon, Madame.'*

'Impertinence does not become you, Katherine,' Isabeau remarked. 'All I will say is thank God the King's madness has drained him of his urges. And one more thing—if Henry brings his associates with him to the bedchamber, don't cower in the bed. You are a Valois princess. We will tie this proud King to this treaty. Now remove your shift and get into bed.'

She rounded on Guille, who still stood at my side, as mo-tionless as a rabbit caught in the eye of a hunting stoat, comb in hand. 'You will strip the bed tomorrow and parcel up the linens. If any one of these proud English should question my daughter's virginity or her fitness to be the English queen, we will have the proof of it in the bloodstains.'

I closed my eyes. It would hurt.

'Yes, Majesty.' Abandoning the comb, Guille folded down the linen, taking a small leather purse from her bosom. Open-ing the strings, she began to sprinkle the pristine surface with herbs that immediately filled the stuffy room with sharp fra-grance.

'What is that?' Isabeau demanded.

'To ensure conception, Majesty.'

Isabeau sneered. 'That will not be necessary. My daughter will do her duty. She will carry a son for England and France within the year.'

I dared do no other. Stripped of my shift, I slid beneath the covers, pulling them up to my chin, and waited for the sound of approaching footsteps with thoroughly implanted terror, my newborn confidence effectively slain.

The door opened. I held my breath and closed my eyes—how impossible was it to honour the King of England when lying naked in a bed—until I realised what was missing. The raucous crack of laughter and jokes and crude roistering of the drunken male guests—there was none of it.

Henry had brought no one with him but the bishop, who proceeded to pace round my bed to sprinkle holy water on both me and the linens that would witness our holy union, and a page, who placed a gold flagon with matching intricately chased cups on the coffer, before quietly departing. When the bishop launched into a wordy prayer for our health and longevity, I glanced through my lashes at Henry, still clad from head to toe in his wedding finery, arms at his sides, head bent, concentrating on the blessing. The candle flames were reflected a thousand times in the jewels that adorned his chest and hands, shimmering as he breathed steadily.

I wished I were as calm. The bishop came to the end.

'Amen,' Henry announced, and glanced briefly at me.

'Amen,' I repeated.

Smiling with unruffled serenity, the bishop continued, raising his hand to make the sign of the cross, demanding God's ultimate gift to us in the form of a son. He was in full flow, but I saw the corners of Henry's mouth tighten. He looked up.

'Enough.'

It was said gently enough, but the holy words came to a ragged halt, mid-petition. Henry's orders, clearly, were obeyed without question.

'You may go,' Henry announced. 'You can be assured that

this hard-won union will be blessed. It is assuredly God's will to bring peace and prosperity to both our countries.' He strode to the door and ushered bishop, Queen and Guille out with a respectful bow.

And I was alone with him at last.

I watched him as he moved restlessly about the room. He twitched a bed curtain into position, repositioned the cups and flagon on the coffer, cast a log onto the dying embers. When I expected him to approach the bed, he sank to kneel before the *prie-dieu*, hands loosely clasped, head once more bent, which gave me the opportunity to study him. What did I know about this man that was more than the opinions of others, principally Isabeau? Very little, I decided. Mentally I listed them, dismayed that they made so unimpressive a comment on my new husband as a man.

He was solemn. He did not smile very much, but became animated when discussing war and fighting. He had been kind to me. His manners were exceptional. God's guidance meant much to him, as did the power of outward show. Had he not insisted on wedding me with all the ritual of French marriage rites? He was never effusive or beyond self-control. He did not look like a man who was a beast in bed. His portrait was very accurate. Perhaps he was even more handsome: when animated he was breathtakingly good to look at.

Was that all I could say, from my personal knowledge?

Henry.

I tried the name in my mind. His brother had called him Hal. Would I dare do that? I thought not. I thought that I would like to, but I had not yet dared to call him more than my lord.

Henry made the sign of the cross on his breast, and looked sharply round as if aware that he was under scrutiny, and I found myself blushing again as I lowered my eyes, foolishly embarrassed to be so caught out. Pushing himself to his considerable height, he walked slowly across the room. And then, when he was sitting on the edge of the bed, he allowed his gaze to run over me. I jumped when he put his hand on mine.

'You're trembling again.'

To my relief he addressed me in French.

'Yes.'

'Why?'

What woman would not tremble on her wedding night? Did he not understand? But he did not seem to me to be insensitive. I sought for a suitable reply that would not make me seem inadequate.

'My mother said you would bring your companions with you,' I said. 'She warned me that…well, she *warned* me.'

'Did she now? I didn't bring them, so you may be at ease.' Still, his expression was unsettlingly grave. 'I did not think you would wish me to do that.'

'That is very kind.' I had not expected such consideration.

'No. Not kind. They were not necessary. I did not want them here.'

And I realised with a flutter of anxiety that it was not a matter of consideration for me so much as a pursuit of his own desires. On this occasion they had coincided, but it had not been to put me at my ease that had determined his choice.

'You were very quiet at the feast,' he observed.

'My mother was watching me,' I said, without thinking, then wished I hadn't when his expressive brows climbed.

'Does that matter?'

'Yes. Well—that is, it did. Before I became married to you.' I thought he must be mad to ask so obvious a question.

'Why?'

Should I be honest? I decided that I would be so, since it no longer mattered. 'Because she has a will of iron. She does not like to be thwarted.' His regard was speculative, not judgemental, but I thought he did not understand what I was trying to explain. 'She has a need to be obeyed.' I gave up. 'Perhaps your mother is more kindly,' I added.

'My mother is dead.'

'Oh.'

'I don't remember her. But my father's second wife was not unkind to me.' A brief shadow of some fleeting emotion crossed his face. 'She was kind when I was a boy.'

'Is she still alive?'

'Yes.'

'Do you see her?'

'Not often now.'

'But she was kind to you.'

'I suppose she was.'

He was not effusive, and I thought there was a difficulty there. There was certainly no close connection with the lady.

'So you will never understand about my mother,' I said.

'Perhaps not.' He picked up my hand, and turned it over within his, smoothing his thumb over my palm. There was a little frown between his brows. 'But the French Queen is not here now. She no longer has jurisdiction over you. You need tremble no more.'

It made me laugh, as it struck home that Isabeau was gone and what passed between us now was not her concern, and never would be again. I no longer trembled; indeed, I admitted to a heady sense of euphoria quite foreign to me. Freedom was a thing of beauty, unfurling like a rose.

'The jurisdiction over you,' Henry stated, 'is now mine.'

My eyes leapt to his face. And I stopped laughing, uncomfortable under that direct stare, for he had not smiled. It had been no pleasantry. Would I find him a hard taskmaster?

'My mother ordered all my days,' I ventured.

'And so shall I,' Henry responded. 'But it will be no hardship for you.'

Releasing my hand, he stood and walked away from me, leaving me not knowing what to say. I searched for something innocuous, since he offered no easy conversation. Perhaps Henry did not have easy conversation. I grasped at the obvious, too nervous to sit in silence.

'Will we go to England soon?'

'Yes. I want my heir to be born in England.'

He was looping a chain of rubies from round his neck to place, very precisely, on the top of a coffer, then sat to pull off his soft boots.

'Tomorrow there is to be a tournament to honour our marriage,' I remarked inconsequentially.

'Yes.' His reply was muffled as he pulled his tunic over his head.

I drew in a breath. 'Will you fight?'

He looked up, lips parted as if to make some remark. Then shook his head and said: 'I expect so.'

'Will you fight for me?'

'Of course. At any tournament you will be guest of honour.'

I thought it a strange choice of wording, but announced what, to my trivial female mind, mattered most at that moment. 'I have nothing to wear to be guest of honour at a tournament.'

He concentrated on placing his sword and belt beside the glittering chain. 'What about the gown you were wed in?'

A man's response, I thought, but, then, he would not know. 'I will not. It is borrowed—from my mother.' I saw his scepticism, so tried for hard logic that might sway him. 'It is French. I am now Queen of England.'

Arrested, and for the first time, he laughed aloud. 'Have you nothing else? Surely…'

'The gown made for me when we first met was abandoned in Paris—when we feared your attack and fled.'

His brows drew into a frown, as if I had reminded him of unfinished business on the battlefield, then his expression cleared. 'Clearly I owe you a gown. I'll send to arrange it.'

'Thank you.' This was not so bad, and I ran my tongue over dry lips. 'I would like a cup of wine.' There were things I wanted to say. Wine might help to dissolve the weight in my chest and loose my tongue.

He tilted his chin, as if he rarely poured his own wine, or if he considered my request unwise, but proceeded to present me with one of the lovely chased goblets with a little bow.

'Don't throw this one on the floor.'

I expected him to smile, making of it an amusement, but he did not, merely returning to pour a second cup for himself. Perhaps it had been an instruction after all.

'The English ladies do not like me,' I announced, sipping the wine.

'They do not know you.'

I took another sip. 'They say my mother is a whore.'

'Katherine.' It was almost a sigh. Was he shocked? 'It is not wise to repeat gossip.'

I sipped again, not at all satisfied. 'I wish to choose my own damsels.'

'Who would you choose?' His brows all but disappeared into his hair again.

'I don't know,' I admitted.

'I have already chosen them—you have already met some of them at the banquet,' Henry remarked matter-of-factly. 'It will be better it they are English as you will reside in England. Lady Beatrice will guide you in your first steps.'

'Will you not be with me?'

'Not all the time.'

So I was condemned to the company of the unknown Lady Beatrice. I hoped she was not the opinionated brunette. I sipped again, the warmth dulling the ferment in my belly as Henry began, moving with an agile flex of muscles, to address the ties of his shirt.

'May I keep Guille?'

'Who is that?'

'My chambermaid.'

'If you wish.' He did not care.

Henry continued to remove his garments until he stood in immaculately close-fitting hose. Nervously I concentrated on the hue of the wine in my cup and dredged up another irrelevant question.

'What is your stepmother's name?'

'She is Joanna. From the house of Navarre.'

'Will I meet her? Does she live at Court?'

'No. She lives in seclusion. Her health is not good.' He took a breath as he stood beside the bed, towering over me. 'Katherine.' It seemed that Henry did not wish to speak of Madam Joanna, and I thought he was growing impatient.

'Has your mother, in her wisdom and undoubted experience, told you what to expect?' My eyes snapped up to his face, all the comforting wine-induced warmth dissipating, seeing that his mouth was set in an uncompromising line of distaste, and not for the first time I wished that my mother had been more circumspect in her amorous dealings. My heart sank but I would not pretend what I did not know. Fear crept steadily back to engulf me, like a winter fog rolling across bleak and chilly water meadows.

'No,' I announced. I thought he sighed again. 'She said you were so experienced that it would not matter that I had none and was raised in a convent.' And I found within me a sudden desire to shake him out of his cold self-possession. I gulped a mouthful of wine. 'She said that you had led a dissolute life.' Nerves—and wine—made me indiscreet. Anything to prolong the time until he joined me in the bed. By now I was trembling uncontrollably.

'She said you had spent a life of lust and debauchery—before you became king, that is, and abandoned your companions.'

'You should not believe all you hear,' he replied, and, although his response was even, I thought I had displeased him.

'Did you?' I asked.

'Did I what?'

'Abandon your companions.' I had never had any companions to abandon.

'Yes. It was necessary. They were not to my advantage.'

I drank again, summoning all my false courage as my head swam a little with the warm fumes of the excellent Bordeaux. 'Am I? Am I to your advantage?'

'Of course.'

'A royal virgin with a dowry of inestimable value.'

His gaze moved steadily over my face. 'I did not know that we were going to talk of politics.'

'I know nothing else to talk about. I have run out of subjects.'

'And drunk too much wine, I think.' He took the cup from me, but his voice was gentle.

'I don't feel drunk,' I said consideringly. 'Do I need to talk of anything else?'

'You don't need to talk at all.' And he pinched out the candles.

I valued the darkness. It was, at the moment when I became Henry's wife in the flesh, an experience that I was not at all sure I wished to repeat. The best I could say was that it was brief.

What did I recall of it?

Pain, of course: the physical invasion; the weight of his body on mine so that I felt crushed to the bed. But was that not the lot of all virgins? But then there was the uncomfortable unpleasantness of it all that made me squirm. My mother would have her stained sheets, and I supposed I would, with time and frequency, become used to it. And I remembered the overwhelmingness of it: the heat; the slide of his hands, roughly calloused, when he made himself master of me. There was the power of his hard-muscled, soldier's body that allowed me no time to catch my breath.

And there was the strange silence, apart from Henry's heightened breathing as he took his pleasure. Henry spoke not one word to me during the whole event. I recalled no pleasure, on his part or mine. It was, I decided, all very prosaic and unembellished.

Well, what did you expect? my mind queried fretfully as Henry withdrew, removed his weight and sank his face in the pillow beside me. I had expected some romance, in the manner of the troubadours, some soft words, even if untrue, to engage my emotions. Some caresses, heated kisses, tender encouragement, not a silent assault delivered with cool skill, driving towards a desired outcome. I would at least have liked him to call me by my name. I did not think that too much to ask.

Perhaps that was how Englishmen made love. Perhaps it would all become more acceptable. Perhaps I might even come to enjoy it. I could not imagine such an eventuality but, then, my experience was lamentable and I would learn from Henry's smoothly practised skills. He deserved a wife who could learn and become what he desired.

★ ★ ★

If I expected some intimate exchange of words after the deed—which I did—I was entirely misled. Henry climbed from the bed, delved into a coffer—one of his own that had been brought to the room—after relighting one of the candles and shrugged into a loose chamber robe that fell magnificently in heavy folds of sable fur and crimson damask to the floor. Fastening a belt that sparkled with rubies and agates, he ran his fingers through his hair to make some semblance of order and returned to look down at me where I clutched the linen to my chin.

'Sleep well.' Smoothing my hair, he leaned to press a light kiss on my forehead—the only kiss during the whole of the proceedings. 'Tomorrow you will need all your resources. It will be a long day.'

Was that it? Was he leaving me without a word? I needed at least to know if he had found me a satisfactory wife. I could not let him go without knowing.

'Henry.' I tried his name in my mouth for the first time. 'Was I, was I…?' But I did not know how to ask.

'You were exactly what I had hoped for, my gentle wife,' he replied, and kissed my hair at my temple, his lips warm, infinitely tender, so that my heart beat long and slow.

The door closed behind him, leaving me miserably bereft, for in my innocence I had not expected to spend this night alone. Perhaps I had not pleased him after all, and he was merely being polite in his cool manner. Or perhaps I *had* satisfied him and he simply did not show it. What would make him show the passion I had seen when he had discoursed on the effective laying of sieges or moving troops into position to attack? I thought I knew. Only if I fell for a child would he rejoice.

I prayed that I would, and quickly.

There was a tentative knock on the door and in came Guille, who must have been watching for just this eventuality. She came slowly towards the bed, curtsied, and we looked at each other. Much of an age with me, short and neat with a managing disposition that I lacked, Guille was the nearest to a friend that I had. I felt that her experience of life was also so much greater than mine.

'Was he pleased, my lady?'

'He said so.' I cast back the covers and ran a hand over the sheets, which were bloodstained enough to please my mother. 'He had his proof that I was a virgin, despite my mother's reputation.'

'I will deal with them, my lady.' She bustled about, pouring tepid water from ewer to bowl for me, generally putting all to rights. 'You will be happier as Henry's wife.'

'I suppose I will.'

'Does he like you?' she ventured.

So personal a question surprised me, and I did not know how to reply. I considered, balancing his thoughtfulness against his lack of animation. Perhaps it was simply that I did not yet know him very well, or that, starved of affection as I had been, I simply did not recognise such an emotion when I saw it.

'I think so,' I said. 'He kissed me when he left.'

'Do you like him, my lady?'

'Yes,' I said. 'I think I love him.' I was nineteen years old.

'That's good,' she said, tucking the clean linens around me. 'It is good if a wife loves her husband.'

'But I think I drank too much wine,' I admitted.

'No one would condemn you for that, my lady. The English King is a cold fish to my mind, but how could he not love so beautiful a lady as you?'

Henry's emotions were too difficult a subject to unpick. I yawned and eventually I slid into sleep, not dissatisfied with the day. My experience as a wife had so far been better than anything else I had known, and I had a new gown promised for me tomorrow when I would take my place in the English pavilion as Henry's chosen bride. And I might not invite my mother to accompany me. I would enjoy the tournament as Queen of England and I would give Henry my guerdon to wear as he fought in my honour. I would reward him when he was victorious—as he would assuredly be. I would learn English so that I could converse with my English damsels.

I think I fell asleep smiling, remembering his final caress, his last words.

You were exactly what I had hoped for, my gentle wife.

3

MY WORLD ON that morning as I awoke, the first day of my married life, was a thing of near-delirious anticipation. It was early when I was awakened by voices, a muted conversation between Guille and a visitor. I started, tempted to hide beneath the covers if it was Isabeau come to interrogate me, but the voice died, and the footsteps receded even before the door closed. The relief was as comforting as a cup of red wine.

I flushed, as I remembered Henry taking the cup from me.

'What is it?' I asked from the depths of the bed.

'A marriage gift, my lady.'

I sat up and looked, with delight, at what she held in her arms.

'From the English King, my lady,' she said.

I slid from the bed to inspect it.

'It's not new, my lady.'

'How could it be?' I did not care. Probably it had been in the travelling presses of one of the English ladies, for it was undoubtedly made in the English fashion, a symbol of my new life. Guille pulled and laced and tied until I felt truly glorious in a blue and gold damask houppelande, its heavy folds banded by an embroidered girdle, its sumptuous sleeves long enough to sweep the floor. Queen Isabeau never wore anything more regal than this. It was a gown fit for a celebration.

At length I stood, my hair braided and veiled in gold and fine gauze, my heart full of gratitude to the unknown lady flooding through me.

'Some colour in your cheeks, my lady,' Guille advised. 'It wouldn't do to look pale at the tournament.'

I submitted to her deft ministrations, impatient to be with him, to experience once again his consideration for me. To talk to him as I had talked last night. Lips and cheeks, enhanced with a delicate tint, I admired my reflection in my looking glass. He had thought about me, he had taken the time to provide me with something close to my heart. He had listened to my foolish complaint and not forgotten. My heart sang a little.

'You look happy, lady.'

I thought about this. 'I think I am.' It was not an emotion I recognised, but if this deep contentment was happiness, then I was happy. 'I need a glove,' I said impatiently. 'I must have one.'

'Why is that, my lady?'

'To give to Henry as my guerdon. He will fight for me today. And he will win.' I enjoyed the sound of his name on my lips. I would make him proud of me as I sat in the gallery, clothed as a queen, and cheered him on to victory.

I perched on the edge of a stool, perfectly still so that I did not crease the intricacies of the embroidered panels, head lifted to catch any sound outside. Would he send for me? Or perhaps he would come himself to escort me down.

The time slid past.

'Will he come for me?' Trying to quell the little ripple of anxiety, I forced my fingers flat against my thighs.

'I expect he will, my lady.'

'Yes. I am valuable to him. He said so.'

I sipped a cup of ale, picked at the platter of bread and meat placed before me, but with no real interest. My mind was already running with the heralds and banners and brave knights. And with Henry.

'It will be on the meadows beside the river,' I said as I brushed crumbs from my fingers. 'They'll be erecting the pavilions—or perhaps they've already done that. I'll have a gallery to sit in, so that I might see. I've never been to a tournament before,' I confided. Another feather of latent concern brushed the nape of my neck. 'When will he come? But listen…' I was conscious of the growing tumult of noise, enough to carry through the walls and glazed windows.

I could sit no longer but crossed the room to look down into the entrance court below. It was full of people and wagons and horses, of banners stitched with vivid heraldic devices, a scene of feverish activity.

'There he is!'

My heart was thudding. Standing at the top of a flight of steps leading from the great door down to the gathering masses, tall, lithe, with his head bent as he conversed with Bedford and with Warwick and the rest of his English friends, Henry was everything I could ever have hoped for in a husband. In a lover. He swept a wide gesture with one arm, at the same time as he laughed at some response from Warwick. His face was alight with the same fierce concentration I had seen when planning the attack against the fortress of Sens. Captivated, I pressed my forehead against the glass, and at my movement, snatching at his attention, he looked up. I raised my hand. He looked back at me, as I thought, then gave his attention back to his brother.

Slowly I lowered my hand.

'He did not acknowledge me,' I said.

'Perhaps he did not see. He is very busy, my lady.'

'Of course.'

I turned back to look again. A shaft of sunlight illuminated the scene, striking silvered fire from his armour. And it came to me that the crowds below were not milling at all. It was a scene of organised and disciplined activity: a force of soldiers with horses, weapons being loaded onto carts. More men mustering every minute.

My mouth dried with the implication.

'It doesn't look like a tournament to me,' I said softly. 'It looks like war.' This was no formal passage of arms. Henry was going to war. I snatched up the fullness of my skirts and I ran.

'My lady...'

'He's leaving me!' was all I could say. And then I was pushing my way through the crowd, refusing to be deterred by the crush, with Guille still remonstrating at my heels, until finally I came to where Henry stood. I climbed the steps out of the crush, pushing aside a rangy alaunt trying to claim his master's attention. I needed Henry's attention more.

'My lord.' I tried for a little restraint. His back was to me as he replied to some comment by my lord of Warwick. 'My lord.' I touched him lightly on his arm.

Henry spun round, and I saw the moment when the laughter was gone.

'What are you doing here?' he asked. 'This is no place for you.'

It was a blow that chilled my blood. How peremptory his command. He did not want to be interrupted. He didn't even address me by my name.

'Are you leaving, my lord?' My voice was amazingly calm. At least he could not see my heart thudding against my ribs, like the insistent tuck of a military drum.

'Yes. Go back and wait in the hall. I will come and take my leave of you shortly.'

Take my leave...!

'But I wanted to—'

'Not now.' He drew in a breath. I knew it was to temper his impatience, but I would not be cowed. A strange boldness took hold of me, born out of panic that he was abandoning me.

'I wish to know what is happening.'

He must have seen the turmoil in me, for his voice became infinitesimally less abrasive, the habitual veneer of courtesy restored to a degree. 'You should not be here, my lady. I'll come to you when I can.' He caught Bedford's attention with a lift of his hand. 'John—escort my wife back to the hall.'

He was already snatching up a document from a squire who'd arrived with labouring breath and a covering of dust from head to foot. Tearing the seal, he scanned it, his mouth clamped like a steel trap as he read, entirely oblivious to me. I felt a flush of shame heat my cheeks, for I had been put in my place so thoroughly. It hurt me to know that he had grounds for his irritation. I should not have been there: a mustering army was no place for a woman on foot. I could hear Isabeau's words ringing in my head. I had acted foolishly, without restraint. It was not becoming in a wife, in a queen.

Without waiting for Bedford's escort, I made my way blindly. I must hold up my head. I must not show anyone interested enough to single me out that I felt slighted, humiliated, and, more importantly to my mind, I must not show that I was ignorant of this change of plan. Why had he not talked to me of this? Surely Henry could have told me, instead of leaving me to believe that the tournament would go ahead as planned? I swallowed hard against an unexpected threat of tears, as angry with myself as with Henry. I must learn to have more pride. I must learn to have composure.

In the hall, skirting the walls and thus keeping out of the way of the comings and goings, I turned into a window embrasure where I sat. Guille hovered.

'You could return to your chamber, my lady. That might be best.'

But I would not. I would make my own decision, no matter how small, no matter how unused I was to doing so. And so I remained there, in all my useless, festive glory, as if carved from marble, my heart a solid lump of it. Cold and uncertain, all my earlier happiness no more than a faded memory, the one question that beat in my head, with the familiar flutter of painful anxiety was: why did he not tell me? This preparation for war had been no instant decision. He had known. He had known when I had confessed my naïve pleasure in the tournament. Why had he not told me the truth then, that the celebration would never take place?

Because he does not care enough about you to be honest with you. It was easier for him, so that he need not explain that he would leave you on the first day of your married life.

It was the only answer that made any sense. He did not care for *me*, for Katherine. Any wife with my blood and my name and my dowry would have sufficed. Why should he have to explain himself to me if he did not wish to? I mattered to him because, by a signature on a document, I had brought him a crown, and that was all.

And then I saw him approaching, followed by a squire and a brace of hounds. By the time he reached me his brow was smooth, but I had seen it, that first moment when he had looked around to discover me, and he had frowned.

'What is happening?' I asked as soon as he was within hearing distance.

'I am leaving.'

'Where are you going?'

'To the fortress of Sens.' He stood in front of me.

'Why?'

'I intend to invest it.' I must have looked puzzled. 'To set up a siege.'

'Were we not to celebrate our marriage today?' Restraint seemed to be beyond me.

'There are more important things to do, Katherine. Sens is a hotbed of Dauphinist sympathies. It needs to be brought under English control.'

'And it has to be today?'

'I think it must.'

I did not think he understood the reason for my question at all. *Why did you not tell me?* The one question I dared not ask, for I already knew I would not like the reply.

'And I think I should know what is expected of me today,' I said instead. Despite the fist that seemed to have lodged permanently in my chest, I held his flat regard, astonished at my brazenness, but I would not be swept aside as an unwanted nuisance. I was his wife and I was a Valois princess. This day, by tradition, as he well knew, should have been mine, and the situation at Sens was hardly an emergency to demand Henry's attention at this very hour. I kept my voice low and cool.

'I was expecting to celebrate my marriage. Now it seems that I am not to do so. I think I should have been made aware of this. Last night you did not tell me. And you dismissed me from the courtyard as if I were an encumbrance.'

Don't dare to tell me that the decision to go to war was made this morning.

As Henry inclined his head, the slash of high colour along his cheekbones began to fade. 'It was obviously remiss of me,' he replied stiffly. 'I ask pardon, lady, if I have given offence.'

It was the nearest I would get to an apology—and I felt he did not make them often—but it was not a reason. I could feel his impatience to be elsewhere, to be involved and *doing*.

'How long will you be gone?'

'It's a military campaign. It is impossible to say.'

I wished he did not make it quite so plain that he thought it was all beyond my understanding.

'What about me?' How hard it was to ask, but what was expected of me? How was I to know if I did not ask Henry? Did I sit at Troyes and wait for news? Stitch and pray as a good wife should, living out her days in fear that her lord was wounded or even dead. That was exactly what he would think. 'I suppose you wish for me to remain here.'

'No. You will accompany me.'

The rock in my chest lurched. 'Accompany you? To Sens?' The terrible constriction eased.

'Certainly. You are my wife and between us we have a duty to perform. An heir for England and France. The misguided efforts of the Dauphin can not be allowed to hinder a political necessity.' He bowed. 'I'll send instructions for your comfort during the journey.'

It was as if he had struck me and I flinched. So my compliance was nothing more than a *political necessity*, a need for me to prove my Valois fertility, and for him to discuss it so blatantly in the presence of his squire and my chambermaid... Because I could do no other, I swept my borrowed skirts in a formal curtsey.

'I will be honoured to accompany you.'

Henry bowed. 'That is good. Good day, my lady.'

And I was once more alone in my window embrasure, wretched with disappointment, watching him weave his way between soldiers and servants. I sank back onto the window seat.

What did you expect? He is at war. A war against your brother. Of course he will be preoccupied. Do you really expect him to pass the time of day with you?

My eyes followed his progress through the hall with, I suspected, a world of longing in their depths that I had not the skill to disguise. At the door, he looked back over his shoulder. Then he paused, gestured for his squire to go ahead, before striding all the way back through the crowd, which parted to let him pass.

I stood. Now what would he say to me? Perhaps he had changed his mind, considering that it would be better for me to remain in Troyes. The frown was still heavy on his brow, if that was any indication.

'My lord?'

Henry stripped off his gauntlets, handed them to Guille and seized both my hands.

'I have abandoned you—and I need to ask your pardon,' he announced. 'I was in the wrong. We will both have to accept that there will be times when I forget that I have a wife. I'll not make excuses, Katherine, but sometimes for me the demands of war will be paramount. I would not have hurt you or made you feel of less worth than you are to me. I did not wish to distress you last night. You were so looking forward to today. There will be other tournaments, I promise you. And I sent you out of the courtyard for your own safety. Do you understand?'

He sighed and at last he smiled. 'I suppose I have not used you well. Preoccupation or selfishness—call it what you will. I ask your pardon, my dear wife.'

'I do understand. I willingly give it.' His apology, the depth of sincerity in his words and expression, astonished me.

'I want you with me in the coming weeks.'

'And I want to be with you,' I replied.

'We will come to know each other better.'

Henry kissed me full on the lips then bowed, his hand on his heart. He would never know how far that gesture went towards healing my uncertainties. There was the explanation

I had so desperately wanted from him, and the acknowledgement that I had been in the right to demand it. For my part I must accept that war was a demanding mistress on Henry's time and concentration and, therefore, I, his wife, must learn to temper my needs.

The hurt of the morning began to lessen, giving way to a soft awareness of my new role in this marriage, and the knowledge that I must try hard to build this new relationship into something solid and valuable, as Henry would try too. He had not thought about me because he could not, but when we were together, every day, on honeymoon…

I took Henry's gauntlets from Guille—Henry had forgotten to retrieve them—and smoothed the stitched and jewelled leather between my palms, before handing them to a passing page with orders to return them to their regal owner. Yes, we would come to know each other better. My spirits lifted.

The opportunity for me to prove my fertility to Henry's satisfaction was no easy matter to accomplish, but I was granted a honeymoon of sorts. As an army wife, a camp follower.

My honeymoon read like a military campaign. Henry, as newly appointed Regent of France in my father's name, and thus leading the attack against my brother Charles, took me with him, much like an item of military equipment. I was at the surrender of Sens—a rapid affair over a mere seven days— in June. Ensconced in a pavilion in his camp, Henry had no time for me, although he did inform me of his victory when the fortress fell. He did not even find the time to visit my bed with a view to procuring an heir. For me it was like living in a constant state of apprehension. Would Henry visit me? If not, was it because I had displeased him in some manner unknown to me?

I sat and stitched and tried to converse with my damsels,

who made little effort to converse back. I was wary of them. Particularly of Lady Beatrice, the lively brunette, owner of the sharp tongue and a blue and gold damask houppelande with trailing sleeves. I returned the gown to her.

'It is lovely. I thank you for your generosity, but you must have it back. I had no opportunity to wear it,' I explained stiltedly.

Her curtsey was perfect, her smile knowing. They all knew of my missed opportunity.

And then we were all packed up and on to Montereau and Melun, where, to my astonished satisfaction, Henry, with an heir strongly in mind after his lengthy absence from the allure of my body, had a dwelling constructed for me, out of earshot of the cannon but near to his pavilion. Thus I was restored to Henry's determined embrace.

Henry proved to be a driven man. His visits to my bed were now so regular that I felt as if I were written into the battle plans, along with the digging of trenches and the ordering up of ale to keep the soldiery content. He was brisk and efficient on those frequent forays into intimate relations over the four months it took to reduce Melun. He never stayed with me longer than an hour, but during that time I was granted his complete attention. He was always gentle with me. As recompense for his rapid departures, at sunrise and sunset he ordered English minstrels to play one hour of sweet music for me.

I enjoyed the music far more than I did the smoothly expert but rapid assaults on my body. They roused nothing in me other than a desire that I might quicken fast and be done with it. Regretting my coldness, I put the blame firmly at my own door but could do nothing to remedy it. The more I worried about my freezing reticence, the worse it became. To be fair to my new husband, he did not appear to notice. Perhaps he had not the opportunity in the short time he allowed himself to fulfil his marital duties. He was never critical of me. I was touched when he ordered two harps to be sent from England.

'I know you play the harp,' he said, snapping his fingers to alert my page, who promptly presented one of the magnificent instruments to me, on one knee.

'I do.' I admitted my surprise, and pleasure, that he had found time both to discover it, and to arrange for their delivery from England.

'My brother John told me.' Henry ran an expert thumb over the strings of the second harp. 'I too have the skill.' He smiled thinly at my raised brows. 'I have other interests besides warfare, Katherine. Perhaps we might play together.'

I flushed with the thought, until disappointment set in. We might have achieved a meeting of souls in music if Henry had had time to run his hand even once across the strings but his hand was firmly on the war pulse. Music—and a wife—were both an irrelevance for most of the time.

And yet all was not uneasy isolation for me: I made one acquaintance due to the intensity of the savage fighting. I did not recognise the young man, some few years older than I, compactly built, with steady grey eyes at odds with the vibrantly curling hair that reached to his shoulders, who was brought to my door under what was clearly a military guard.

'Lady Katherine.' He bowed with the sweetest of smiles, his escort unexpectedly abandoning him to my care. 'I apologise for my presence here. I am ordered to stay.'

'Who are you?' I asked. He clearly knew me.

He executed another flamboyant bow. 'I am James Stewart.'

'Yes?'

'King of Scotland.'

'Oh.' I was no wiser. 'Why are you here?'

'I don't suppose he's told you, has he?' I shook my head: 'Because I am a prisoner of your husband.'

'Are you?'

James explained with cheerful insouciance. Taken captive by English pirates on a ship bound from Scotland to France, he had been handed over to the English King and had been a captive ever since, too dangerous to be sent back to Scotland. And now, his nationality and title of an advantage to England, he had been escorted from London to the war front, where he had been instructed by Henry to command the obedience of the Scots mercenaries who were fighting for the Dauphin. To demand, as their King, that they lay down their arms.

'Did it work?' I asked, fascinated, imagining this lively individual addressing his wayward fellow countrymen on the opposite side.

'Not that I could see. And why would they? Since they're fighting for money, they don't acknowledge my authority. Henry was not overly pleased.' He did not seem particularly concerned over any royal displeasure, and I said as much. 'I've been a prisoner of the English for fourteen years—since I was twelve years old,' James explained. 'I have to keep things in perspective, my lady.'

It made little sense to me, not understanding the situation between England and the Scots. 'You are not well guarded,' I pointed out. 'Can you not escape?'

'How would I get back to Scotland without English aid?'

'Will you be a prisoner for ever?' It seemed a terrible predicament. 'Will Henry never release you?'

James Stewart shrugged lightly. 'Who's to say? Only on his terms.'

'And what are they?'

'I don't know that yet.'

I admired the young man's sangfroid.

'Since we're both here for the duration, can I be of any use to you, Lady Katherine?' King James asked.

His grin won me over. 'You can entertain me, sir. Tell me about England.'

'You'll not get an unbiased view. I'm the enemy and a prisoner, Lady Katherine.'

I liked him even more. 'I'll get more from you than I will from my damsels. And you must call me Katherine.'

'Then you must call me James.'

And so I fell into the first friendship I had ever had.

'Will I enjoy living in England?' I asked, my anxieties multiplying now that the time was approaching. James had described for me the great palaces of Windsor and Westminster, the massive Tower of London, the places I would soon call home.

'Why not? The English are kind enough. In a cool manner, and as long as they see some personal gain in engaging your support. They don't *like* you as much as tolerate you.'

'I think Henry only tolerates me.' Shocked, I covered my mouth with my fingers. 'I did not mean to say that. You must not repeat it.' How unguarded I had been. How unwise to say what was in my heart. I looked at James anxiously. Would he think me impossibly unpolished?

But James returned my regard, suddenly very serious. 'He will do more than tolerate you. He will fall in love with you— when he gets the battles out of his system. I would love you if you were my wife.'

My face flushed brightly, my breath caught in my throat.

'Really?' I knew I was ingenuous, but how could I not respond to such unexpected admiration? 'How kind you are.'

I smiled at James, and he smiled back at me. From that moment he became a welcome addition to my battlefield household, which was further enhanced by the arrival of Dame Alice Botillier, her husband and full-grown son both being in Henry's service.

Her role became something between nurse and superior

tirewoman, her position arranged by Henry to promote my well-being and to care for me when I became pregnant. Stern and acerbic, every inch of her tall figure encased in austere black with a crisp white coif as if she had taken holy vows, I found her presence agreeable, although her first words were caustic enough.

'There's not enough flesh on your bones, my lady, to feed a starving lion. If you are to carry a child, we must build you up.'

'If I am to carry a child, I need to see more of my husband,' I replied crossly. Henry had been absent for almost a week.

Alice pursed her lips. 'I expect he does his best in the circumstances.'

Her reply warned me that I must take care never to be openly critical of my heroic husband. The loyalty of the English to their masterful king was chiselled in granite, like the blank-eyed statues on Westminster Abbey. Accepting my silence as compliance, Alice dosed me with an infusion of feverfew, the yellow-centred white flowers gathered from the hedgerows.

'If the King is to plant his seed, the earth must be rich and strong to nurture it.'

I shuddered at the rank smell!

'Drink up! This will heat your belly and your blood. You'll carry a child in no time.'

At a lull in the siege operations, Henry planted his seed with thorough attention to detail. I prayed fervently for a satisfactory result.

'Are you happy here?' Henry asked as he pulled on his boots and reached across the bed to retrieve his sword. There had not been much in the way of undressing, time being at a premium.

Happy? I did not think I was, but neither was I unhappy. Lonely, yes, but less so in the company of the splendidly garrulous Scottish King. My facility with English was improving in leaps and bounds, as James would say.

'I am not unhappy,' I offered, regretting my nervousness, wishing that I could be more loquacious in my stern husband's company.

'Good. I would not wish that.'

It had the effect of a warm caress, and encouraged by it I touched his wrist. Henry stroked his hand along the length of my hair.

'A child will bring you happiness,' he observed. And then: 'You're not afraid of me, are you?'

'Afraid?' My cheeks became a puzzled pink.

'I have never yet beaten a wife.'

His humour was heavy but I laughed and reached up to kiss his cheek. Henry appeared surprised. His mouth was firm, his embrace strong and, abandoning the sword and any thought of returning to the fray quite yet, his renewed possession of me was more than flattering.

'Pray for a son, Katherine. Pray for an heir for England.'

And I did, fervently. And that Henry would miraculously fall in love with me if I could laugh with him and fulfil this apex of his desire. While I was thus engaged in bright thoughts of the future, Melun fell at last. Rejoicing, I tolerated Alice's astringent draughts, dressed with care, and was unpacking the harps when Henry arrived.

'We leave tomorrow,' he announced.

'Where are we going? To England?'

Mentally repacking the harps, I experienced a sudden desire to see my new country. To settle into a new home where I might raise my children and have some time for what could pass for a normal wedded life even if I was a queen. Henry was preoccupied, reading a letter just delivered.

'Do we go to England?' I persisted.

'Paris first,' he said. His eyes gleamed. He must have seen my doleful expression for, surprising me, he wound an arm around my waist and drew me close, rubbing his face against my hair. 'You will enjoy going home to Paris. We'll celebrate our victory, and put on a show for the citizens.' He kissed my mouth with obvious passion, perhaps for me as well as for his victory. 'And then we will return to England. To celebrate our triumph. Perhaps we'll have a child to celebrate too.'

It was lightly said, but I could feel the beat of his blood under my palm, and I felt a blossoming of incipient joy within me. Of anticipation for a love that would surely mature and develop between us. This would be the real beginning of my marriage, when we were in England, when we would be able to spend time together, to grow to know each other.

I laughed, making Henry smile too.

'I would like very much to go to England. I'm sure I will quicken soon.'

4

'I DON'T WANT that tradition, my lord. I would like you to stand with me.'

'There is no need to be emotional, Katherine.'

Our first disagreement on English soil. Our first full-scale quarrel because, instead of my habitual, careful dissimulation, I said the first words that came into my head.

'What do you wear for this occasion?' I had asked, surprised at the informality of Henry's tunic and hose when I was clad from head to foot in leopards, fleurs-de-lys and ermine. I stood before him, arms lifted to display my finery, as he broke his fast with a hearty appetite in our private chamber. It had taken an hour for my damsels—Beatrice, Meg, Cecily and Joan—to dress me. Now Henry and I were alone.

'Do you not have a part to play in this?'

'No.' Henry looked up from a platter of venison, knife poised. 'I won't be there.'

'Why not?'

'It is your day. I'll not take the honour from you.'

I tensed against a tremor of anxiety. I would have to face this shattering ordeal on my own. Already I felt perspiration on my brow and along my spine beneath the heavy fur. Would

I ever be able to face such public display with the equanimity that Henry displayed? I did not think so.

'If I asked you to come with me,' I tried, 'would you?'

Henry shook his head. 'It is the tradition. A King does not attend his Queen's coronation.'

'But I don't want that tradition, my lord. I would like you to stand with me.'

I heard the quiver in my voice, flinched at the formality I still clung to in moments of fear, as I envisaged the hours of ceremonial that I would have to face alone. So did Henry hear it.

'There is no need to be emotional, Katherine.'

'I *am* emotional.'

I felt as if I was being been abandoned in a cold and friendless place, a lamb to the slaughter. I had left the country of my birth with my sister's ring, a portrait of Henry given to me by Lord John and a desire in my heart to prove myself worthy of my husband's regard. At first I had looked to Henry, but he had his own affairs and his own manner of dealing with them.

Hardly had we set foot on English soil than it was writ plain. He left me at Canterbury, going on ahead to prepare my reception in London. I wished he hadn't. I would rather forgo the reception and have him with me. The constant critical concern over my presence, my appearance, my knowledge of how I should comport myself, unnerved and baffled me.

Henry placed his knife carefully beside the platter, aligning it neatly as he sighed. 'Your damsels will surround you and support you.'

I had enough acquaintance with my damsels to answer smartly, 'My damsels sneer and scoff at my lack of confidence.'

'That's nonsense, Katherine.' Impatience was gathering like a storm cloud on Henry's brow. 'They are only your servants. They will obey you.'

'But they do not like me.'

'They don't have to like you. Their opinion is irrelevant.'

Ridiculously, I felt tears press against my eyelids. This momentous day was being ruined by my lack of assurance and Henry's lack of understanding. My enjoyment was fast sliding away between the two.

'My brothers will stand beside you. The archbishop will do all that needs to be done. And you, Katherine, will play the role to perfection.' Henry rose to his feet and, collecting the pile of documents from beside his platter—of superbly inscribed gold craftsmanship, of course—walked from the room. At the door he halted and looked back. 'We have been wed for six months now. It is time that you were able to present yourself with more regal authority.'

Henry stepped out, then stopped again to add, 'You have a duty to this country as Queen and as my wife. It is time that you fulfilled that duty. In all its aspects.'

It was a final, blighting condemnation of my failure to bear a child for him. It was also an order, stated with cold exactitude, leaving me feeling awkward and foolish. And ungrateful, despite having been plucked from obscurity and made Queen of England with all the splendour of rank and honour. Yet how cold was English precedent! How rigidly formal the demands of ceremonial, when my husband was prevented from standing at my side to imbue me with his grace and confidence. Would I ever grow used to it? Growing up enclosed behind Poissy's walls, I knew nothing of living so prominently in the eye of the Court.

'I will fulfil my duty. Of course I will. But I do not wish to be there alone.' I addressed his squared shoulder blades and formidably rigid spine.

Henry did not hear me. Or chose not to.

And now my coronation banquet, which should have filled

me with a sense of my achievement, merely enforced my un-worthiness. As I sat in the place of honour and smiled at my guests, all I could think of was who was there and who was not. These high-blooded members of the English royal family, these English nobles and princes of the church, would people my future existence and dictate the direction of my future life. I had no one of my own.

So I must become English.

There was Lord John, who had made me welcome from that very first occasion when the war between hunting cat and wolfhound had filled me with fear. He smiled at me and raised his cup in a silent toast. I could call him John and trust his friendship.

I slid a glance to my right, to Henry Beaufort, clad in all his magnificence as Bishop of Winchester. Thin-faced, sharp-eyed, quick and keen as a fox, this was Henry's uncle, a man very close to all the Plantagenet brothers. He had welcomed me like a niece, assuring me of his good offices. I think he meant it but I sensed a strong streak of ambition, a man who would let no one stand in his path. He had a wily eye. He patted my hand and nodded his encouragement.

On my left was James, hopeful King of Scotland. Dear James. His jaunty irreverence was balm to my sore heart.

I tried not to look across the table, in case I caught his eye, for there sat Lord Humphrey, Duke of Gloucester, another of Henry's clutch of brothers, easily recognisable with the family traits of nose and brow, but his mouth had a sour twist. I recognised his dislike of me behind the false smile. Perhaps because I was French. Or my mother's daughter. I was wary of him, and he was cool with me.

The one figure I looked for, and did not find, was that of Queen Dowager Joanna, Henry's stepmother. Perhaps there was a reason for her absence. Perhaps her health was not good. I determined to ask Henry.

The banquet began. Because it was Lent, the range of magnificent dishes that were brought for our delectation was composed entirely of fish. Salmon and codling, plaice and crabs, sturgeon cooked with whelks—the variety was astonishing. And after each of the three courses a subtlety to honour me, a confection that elicited cries of wonder. A figure of me as Saint Catherine seated amongst angels, all constructed cleverly out of marchpane, then another of me holding a book. I hoped Saint Catherine was better able to master the contents than I. And then another Saint Catherine with her terrible wheel and a scroll in her hand, with gold crowns and fleurs-de-lys and a prancing panther, which made me laugh.

And where was Henry, to enjoy this moment with me? He would not be there because this was my day and he would not impose his own presence on it. The exchange, becoming increasingly impatient on his part and increasingly hopeless on mine, had ultimately undermined all my pleasure.

Oh, I wished I had more confidence. The weight of the jewelled crown on my head did nothing to enhance it. Why did I not have the assurance of Beatrice, who was laughing and simpering with the gallant on her right? How could a newly crowned and anointed Queen of England be so gauchely tongue-tied? I picked at the dish of eels roasted with goujons of turbot.

I made a token gesture of eating, yet when another dish, a crayfish in a golden sauce, was placed before me, I abandoned my spoon. This roused unsubtle debate over possible reasons why my appetite was impaired. Could it be that I carried England's heir?

No, it could not. My ability to quicken was becoming an issue.

★ ★ ★

'You were magnificent, Katherine.'

Back at the Tower, leaping to his feet as the little knot of us, full of laughter and comment, entered the room, Henry abandoned his cup of wine—for once he had been lounging at ease, ankles crossed, a hound at his feet—to clasp my shoulders in his strong hands and kissed my cheeks.

Delighted at such a show of spontaneous admiration, I returned his smile. The apprehension that had dogged me through the whole performance dropped away, along with the ermine cloak that Beatrice bore away to preserve for the next occasion. Henry's praise expressed with such immediacy was a rare commodity and to be valued.

'I think I did nothing wrong,' I replied hopefully, as his hands slid down my arms to link fingers with mine. Joy spurted in my affection-starved heart.

'You did it to the manner born,' John assured me.

'Very gracious, Your Majesty!' James grinned.

Humphrey said nothing, busying himself with cups of Bordeaux.

'You made a magnificent Queen,' Bishop Henry added. 'You would have been proud of your wife, Hal.'

'So I am.' Henry had forgotten our clash of the early morning and was in good humour, reminding me of our first meeting when he had allowed his admiration for me to shine in his eyes. 'And a more beautiful one I could not have chosen. Did I not say from the beginning that you would make me a superb wife?'

He kissed my fingers, then my lips. He was proud of me. More than gratified, I tightened my hold, heart throbbing and my whole body flushed with my achievements and my love for this man who saw through my fragile facade to my possible strengths and encouraged me to stand alone. With him I would be confident. I would hold my head high.

'Oh, Henry…'

What I would have said I had no idea, for I could hardly pour out my love at his feet, but Henry released my hands and turned to look at John. 'About tomorrow…'

'Bishop Henry said we would go on progress,' I said, emotion still bubbling inside me. 'So that the people of England will know me.'

'I leave tomorrow,' Henry said with a quick glance, taking the cup offered by Humphrey.

My belly lurched, clenched, but I kept my expression impassive. A Queen of England must exercise composure. 'And what do I do?' I asked carefully. My smile was pinned to my face.

'Remain here. I intend to make a circuit of the west. And then I'll go on to…' I closed my eyes momentarily, accepting that Henry's discussion of his itinerary was more for the benefit of his brothers and uncle than for mine. 'They need to see me after so long in France. And I hope to call on their loyalty in hard cash. The army's a constant drain—will you organise a body of royal commissioners to follow on behind to receive loans that are freely offered—or not so freely? It's quicker than going cap in hand to Parliament.'

'I'll organise it,' Humphrey offered.

'Do I go with you?' James asked wistfully.

Henry shook his head. 'Stay in London.'

So he was rejected too. Since there was no reason for me to stay with what was fast becoming a discussion of financial and military policy, masking my raw dismay behind a spritely step, I made my way to the door.

'If you will excuse me, my lords.'

Henry looked up from the list of loans already promised,

handed to him by Humphrey. He promptly cast the list aside and covered the space between us.

'Forgive me, Katherine. How unthinking I was, and after your glorious day.' His smile was wry. 'I know you'll understand by now that when I am focused on the next campaign, I forget the needs of those around me.' The smile twisted, even more ruefully, appealingly. 'I'll not abandon you completely,' he said. 'I have made plans for you to join me at Kenilworth. We will go on from there together to the north. We'll enjoy a somewhat late honeymoon, without the pressure of battles and sieges. You'll like that, won't you?'

'Oh, yes!'

All my hopefulness returned. So I was not to be entirely cut out of his life. If we travelled slowly together and he was not engaged in warfare, if I could match the sort of wife he wanted and show him that I loved him, then he would come to love me. I knew that he would.

Henry came to me that night, entering my room without a knock, and I was pleased to stretch out my hand in greeting. Stripping off his clothes, he assuaged his need with customary efficiency and speed.

'Stay with me,' I invited. 'Stay with me because tomorrow you will leave me.'

'I cannot, Katherine. Not tonight. When we are on progress, then I will. But I have too many demands on my time as yet.'

And I am not one of them.

'Will you miss me?' I asked, ingenuously. 'Will you miss me just a little?'

He looked surprised. 'Of course. Are you not the bride I always wanted?'

'I do hope so,' I replied.

'You are, without a doubt.'

With a kiss to my lips, a smile and a graceful bow, at odds with his informal chamber robe, Henry left me holding tight to his assurances. As it must with any woman, it crossed my mind: did Henry, handsome and powerful, perhaps have a lover? Did he go from my bed to the arms of one of the palace servants who could entice him with sharp wit and languorous caresses?

I did not think so; I had no earthly rival. I had to fight against a God-ordained obligation to England and Henry's vision of his country as the pre-eminent power in Europe. I did not think I would ever emerge the victor in such a contest.

Holy Mother, have mercy on me. At my *prie-dieu* I prayed harder than I had ever prayed. If I carried the heir he so desperately desired, Henry might acknowledge me as part of his dream for the future, rather than as a burden to be shouldered or put aside as time and necessity dictated.

'How does a woman fall for a child?' I asked. Alice's much-vaunted feverfew was not working. 'What must I do to ensure my fertility?'

What a collection of raised brows and rounded mouths. Prayer was good, but I knew I must take counsel elsewhere. I steeled myself to it.

There was a silence in the artlessly decorative group of damsels, stitching and reading in the late afternoon.

Had I shocked them? Did English Queens not ask such intimate questions? I felt my face colour with heat but my need was greater than my shame. They—my damsels—had been universally cool since our establishment back in their own *milieu*. Poised, at ease in the ceremonial ways of the court, I thought that they scorned my lack of aplomb. Respectful for the most part, for they would not deign to be less than deferential towards the King's wife, there was no warmth for their foreign mistress. I found them hard to read. I had made no friends there. With no practice in making friends, I had no pattern of experience to use to court and win affection.

But this was urgent. I needed advice.

Meg pursed her lips. 'Your hips are very small, my lady, for sure. It can make childbearing difficult.'

My hands clenched into fists, well hidden in the soft silk of my skirts. So the fault was mine that I did not conceive. As perhaps it was, but I heard the disdain for my failure behind the carefully phrased fact.

'His Majesty is capable, my lady,' Beatrice observed. They would know how often Henry came to my bedchamber, of course.

'Yes.' The heat in my face became more intense.

Joan, the youngest of my damsels, with a kinder eye, spoke up. 'My sister says that if you grind the dried testicle from a wild pig into powder, mix it in wine and drink it, the result is excellent.'

'Do we have a testicle of a wild pig?' I heard myself asking, unnerved at the advice.

A silence. A pause. Then my damsels erupted into laughter, with an edge that was, to my mind, not kind at all. I thought they looked at me with pity, even when Alice took them to task.

'I have heard of such a nostrum, Joan, but that was not helpful. Unless you are volunteering to go and kill a wild pig for us? And you can take Beatrice with you. Her scowl will kill a boar at twenty paces. I think we can do better. If you carry a walnut in its shell, my lady, it will strengthen your womb and aid fertility.'

'If you eat walnuts, it is said to cure madness.'

I froze, heated skin now pale and cold at this unexpected wounding. Anguish ripped through me that Cecily would make it so personal an attack. Could they be so deliberately cruel? I turned to her, prepared to defend my father.

'Enough, Cecily!' It was Beatrice who came to my aid. 'Your manners are not what your mother would wish for you. I suggest you say a rosary before dinner and pray to the Holy Virgin for humility.'

While to me, with compassion in her face, Alice advised, 'We will tuck some leaves of *polygonum bistorta* into your sleeves. And if you will eat some of the seeds of the *Helianthus* flowers, my lady...'

'And you, Cecily, might pray that fragility of mind never touches one of your family.' Beatrice continued her admonitions to my pert damsel. But I knew that Beatrice's loyalty was to Henry and the as yet unconceived heir rather than to me.

'Forgive me, my lady.' Cecily's eyes dropped before mine.

'Thank you,' I said to Alice, smiling at Beatrice, hanging on to dignity.

'It's early days,' soothed Alice. Then added sternly, 'And this flock of clucking fowl should know better than to mock a woman in such need.'

My damsels sniffed at the reprimand and laughed in corners, even when they knew I would hear them.

No, I made no friends with my ladies in waiting.

Perhaps it was at Leicester where I eventually caught up with Henry on his progress. Or perhaps it was York. Or even Beverley. Or perhaps I did not actually go to Beverley. I remember Henry enveloping me in his arms, lifting me from my litter, welcoming me with gratifying heat, but in the end one town merged with yet another, towns I did not know and have little memory of, where the inhabitants thronged the streets to cheer us, fêting us with banquets and entertainments and lavish gifts of gold and silver. So pleased they were to see and entertain their King after so long an absence.

And his new French wife, of course. Henry continued in good mood, receiving the professions of loyalty with gracious words, before demanding taxes and reinforcements for the renewal of war. I knew the direction of Henry's thoughts. How could I not, when boxes of documents accompanied us, packed into carts that lumbered along in our wake? But Henry smiled and bowed and was careful to wish me good morning and ask after my health.

After my failure to fulfil his hopes on that last night in London at the Tower, Henry occupied my bed with flattering frequency, his desire for an heir taking precedence even over the Exchequer rolls. With tender kisses and chivalrous consideration, he put me at my ease, and I felt more attuned to Henry than I had ever been.

'I am proud of you, Katherine,' he said more than once when I had helped him charm the citizens of some town into subscribing to the royal coffers.

'That pleases me,' I replied.

Henry kissed me on my mouth. 'I knew you would be an excellent wife.'

And my heart kicked against my ribs in a not unpleasant reaction. *This* was the closeness I had looked for. When he took the time to escort me through the fine streets of York and into the magnificent Minster, I could not believe my good fortune. Henry was indulgent and I relaxed when he held my hand and introduced me as his incomparable wife.

But at Beverley—or perhaps it was York—there was an unnerving change. I saw the exact moment it happened.

We had taken possession of yet another suite of chilly and inconvenient rooms in the accommodations belonging to the church, and letters arrived at daybreak as we broke our fast after Mass. There was nothing unusual in this to draw my attention from the prospect of two hours watching the craftsmen of the town perform yet another play of their own devising. Noah and the Flood, and the whole array of animals—or at least a goodly sum of them portrayed by the masked children of the guild families.

Henry opened the documents one after the other, one hand dealing efficiently with bread and beef, the other smoothing out the well-travelled parchments. He read rapidly, with a brief smile or a grunt and a nod, pushing them aside into two neat piles, one for immediate attention, the other for disposal. Henry was nothing if not meticulous.

And then he hesitated. His hand clenched the letter he held. Very carefully he placed the bread and the letter on the table, and brushed the crumbs from his fingers. His eyes never left the written words.

'What is it?' I asked, putting down my spoon. The stillness in him was disquieting.

I might not have spoken. Henry continued to read to the end. And then started again at the top. When it was finished, he folded the document and tucked it into the breast of his tunic.

'Henry?' By this time I had progressed from the formal address of 'my lord'.

Henry slowly raised his eyes to my face. His expression did not change by even the least tightening of muscles but I thought the news was ill. The opaque darkness of his eyes, reminiscent of the dark pewter of the puddles in the court-yard of my childhood home under a winter sky, told of something that had displeased or worried him. His lips parted as if to speak.

'Is it danger?' I asked.

He shook his head. 'No danger. No.' It was as if he shook

his reactions back into life, to re-engage his senses. Bread and meat forgotten, he clenched his hand round the cup at his elbow and gulped the last of his ale.

'Is it bad news, then?' For however much he might struggle to maintain it, something had unexpectedly shattered his impassivity.

Stiff-limbed, Henry stood. 'We are expected to attend the mummers and official welcome this morning.' As if I did not already know. 'Be ready at eleven of the clock.'

He walked from the room with no further comment or explanation, my astonished gaze following him. And the day passed as so many before, with Henry the ultimate monarch, charmingly attentive to his loyal subjects, delighting them with his attention to their preparations but completely devoid of emotion. Noah's ark might have sunk without trace and the animals met a watery death for all the enjoyment he had in it.

'Henry.' I tried as we sat side by side to sample the meats and puddings at the formal banquet. 'Has something happened to disturb you?'

I could not imagine what it might be. The obvious answer was a reversal in English interests in France, but that would have prompted a council of war, not a withdrawal into oyster-like silence. Was it rebellion in England? If so, we would not be sitting here calmly eating the beef and toasting the health of our hosts, who still wore the costumes of their lively play. So not rebellion.

'Not a thing,' Henry replied, *sotto voce*, 'unless it is the toughness of this meat. I advise you to try the fish.'

I gave up.

Henry did not honour me with his attentions that night. I had hoped he might. Could I not persuade him to tell me what was in his heart? But he did not come.

Next morning, when we were to attend Mass, as I made my

way to the private chapel we had used on previous mornings, I was informed by one of Henry's squires that Mass would be celebrated in the body of the church with a full congregation from the town.

Escorted there, I found Henry already kneeling. Conscious of my tardiness, I knelt at his side without comment. He acknowledged me with an inclination of his head, no more than a glance, but there was time for nothing more as the polyphony began and the bishop took his place before the altar. A quiet stillness settled in me as the familiar words and gestures of the priest wrapped round me and my mind was overwhelmed by the intense colours from the great east window. The blue of lapis and cobalt, the blood red of rubies and garnets. Everything was as it should be. Of course nothing was amiss. Would Henry not have said?

There—there were the prayers for Henry and England, for me his Queen and—

My breath caught on an inhalation as the bishop's less than sonorous tones rolled out.

'We pray for the departed soul of Thomas, the Duke of Clarence.'

Thomas, Duke of Clarence. Henry's brother. Dead! When had this happened? Hands gripped tight, I glanced across at Henry, but his gaze was fixed on the altar.

'…cruelly done to death in France. We thank God for his courageous life and pray for his departed soul.'

Henry's brother was dead. So that was the news that had arrived. He had known since the previous morning and had said nothing to me. I might have no experience of family relations with my brothers except for suspicion and hostility, but Henry had a keen closeness with his brothers. How could he show so little grief? If Michelle were dead, would I not grieve? I would not be silent. I would weep, howling out my hurt for all to hear. My chest was tight, my breathing shallow, my emotions all awry: my sorrow was for Henry, but why had he not told me the truth?

The Mass proceeded to its end, and as we walked side by side from the vast arch of the church into the sunlit warmth of the churchyard, I stopped, caught hold of the fullness of Henry's tunic and faced him.

'You have known of this since yesterday,' I stated. 'Since the letter arrived.'

'Yes.'

'Was it a battle?'

'Yes. At Bauge.' He was silent for a long moment, looking back towards the precise carving of leaves and flowers, interspersed with grinning stone faces, that rioted around the doorway, but I did not think he saw them. His mind was in France, on a battlefield where English pride had been trampled in the dust and a royal brother done to death, and behind his implacable mask I saw his sorrow. Would I actually have to ask if it was an English defeat?

'Was it...?'

'It was a rout,' he remarked impassively, gaze snapping back to my face. 'Your inestimable brother the Dauphin all but destroyed my army and killed my brother. Thomas rode against superior forces and was cut down in the thick of it. He was one of the first to die. Bad tactics, I warrant you—he always had more courage than sense and to wear a jewelled coronet on his helmet was downright foolhardy. But still. My army was beaten and my brother slain.'

'Oh.' It was worse than I had thought, and for a moment Henry's features were raw with the grief he had so effectively hidden.

'His body was recovered. It will be brought back to England for burial.'

'Good. That's good, of course.'

But the grief had gone and Henry's eyes were cold and searching, as if he could find the answer to his question in my face. 'It is a great loss. Such a defeat is catastrophic for us at this point in the war. Are we so vulnerable? It will make my task so much harder...'

'Henry!'

I did not care. I did not care about the war. I did not care about our escort of knights and servants and men-at-arms who thronged behind us, hindered from leaving the church by our halting. All I cared about was his incomprehensible silence on so personal a matter that must have wounded him. Why could he not tell me? Was I, his wife, not to be allowed to give him comfort? But when I placed my hand softly on his forearm in compassion, I felt the muscles beneath the fine cloth instantly stiffen against me. I let my hand fall away.

'Why did you not tell me?' However much I might try to suppress it, I could hear the anger in my low-voiced interruption. 'When I asked you yesterday, you said there was nothing untoward. The whole day passed, and you did not tell me.'

He looked at me as if he could not understand my complaint.

'I did not tell you. I told no one.'

'But why not me? I am your *wife*. And your brother is dead. Did you think I would not *care*?' My heart was sore for him. 'I would mourn with you. I would—'

'What could you have done?' he interrupted.

'I could have given you comfort. Am I incapable of giving you some solace?'

His smile was bleak, barely a smile at all. 'I did not need it. I don't need it now. What I need to do is take action to forestall the French advance.'

Thoughts crept into my head. Chilling doubts. The defeat

had, of course, been at the hands of my brother. However hard it was, I looked into Henry's eyes. Had he decided that my Valois blood was more of a danger than a blessing? But his eyes were lightless, empty of either understanding for my predicament or judgement of my possible loyalties. I did not think that he understood at all.

'Come,' he said.

I held my ground. 'Did you not trust me with the news?' I asked. 'Is that it? Did you think I would cry it from the roof-tops to cast your precious English citizens into despair?' And an even worse thought joined the others. 'Or did you think I might secretly rejoice at a French victory over your brother and crow over his death?'

'Don't be foolish, Katherine.' The tone, thick with disdain, slithered over me.

'I am French, am I not? Is it not possible that I would wish my brother well?'

'Curb your tongue,' he ordered. 'Such thoughts are un-worthy of you and demeaning to me. And we are drawing attention to ourselves. We will give the populace no cause for prurient interest.'

His fingers closed around my arm and he propelled me through the churchyard, so fast that I was forced to lengthen my stride to keep up with him. He was smiling for the sake of those who had come to bow and scrape, but his hand gripped like a vice. As soon as we had reached our accommodations and closed the outer door on the populace, he released me as if his hand was scalded. But I continued, driven on by a cold grip around my heart.

'I am so sorry. I did not intend to demean either you or myself, Henry.'

'Katherine.' He turned his back on me, weariness now in his voice. 'It is done. Leave it now. My brother, God rest his soul, is dead. The battle was a disaster. What more to say, for either of us? You can do or say nothing that could give me comfort or make it more acceptable to me that Thomas is dead. Let it lie.'

I bit down on my lip, silenced at last. 'I am sorry. I am so sorry for your grief.' Nothing could have made it plainer that he did not need me, or even want me with him. I waited, expecting him to say more, but he did not.

'Will you go to France?' I asked eventually.

'No. I told your father that I would return in midsummer to restart the campaign, and that is when I will go. Now I have business to attend to.' And I was shrugged off, the door to his chamber closed against me.

Did he find no value in any words of consolation I might offer, or even in the simple touch of my hand on his? As I stood outside that closed door, all I was aware of was a vast tide of loneliness sweeping up to enclose me. Why are you waiting here? I asked myself. What is there to wait for?

Nothing.

Henry came to my bed that night. I did not think his heart was in it even though his body responded magnificently. It took very little time.

'Stay with me,' I invited in despair, as I had once in London, as he shrugged into his chamber robe.

Why would he not stay with me? It was what I wanted more than anything, to lie in his arms and listen to him talk, of his own ambitions, of the loss of his brother. That was what I wanted more than anything in the world, and if I could show him that I was not treasonably French but a loyal wife who cared for his grief and the destruction of his plans, then it was all I could ask for.

I watched from my bed as Henry, pulling up a low stool, sat

to slide his feet into a pair of soft shoes. He stopped, arms resting on his knees, and looked down at his loosely clasped hands.

'Stay,' I repeated, holding out my hand. 'I'm sorry I was
angry. Perhaps I did not understand.'

When he shook his head, I allowed my hand to fall to the
bedcover, my heart falling with it, remembering that Henry
did not like to be touched unless he invited it. Yet still I would
try. 'Do we go on to Lincoln by the end of the week?' I asked.

'I will go to Lincoln, yes.'

'Where will we stay? Another bishop's palace with no heating and poor plumbing?'

'I will go to Lincoln,' he repeated. 'And you will return to
London.'

I felt the cold begin to spread outward from my heart. 'I
thought I would travel with you, to the end of the progress.'

'No. It's all arranged. You'll travel to Stamford, then through
Huntingdon and Cambridge and Colchester.' Henry listed
them, all already planned, everything in place, with no room
for my own wishes. 'They are important towns and you will
make formal entries and woo the populace in my name. It is
important that you are seen there.'

'Would it not be better for me to be seen at your side?' I
asked. 'A French Queen, whom you hold in esteem, despite
the defeat?'

'Your loyalty is not in question,' he stated brusquely.

I sat up, holding out my hands, palms up, in the age-old
gesture of supplication. 'Let me come with you, Henry. I don't
think we should be parted now.'

But Henry stood and moved to sit on the bed beside me. At
first he did not touch me, then he reached out a hand to stroke
my hair, which lay unconfined on my shoulders.

'Why would you wish to? You'll be far more comfortable
at Westminster or the Tower.'

'I want to travel with you. I have seen so little of you since we were first wed, and soon you'll be back in France.'

'You'll see enough of me,' he remarked, as if it was a matter of little consequence how many hours we spent in each other's company.

'No.' I twisted my fingers into the stiffly embroidered lions on his cuff, and said what I had always resisted saying. 'I love you, Henry.' Never had I dared speak those words, or even hint at my feelings, fearful of reading the response in that austere face. Now I said them in a bid to remain with him, to make him realise that I could be more to him than I was, and I waited wide-eyed for his response.

'Of course. It is good that a wife loves her husband.'

It was not what I had hoped for. Merely a trite comment such as Guille had made on my wedding night. My belly clenched with disappointment.

Do you love me, Henry?

I dared not ask. Would he not tell me if he did? Or did he simply presume that I knew? A voice whispered in my mind, a voice of good but brutal sense: *He does not love you, so there is nothing to say.* I held tight to the emotions that rioted nauseously within my ribcage.

'Then stay with me tonight,' I said before my courage could die. 'If we are to be parted, stay with me now.'

'I have letters to write to France.'

I swallowed the disappointment that filled my mouth. I would not ask again. At that moment I knew that I would never ask again.

'You must make ready to leave at daybreak,' he said.

'I will do whatever you wish,' I replied, weakly compliant. But I knew in my heart that there was no changing his mind.

'You will prefer it.' Henry stood. *You* will prefer it, I thought.

'I will be ready. Henry…' He halted at the door and looked back. 'You don't really think I would rejoice in my brother's victory, do you?'

For a moment he looked as if he was considering the matter and my heart lurched. 'No,' he said. 'I don't suppose you would. I know you have no love for the Dauphin. And I think you have little interest in politics and what goes on in the war.'

I forced myself to show no reaction, no resentment. 'So you don't condemn me for my birth and past loyalties.'

'No. How should I? I knew the complications when I took you in marriage. Don't worry about it, Katherine. Your position as my wife is quite secure.' He opened the door. 'And will become even stronger when you give birth to England's heir.'

And he closed the door at his back, reinforcing the reason he had come to me when his heart was heavy with grief for his brother. Not for comfort, or to spend a final hour with me, but to get a child on me before he parcelled me off to London so that I might sit in the vast rooms of Westminster with the heir to England growing inside me.

A bleak fury raged within me, a desolation so deep that I should ever have thought that he could love me. He did not. He never had, he never would. Even affection seemed to be beyond what he could give me. He could play the chivalrous prince and woo me with fine words, he could possess my body with breathtaking thoroughness, but his emotions were not involved. His heart was as coldly controlled as his outer appearance.

And—the anger burned even brighter—he had judged me to be nothing more than an empty-headed idiot, incapable of comprehending the difficulties of his foreign policies or the extent of his own ambitions. I was an ill-informed woman who had little wit and could not be expected to take an interest. I may have been ill informed when he first met me, but I had made it a priority to ask and learn. I was no longer ignorant and knew very well the scope of Henry's vision to unite England and France under one strong hand.

It was during that lonely night that I accepted that, even as I grieved for Henry's loss of a beloved brother, my marriage was a dry and arid place. Why had it taken me so long to see what must have been obvious to the whole court?

I rose at dawn, my mind clear. If all Henry wanted was an obedient, compliant wife who made no demands on him, then that was what he would have. Not waiting for Guille, I began to pack my clothes into their travelling coffers. Obedient and compliant? I would be exactly what he wanted, and after Mass and a brief repast, both celebrated alone—Henry was elsewhere—I stepped into the courtyard where my travelling litter already awaited me. Before God, he was thorough.

It crossed my mind that the accounts of taxes paid and unpaid might prove a more beguiling occupation than wishing me Godspeed, but there he was, waiting beside the palanquin, apparently giving orders to the sergeant-at-arms who would lead my escort. It did nothing to thaw out my heart. Of course he was conscious of my safety: after last night—might I not be carrying the precious heir to England and France?

'Excellent,' he said, turning as he heard the brisk clip of my shoes on the paving. 'You will make good time.'

My smile was perfectly performed. 'I would not wish to be tardy, my lord.'

'Your accommodations will be arranged for you in Stamford and Huntingdon. Your welcome is assured.'

'I expect they will.' I held out my hand. Henry kissed my fingers and helped me into the litter, beckoning for more cushions and rugs for my comfort.

'I will be in London at the beginning of May, when Parliament will meet.'

'I will look for you then, my lord.'

The muscles of my face ached with the strain of smiling for so long, and I really could not call him Henry.

At a signal we moved off. I did not look back. I would not wish to know if Henry stayed to see my departure or was already walking away before my entourage had passed from the courtyard. And thus I travelled quite magnificently with a cavalcade of armed outriders, servants, pages and damsels. The people of England flocked to see their new Queen even though the King was not at her side.

In Stamford and Huntingdon and Cambridge I was made to feel most welcome, I was feasted and entertained most royally, my French birth proving not to be a matter for comment. It should have been a series of superb triumphal entries, but rather a deluge of rejection invaded every inch of my body. I meant nothing to Henry other than as a vessel to carry my precious blood to our son, so that in his veins would mingle the right to wear both English and French crowns. I should have accepted it from the very beginning. I had been foolish beyond measure to live for so long with false hopes. But no longer.

My naïvety, constantly seeking Henry's love for me when it did not exist, was a thing of the past. His heart was a foreign place to me, his soul encased in ice.

Why had I not listened to Michelle? It would have saved me heartbreak if I had. And although I knew from past experience that tears would bring no remedy, yet still I wept. My final acknowledgement of my place in Henry's life chilled me to the bone.

5

HE WAS BACK. Henry was in London. I knew of his approach to the city even before the cloud of dust from his retinue came in sight of the guards at the gates, since couriers had been arriving for the whole of the previous week, issuing a summons in the King's name for a Parliament to meet to ratify the Treaty of Troyes. I knew of his arrival at Westminster, where I had already taken up residence, knew of the unpacking and dispersal of his entourage, Henry's own progress to his private rooms. What I could not hear and deduce from my windows, I ordered Thomas, my page, to discover for me. The King was once more in residence in his capital.

I had a need to speak with him.

'How did he look?' I asked, hoping my urgency would extract some specific detail.

'He was clad in armour and a surcoat with leopards on it,' Thomas reported with single-minded attention to the accoutrements of his hero, 'and he wore a jewelled coronet on his helm and a sword at his side.'

'Is he in good health?' I asked patiently.

He thought for a moment. 'Yes, my lady. His horse is very fine too.'

So why was I not waiting for Henry in the courtyard, a Queen to welcome her King? Because I now knew enough of

Henry's preferences to allow him to arrive and settle into his rooms in his own good time, without any distraction, as he brought himself abreast of messages and documents.

I knew, with my newborn cynicism, that I might be awarded at best a cursory bow and a salute to my cheek, at worst a request that I return later in the day. Besides, I wanted my first meeting with him to be alone, not with the whole Court or his military escort as an interested audience.

I waited in my chamber for an hour. He might come to me, to see how I fared, of course. Foolish hope still built like a ball of soft wool in my chest, only to unravel. Another hour passed. I could wait no longer. The excitement that had hummed through my blood for as many weeks as I could count on the fingers of one hand rippled into a warm simmer. It was, I acknowledged with some surprise, as close to happiness as I could expect.

I picked up my skirts and I ran.

I ran along the corridors, as I had once run out into the courtyard on the day after my marriage, my heart sore that Henry was leaving. Now I ran with keen anticipation through the antechambers and reception rooms to the King's private apartments. The doors were opened for me by a servant who managed to keep his astonishment under control. Obviously queens did not run.

'Where is the King?' I demanded of him.

'In the tapestried chamber, my lady.'

On I went, walking now, catching my breath. Pray God that he was alone. But when I heard the sound of voices beyond the half-open door, irritation, disappointment slowed me. Should I wait? I hesitated, considering the wisdom of postponing this reunion, then knew I could not. I wanted to speak with Henry now. I pushed the door open fully and, not waiting to be invited, I entered.

Henry was in conversation with his brother Humphrey of Gloucester and Bishop Henry. He looked up, frowning at the unwarranted disturbance of what was clearly a council of war, then, seeing me, his brow cleared.

'Katherine... One minute.'

'I have news,' I stated, with only a modicum of grace.

'From France?' His head snapped round. 'From the King? Is he still in health?'

'As far as I know.' The state of my father's wits was of national importance, of course. 'No, Henry. Not from France.'

Since it was not from France, he looked at me as if he could not imagine what I might have to tell him of such importance to interrupt his own concerns. He addressed a scowling Humphrey. 'There's this matter of the Scots supplying arms to the Dauphinists. It must be stopped.'

I walked forward until I could have touched him if I had chosen to. 'I wish to speak with you now, Henry. I have not seen you for weeks.' His brows climbed, but I stood my ground. I smiled. 'I would like it if you were able to spare your wife five minutes of your time.'

'Of course.' His brief smile stretched his mouth. 'If you will attend me here in the hour after noon.'

I was neither surprised nor shocked. Nor was I reduced to easy tears. I had come a long way from the girl who had stood beside him in the church in Troyes. I had more confidence than the girl who had feared sitting alone at her own coronation feast. My weeks alone since my curtailed progress had at last added a gloss of equanimity, however fragile.

'Now, my lord.' I raised my chin a little. 'If it please you.'

I thought he might still refuse. I thought he might actually tell me to go away. Instead, Henry nodded to Humphrey and the bishop, who left us alone.

'Well? News, you said.'

'Yes.' The bite of my nails digging into my palms was an acknowledgement that my courage was a finite thing. 'I am carrying your child.'

It was as if I had stripped to my undershift in public. The stillness in the room prickled over my skin. Henry allowed the list he still held to flutter from his fingers, and for the first time since he had entered the room he really looked at me.

'I carry your child,' I repeated. 'Before Christmas I think your child—pray God a son—will be born. You will have your heir, Henry.'

My words, as I heard them spoken aloud, stirred within me such exhilaration that at last I would achieve something of which he would approve. Surely this would make the difference. This would bring his attention back to me, even if not his love. If I carried a son for him he would be grateful and attentive so that I would not be swept away, like a lazy servant sweeping dust behind a tapestry. I knew that this was the best thing I could do for him, for England.

Since my discovery I had been counting the days to his return, telling no one but Guille, who held a bowl for me every morning as nausea struck. I would have Henry's child: I would have his gratitude, and prove myself worthy of the contract made at Troyes that Parliament was about to ratify, not just for the crown I brought him but for the heir I had given him. Our son would be King of England and France.

I ordered myself to stand perfectly still as he watched me from under straight brows. I did not even show my pleasure. Not yet. Why did he not say anything? Was he not as delighted as I?

'Henry,' I said when still he did not respond. 'If I have a son you will have achieved all you have worked for. To unite the crowns of England and France.' What was he thinking? His eyes were opaque, his muscles taut, the stitched leopards immobile. 'Our child—our *son*—will be King of England and France,' I said, unnerved. 'Are you not pleased?'

It did the trick. His face lit up in the smile such as he had used on the day that he had first met me, when it had turned my knees to water. It still did, God help me. It still did. He crossed the space between us in three rapid strides and seized my hands, kissing my brow, my lips with a fervency I had not experienced before.

'Katherine—my dear girl. This is the best news I could have had. We will order a Mass. We will pray for a son. A son, in God's name! Go and dress. We will go to the Abbey and celebrate this momentous event.'

One brush of his knuckles across my cheek, one final salute to my fingers and he released me, leaving me with a yearning that almost succeeded in reducing me to tears. Oh, how I wished he would take me in his arms and kiss me with tenderness, and tell me with intimate words that he was pleased and that he had missed me, even that he was grateful to me for fulfilling my royal duty to him as his wife.

Instead: 'I need to finish dealing with these,' he said. His face was vivid with emotion, but his hands and eyes were for the documents. 'Then we will celebrate with the whole country your superlative gift to me.'

Superlative gift. That did not stop him closing the door behind me as he ushered me out to find something suitably celebratory to wear. I did not run back to my rooms. I walked slowly, considering that my place in Henry's life would never be important enough to distract him from his role as King.

When the child was born, perhaps?

No, our weeks of being apart had changed nothing between us. I had read love where there was none, as a deprived child would seek it, when all that existed was tolerance and mild affection. I had given up on hope for more at Beverley, when he could not tell me of his grief. Now I abandoned my empty longings, even as I celebrated, clad in the blue of the Virgin's robes and cloth of gold, my ermine cloak wrapped regally around me, as the voices in the Abbey rose about me in a paean of praise to announce that I was Queen and would soon be mother to the heir.

Even my damsels smiled on me.

'You will stay here at Westminster,' Henry informed me as he escorted me back to my chamber at the end of one of the interminable banquets to shackle the foreign ambassadors to our cause, very much in the tone that he had been issuing orders for the past hour. 'You must send word to me as soon as my son is born.'

Henry was making preparations for his—and his army's—imminent departure to Calais. I did not waste my breath asking if I would accompany him. If Henry did not want me with him on a progress through peaceful England, he would not want me on a military campaign beset by unknown difficulties. The days of our honeymoon when he had serenaded me with the best minstrels he could set his hands on so close to a battlefield seemed very far away.

I was now too precious to be risked, as the vessel that would produce the gilded heir. The child who would fulfil Henry's dreams of an English Empire stretching from the north to the shores of the Mediterranean. I became part of his preparations.

'Of course.' There was no doubt in his mind that the child would be male. I tucked my hand into his arm, trying for a lighter mood. His brow was creased with a strong vertical line, his gaze distant. 'You will be able to celebrate his birth at the same time as that of the Christ Child.'

'Yes. Before I leave I will order a Mass to be said.'

'Will you not return before then?' It would be a good five months. Surely he would return.

'If it is possible—I will if I can.'

In truth, I did not think he would. The preparations were for a long campaign, and once winter set in there would be no crossing of the Channel unless it was of absolute necessity. As we walked past one of the glazed windows, I looked out over the Thames, grey and drear for it was a cloudy day, and thoughts of winter lodged in my mind. I imagined Westminster would be a cold and inhospitable place in winter.

'I think I will go to Windsor when the weather turns,' I said.

'No.'

I glanced up. Surprisingly, I had his entire attention. 'Why not?'

'It is not my wish.'

I felt a little spirit of rebellion stir in my belly. If Henry would not be in England, why should I not choose my residence? Perhaps he had not thought about it carefully enough, and if his concern was for my comfort then he must be open to persuasion. 'The private rooms are more comfortable and less...' I sought for a word '...less formidable at Windsor. Here I feel as if I am living in a monument rather than a home. The drainage is better at Windsor. I like the countryside too.'

I glanced up and tried a final thrust. 'The chance of disease, I imagine, is far less at Windsor than living here in the middle of London. The child will thrive there.'

'No.' He was no longer even listening. 'Stay here. Or go to the Tower if you wish. But not Windsor.'

'I dislike the Tower as much as Westminster,' I persisted. 'And what if plague threatens London again?'

'I'll not be persuaded, Katherine. I expect you to be obedient to my wishes. Your reputation must be beyond reproach in all things,' Henry replied. 'I do not expect you to take matters into your own hands and set up a separate court.'

'That was never my intent.'

Taking in his severe expression, I knew he considered that there was enough notoriety in my family with my mother living apart from my father in her own household, and was instantly filled with shame. Would I never be free of my mother's notorious amours?

'My reputation is beyond reproach,' I retorted. 'My mother's morality is not mine.'

'Of course. I implied no other,' continued Henry, starkly disapproving. 'Merely that the mother of the heir must be as pure as the Holy Virgin.'

'But I don't see why it would make a difference if I was at Windsor or Westminster.'

Henry stopped, his hand around my wrist, and for a long moment was caught in a tight-lipped silence as his eyes, bright hazel, searched my face.

'I order it, Katherine. You will not go to Windsor.'

So much for my brief moment of subversion. I slid back into obedience. 'Very well,' I agreed stiffly. 'I won't if you don't wish it.'

'I will make all the arrangements before I go.' Henry released my arm and we walked on. I could not see the need for the little lick of temper in his eyes, but if that was what he wanted, I would remain in Westminster and shiver through the cold. I would not go to Windsor. I would be as virtuous as the Virgin herself, cosseted and protected, an example to all womankind. Disillusion might keep me close companionship, but now I had a child to fill my thoughts. A child who I would love as my parents had never loved me.

Henry left me and went to war in a flurry of gilded armour, blazons and caparisoned horses. I received a publically formal bow and a peck on the cheek, impeded somewhat by the feathered war helm he carried, before he mounted. Once I would have been impressed. Now I knew that in his mind would be the superb chivalric impression his leavetaking would make on his subjects.

A pity about Windsor.

But the seed had been sown, and it blossomed more strongly in my mind every day. I began to think of the bright rooms, the large fireplaces, the warm water brought by a spigot so that bathing in a tiled chamber constructed for the purpose became a pleasure.

Why should I not? Henry could not have considered. His mind had been taken up with the French war—he must have been distracted when he had forbidden me, and would surely not object if I ran counter to his orders. He might even forget that he had actually objected. I might like to decide for myself…

A week of constant rain made up my mind. Westminster became a cold grey domain of draughts and streaming walls and icy floors. My growing bulk barely showed under the layers of furs and mantles that Alice heaped on me. Fur-lined slippers did not stop the rising cold as we huddled next to the fires. No one was tempted outside: exercise was taken in the Great Hall, our breath rising in clouds of vapour. And then there was the day when there was ice skimming the water in my ewer. Enough was enough. I could easily travel—it was still two months before the expected birth of my child and I could take to the seclusion of my suite of rooms in Windsor quite as well as in Westminster.

'We will go to Windsor,' I announced to Beatrice, suddenly much more cheerful.

'Yes, my lady.' And she departed with alacrity to supervise the packing.

'Will we?' Alice asked, surprised at this change of plan but willing to see its merits.

'No, my lady.' Mistress Waring was adamant, her frown formidable.

Mistress Johanna Waring. If Henry had thought he had made every preparation for my *accouchement*, he had been wrong, for this self-important individual had arrived in my expanding household the day after Henry's departure, with much baggage heaped in two large wagons, and a shortage of breath due to her advanced age and considerable girth. Mistress Waring—I would never have dared address her as Johanna— nurse to the infant Henry and his brothers, and one time tire-woman to Lady Mary Bohun, Henry's mother.

'A great lady,' she had informed me, sighing gustily, ousting Alice from her favourite seat and lowering her weight onto it on that day of her arrival. 'Dead too young. And Lord Henry not yet eight years old.' She fixed her eye, which brooked no dissent, on me. 'I expect that you will be a great lady one day.'

And Mistress Waring had brought with her a package.

'Can't have the heir born without this, now, can we?' She pulled at the ties and cloth with surprisingly nimble fingers for a lady of her bulk and years. 'It was Lord Henry's, of course. He was such a lovely boy. I always knew he would be a great king. See? When he was old enough to pull himself up?'

There were faint teeth marks in one of the little birds' heads.

I touched it with my fingertip so that the little wooden box rocked gently on its two falcon-headed supports. I could not imagine Henry so small, so helpless that he would fit into this crib. It swung smoothly against my hand, as my baby would be swung to sleep here. I could not recall if I had had a cradle. Neither did I recall a nurse who had held me in such affection as Mistress Waring had held Henry. And as I was now Henry's wife, Mistress Waring took me in her briskly solicitous hand and laid down the law.

'She's nought but an old besom,' Beatrice sneered down her narrow nose. 'She has instructed me to ensure that all windows are kept tightly closed in your chamber, my lady, to allow no foul air to permeate.'

'Is that not a good thing?' I asked, quick to pour oil on potentially troubled waters.

'I don't see why *I* should do it. It is the work of a servant.'

'But she is favoured by the King,' I replied.

That was enough to restore peace to my dovecote. I was, to my pride, gradually learning to manage my disparate household. Beatrice might have little respect for my opinions, but Henry's word was law. The windows were kept tightly shut. But as for Windsor, now that I had decided, I would not be put off. Not even by Henry's officious nurse.

'Why ever should I not go?' I asked.

'Lord Henry will not like it,' Mistress Waring stated.

'Lord Henry is not here with frozen feet,' I replied sharply, rubbing my toes through my fur slippers. I had chilblains.

'I can heal your chilblains with pennyroyal, my lady,' Mistress Waring admonished.

'Then you can heal them in Windsor.'

I left the room, but Mistress Waring followed me to my bedchamber where I directed Beatrice and Meg to select the clothes I would need. Henry's nurse stood at my shoulder, where she could lecture me without being overheard.

'What is it, Mistress Waring?' I asked wearily.

'My lady, it must not be.'

'Mistress Waring—my child will thrive at Windsor because I will be more content.' She folded her lips. I eyed her. 'What? I can always come back to Westminster when Henry returns from France, if that's your concern.' It had crossed my mind. Indeed, he need never know I had defied him. I really could not see the importance of where I bore this child.

But when Mistress Waring made the sign of the evil eye, I looked aghast, a chill brushing my skin that had nothing to do with the draught whistling round the open door or the grey mist, like an unpleasant miasma, that had blanketed the Thames.

'It's the old prophecy, my lady,' she whispered.

'A prophecy?' I whispered back.

'Made when Lord Henry was born. Come with me.' I followed, out of my chamber and into my private chapel. 'I'll tell you here, because it does not do to speak of some things except in the sight of God.' She lowered herself awkwardly to her knees before the altar, and I did likewise.

'Lord Henry was a delicate child—there were fears for his life. An old wisewoman gave a prophecy to his mother, the Lady Mary, to reassure her that the child would not die.'

Mistress Waring made the sign of the cross on her ample bosom.

'But this has nothing to do with me,' I replied, puzzled.

'It might have to do with your child.'

'And this wisewoman's sayings will stop me going to Windsor? I think this is nonsense,' I remarked.

'It made the Lady Mary weep,' she asserted.

I would have none of this. I stood and walked from the chapel, back to my chamber where the packing went on apace. By the window, a little ruffled by the strange incident, I let my hand fall to stroke the head of the nearest little falcon on the supports of the cradle. They must have looked over the child that Henry had been, I thought fancifully, keeping watch. Who was keeping watch over him now?

My thoughts winged their way, imagining him in full armour, his battle helm in place, facing my brother's army. Who would keep him safe? Some wisewoman's mutterings would have no influence over him, of that I was certain. I offered up a silent prayer, my hand spread wide on my belly.

Holy Mother, keep him safe. Bring him home to me and this child.

Then smiled, a little sadly. His own confidence and his talent in the battlefield would keep him safe. But there was Mistress Waring, her large bulk again looming at my side.

'The prophecy,' she hissed.

So I would humour her. 'What exactly did the prophecy say?' I asked.

'I don't know. But the Lady Mary said that Windsor was not the place for the heir to be born.'

'I cannot believe that my child will suffer for being born in one place or another. I'm sure the Lady Mary had more sense than to give credence to it. If you are so anxious we will say a rosary to the Virgin to ask for her protection.' I was beyond being dissuaded. I would not be swayed by anything less than good sense.

Mistress Waring drew in a breath. 'Queen Dowager Joanna knows the truth.'

'I have never met her.' Queen Dowager Joanna, Henry's reclusive stepmother. I recalled her absence at my coronation, and our paths had not crossed since, for which I was probably remiss. I had meant to ask him, and had forgotten.

'Nor would you,' Mistress Waring advised bleakly. 'She is a prisoner.'

'A *prisoner*?' I thought I had misunderstood the word.

'She is kept in confinement.'

It made no sense to me. 'Does Henry know?'

'Of course. It is by his order. She is accused of witchcraft. Against the King himself.'

I could think of nothing to say. Henry had led me to believe that it had been her choice to live a secluded life, not that she had been incarcerated for so terrible a crime. And I could prise no more information from Mistress Waring other than a reiteration that Madam Joanna would know all about the prophecy. And that I must on no account go to Windsor.

'You must ask the Duke of Bedford for permission, my lady.' Lord John was still in England, thus a final throw of Mistress Waring's dice. 'I wager he will not give it.'

Alice approached to enquire if she should organise the transport of the cradle that still sat, rocking gently, under my hand. Lord John was out of London, visiting the north. Madam Joanna's predicament was something I must consider at more leisure. As for Windsor as my destination—why should I not make my own decision?

'Pack it,' I said.

I was packed up and gone to Windsor long before Lord John returned.

My lord.
I am well. Mistress Waring expects our child to be born early in December.

What more could I write? Nothing I did here at Windsor could possibly interest Henry. Windsor was everything I had remembered and anticipated from my brief visit on my first arriving in England, a place of seductive comfort and royal extravagance, nicely balanced. Painted and tapestried, the rooms that looked out over the River Thames closed around me like a blessing.

Four were put aside for my own use, apart from my bedchamber. One was hung entirely with mirrors, a room that I avoided as my girth grew and I became more clumsy, so I commandeered the Rose Chamber, glorious with paint and gilding, instead. One chamber was for dancing, constructed

by Edward III for his wife, Philippa. There was no dancing
for my little household, but perhaps at Christmas there would
be celebrations. Perhaps Henry would be there to see his firstborn child.

Fat and indolent, I withdrew and settled into Windsor like a
bird into her nest, in a world from which all men were barred
as my time drew closer. My chilblains responded to the pennyroyal ointment. Alice and Mistress Waring clucked around
me. Even my damsels regarded me with smiles of approval and
a willingness to entertain me with music and song as the arrival of the heir approached. It amused me that everyone presumed the child would be a son. I hoped so, I prayed so, for a
son would assuredly win me Henry's approval.

Occasionally my thoughts turned to Madam Joanna, shut
away from the world much as I was, but for necromancy.
Necromancy! The use of the Dark Arts. What had she done?
And why had Henry remained so determinedly silent about
it? When my child was born, I decided, I would make it in
my way to visit this intriguing Queen Dowager.

I wrote to Henry. I felt a need to tell him, to remind him
of my existence, yet found it strangely difficult to write. My
skills were limited, and I struggled with the words as well as
the sentiments.

*I pray for your safety, and that of the coming child. I trust that
you are well and in good heart. I look to the day when you return to England in victory, as do all your loyal subjects.*

It was deplorably stilted, but all I could do. I did not know
where in France he was at that moment but thought him still
to be tied down at the siege of Meaux, where my brother's
forces were holding out against Henry's assault. And how to
finish this worthless little note?

Your loyal and loving wife,
Katherine

I sent it by courier and set myself to stitching for the child that moved restlessly under my hand. Perhaps Henry would even find time to reply. And when he did, I opened the letter enthusiastically, scattering wax on my skirts as the royal seal broke.

To my wife Katherine,
I rejoice to hear of your good health and trust the arrival of the
child will be soon and not too difficult for you to support. I will
order a Mass to be said for your strength.

The writing was uneven, the uprights less forceful than I thought I remembered, not that I had seen Henry write often. Well, I considered. He would not be free to sit and write at leisure. And, no, for he continued:

I am at Meaux but we are hampered by heavy rains that have
caused the river to flood. We are troubled by dysentery. I will
return to Westminster when affairs permit.
Henry.

The tail on the *y* slid abruptly away with a blot and a smear.
I rubbed my thumb over the smudged letters of his name. Not much here. I frowned at it. Then at Alice, who had delivered it from the courier who had remained shut out beyond my closed doors.
'Was the King in good health? Did the courier say?'
'Yes, my lady.'
'Good. Do we know anything about the King of Scotland?'
For James, restless at the endless curtailment of his freedom, had begged to be allowed to accompany Henry to France.

Henry had finally agreed, and given consent to James's release from captivity. Within three months of Henry's return to England, and presuming that the Scottish forces had fought well in England's name, James would be restored to Scotland, if hostages were given for his loyalty.

And providing that James agreed to wed my damsel Joan Beaufort, daughter of the Earl of Somerset and niece to Bishop Henry, it was a neat way of keeping an independent James loyal to English interests. Not that that bothered him particularly. James thought Joan Beaufort to be a remarkably pretty girl.

'Yes, my lady. Lord James sent a poem for the Lady Joan.' With a sly smile Alice removed from her sleeve a folded and sealed square of parchment. 'I have it here.'

'How very thoughtful of him.'

I beckoned Joan, who had been watching, anticipating my every move. A solemn girl in a yellow gown, she was marked by the distinctive Beaufort features of heavily hooded eyes and softly russet hair. One day she would make a lovely bride.

And I smiled, my heart a little sore, as she fell on the dog-eared parchment as if it would save her life, instantly engrossed as she read and re-read with flushed cheeks. I wished that Henry had sent me something rather than a mere half-dozen lines, written about dysentery and flooding.

'"*Now was there maid fast by the wall,*"' Joan read aloud so that we might all admire.

'"*A garden faire, and in the corners set a herbery green.*

And on the small green branches sat

The little sweet nightingale, that sang so loud and clear..."'

James's poetry was not good, he would never threaten the reputations of the troubadours, but if nothing else it proclaimed the direction of his heart.

Should I read aloud from Henry's note to me? I thought sourly. But I was instantly regretful of the jealousy that nipped at my thoughts. They were both young, and no doubt the love that bound them together was a fine thing.

Whatever the state of the chilly rift between us, Henry would be far too busy to mend it, and neither had I made any effort with intimate thoughts in my writings to him. How could I? The campaign took precedence over everything: I must understand that and not be a burden on him. Yet I felt moved to leave the room as Joan launched into the third verse. I could not bear to listen to the passion of a lord yearning for his lady, however badly written the sentiments.

My dear Katherine,
I can think of no better news.

The baby kicked and blinked myopically in his cradle—Henry's cradle—at my knee on which Henry's letter lay open.

A son, an heir to inherit the thrones of England and France, is the greatest possible achievement of our marriage.

The heir, a boy, born on the sixth day of December at four hours after noon, sneezed.

He must be named Henry.

Henry snuffled and waved his tiny hands.

Order a Mass to be said in grateful thanks.

Henry stuffed the corner of the embroidered coverlet into his mouth.

My heart is filled with great gladness.
Henry.

I had not needed to write to inform Henry of this blessed event. The news had been official, carried fast by one of the heralds in full panoply of tabard and staff of office, and here was the reply, even before we were to celebrate the Birth of the Holy Child.

'Where is he?' I asked, noting that Henry's writing had returned to its usual force.

'Still at Meaux, my lady,' Alice reported. 'They are dug in for a siege. A lengthy business.'

So there was no suggestion that Henry would return soon, but I had not expected it. The festivities were almost upon us.

'Was the King in good heart? Did the courier say?' I asked automatically. If he was engaged in a siege, he must be.

'Yes, my lady. The siege goes well. But...'

My eyes snapped to Alice's face at the hesitation. 'But?'

'Nothing, my lady.'

'What would you have said?'

'I think—from what was said—that the King had been unwell, my lady.'

'Unwell?' A little jolt to my heart. I could not imagine Henry unwell. His strength had always been prodigious.

'The courier may have been mistaken, my lady.' Alice nodded reassuringly. 'I think they all lack a good night's sleep and the food leaves much to be desired. His Majesty was well in command.'

I leaned on her reassurance. So no cause for concern, just the usual strains of a long campaign when the body was worn down by the need for constant vigilance. Henry was stronger than any man I knew. I hoped he would come home. I wanted him to smile on the infant Henry and on me.

I lifted the baby from his cradle, holding him so that I could look into his face.

'You are Henry,' I informed him. 'Your father wishes it

to be so. His heart is filled with gladness at the news of your birth.' He seemed to be too small to be Henry. 'I think I will have to call you Young Henry,' I informed him.

The baby squirmed and fussed in his wrappings, so I placed him on my lap. I could see nothing of Henry's face or of Valois in his features, which were still soft and blurred, his eyes the palest of blues and his hair a fair fluff of down. His head was heavy and warm where it rested on my arm, and there was the faintest frown on his brow as if he could not quite see who held him. He began to whimper.

'I'll take him, my lady.' Mistress Waring hovered anxiously, conscious of my lack of experience, but I shook my head and drew the child close to my breast. 'It is not fitting that you nurse him.'

'No. Not yet.'

The whimper became a snuffle and the baby fell asleep. Two weeks old—he was so small—and I felt my heart shiver with protectiveness.

'You are mine,' I whispered as Mistress Waring moved away. 'Today you are mine.'

And I knew that my ownership would be a thing of a temporary nature. Soon, even within the coming year, he would have a household of his own with nurses and servants to answer his every need, perhaps even far from me in his own royal castle if that was what Henry wished. It was not unknown.

He would be educated and trained to be the heir, his father's son, in reading and writing and military pursuits. Henry would buy him a little suit of armour and a small sword and he would learn to ride a horse.

I smiled at the prospect, but my smile was quick to fade. I would lose him fast enough, but for now he was mine, dependent on me, my son quite as much as he was Henry's, and love for this small being suffused my whole body. I thought he would never be as precious as he was to me at that moment before life stepped between us. Born at Windsor he may have been, but I could see nothing but a glorious future for him.

'You will never be hungry or afraid or neglected,' I informed my son.

I kissed his forehead where his fair brows met, and remembered that Henry had not asked after my health at all.

We held the Mass as instructed in the magnificence of St George's Chapel. The Court celebrated the birth of the Christ Child and the start of the New Year and then the riotous junketings of Twelfth Night without either the King or Queen in attendance.

Henry was still pinned down by my brother at Meaux, while I kept to my chambers for I had yet to be churched before emerging into the world again. Baby Henry thrived. Alice cared for me, and Mistress Waring waxed tiresomely eloquent in her comparisons between father and son, how Henry had learned to sing and dance as a child with such grace. I regretted that I had never seen Henry sing or dance. But there was time. Young Henry's birth had blessed me with a new sense of optimism.

I planned my churching with care and an anticipation of my release, and I wrote to Henry.

My lord,
It is my wish to be churched at Candlemas, the Blessed Virgin's own Feast of Purification. If events in France are such that you could return for this thanksgiving, I would be most gratified.
Your loving wife,
Katherine.

I did not quite beg, but I thought it plain enough. So was the reply.

To my wife Katherine,
I am unable to be in England in February. I will arrange for alms to be given to the poor and prayers to be said for your health and that of my son.

I read no more, for there was not much to read before the signature.

'What is he doing?' I asked, unable to hide my chagrin.

'Besieging that thrice-damned fortress of Meaux, so the courier says,' Alice informed me. 'A nest of Dauphinist vipers if ever there was one. It's proving to be a thorn in English flesh. As well as losing Avranches and regaining it. It's all a bit busy.'

And my family was causing Henry much annoyance. I could imagine the line digging deep between his brows, even at this distance. So I was churched without much of festivity, and gave candles for the Virgin's own altar. The prayers were duly said and I expect the alms were given to the poor. Henry was always efficient.

After my release from confinement I remained at Windsor and I wrote.

My lord,
Your son is healthy and strong. Today he is three months old. He has a gold rattle that he beats on the side of his cradle. He also gnaws at it so perhaps his teeth will appear soon.
Your loving wife,
Katherine.

And did I receive a reply? I did not. Whilst I told Henry of the daily minutiae of his son's life, Henry sent me not one word. I understood his needs, the ambition that drove him on, the pressure of war on his every waking moment. Of course I understood. I would not expect him to expend too much energy in considering my state when he knew that I was safe, and that both I and the child were healthy. I was not selfish.

But it had been almost a year since we had been in each other's company. Our relationship was so fragile, based on so little time together, how could it survive such absence? Neither was there any indication of when we would be reunited. I accepted that Henry did not love me, but he did not know me. Neither did I know him.

Were we destined to exist like two separate streams, running in tandem but never to meet? Sometimes I wept that we were such strangers to each other.

Desolation throbbed in my blood. Frustration kept me restless. My foolish attempts to send my thoughts to Henry, as if I might find some echo of him, make some ephemeral consummation of the mind with him, failed utterly. But of course, I admonished myself, both parties would need to be open to the conversation. Henry would not be thinking about me.

How long could I wait?

6

I WROTE TO Henry, taking the matter into my own hand with a direction that shook me.

> My lord,
> Now that the roads are dry and passable, I think it would be good for me to visit with my parents in Paris. And with you too if you deem it possible. I understand that the fortress of Meaux has at last fallen to English hands. Perhaps you will have a short time to welcome me to France.
> Your loving wife,
> Katherine.

Spring had arrived. Travellers began to people the roads, groups of merchants and pilgrims about their business, travelling together for safety. The market in Windsor was thronged with townsfolk glad to emerge after the winter. I watched them from the walls, listening to the cries and music that spoke so eloquently of life going on outside the castle, and with them had come that urgency, to lodge in my mind like a burr under a saddle.

My letter received a reply, and smartly, delivered by Lord John. Yes! Henry would give me leave to join him at last. I tore open the single sheet, scattering the wax in my joyful haste.

To my wife Katherine,
It is not a good time for you to travel in France. Meaux has
fallen but matters between your brother and me are by no means
settled. I would not wish you to be placed in any danger.

No! I swallowed against the intense disappointment and
read on.

I think you will see the wisdom of remaining in England until
I consider it safe for you to arrive. Your safety is my prime con-
cern, you understand. I will send a courier when time and events
permit.
Henry.

So my safety was his prime concern, was it? He would send
a courier, would he? Then why did I get the impression that
such an invitation would never happen? My desolate rest-
lessness was replaced by fury. It blazed, for by now I had not
seen Henry for over a twelve-month, so long ago that when I
closed my eyes I had to concentrate to bring his features into
focus. Would I eventually forget that direct stare, the straight
nose and uncompromising mouth? Would I need his portrait
to remind me?

Oh, Henry! You have not even given me a sound reasoning why I
should not, merely it is not a good time. When will it be a good time?

'He says no.'

'I know.'

'What is he doing now?' I asked Lord John, looking up from
the brisk refusal that he had brought. 'I thought Meaux had
asked for terms at last.'

'Yes. It's taken.'

'But he has no wish to see me. You don't have to deny it,'
I said, seeing John's failure to find a soft reply, trying not to

read the pity in his face. 'I know that his feelings for me are…
mild.' How painful it was to admit that in public. 'But I cannot accept his reasoning. In fact, I will not accept.'

There was a lull in hostilities. If Henry would not come to
me, then I must go to him, and it seemed to me to be high
time Henry came face to face with his son. It was time my
baby travelled to the country that he would one day rule. It
was time he became acquainted with his Valois grandparents.

How easy it was to make that decision, and to inform John
of my wishes, refusing any advice to the contrary. My energy
restored with the prospect of action, I marched to Young Henry's room, swept the baby up from his cradle and took him
to look out of the window in the general direction of where
his father might be at that very moment. Young Henry was
growing, I noticed. He was heavier in my arms now.

'Shall we go to France? Shall I take you to see your father?'
He grinned with toothless gums.

'Then we will go.'

But first, before I saw Henry again, I knew I must discover
the truth to some unanswered questions. After months of in-
activity, I was swept with a desire to discover what was hidden, and perhaps to build some bridges.

It was not at all what I had expected when, accompanied by
an impressive escort, including both Gloucester and Bishop
Henry, I made a bid to discover all I could about Henry's imprisoned stepmother and the troubling prophecy.

Leeds Castle, a beautiful little gem set in a sapphire lake
created by two encircling arms of a river, the waters reflecting
the blue of the sky, was no grim dungeon for Madam Joanna.
A soft imprisonment—yet still, all in all, it was an imprisonment if she lived under the custody of Sir John Pelham, as
Bishop Henry informed me, and was not free to travel. I was

both intrigued and anxious. What would this visit reveal about Madam Joanna—or indeed about Henry?

We were announced into her chamber: Joanna of Navarre, Queen Dowager of England and second wife of Henry's father. She did not rise from her chair when Gloucester and Bishop Henry kissed her cheeks with obvious fondness. And I saw why she did not stand when she placed an affectionate hand on Gloucester's sleeve.

Elegant she may be, her pure white hair coiffed, the folds of her houppelande rich with embroidered panels, jewels gleaming at neck and wrist, but her hands were crippled into claws and her shoulders rigid, and any movement deepened the lines between her brows. Discomfort notwithstanding, I was welcomed with a smile and a speculative regard from direct grey eyes. Entertained with music and wine, Gloucester and Bishop Henry proceeded to enliven her existence with news of court trivia and some comment on what Henry was doing in France.

Madam Joanna absorbed it all, then announced with quiet authority: 'I wish to speak with Katherine.' And when we were alone, duke and bishop obediently departing: 'Sit next to me. I hoped you would come and visit me.'

I moved to the stool at her side. 'I did not realise, my lady.' What a poor excuse it sounded even to my ears, and what an appalling situation. 'I did not even know—'

'That I was a prisoner.' She completed my thought with astonishing complacence.

'Henry told me you chose to live a quiet life.'

'Perhaps I would, in the circumstances.' She lifted her arthritic hands with a little *moue* of distaste, before allowing them to fall gently back into her lap. 'But this is no choice.' Her smile was wry and humourless, her eyes sharp, demanding an honest response. 'And no doubt you wish to know why my stepson keeps me under lock and key?'

'Mistress Waring said that…' How could I voice something so terrible?

'I was accused of witchcraft.' Madam Joanna frowned as if the words pained her. 'It is true. So I am accused. Do you believe it?'

'I don't know. I don't think Bishop Henry does. Or Gloucester.' Their warm acknowledgement of the Queen Dowager, their affection for her, could not be ignored.

'I don't think Henry believes it either,' Madam Joanna added dryly. 'But he needed me to be vulnerable.'

Again, I was lost for words. 'But why?'

'So that he could confiscate my dower lands and income, of course.' Her candid explanation startled me, even more her calm acceptance of it. 'England needed as much gold as she could raise in order to pursue the French wars. The easiest source to plunder was my dower. So how to get his hands on it? It was so simple. He had me accused of threatening his life with necromancy.'

'But that's despicable.'

'I cannot disagree. And—do you know?—I have never been put on trial. I have been unfairly accused and incarcerated for more than two years in one castle or another.'

It was too much for me to take in. 'I can't believe that he would do that.'

'How long have you lived with Henry? Have you not yet learnt that he can be ruthless?' Madam Joanna's smile and voice acquired an edge worthy of a honed sword. 'Where do you think he got the money for your dower?'

If I was horrified before, now I was shocked almost into disbelief. It was a shattering revelation, undermining all my pleasure in what I had once considered to be Henry's true consideration for me.

To compensate for my lack of a dower in gold coin, Henry

had provided me with the vast sum, to my eyes, of a hundred thousand marks to spend every year, as well as gifting me lands and estates, manors and castles, put aside for my own personal use. Henry had ensured that I was not a penniless supplicant, and once I had marvelled at his generosity. Now I learned that it was at the expense of this tragic lady.

'My dower was exploited and I remain under duress until Henry decides to free me.' Madam Joanna tilted her chin, wincing a little. 'I'm not sure I can ever forgive him for that.'

I could think of nothing to say that would assuage my guilt or add to Madam Joanna's comfort. Her situation was truly deplorable. All I could manage was, 'I am so sorry.'

'Why should you be? It was not your doing. Henry needed to fund your dowry, and mine was the obvious source. He is a man driven to reclaim the possessions of his ancestors and ensure England's greatness,' Madam Joanna continued. 'The French war and England's victory is his only concern.'

'I know it is,' I murmured. 'Do you think I have not seen it for myself?' It seemed disloyal to admit it, but Madam Joanna's plain speaking encouraged me.

Seeing my unease, Madam Joanna leaned to close her hand awkwardly over mine. 'That is not good. You should go to your husband,' she said, as if reading my thoughts. 'It is almost a year now, is it not, since you last saw him? I know Henry very well, and I know that you should be with him. He allows his mind to be taken up with the here and now—and sometimes he needs to be reminded that there are other people who need his attention.'

'But I don't think he wants me with him.' For the first time I confessed my fears aloud, seduced by the compassion in this gentle woman. 'He does not love me, you see. He never has…'

Her brows lifted. 'How could he not love so beautiful a wife as you?'

'He never pretended that he did. I thought he did, and I was naïve enough to think that he might. He was kind and chivalrous, you see.'

Her hands tightened imperceptibly. 'You poor girl. How could you know what was in his mind? I never could. As a young man he never permitted anyone to see what was important to him—almost in case it was snatched away and he lost it. And he has excellent manners. How does one read what he is thinking behind that impossible facade of dignified control? I don't suppose he has changed.'

Madam Joanna paused, then urged, her voice no longer soft, 'Go to him. If you wish to make anything of your marriage other than a distant circling of minds that never meet and have no understanding of each other, go and be with him in France. It's too dangerous to take the young boy, but Mistress Waring will care for your child. She will let no harm come to him.'

'Yes. I will.' It seemed such wise advice, such an intuitive reading of my life and Henry's. And such solace to my heart that I was not the only one to be misled by Henry's excellent manners.

'Make him notice you. Beguile him. Lure him from the battlefield, if only for a little while.' She smiled with a touch of very female mischief, which sat oddly on her weary features but hinted at her charm as a young woman. 'It should not be beyond a beautiful woman.'

Yes, Madam Joanna was wise indeed. Perhaps if Henry and I were to live together again, away from battlefields and campaigns, we could build a closeness, an understanding. Perhaps he would even grow to have an affection for me. Were not all things possible with God's grace?

'I will do it.' The resolve settled in my belly.

She patted my hand carefully. 'Henry, I am certain, does know what a jewel he has in you. You are still young, with all your life before you. All you have to do is remind him and bring him home to England once in a while.' We smiled our understanding. 'And now I expect you must go. Your escort will be champing at the bit and damning gossiping women to the very devil. But you must come again. Sometimes I am lonely.'

This brought to my mind what had been hovering over my head during the entire visit.

'Mistress Waring said I should ask you about a prophecy,' I said.

'Did she?' Madam Joanna's all but invisible brows drew down into a line.

'I gave birth to my son at Windsor. Henry forbade it and Mistress Waring disapproved. Henry gave no reason but Mistress Waring said there was a prophecy...'

Madam Joanna's features sharpened as she looked away beyond the window, to the scene of freedom denied. 'I have no truck with such things, even though some would have me guilty of a far worse crime. But, yes, there was such a prediction made to poor Mary de Bohun who did not live to see her son grow to adulthood. A venomous little comment, I would say, product of some malicious mind that had no good thought for the House of Lancaster. It was told to me by Mary's tire-woman in a moment of unedifying gossip over a cup of ale. From what you tell me, it seems that Henry too knows of the calumny from some source—I was not aware. Do you wish to know?'

And she told me.

It did not make for comfortable hearing, thus my first instinct was to reject it. I could not believe it. I *would* not believe it. I need have no fear for Henry, I decided; no decision that I made would have any influence over his future achievements. But what of my son? I tucked the disquieting words away, to consider at some later date if I, insisting on having my *accouchement* at Windsor, had wilfully put my hand to a pattern of events that could bring no good to Young Henry.

The prophecy, known to so few but clearly to Henry, baffled me, with its enigmatic warnings and dire predictions. But then I comforted myself. Madam Joanna discarded it as no more than mischief-making. I, guided by her good sense, would do the same.

And I would take Madam Joanna's advice. At the beginning of May, leaving my son in the care of his besotted parcel of nurses, escorted by Lord John and with a fair wind behind us, I sailed to Harfleur. Before I left, I wielded a pair of shears with great care.

I had learned much that disturbed me about Henry's treatment of Madam Joanna, yet she bore no grudges. Could I be equally tolerant, knowing his obsession with the campaign in France drove him in all things? I did not know. But in spite of everything that lay between us, I knew that I must make Henry notice me.

The closer I got to Paris, the more nervous I became. In the year in which we had lived apart, I had changed and I now accepted Henry's coolness towards me. It was a fact that could not be denied, and surely I was now mature enough to shoulder the burden that my regard for him might not be returned. And yet I continued to hope that Henry would at least rejoice at seeing me, even when it was a hope difficult to maintain.

I could imagine Henry rejoicing at nothing but a hard-won battle, a successfully completed siege. In my head I could hear the timbre of his voice but not the greeting he would offer me. And what would I say to him? He had, after all, forbidden me to make this journey.

And then there was the whole weight of Madam Joanna's

imprisonment. I suspected, as did she, that witchcraft had been a carefully crafted ploy to remove her dower lands from her because Henry had needed them for me. I felt the guilt of it, even though the lady had absolved me. I wondered if I would have the courage to challenge Henry with his calculated cruelty towards a woman who had done him no harm.

I could not excuse Henry, however hard I tried, from an act of such arrogant self-interest that it took my breath. He could indeed be ruthless when pursuing his own set purpose, and how difficult it was to sustain a regard for a man who could be so coldly unscrupulous. I had seen his vicious temper in war; now I had experienced it in the very heart of his family.

I thrust that unsettling thought away. Henry must be pleased with his victory at Meaux, with his son. Would that not cause him to smile at me and kiss me in greeting?

'He'll not send you home, you know,' Lord John said, apparently seeing my anxiety. 'You don't have to fear that he will not treat you with respect.'

'That is not my fear,' I replied. My fear was that he would treat me with too much respect. That he would freeze me to the spot with frigid courtesy and an oppressive outward display of his kingship.

'He'll enjoy your company when he has time to think about it.'

I smiled at him sympathetically. John was trying very hard.

'I know he does not wish me to be here. But I thought that I must.'

'You are a courageous woman, Katherine.'

'I assure you I am not! My heart is thudding hard enough to crack a rib.'

'There are many forms of courage.'

When Lord John took hold of my hand, to fold it warmly

in his as he helped me to dismount, I held on tightly. I would need all of his strength behind me when I came face to face with Henry.

Henry and I met just outside Paris, at the palace at Blois de Vincennes, our joint arrival coinciding fortuitously, although Henry's was far more impressive for he had moved his whole court there after the fall of Meaux.

I was able to slip almost invisibly through the throng of military and baggage wagons, artillery and horseflesh, catching a glimpse of Henry in the midst, so that my heart lurched in familiar fashion at the sight of him, but I knew better than to approach. Henry was more amenable when things were done on his own terms.

For a moment I simply looked, held fast in fascination. He was listening to one of his captains, then pointed and issued an order. Another captain claimed his attention before marching off to carry out some instruction. I grimaced silently then left him to his arrangements.

See what an amenable wife you are becoming. Perhaps one day he will actually love you if you efface yourself enough and jump to obey.

I shook my head and settled myself with John in one of the audience chambers, and was delighted when James of Scotland found his way to join us, with all the pleasure of reunion and a cup of wine. As lively as I remembered him, his curly hair still rioting, he had grown, in height and breadth and in confidence.

'We have missed you,' I told him.

'I enjoy soldiering,' he announced.

'Good. Are you better at it than writing verses?'

He laughed. 'I can't help it if you do not recognise the hand of a master.' Then: 'How is Joan?'

'Languishing in London.' And I told him of her, yet all the

time my senses stretched for the sound of Henry's footsteps, every muscle tensing when I finally heard them.

Henry walked into the room, bringing with him all the authority and regal bearing I recalled from the past. Assured, proud, supremely powerful: that was the Henry I remembered. And I stood there, wishing John and James would leave us alone together, terrified that they would. Eleven months since I had last seen him, and I had only spent a little longer than that with him as his wife. Even that had been interrupted by siege and royal progresses. Now, in the wake of such distancing, I was seized by terrible uncertainty. Predictably, my confidence drained away as he strode in, his eyes taking in every detail of who was there to meet with him. They moved to me, then over my face to John and James.

Keeping my own face carefully welcoming, I watched his expression, searching for pleasure or disinterest. Or—my belly clenched—would he castigate me for disobeying his express order to remain in England? All I could do was to sink down into a deep obeisance. I was here. I would not retreat. I rose to my full height, spine firm. Henry and John embraced, smiling, exchanging words of greeting. He clipped James on the shoulder in warm acknowledgement.

Henry walked slowly to where I stood. I said, before he could speak to me, to forestall any reprimand, foolishly, as a child might, 'I persuaded John to bring me.'

Henry's reply was light and cool. 'You shouldn't have come. And he should have known better.'

'I wanted to see you. It is well nigh a year since…' I said precisely. And then my mind was seized by something quite different. Fear of rejection was wiped entirely from my thoughts.

'There were no dangers, Hal,' his brother interposed. 'We travelled via Rouen—the peace seems to be holding there.'

'It is, thank God.'

Now, at last, Henry took my hands in his and, with a strained smile, saluted my cheeks.

'You look well, Katherine.'

And you don't look well at all.

I stopped myself from saying it, but the impulse was strong. He looked immensely tired, the lines at the corners of his eyes a mesh of crow's feet, his skin pulled taut over cheekbone and jaw, and a line between his brows did not smooth away, even when he smiled at me at last. I thought he had lost weight. Always tall and slender rather than heavily muscled, his frame could ill-afford to lose flesh. His hands around mine looked as finely boned as a woman's.

'We got tired of waiting,' explained John, and when Henry turned his head to respond I was horrified by the translucence of his skin at his temple. He looked stretched and weary to the bone, with an uncomfortable pallor beneath his campaigning bronze.

He kept hold of my hands. 'How is my son?'

I dragged my mind from Henry's appearance to reply with a smile, 'He thrives. He is safe at home. Look—I have brought this for you.' I released myself from his hold to draw from my sleeve a screw of parchment that I gave to him, explaining as he opened it, 'It's Young Henry's. His hair will be like yours.'

Henry smoothed his thumb over the curl of hair and, to my relief, laughed softly. 'Thank you.' He tucked it into his tunic.

'When will you come back to England to see him?' I asked, before I could stop myself.

And there was the bleak lack of emotion that I so feared. 'I don't know. You should know better than to ask.'

'What are your plans?' John added with the slide of an apologetic eye in my direction.

Henry turned his head as if to reply. Took a breath. Then frowned.

'Later, I think,' he responded curtly. 'We'll talk later.'

'Of course. Shall we share a flagon of good Bordeaux?'

Henry shook his head. 'In an hour. I'll find you.' And strode swiftly from the room. We heard him shouting for his squire to order the disposal of his baggage—and then silence. With a little shrug, James followed him.

John and I looked at each other.

'He worries me,' I said simply.

'He is weary. Long campaigns—particularly sieges—take it out of the best of soldiers. A rest will restore his good humour.'

I thought that Henry had little humour at the best of times. 'I thought he looked ill.'

'Lack of food, lack of sleep, that's all.'

That was what Alice had said. I supposed she was right.

'He was pleased to see you.'

'Was he?'

'It will all work out well. You'll see. Give him time to settle in here. His victory at Meaux was a great one but draining. Sieges always are. Give him time.'

I was not convinced, and thought that John's repetitions were an attempt to allay his own fears. I walked in front of him from the room so that he would not see the threat of tears.

When we met for supper Henry seemed much restored, although he only picked at the dishes and drank little. He left us before the end without explanation or excuse. In nervous anticipation I sat in my sheets, trembling, my hair loose and gleaming, as seductive as any bride, but Henry did not come. I had been so sure that he would. I thought the need to converse with me about Young Henry, even to take the necessary steps to produce another son, would be important, but he did not come. All my tentative hopes for our reconciliation after so long a time were dashed, ground like shells into sand under the unstoppable onslaught of the sea.

★ ★ ★

There was no leisure to be had at Vincennes. We moved on to Paris almost immediately for a ceremonial entry in the heat of May, our arrival timed to match that of my parents. We stayed at the Louvre in cushioned luxury, Isabeau and my father consigned to the worn and shabby rooms of the *Hôtel de St Pol*. My father was too indisposed to notice. Isabeau merely scowled her disapproval when Henry bowed to her.

Henry and I received visitors, both English and French, we attended banquets too many to count and we watched the Mystery of St George. Henry shuffled throughout and made his excuse before the final bow of the brave knight after his dispatch of the terrible dragon.

'I'll sit through this no longer,' he growled, and stalked from the chamber, leaving me to smile brightly to smooth over any ill feelings. The next day we packed up and, detouring to visit the tombs of my ancestors at St Denis, travelled on to Senlis, where Henry made it clear that we would remain for a short time.

'Thank God!' I remarked to John. 'At least we can draw breath.' Even though Isabeau and my father had followed hard on our heels. 'Perhaps he can rest at last.'

In all this time Henry had not shared my bed for even an hour, which in itself was a source of anxiety for me. One son left a throne weak. I would imagine that Henry would want more, and that this would be too good an opportunity for him to miss. How many more days could we guarantee that we would be together? But he did not. Fine drawn, strung with nerves, Henry avoided me, and I knew better than to suggest any of Alice's nostrums. I dared not. The tension around Henry was sharp as his goshawk's talons.

★ ★ ★

I dared not, not even when Henry came to my room that final night, when I least expected it, when I had given up hope. As I was kneeling at my *prie-dieu*, he entered quietly, pushing the door closed at his back and leaning against it. His face was in shadow but I could not mistake the dark smudges of exhaustion below his eyes. Where his chamber robe fell away from his neck, the tendons stood out in high relief. For a long moment he did not move. He was looking at me but I did not think he saw me.

'Henry...'

It was the first time we had been alone together since I had returned to France. Unnerved, I stood and I stretched out my hand, my mind suddenly flooded with compassion. Where was the pride, the stern composure? Here was a man suffering from some terrible weight, but whether of mind or body I did not know. Instinct told me that he needed me, and I would respond with all the generosity in my heart, but would he tell me what troubled him?

'Forgive me,' he said softly.

For what I was uncertain, neither did I ask when Henry took my hand and led me to the bed, where he pushed me to sit on the edge. I would allow him to do as he wished if it would bring him relief from the pain in his clenched jaw and tired eyes. He sat beside me, his actions spare and controlled, and, leaning, he pressed his lips where my pulse beat at the base of my throat, his hand pushing my shift from my shoulders. When his kisses grew deep, almost with desperation in them, I clung to him. Then Henry groaned against my throat, becoming still. His eyes were closed, every muscle braced.

'Henry?'

He flung away, to lie supine beside me. Then: 'Before God,

I cannot do this.' And turned to press his face against my hair. 'I can't. Do you know what it takes for me to admit that?'

Despite the nerves that were clenched hard in my belly, compassion ran strong through my blood. There was some problem here, one even greater than I had feared, that Henry could not control. My hands, holding tight to his shoulders, becoming aware of the sharpness of bone and sparseness of flesh, told their own story.

'You are unwell,' I murmured. I slid my palms down from his shoulders, along the length of his arms where the muscles had wasted. I pushed the robe away from his chest, and I could see his collarbone stark beneath his skin. 'What is it?' I whispered, horrified.

His attempt at a smile, perspiration standing out on his forehead, was a poor one. 'The usual soldiers' disease—a bout of dysentery. But I'm on the mend—although this seems worse than I can ever recall.'

'But you are not on the mend,' I observed carefully, fearful of driving him away in a bout of pride. 'It has gone on too long, hasn't it? I think we should send for your doctor from England.'

He stiffened. I thought he would refuse, then he capitulated, which said much for his state of mind. 'Yes. I can't say no, can I?'

'I will send for him. To come here—or to Vincennes?'

'Here—to Senlis. I will come back here after the next battle. It shouldn't be long.' His voice was a mere thread, the old scar on his face standing out, angry and livid.

'I don't think you should go,' I remonstrated, but again gently. Henry was in no state to be harangued, even if I thought it would do any good. 'You are not well enough. You drive yourself too hard. You should stay here and recover your health.'

His response, on a laboured intake of breath, was predict-able. 'It has to be done. I'll fight your brother at Cosne, and defeat him.' He kissed me, a perfunctory brush of lips, on my brow. 'God will give me the strength I need. I'll deal with the rebels and then I'll come back here.'

'We should go home.' I tried to keep the distress from my voice. 'You should see your son.'

'Yes. You're right, of course. I'll leave John in command here.' He kissed me again. 'I can't rest... I can't sleep.' I had never seen him so close to despair.

'Stay,' I said, as I had so many times before, but now with a difference. 'Stay and sleep.'

And he did. For the first time Henry spent the whole night in my bed. Restless and plagued by dreams, he found little healing, but I stayed awake at his side in an anxiety-filled vigil, trying to quell my mounting fears. His flesh was heated, his hands curling into claws as his head thrashed on the pillows. As I covered Henry once again with the disordered bed lin-ens, all I could see was a man driven beyond endurance by some monstrous assault.

He is strong. He will overcome this.

Henry cried out, shouting in anguish, as if wounded or fac-ing an enemy on the battlefield.

My heart sore, I kissed his cheek, smoothed back his mat-ted hair and wept.

The next morning, somewhat restored, although still ice pale, Henry went to Vincennes with his army, taking John and James with him. I sent to London for his doctor, who arrived and waited with me. We both waited, with my mad father and my ever-complaining mother for company, through the long, hot month of August. All I knew was that Henry was still at Vincennes, and that I had never found time to talk to

him about the injustice of Madam Joanna. But I would when
I saw him again.

I prayed. The beads, carved ivory and jet, clicked through
my fingers in perpetual petition that the Blessed Virgin would
watch over my husband and restore him to health.

When Lord John was announced in the solar of the old palace
where I sat with my mother and the handful of damsels who
had accompanied me, the silence between us—for what had
we to say to each other?—masked by a lute player, I sprang
to my feet, delighted to see a familiar face, abandoning my
needlework to Beatrice's care. John would have news of the
campaign and perhaps a message from Henry. He would also
have some conversation to while away even an hour of my
time. He came to an abrupt halt just within the door, pushing gauntlets and helm into the hands of the surprised servant
who had announced him.

'John.' I approached with hands outstretched in welcome,
my heart light. 'What brings you? And James too.'

For there behind him, similarly clad in a metal-riveted
brigandine, gripping gloves and sword, was James Stewart.

'My lady.' John bowed to me, and to my mother. James's
inclination of the head was cursory in the extreme.

'What are you doing here?' I asked. 'We didn't expect you.
Is the battle at Cosne won?'

'No, my lady. The battle has not been fought,' John replied,
lips stiff, voice raw.

It seemed to me that there could be only one reason. 'Has
my brother then surrendered?' But a sudden touch of apprehension prickled over my skin. How formal he was. But perhaps it was simply the presence of my mother that had made
him circumspect. It was hard to read anything from the dust-

engraved lines on his face, unless it was weariness from the journey.

'No, no.' Lord John hesitated. 'The Dauphin has withdrawn from the siege. There will be no battle.'

'Then what…?'

'I am here…' As he stepped forward into an angled shaft of light from the high window, I saw that his face was a graven mask, imprinted with far more than weariness. 'It is the King, my lady. The King.'

What was this? I frowned at the unaccustomed formality. 'Henry—has he then recovered? Do I go to join him?'

'No, my lady. Not that.'

Dark dread began to close around my heart, but I clung to what I knew must be the truth. Henry would control the situation, the reins firmly in his hand, as skilfully as a knight would direct his mount when riding in the lists. How could the news be bad if both sides had withdrawn from battle? 'Does he come here, then, to Senlis?' I asked.

John drew in a breath. 'No…'

The sense of terror, dark and bottomless, began to grip harder, so hard that I could barely take a breath. 'What is it, John?' I whispered with a terrible premonition. 'James?' I glanced at the silent King of Scotland. 'Will you not tell me?'

James looked away.

'Have pity,' I whispered.

It was John who told me in the end. 'Henry is dead.'

The words dropped like a handful of pebbles, cast to clatter onto the floor in an empty room. I looked up, away from John, my attention caught, as if I had missed something. Perhaps a bird flown in through the open window to flutter and cheep in panic. Or a murmur of gossip from the damsels. Or Thomas entering with a platter of wine and sweetmeats. Or even my father, come to discover where in France he actually was.

No bird. No conversation. No page or father. No sound except for an echoing silence. Every detail of that room seemed to be fine etched in my mind. My mother was staring at me, her embroidery abandoned in her lap. My damsels seemed frozen in time and space, silent and still as carved statues.

Inconsequentially I marked that the lute player had stopped playing and was looking at me, open-mouthed. That John's boots and clothing were mud-spattered, that James's hair, curled on his neck, was matted and sweat-streaked. They must have ridden hard and fast. How strange that they had not sent a courier to tell me about this vital matter that had brought them hotfoot from Vincennes to Senlis... But— I shook my head, trying to release my thoughts from some muffling cloud.

What was it that John had just said?

'I'm sorry. I don't...' I heard myself murmur.

'Henry is dead,' John repeated. 'He died two days ago. I am here to tell you, Katherine. I thought it was my duty to come in person.'

Duty! All was black. My sight, my mind. These words, so gently spoken by a man whom I would call friend, could not be true. Was it a lie? Had it been said to deliberately cause me hurt? My mind shimmered, unable to latch onto the meaning of those three words.

Henry is dead.

'No.'

Although my lips formed it, I could not even speak the denial. The floor moved under my feet, seeming to lurch towards me as my sight darkened, sparkling with iridescent points of light, jewel bright, that all but blinded me. I felt my knees weakening and stretched out for something solid to catch hold of… And as I felt John clasp my arm, in a rush of silk damask my mother was at my side, catching hold of me with her nails digging into my hand, her voice as harsh as that of a crow's warning in my ear.

'Katherine!'

I heard a mew of pain—my own voice.

'You will not faint,' my mother muttered. 'You will not show weakness. Stand up straight, daughter, and face this.'

Face what? *Henry is dead.* It couldn't be.

A cup of wine was pushed into my hand by Thomas, but I did not drink, even though my throat felt as raw as if it was full of sand. Unheeded, my fingers opening numbly, the cup fell to the floor and liquid splashed over my skirts.

'Katherine! Show the courage of your Valois blood!'

And at last, at my mother's command, I drew myself up and forced my mind to work.

'Two days ago,' I heard myself say, slowly. 'Two days.'

Why had I not known? Why had I not felt some powerful essence leach out of this world when so great a soul left it? What had I been doing two days ago? I frowned as I tried to recall. I had ridden into the forest of Chantilly with a group of my mother's courtiers. I had visited my father, who did not know my name. My mother had bemoaned the quality of my embroidery. I had done all of that and felt no sense that Henry was dead, that Henry's soul, at some point in those meaningless events, had departed from his body…

How could he? He was young. In military skill he surpassed all others. Had it been an ambush? A chance attack that had gone wrong?

'Was it in battle?' I asked. But surely John had said that there was no battle. I must have misunderstood. 'Did he lead the army against Cosne after all?'

'No. It was not a wound,' John explained, relieved to be

asked something that he could answer. 'He was struck down with dire symptoms. The bloody flux, we think. A soldier's disease—but far more virulent than most.'

'Oh.' I could not take it in, that he was dead of some common ailment. My magnificent husband cut down by the soldiers' flux.

'For the last three weeks he could barely rise from his bed,' John continued to explain in flat tones that expressed nothing of the agony Henry must have suffered. Or the anxieties of his captains.

'I sent for a new doctor from England,' I said. 'Henry said that he should wait here. I should have sent him to Vincennes...'

'I doubt he could have reversed the illness,' John soothed. 'He was failing for three weeks. You must not blame yourself.'

The words swirled around me, pecking at my mind like a flock of insistent chickens. This made no sense. Three weeks!

'He could barely ride when he left here—he was too weak in spite of his insistence,' John continued. 'We travelled to Vincennes by river in the end, which was easier. Henry tried to ride the final miles into camp but it could not be.' John passed his tongue over dry lips. 'He was carried the last distance in a litter.'

'And that was three weeks ago.'

'Yes, my lady. On the tenth day of August. He did not leave his bed again.'

But...it made no sense. He had been so ill that he could not ride a horse for three weeks? For a moment I closed my eyes against what I now understood... Then opened them and fixed John with a stare, for I must know the truth and I would not allow him to dissemble.

'My husband was bedridden for three weeks.'

'Yes.'

'Who was with him? At the end?'

'I was. His uncle Exeter. Warwick. His captains. James, of course.' His eyes slid from mine. Dear John. He knew exactly what I was asking. 'I think there might have been other members of his council, and of course his household. I forget…'

'And what did you speak of?'

'What use is this?' my mother demanded, still at my side, her hand still gripping mine. 'What use to know what he said? I swear it will give you no comfort.'

I shook her off, stepping to stand alone with a bleak resolve. 'I need to know. What did you discuss in all those three weeks, John?'

'Matters of state. Government affairs, of course. The direction of the war…'

'I see.'

Henry's brother, his uncle, his friend and captains had all been summoned to his side, but not his wife. They had discussed matters of state, but nothing as personal as the ignorance of a wife who had not been invited to attend her husband's deathbed. His *wife*, who could have made the journey within two days if she had been informed. Emotion throbbed behind my eyes: shock that a man who had seemed untouchable should live no more; anger that I should be the last to know.

'Did he speak of me at the end?' I asked, my voice perfectly controlled, knowing the answer by now. 'Did he talk of me or of his son?'

'Of his son, yes. It was imperative to consider the position of the new king.' John's eyes were full of misery as his gaze met mine. I admired his courage to deliver that blow so honestly. I needed honesty beyond anything else.

'It was not imperative to consider my position. He did not talk of me,' I stated.

'No, my lady. Not of you.'

I took a breath against the dark shadows that hovered. 'What did Henry say at the very end? Did he know he was dying?'

'Yes. He said that he wished he could have rebuilt the walls of Jerusalem. He begged forgiveness for his sins. He said that he had wronged Madam Joanna.' John smiled grimly. 'He has released her. You will be relieved to hear that, I know. She never deserved her imprisonment.'

I laughed harshly, mirthlessly. At least he had remembered Madam Joanna.

'That was all he said, until he committed his soul to Christ's care.' John took my hand. 'Forgive me, Katherine. There was no easy way to deliver this catastrophic news. I cannot imagine your grief. If there is more I can tell you...'

There was really nothing more to ask. Nothing more for me to say. But I did, because the dark clouds were rent and the true horror had struck home.

'Why did he not tell me that he was near death? Why did he not send for me?'

It was a cry of anguish.

Shamed, because there was no answer that could be made, I covered my mouth with my shaking hands. And walked from the room.

I did not weep. I could not sit, could not lie down on my bed. I stood in the centre of the floor in my chamber and let the realisation wash over me as the sun covered me with its warm blessing from head to foot. I did not feel it. I was shocked to ice, blood sluggish, my heart nothing more than a lump of frozen matter. How could the sun be so warm on my skin when all feeling, all life seemed to have drained from me?

Eventually I discovered that I was sitting on the floor, staring at the barred pattern made by the light and shadow on the tiles. Bars, such as those making a prison cell of a well-furnished room. But now the bars for me were open and for the first time since I had stood before the altar at Troyes I allowed myself to see the truth in all its rawness. I could pretend, I could hope no longer. Henry's death had written it plain.

My life with Henry had been built on a swamp, all its footings unsure except for the legal binding in the eyes of the church. I had worshipped him, been blinded by him, made excuses for his neglect.

And had he not drawn me into the mirage? He had treated me with such chivalric respect when we had first met and he had wanted to woo my consent—not that he had needed it—but perhaps it had pleased him to acquire a besotted bride. Henry had enjoyed being lauded on all sides, and requiring unquestioning obedience had been part and parcel of his life.

My mind ranged over the times when I had been an encumbrance or, even worse, a person of no real importance to him. No, he had not been cruel, I admitted with painful honesty, he simply had not seen the need to consider me as part of his life. I had never been part of his life. It had been John who had sent me the portrait, James who had kept me company during the sieges of my honeymoon and played Henry's harp with me.

What need to tell his wife of any change of plan? Why tell her that his brother was dead in battle? And as soon as my body had co-operated with the promise of a child, he had abandoned me for the demands of the battlefield. Oh, I knew his commitment to England had been strong, and had he not had a God-anointed duty to his country as King? But did he have to leave me for a year of our young marriage?

And I, not guiltless in this, had been too immature to forge a relationship with him. I had been obedient and subservient, I had never forced him to notice me as Katherine because I had not known how. I had never dared call him Hal, as his

brothers had. And now all my chances to build a loving marriage with Henry were destroyed.

Perhaps there had never been any real chances.

A howl was rent from me, hot with fury and grief. I swept
my lute from coffer to floor, the strings twanging in complaint.
I dragged the curtains of the bed closed. He would never lie
there again with me.

How could this be? How could I have fooled myself for so
long? His family, his captains, his confessor all summoned to
his bedside. But not me.

And at last true horror laid its vicious hand on me, and the
degradation, for I had not been ousted from his affections by
another woman, or even by another man. Or even by a cold
and distant duty laid down by God. War and conquest and
English glory had proved to be a demanding mistress, against
whose enchantment I had never been able to compete. At last
I sat and wept, my infatuation for Henry as dead as his earthly
remains, my body an empty shell.

Saddest of all, Henry had never even set eyes on the son he
had so desired.

All the structure of my life lay in pieces, the pattern of my life
as Henry's wife and Queen of England.

What was expected of me now?

'Do I go to him at Vincennes?' I asked John next morning. Surely I could make this decision for myself. Of course I
would go. As my last office to him as his wife, I would kneel
beside his coffin and pray for his departed soul.

'No,' John replied. 'They will have already begun the journey back to England. I advise you to make your way to Rouen.'
I had found him in the entrance hall, already dressed to leave,
shrugging into a heavy jerkin, pulling on his gauntlets, out-

side in the courtyard, his horses and entourage already drawn up. 'I'll leave James here. He'll escort you when you're ready.'

So I would go to Rouen. The customary flutter of apprehension that attacked me when all was not clear was beating against my temples, warning me of imminent pain. I realised that I had not even asked John what provision had been made for me on my return to England. I had no idea what would be expected of me there.

'What will I do?' I asked Isabeau in despair. My mother was already making her way towards the chapel for her daily petitioning of the Almighty, but she turned and considered, head tilted, a little smile on her mouth.

'Do you not know? You are more important now, Katherine, than you ever were before the English King's death. Are you not the living, breathing symbol of all that was agreed between Henry and your father?' She sneered. 'They'll put you on a pedestal, place a halo around your head and clothe you in cloth of gold. Glorious motherhood personified.'

Her brutal cynicism horrified me. 'I can't...'

'Of course you can.' A sour twist of her mouth, wrecking the smile, coated Isabeau's words in disdain. 'What is your alternative? Better that than to be driven to return here to France, to live out your days in penury in company with a bitter, aging woman and a witless man.'

It shook me into a terrible reality I could not envisage.

As advised—or instructed—by Lord John, and accompanied by a silent James, for once robbed of all his high spirits, I travelled to Rouen. I was there, in the position prepared for me at the door of the great cathedral, when the remains of King Henry of England arrived.

I watched the scene unfold, all in sharp detail but as if at a great distance from me. The vast doors had been opened wide to receive the procession. It was truly magnificent: a mighty host of mourners. If I had not realised before the honour in which Henry of Lancaster was held in Normandy, I did now. Bells tolled, clergy chanted, while beneath it all simmered a dark and doleful sense of doom as a carriage drawn by four burnished black horses came to a halt.

A canopy of rich silk was held aloft. Behind it they came, John of Bedford, James of Scotland, the Earl of Warwick, all the English lords and royal household who had been there at my husband's death, sombre in black. They bowed to me as they approached and stopped.

I walked forward, my limbs stiff, to where the bier lay draped in black silk. My errant heart, lodged in my throat, beat louder still. For upon it there was an effigy, a more than life-sized effigy, of Henry, fashioned in leather. I took in the details of it as if it were Henry himself, clad in royal robes, furnished with crown, gold sceptre and orb.

Slowly I placed my hand on the arm, as if it might be a living body. It was warm from the sun, but rigid and unresponsive. How could this stiff facsimile contain all Henry's exuberant life-force? The austere features would never again warm into a smile that could pierce my heart as it had in that long-distant pavilion, with the hound and the hunting cat, at Meulan. How strange that now I was free to touch him without redress—except that this creature was not real.

'Is he…?' I tried to ask. How ignominious it would have been for him if he had been dismembered as the dead sometimes were. His pride could not have tolerated it. 'Is he…?' I could not think of the words to ask.

John came to my rescue. 'Henry has been embalmed. He was very emaciated at the end. And it is a long journey.'

Of course. His body would have been packed with herbs against putrefaction, but still my mind could not encompass it. All that life snuffed out. Too young, too young. And as the procession passed by into the dark interior, there was James of Scotland at my side, as he had been for the whole of that terrible journey from Senlis.

'Are you strong?' he asked, closing a hand around my arm. I must have looked on the brink of collapse. I could not remember when I had last slept through a night.

'Yes,' I said, my eyes following the preserved remains of my husband.

'When did you last eat?'

'I don't recall.'

'It will be all right, you know.' He stumbled a little over the words. 'I know what it is to live in a foreign country—without friends and family.'

'I know.' The cortege had now made its ponderous way into the cathedral where Henry's body would lie in state.

'You will return with us to England?'

I did not think I had a choice. I raised my head and watched the effigy still moving away from me into the shadowed depths, until a bright beam of light illuminated it with colour from one of the windows, and for that brief moment the effigy was banded majestically in red and blue and gold. It woke me from my frozen state and with it came an inner knowledge of what I must do.

'I was his wife. I am the mother of his son, the new king. I will make his return to England spectacular because that is what he would have wanted.'

James's hand was warm on my cold one. I could not recall when I had last been touched with such kindness, and I said it to him because I could say it to no one else.

'Henry did not think of me, but I will think of him. Is it not the duty of a wife towards her husband in death as in life?

I will carry out his last wishes—whatever they are—because that is what he would have expected of me. I will do it. I will come home to England. Home to my baby son, who is now King of England.'

'You are a brave woman.'

I turned my head and looked directly at James, seeing a depth of compassion in his face as I remembered John expressing similar sentiments. How wrong they were. I was not brave at all. 'Why could he not have loved me?' I asked. 'Am I so unlovable?'

It came unbidden to my lips, and I expected no answer but, surprising me, James replied. 'I don't know how Henry's mind worked. He was driven by duty and God's will for England.' He hitched a shoulder. 'No one held centre place in his life. It's not that he could not love you. I doubt he could love anyone.' His smile was a little awry. 'If I did not love Joan, *I* would love you.'

It was an easy response, and one he had made before, but it struck at my heart. And I wept at last under the arch of the cathedral door, tears washing unhindered down my cheeks. I wept for Henry, who had not lived to see his visions fulfilled, and for myself and all my silly shattered dreams: the young girl who had fallen in love with the hero of England, who had wooed her as a political necessity.

'My lady.' Made uneasy by my tears, James handed me a piece of linen. 'Don't distress yourself.'

'How can I not? I am French. Without Henry, I will be the enemy.'

'So am I the enemy. We will weather it together.'

'Thank you,' I murmured. I wiped my tears and lifted my head as I followed my husband's body into the hallowed darkness. All I wanted was to be at Windsor with my son.

★ ★ ★

When we buried Henry in Westminster Abbey, I gave him everything he rejected from me in life: all the care and attention that a wife could lavish on her husband. Henry had arranged it all, of course—how could I ever think I would be given a free hand?—but I paid for it out of my own dower, and I watched the implementation of his wishes with a cold heart as I led the mourners in procession to the Abbey, with James at my side, Lord John behind.

I arranged that Henry's three favourite chargers should be led up to the altar. I considered that he would be more gratified with their presence than with mine.

Henry had put in place a plan for a tomb and chantry chapel in the very centre of the Abbey. So be it. I arranged for the workmen and paid their wages for the very best work they could achieve. No worshipper in the Abbey would ever be able to ignore Henry's pre-eminence in death as in life.

I also took the effigy in hand: carved in solid English oak, plated with silver gilt, head and hands in solid silver. And above this magnificent representation were hung his most treasured earthly possessions. His shield and saddle and helmet. Trappings of war.

Completed at last, gleaming as it did with dull magnificence in the light from hundreds of candles, I stood beside the remarkable resemblance of his effigy. I placed my hand on his cheek then on his chest, where once his heart beat. The heart beneath my hand was still, stone-like in its oaken carcase, but mine shivered within the cage of my ribs.

'I am sorry, my lord. I am sorry that I could not mean more to you. Your heart never beat for me—but I vow that I will raise your son to be the most powerful king that England has ever seen.'

It was all I could do for him, and I would not be found wanting in this.

Then, distressingly, clearly into my mind came Madam Joanna's memory of the old prophecy:

Henry born at Monmouth shall small time reign and much get.

The accuracy of the old wisewoman's reading of Henry's lifespan took my breath. So short a life, so great an achievement. But would her further insight come to pass also?

Henry born at Windsor shall long reign and all lose.

What a terrible burden this placed on me, for was I not helpless to alter the course of such predestined events? But my protectiveness towards my son was reborn with even greater fervency. I would protect him and guide him and pray to God that his reign would be as glorious as his father's. As the whole country mourned the passing of its acclaimed King, I decided that that must be the course of my life, to protect and nurture. And I banished the unsettling prophecy from my thoughts. I would simply not let it happen.

7

'WHAT AM I?' I asked Humphrey, Duke of Gloucester, Henry's youngest and least appealing brother, and now the newly appointed Protector of England. King in all but name as far as I could see, but it had been Henry's wish, and so I must bow to it. And to him. It was exactly one week since I had accompanied Henry's coffin to his burial in Westminster Abbey.

'You are Queen Dowager.' He spoke slowly, as if I might not quite understand the significance of it, and looked down his high-bridged nose. He would rather not be having this conversation with me. I did not know whether he still doubted my facility with the language or questioned the state of my intellect.

Of one fact I was certain: Gloucester was a bitter man, bent on grabbing as much power for himself as he could. Henry, in his final days, had conferred on this younger brother the *tutelam et defensionem* of my son. On the strength of that, Gloucester had claimed the Regency in England when Lord John of Bedford had shouldered power in France, but Gloucester was not a man to make friends easily.

The lords of the Royal Council declined—very politely but firmly—to invest Gloucester with either the title or the power to govern in this way, only agreeing to him becoming principal counsellor with the title of Protector. Gloucester had not forgiven them, directing most of his animosity at Bishop Henry Beaufort, whom he suspected of stirring up the opposition.

'You are the supremely respectable, grieving widow of our revered late king,' he continued, in the same manner.

His explanation was straightforward enough, but it did not make good hearing. *Queen Dowager.* It made me sound so old. As if I had already lived out my life and my usefulness, and now all I had left was to wait for death, whilst I eked out my existence with prayer and the giving of alms to the poor. Much like Madam Joanna, I pondered, now enjoying her freedom but with increasing ill health. But she was fifty-four years old. I was twenty-one.

Still, I was not sure what Gloucester—and England—expected me to do.

'What does that mean, my lord?' I pressed him. I was at Windsor with my baby son, now almost a year old, in a court in mourning. My future too, to my mind, was heavily shrouded, like the winter mists creeping over the water meadows, obscuring all from view. Gloucester had descended on us from Westminster to assess for himself the baby king's health. He was announced into my solar where I sat with my damsels, Young Henry at my feet, busy investigating a length of vivid purple silk from my embroidery. 'What role do I have?'

Gloucester pretended, in his supercilious manner, to misunderstand me. 'You have no political role, Katherine. How would you? I'm amazed that you expect one.'

'Of course I didn't expect a political role, Humphrey.' Since he would be informal, so would I. 'All I wish to know is what place I have at Court. What it is that I am expected to do.'

His brows rose and he waved a hand around the well-appointed room as if I were particularly stupid to ask. With its beautifully furnished tapestries and hangings, vivid tiles beneath my feet and the polished wood of stools and coffers, indeed I could have asked for nothing more sumptuous to proclaim my royal state. The windows in this room were large, admitting light even on the dullest of days. I followed Gloucester's gesture, appreciating all I had been given, but...

'What do I do for the rest of my life?' I asked.

Henry was dead. I did not miss him: I had never had him to miss, except as an ideal of what I had expected my husband to be. His funeral was over, the silver death mask gleaming in Westminster Abbey, but his legacy for England and his heir dogged my every step. He had been busy indeed on his death-bed when the future government and security of England had been mapped out in every possible detail.

During Young Henry's infancy, England would be governed by the Council, and those holding the reins of power would be Henry's closest family. Lord John of Bedford would rule as Regent of France and control the future pursuit of war.

Humphrey of Gloucester, my present reluctant companion, was Protector of England but subordinate to Bedford in all things—which was the reason for Gloucester's sour expression. And added to the mix was Henry's uncle, Henry Beaufort, Bishop of Winchester, who would be tutor to my young son. I liked Henry Beaufort—he was a shrewd politician, a man ambitious for promotion, but a man not without compassion. Whereas in Gloucester there was no compassion, only a driving need for personal aggrandisement.

Thus Henry had laid down the pattern for how England should be governed until his baby son came of age.

'Is there no part for me in my son's life?' I asked.

For there was no mention of me in the ordering of the realm. Should I have expected one? I saw Henry's reasoning well enough when he carefully omitted me. I was too closely tied to the enemy in the person of my brother the Dauphin, and as a woman——a woman whom Gloucester still considered incapable of understanding all but the most simple of English sentences—government in any capacity would be entirely beyond me.

'What do I do with the rest of my life, Humphrey?' I repeated, enjoying his reaction as he flinched when I called him Humphrey, but he considered my question.

'You are the Queen Mother.'

'I know, but I wish to know what that will mean. Am I...?' I sought for the word 'superfluous' and he must have seen my agitation for he deigned to explain.

'You, Katherine, are of vital importance to England. It is your royal Valois blood that gives the new King his claim to France. And now that your own father is dead...'

For so he was, my torment-ravaged father. His body and mind had been eaten away by those invisible terrors, until eventually he had succumbed to them. My father had died two short months after Henry's own demise, leaving my little son at ten months with the vast responsibility of kingship over both England and France. I suspected Gloucester considered it a most convenient death.

'And since your brother the Dauphin refuses to recognise our claim to France and continues to wage war to wrest France from us...'

True. Brother Charles—Charles VII as he now claimed—had an army in the field against us.

'...we must use every weapon we have to assert our claim for the boy. *You* are that weapon. Your blood in this child's veins is the strongest weapon we have to enhance Henry's son's claim to the French throne.' Henry's son, I noted with a twist to my heart. He would always be Henry's son. 'There are many in France who will argue that the boy is too young. That he is English. But he is part Valois too, and so his claim to the French Crown is second to none.'

I nodded slowly. I was to be a symbol, exactly as my mother had painted for me. A living, breathing fleur-de-lys to stamp my son's right to sit on the French throne.

'I do have a part to play, then.'

'Undoubtedly. And I must call on you to play that part to perfection. You must make yourself visible in public, as soon as your deepest mourning is over.'

'And how long will that be?'

'I think a year will be deemed acceptable. You must pay all due respect to my brother. It will be expected of you.' Gloucester smiled thinly. 'Remaining here at Windsor with the Young King should be no obstacle for you.'

A year of mourning. My heart fell. No dancing or music for a year, no life outside Windsor. As the widow of the hero of Agincourt I must be honourable and virtuous. Being enclosed in a convent could be no worse.

'Then, you must attend the Young King in all ceremonials, standing with him, reminding the country of the child's rich inheritance,' Gloucester continued. 'You will remain close to the boy. You are the female embodiment of his royal power and will be given a high political profile when it is considered necessary.'

I could have been a statue in Westminster Abbey. Or an armorial in the glazed windows, an embodiment of French royal blood, engraved in stone or coloured glass. It chilled my blood.

'And when not necessary?' I asked. 'When I have observed my days of mourning and am not engaged in ceremonial?'

'You must be circumspect at all times, Katherine. You must not draw attention to yourself for any but the highest of reasons. There must be no cause for suspicion of your interests or behaviour. I am sure you understand me.' He was already drawing on his gloves, preparing to return to Westminster, presumably to report to the Council that the Queen Dowager had been made thoroughly cognisant of the future pattern of her life to enhance the glory of England.

'You mean, I presume, that I must not draw attention to my Frenchness.'

'Exactly. And you will remain in the Young King's household. My late brother insisted on it.' His tone, now that he had informed me of the lack of freedom, was brisk and business-like and he strode to the door. 'You will retain your income from your dower properties. It will be a satisfactory sum to pay for your small entourage. It is considered that four dam-sels will be sufficient for your needs as you will live retired. Do you not agree?'

'Four…?' I was used to more than that.

'You will keep no state. Why would you need more?' Gloucester drove on. 'We have appointed a steward and chan-cellor for you from my late brother's household. John Leven-thorpe and John Wodehouse will deal with all such matters appertaining to your household and your dower lands. They will have all the experience you will need to preserve a house-hold worthy of the Queen Mother.'

I knew them both. Aging men now, meticulous and gifted, with long service to Henry and to his father before him.

'We have appointed a new Master of the Queen's House-hold to order and arrange all things for you. One Owen Tudor, who served under my brother.'

I knew him too. A dark young man with a dramatic fall of black hair and an air of ferocious efficiency, who said little and achieved much, and who had gained his experience in service with Sir Walter Hungerford in France. As steward of Henry's own household, Sir Walter had an eye for an able man, even though this choice of Gloucester's, Owen Tudor, seemed to me to be young for such a weighty position. But what did it matter to me? I was hemmed in by Henry's world as much now as I had been before his death.

'I expect you will choose your own confessor and chaplain, and your chamber women,' Gloucester continued, surveying me dispassionately. 'You will have your own suite of rooms, and there you will be expected to keep queenly state. Beyond that you will obey the instructions sent to you and present the dignified face of Queen Mother to the world.'

I nodded, barely taking this in but holding on to the sweet kernel in the nut. I would accept the period of mourning: it was what Henry deserved, and I would mourn him with due diligence as befitted a French princess. I would accept my ceremonial role and play it to perfection. I would accept that I was to be given no choice in the appointment of officials to my household, except for my chaplain and chamber women. I would tolerate all of that because in Gloucester's chilly portrayal of my life he had made one pertinent comment.

You will remain close to the boy.

'I can play that role, my lord,' I said with formal dignity.

'We are gratified, my lady.'

I did not like the look in his eye. Neither did I like it that not once had Gloucester shown any interest in his nephew beyond a cursory glance.

When the door closed at Gloucester's back, I picked up my son, holding his body close, his fair curls soft against my cheek. He was mine: he would always be mine and I would lavish all the love on him that I had.

As the years passed I would watch him grow, learning his lessons, able to wield a sword and ride a horse. One day he would be as great a soldier as his father had been. My days would be well spent in setting his tiny feet on that path. The prophecy would come to nought.

Young Henry patted my cheek then struggled to be set down.

'You will be a great king,' I whispered in his ear, holding him tightly, ashamed at the tears that gathered in my eyes.

Young Henry crowed against my shoulder, gripping the folds of my robe.

It came to me that if it had not been for my little son I would have sunk into despair.

I had expected to be pre-eminent in the upbringing of my son. Was I not his mother? Was I not the embodiment of virtuous and noble motherhood, like the Blessed Virgin herself? Not so. At the turn of the year I received a document, which I handed to Master Wodehouse, my new Chancellor: a kindly man, if content to sit with a cup of ale beside a fire in his latter years. Fortunately my demands on him were few.

'What is this?' I asked.

It was formal and official in a clerkly hand, and beyond my deciphering.

'It is the appointment of a legal guardian for the Young King, my lady.'

'A guardian?'

'The young King has a new guardian, my lady. Richard Beauchamp, Earl of Warwick. A good man.'

Well, of course he was. I knew Warwick. But his goodness was not an issue. I did not care if he was good. 'Who says this?' I demanded.

'The Council, my lady. It was to be expected,' Master Wodehouse advised gently, wary of my irritation. And he read on to the end of the Council's statement while I brooded in silence. It may have been expected, but not by me. I had not been consulted, but I was given to understand that Henry had wished it; Henry's brothers and uncle wished it. But I did not.

I could not see why my son would need a guardian when his mother was perfectly capable of guarding his interests.

How dared they go over my head and appoint a guardian who would effectively oust me from my son's side, who would have the power to overrule any decisions I might wish to make?

'It is an excellent choice, my lady.' Master Wodehouse was still regarding me with some concern. 'There could be no better man in the whole of England to protect and advise your son as he grows. Supervising his education and training in all aspects of kingship. It is beyond you, my lady.'

I frowned at him, and the document.

'Indeed he is the best man possible, my lady.'

And as I considered it, I saw the sense of it—as I must, for I was not entirely without insight into my son's needs. As he grew my child would need a man to guide and instruct him in all aspects of warfare as well as in government. Bishop Henry was well intentioned but too entangled in clerical matters and too self-interested, Gloucester too pompous for my taste. Lord John was committed to events in France.

'Could you find any fault in him, my lady?' Master Wodehouse asked.

'No.' I sighed. 'No, I cannot. It is just that...'

'I understand. You do not wish to let go of the boy.'

No, I did not. There was nothing much else in my life.

I pondered on what I knew of Richard Beauchamp, Earl of Warwick, who had been at Henry's side since that very first day in the pavilion at Meulan. A man of erudition, a man of considerable reputation, he was barely forty years old, even tempered with considerable personal charm, with all the experience and knowledge I could have asked for. I was forced to admit that Warwick was the perfect choice to teach a growing boy everything a young prince should know. To study, to choose between right and wrong, to fight as a knight to inspire his people, and all the military things that a man must learn that I could not give him.

Besides, I liked Warwick.

And so I allowed him his jurisdiction—since I had no power to circumvent it—but still I had to fight the resentment in my heart. The distancing from my son was hard to bear, even though Warwick applied his power with a light hand, often leaving Young Henry in my care when state matters demanded that he be at Westminster. Young Henry was still too young to wield a sword, even a wooden one, and his daily routine continued to rest with me and the coterie of nurses, supervised by Joan Asteley, who spoiled and cosseted him.

So my initial resentment settled, and I decided that the Council's decisions could have been far worse. But my complacency could not last. In my heart I knew it and Warwick warned me as we stood in the nursery on one of his visits.

'He looks well,' Warwick observed as he stroked his hand over Young Henry's head. My son was asleep, hooded eyes closed, lips relaxed, reminding me how like his father he was in repose.

'He is. Soon he will be running through the palace.' But not like I had run at the *Hôtel de St Pol*. Never like that.

'I must buy him a pony.' Warwick laughed. Then became serious as if he knew I would not like what he said. 'The time has come, my lady.' I regarded him quizzically, suddenly aware. 'Now that the Young King is more than a year old, he must be put under the guidance of a governess.'

At first I did not quite understand. 'Do I need more servants?' I asked. 'If so, my steward will appoint—'

'The governess will be appointed by the Council,' he said gently.

I felt that unpleasant shiver of apprehension. Warwick, as

guardian, was a distant figure, willing to allow me a degree of influence, but a governess appointed by the Council would be ever present, a real and constant authority.

'My son has a whole parcel of nurses to see to his needs,' I remarked coldly. 'Joan Asteley has my complete confidence. Mistress Waring, of course. Young Henry loves her.'

'He needs more, Katherine. Mistress Waring's influence must end.' His gentle use of my name warned me. 'He needs a governess to nurture him in courtesy and good manners. Most importantly he needs a governess who has the power to chastise the Young King if necessary.'

Courtesy. Good manners... My authority as his mother counted for less and less. 'She would chastise my son?' I was outraged. Yet had not our servants in France chastised me, and not always with a light hand? As I remembered the slaps, the sharp blows of a whip, my hands tightened into fists.

'Only within reason, my lady.'

'And what is reason?' Abruptly I turned my back on him to walk to the end of the room. 'She is not his mother. How will she know?' I raised my voice. 'I do not agree.'

Warwick followed me, eyes soft with sympathy, but he spoke plainly, as was his wont. 'This is no argument here, Katherine. It will happen with or without your consent—and it must be no surprise to you. It is customary for princes to be raised in their own households. You cannot expect to keep him close to you, even though you live in the same palace. He will be raised with his own staff, eventually with youngsters of noble blood of his own age. He will learn what it is to be King. You know this. Surely you were brought up with your royal brothers and sisters in a similar manner?'

'Yes,' I admitted abruptly. Did he not realise? That was my reason for resisting. I remembered my own childhood far too vividly. 'I know exactly what it can be like. I would not give my son to the possibility of such neglect. Or *chastisement*!'

'It will not be like that.'

I took a turn to the window and back, hemmed in by the shadows of the past. 'I hear what you say.' I tried to hide the hopelessness that lapped against my heart. 'Do I have any influence over who will be governess?'

'The appointment will be decided by the Council,' Warwick repeated.

So, no. The answer was no. I pressed my fingertips against my lips to still their trembling. I would not weep. I would remain strong, for my son's sake, and I frowned at the idea that encroached, and not for the first time, since Gloucester's dislike of me bit deep.

'Is it because I am my mother's daughter, and her reputation is not of the best? Is my influence not trustworthy?'

Warwick considered his answer.

'I think you have to accept that there are those in the Council who wish to supersede your influence.' He shrugged uneasily, aware that his reply had hurt. 'You must accept it, Katherine. The governess chosen by the Council will deal well with the boy. He is growing quickly; he needs more than clean clothes and regular meals. He needs discipline and education, and he needs to be raised with all the tenets of an English prince.'

But did I not have the right to nurture him and see him grow out of babyhood? My mother had never watched me. I would watch my son, for he was all I had. In that moment I felt like resting my head on Warwick's shoulder and weeping out my sorrows.

'It will not be a bad thing,' he told me. 'They will appoint someone who is wise and kind and has experience of children.'

'You are a member of the Council. Will you have a voice in who is chosen?' I asked, raising my chin. I would not weep.

'Yes.'

'Can you sway them against any choice made by Gloucester?'

Warwick smiled dryly. 'I am not without influence.'

It was my one hope.

I knew what I wanted, what I must do, for my own peace of mind. All that was required was a little careful intrigue. A week later, during which I was not inactive, I requested Warwick's attendance at Windsor again, waylaying him as he entered the palace and crossed the Great Hall.

'I have been considering my son's governess, sir.' He bowed with his customary grace, but his glance was more than a little wary, probably preparing for another battle with the Queen Mother, who ought to have the sense to accept the decisions made for her son. 'Has the Council made its choice?' I asked.

'Not to my knowledge, my lady.' He slid another glance in my direction.

'Then come with me.'

I led him to the nursery where Joan Asteley and her minions were occupied in the constant demands of a young boy that filled their day. But there, in the midst of the activity, a woman was seated on a stool with Young Henry on her lap. A tall, spare lady in sombre garments, straight-backed and authoritative, her hair hidden in the pristine folds of her white coif. When we arrived she was speaking with my son, allowing him to work his hands into her gloves, laughing with him when he laughed. When she heard the door open, she looked up.

'I do not need to introduce you, sir,' I said, admiring the picture they presented. Henry, appealingly angelic today, had a new blue tunic and a matching felt cap flattening his curls. His cheeks were flushed, his eyes alight with his occupation.

The woman's stern face was softened with laughter, the sharp gaze holding a glint of unexpected roguishness at what we had plotted together.

Warwick came to an abrupt stop, then strode in with a bark of a laugh.

'No. You do not. Perhaps I should not be surprised to see you here, Alice. Can I guess why?'

Dame Alice Botillier placed my son on his feet at her side, and stood with a smile, holding out her hands. Warwick took them and kissed her on both cheeks.

'You don't need to guess,' she said. 'You are a man of considerable foresight.'

'So?' Warwick surveyed me, and then Alice. 'Do I scent a scheme here? Am I being outmanoeuvred?'

'No scheme, sir. Here is my son's new governess.' I repeated Warwick's words back to him. 'She is wise and kind and has experience of children.'

'As I know.'

'Mistress Alice has served me before, during my confinement. Her husband was well regarded by the King.'

'Indeed. I know that too.'

'If you would be so good as to recommend her to the Council.'

Warwick's agile brows rose. 'And how could I not as she is a kinswoman of mine?'

I smiled. 'Exactly so!'

So Mistress Alice Botillier, at my instigation and as a more than willing ally, joined my household when Warwick's recommendation was accepted by the Council. Alice had left my service in France, remaining with her husband, Sir Thomas, and her son, Ralph, when I had returned with Henry's body, but she had taken little persuading to join me once more. I liked her and respected her: she was for me the perfect choice, and closely connected to Warwick's family as she was, the Council would see no difficulty. Alice would raise my son as she had raised her own.

Yet still I seethed with jealousy. For her authority over every action of my son was supported by the Council and by law, and it hurt my heart to watch Alice's influence grow. Young Henry ran to her rather than to me. When he wept, it was her lap in which he burrowed for comfort. She soothed him when he woke in fear from bad dreams. I did not think he cried for me. I did not think that he noticed when I left him to his nursemaids. I was being pushed further and further back into the shadows, shadows that were increasingly difficult to disperse.

Holy Mother, grant me your strength to live this life with some vestige of inner peace.

And for the most part I did, but oh, I wept with savage grief for my sister. My beloved sister was dead. Suddenly, shockingly, a report had come that Michelle was dead. I could not comprehend it; I could not accept that her loving nature and bright spirit were quenched for ever. My first impulse was to go to France—but to what purpose? My sister was dead and I would not mourn with my mother.

I wept and for a little while Alice comforted me as she comforted my son. Sometimes I despaired. All gone—my father, my sister, my husband. Who was left with whom I could open my heart?

Blessed Virgin, have mercy on me. Keep my son safe.

But Young Henry was increasingly less and less mine.

What have you done with your clever arrangements, Henry? What vile future have you wrought for me? You have left me nothing, not even my child. If I lose Young Henry, what do I have left?

★ ★ ★

I fell into melancholy. The shortening days of winter, which had always induced a weight on my spirits, now pressed me down so low that I could hardly stand upright to bear them. As darkness invaded every day, I could not shake off my desolation. I slept badly, yet when daybreak came I felt no urge to rise and face the new day.

I ate little, my gowns began to hang on my shoulders, and I felt a tremor behind my eyes before the onset of such pain that I must take to my bed. When restored, I felt no lighter. Sometimes I could not order my thoughts in my mind. Sometimes I forgot what I was about to say, at others I forgot the reply. I kept to my bedchamber on those days, afraid of stumbling over simple words that would cause my four damsels to exchange anxious glances.

The dark nights of my loneliness, the winter cold of my isolation, gnawed at my mind.

'Walk in the gardens, my lady,' Alice ordered when the morning acquired a gleam of pale sunshine. 'It will do you good to get out of this room.'

So I did, with reluctant steps, my women trailing equally reluctantly in the damp chill.

'Ride along the riverbank,' Alice suggested.

So I did that too, but horsemanship was not something I excelled in and I felt the cold bite into my bones as we plodded along at a snail's pace. I had no wish to exchange meaningless gossip with those who rode with me.

'Drink this.' Alice, seeing me wan and desolate on my return, presented me with a cup of some foul-smelling substance.

So I drank, not asking what it might be—I had no interest—choking over the bitter aftertaste of herbs that made my belly clench.

'Look at you!' she admonished. 'You must not allow this, my lady. You must eat.'

I studied my reflection in my looking glass. My skin was pale, my hair lank and dull. Had my cheekbones always been as sharp as that? Even the blue of my eyes seemed to have leached into pale grey. I tried to pick at the platter of sweet fritters for fear of Alice's sharp tongue, but stopped as soon as her back was turned. In those days she was as much my nurse and mentor as Young Henry's.

I was allowed to accompany my son to the formal opening of Parliament at Westminster. A magnificently formal occasion, it was eminently threatening for a child so young, and I was full of trepidation that Young Henry would fail to impress his subjects. Would not any failure be laid at my door? Perhaps he would even be sent away from me.

'Did you approve?' I asked Warwick, who had returned with us to the royal accommodations at Westminster after the event, sitting with us as we sipped a cup of ale. Henry, almost asleep on his feet, was dispatched with Joan to the nursery while Alice and I exchanged glances of sheer relief. Young Henry's fit of childish temper on the day of his entry into London had terrified me with its frenzy, but now pride in my son was a warm fire in my belly.

'How could I not?' Warwick smiled at some memory. 'He was every inch a king. His father would have been proud of him. What a sovereign we will make of him.'

'He wooed Parliament, didn't he?' Young Henry had clapped his hands when the Speaker had bowed before him.

'And so did his mother.' Warwick lifted his cup in a silent toast.

I blushed, surprised at the gathering of tears in my eyes. What an emotional day it had been, and such praise meant more than I could express for my own confidence. I had played

my part, made a good impression. My fears of losing Young
Henry receded.

Alice left us. The short day grew dark, and Warwick stood
to make his departure.

'Is that it?' I asked. 'Do we now return to Windsor?'

Warwick tilted his head. 'Until next year. We'll not over-
burden the boy.'

'No.' Of course we would not. I clasped my hands tightly
together, as if in a plea, and looked up at him. He was the only
man I could ask. 'I need to do more, Richard.'

'You will, as he grows older and can cope with more demands.'

'I think I will do less,' I admitted sadly. 'As my son grows,
he will stand alone.'

'But not for many years.'

The day, with its step back into the world of the Court
and politics, the bustle and excitement of London, had been a
two-edged sword for it had stirred me to life again. Returning to Windsor was like closing the lid of a newly opened coffer, dimming the sparkle of the jewels within, and it would
remain closed for the foreseeable future. What a narrow path
this was for me to follow.

As my son grew he would willingly cast off the need for
his mother's presence on such occasions as this. At some point
in the future my son's wife would oust me completely, and I
would be nothing. Today I had been honoured with my child
on my knee, but I was restless, unsettled. Fearful of a future
that promised nothing.

'Will I marry again?' I asked.

It surprised me, much like the brush of moth's wings against
my hair in the dusk, the thought alighting from nowhere in
my mind, like a summer swallow newly returned. I had never

thought of remarriage before. But why not? Barely into my third decade, why should I not?

'Do you wish to? I had not realised.' Warwick looked equally startled.

'No, no. I have no such plans, or even thoughts of it. But… will I be allowed to? Will the Council allow it? At some future time in my life?' Suddenly it seemed of major importance that I should have this promise of possible fulfilment and companionship—even of love—somewhere on my horizon.

'Why not? I can see no reason why you should not.' Warwick paused, the moment marked by a thin line between his smooth brows. 'As you say, as Henry grows he will become more independent. Why should you not remarry?' Another pause. 'If a suitable husband is found for you, of course.'

His obvious unease comforted me not at all.

If a suitable husband is found for you.

The qualification found a fertile home in my mind, for was that not the essence of it? Who would be considered suitable? I recalled Gloucester's inflexible portrait of Katherine, the Queen Dowager. I did not think my remarriage was something he would tolerate when he had painted me into a lonely, isolated existence, a gilded figure in an illustrated missal.

I forced myself to pass my time in useful pursuits. No dark night, no cold winter could last for ever. I made myself appear to be busily employed, and so I turned the pages of a book but found no interest in the adventures of Greek gods or heroes who fell in and out of love with envious verve.

I ordered music but I would neither sing nor dance. How could I dance alone? I played with Young Henry, but he was now being drawn into a regime of books and religious observance. I applied my needle with even less enthusiasm, the leaves that blossomed under my needle appearing flat and lacking in life, as if the imminent approach of winter would cause them to shrivel and die. It seemed to me that my own winter approached, even before I had blossomed into summer.

This would be the tenor of my life until the next opening of Parliament, when Young Henry would journey to London and I would again accompany him. Year after year the same. Henry had used me to further his ambitions in France. Now I would be used to bolster the authority of my baby son.

Sometimes I wept.

'You need company, my lady.' Alice was fast losing patience.

True, but I was unlikely to get it. Oh, I tried to smile and join in with the damsels, when Meg and Beatrice and Joan whispered their endless gossip and Cecily spoke of love, unrequited for the most part. I tried to force myself to enjoy a cup of spiced wine and the scandalous tale of Gloucester's matrimonial exploits to while away the November evenings. And indeed I was momentarily diverted with the reprehensible issue between Lord Humphrey and his wife, Jacqueline of Hainault, a bigamous union, for she was already wed to the Duke of Barbant, and there had been no annulment.

But my interest was tepid at best and they gossiped without me when they found me poor company. I could not blame them. Their chattering voices with their opinions and comments and lewd suggestions barely touched my soul. They, I suspected, were as bored as I, shut away as we were at Windsor at the court of a baby king.

Warwick—dear, kind Warwick—sent me a gift, a lap dog with curling chestnut hair and sharp eyes, and equally sharp teeth. Probably, in a fit of remorse, to take the place of a husband, since the possibility of one had been so far into the future as to be impossible to envisage. I suspected Alice's involvement too, hoping it would entice me from misery, and indeed it was a charming creature, still young enough to cause havoc in my chamber, pouncing on embroidery silks and chewing anything left in its path, but it did not distract me.

You are a poor creature! I castigated myself. *You have no cause to be so lacking in spirit.*

Loneliness wrapped itself, shroud-like, around me, and I covered my face with my hands so that I could not see the aimless path that I must follow until the day I died.

Holy Virgin, I prayed at my *prie-dieu* every morning. *Holy Virgin, grant me some solace. Grant me resolve to see my life as a more purposeful journey.*

'Perhaps you should take the boy and go to Westminster for the Christmas festivities,' Alice growled as November moved into December. 'My lord of Warwick will allow it, I'm certain.'

'No,' I replied, my voice as dull as my mind. 'I will not celebrate.'

She strode from my chamber, eyes snapping at my intransigence. I felt no guilt.

A week later the space of Windsor's Upper Ward was full of people and horses. The sudden burst of voices and clattering hooves on the cobbles could be heard even through the glazed windows of the chamber where my damsels and I sat to catch the final spare gleams of the afternoon sun, but I was disinclined to stir myself to look to find out the reason. Probably Warwick come to check on the progress of Young Henry, hopefully without another lap dog. The cheerful activity was, however, too much for my damsels to ignore.

'My lady?' Meg asked, already on her feet.

'Look, if you will,' I said, not that they needed my permission. My hand of authority was a light one.

A shriek of joy from Joan made all clear.

'I take it that the King of Scotland visits us,' I remarked fretfully. I had not seen him for months.

'May I, my lady?' she asked. She was already halfway to the door.

'Of course. Try to be...' the door shut behind her '...maidenly and decorous.'

And she ran, leaving me with a few sharp pangs, firstly that my mood was so churlish, and even more that the arrival of a visitor should give her so much pleasure yet hardly move me from my chair. But I must. I placed the lute I had been idly strumming on the coffer and fixed what I hoped would be a welcoming smile on my mouth.

Would it not be good to see James again? I could not expect him to dance attendance on me as he had done in those early months after Henry's death, for he had his own life to lead, even if it was curtailed and hemmed about with watchful eyes. I must make him welcome—and there he was, hair curling energetically onto his shoulders, dark eyes gleaming with some personal satisfaction, and Joan looking flushed and eager and youthfully pretty, almost clinging on to his arm. My advice to her had clearly gone unheeded. And then, before I could frown a warning at her, heralded by a burst of vigorous conversation, my chamber was invaded by a group of young men. Around them the damsels glowed, as if the flames of a score of candles had been set ablaze.

I blinked. I had grown unused to such vitality or such lack of rigidly formal courtesy. They were like my puppy, overwhelming in their energy that smashed against my staid walls, ringing from the rafters. Their faces were vivid, their voices sharp and confident, and even their clothing was bright, eye-catchingly fashionable, bringing in a breath of freezing air to prod us into wakefulness after a winter's hibernation. It was as if a heavy curtain, muffling my chamber from the outside world, deadening every sound, had been rent apart.

Meanwhile, approaching with long strides, James lost no time in polite greeting but flung out his arms before me.

'It has been agreed!'

'What has?' My thoughts refused to drop comfortably into line.

'Katherine!' He seized my hands and saluted my fingertips. 'How can you not know? Are you so isolated here? Or deaf to what's going on without?'

'Deaf, I expect.' I managed to smile apologetically.

'Never mind. I'm here to tell you in person. They have come to an arrangement at last.'

His face was alight, so much so that my forced smile became a true one as, finally, I caught the gist.

'Oh, James! I am so pleased for you. I take it you are to be released.'

'Yes. Freedom, by God.' His arms around my waist, he spun me round and replaced me on the same spot. 'I have attended every lengthy, tedious, impossibly dull negotiation between the long-winded but puissant commissioners from Scotland and England—and am come to tell you first because I knew you would wish me well.'

'Come and tell me,' I invited, because that was what he wanted from me, and I signalled for wine to be brought. His delight was infectious, stirring even my subterranean depths. Tucking my hand through his arm, I led him to sit beside me on a cushioned settle beside the fire.

'I've harried them from Pontefract to York and back again, until I swear they were weary of the sight of my miserable features. They have finally announced that I'm free to return to Scotland.' James, running his hands through his unmanageable hair, could barely sit still with the news. He was twenty-nine years old: he had survived fifteen years of cushioned captivity. I had no difficulty in imagining his pleasure, as if the door of a birdcage had been suddenly flung back to allow this glossy singing finch a glimpse of freedom.

And I thought that I too would like such a glimpse of freedom. Not to return to France—there was nothing to draw me there—but to live my life without restriction and to my own will.

'They'll make me pay, of course,' he was continuing as I surveyed the group of young men, his companions, who were making free with the wine at the far side of the room, enjoying the fluttering attentions of the damsels. I recognised most of them—sons of high-blooded English families—but I might have to search for a name or two. There was a loud burst of laughter and in that moment I wished I were there with them, simply a lady of the Court free to flirt and attract the eye of a handsome man.

Wistfully, I turned my attention back to James, who continued to expand on his good fortune. 'An extortionate ransom of sixty thousand marks.' He laughed with a sardonic bark. 'Good to know they see my worth. In their generosity, I get to pay it in annual instalments.' His cynical smile sat strangely on his youthful features, but he had learned cynicism before all else in his protracted exile. 'I hope it won't beggar Scotland. They'll not want me back if it does.'

'Of course they will,' I assured him, my attention snagged by a raucous burst of laughter.

One face in the *mêlée* of young men, and younger than most, caught my eye. A vital face with fine dark brows and russet eyes that glittered with high spirits.

'And do you know the best of it?' James continued, unaware of my wandering appreciation. 'I get my wife. I get Joan.' He leaned to where Joan hovered, close enough to overhear, snatched her hand and pulled her closer still until his arm was wound around her waist. 'I never thought I'd see the day. Or if I did, we would both be in our dotage before we climbed into the marriage bed together and I would be incapable.'

Joan giggled, her cheeks pink, and I smiled on them, even as claws of jealousy raked at my heart. Joan positively shimmered with happiness and James's love for her was written on his face far more clearly than it had ever been in his verses. I clenched my fists in the folds of my skirts. I would curb such instincts as base as envy.

'Have they set a date for your marriage?' I asked, aware now of a frown between James's eyes, but again my interest was caught elsewhere.

The young man with russet eyes and hair to match had snatched off his cap, flinging it to one of his friends, and was demonstrating a flamboyant thrust of an imaginary sword. He lunged, overbalanced, righted himself with a graceful turn of foot and burst into laughter. His companions mocked but slapped him on the back in easy camaraderie. He might be younger than most of them but he had a place in their society. When he retaliated with a series of quick punches to those who tormented him, I found myself smiling because I could do no other.

And, of course, I knew those features. When he turned to face me, repeating the thrust with an agile wrist, I saw the Beaufort family resemblance was strong. Joan's hair might be lighter, her eyes more brown than russet, but the smile was the same, the quick winging brows.

Here was her brother.

'No, they have not set a date for the marriage yet,' I heard James remark in reply to my question. 'They say it will be as soon as it can be arranged—although I have my doubts.' He shook off his concern, probably for the sake of Joan, who had begun to look anxious again, and he seized my hand and squeezed it. 'We'll live in hope—have I not done so for the past dozen years and more? And I'll expect you to dance at my wedding.'

'I don't dance,' I said flatly. My baser nature was still lurking around my mood, reluctant to let go and be banished.

'Well, you should.' For the first time he really looked at my face. 'What's wrong, Katherine? You don't look happy.' I shook my head. This was no day for my unreasonable miseries. 'In fact...' he pursued, frowning.

Immediately I stood, more than a little embarrassed that he should see so great a change in me. 'Perhaps you should introduce your friends.'

As a distraction it worked well enough. 'Most of them you know.' He complied, drawing the young men forward to make their bow. 'And here,' he announced, 'is Edmund.'

'My brother thought he ought to come to wish me well, my lady,' Joan said, pulling the young man before me. I saw love and admiration in her face, and was not surprised.

He bowed, more ostentatiously than was necessary in so intimate a setting, and I remembered his flamboyance with the invisible sword. Clearly he was a man to draw attention to himself, as was proved when the feathers of his velvet cap swept the floor, his arms spread in the deepest respect, until he looked up at me beneath his well-etched brows. He laughed aloud, his eyes full of mischief.

'My sister does me a disservice, my lady. I am not at her beck and call. Neither am I under orders from the newly restored King of Scotland.' His smile touched my heart as he took my hand and raised it formally to his lips. They were warm and dry against my skin and I shivered at their light brush as Edmund Beaufort continued, smoothly courteous, holding my gaze with his. 'I am come to pay my respects to the Young King. And, of course, to his lady mother.'

He hesitated as if he was lacking in assurance, but I knew

he was not. None of the Beauforts lacked assurance. 'If my lady will receive me here as a guest, in her household, as the King's cousin?'

The question made my heart flutter. How strange that he should ask it, and in so personal a manner. Why would I not receive him? The strange intensity of him undermined my habitual polite response, and I found myself searching for a reply, caught up in his stare.

His family history was not unknown to me, redolent as it was with past scandals. The Beaufort bloodline was descended from John of Lancaster and his mistress of many years Katherine Swynford. A scandalous, illegitimate line, of course, but on the marriage of the infamous pair the children had been subsequently legitimised and had married into the aristocratic families of the realm. Now, formidably ambitious, precociously gifted and intelligent as well as blood related to the King, they were one of the foremost families in the land.

And this was Edmund Beaufort, son of the Earl of Somerset and nephew of Bishop Henry, and of course Joan's brother. And second cousin to my son. A young man from a family skilled in warfare and politics, obviously destined for great things, as were all his family, although he had been too young to fight in the recent wars in France at Henry's side.

How old was he? I considered the years behind the supreme confidence, beneath the fluid line of muscle given attention by his fashionable tunic with its luxuriant sleeves and jewelled clasps. Less than twenty years old, I thought. Younger than I. But he had grown up since I had last seen him, a youth under Bishop Henry's care, when I had first come to England. Taller and broader, he would make a fine soldier now that he was grown into his strength.

'My lady?'

I had been staring at him. 'You are welcome,' I managed as

he bowed low again over my hand, brushing my fingers once more in chivalrous salute. And he did not release his clasp until I tugged my hand away, and then he did so with a rueful smile.

'Forgive me, my lady. I am sorely blinded by your beauty. As is every man here.'

It took my breath. I could only stare at him, as he stared back at me. Men did not flirt so openly with the Queen Dowager. Men did not flirt at all.

James, still caught up in his own woes and oblivious to any undercurrents, continued to expound. 'I still thought they would never release me, even with the document and the pen to hand.'

'Of course they would.' Edmund, abandoning me with a charming smile much older than his years, punched him on the arm. 'Have sense, man. Think about it. What will your return to Scotland bring of benefit to England? Peace between the two countries. Particularly if you decide you were well treated here.'

James gave a shout of laughter. 'So that's why the Exchequer has agreed to provide me with a tunic in cloth of gold for my wedding.'

'Of course. And in grateful thanks for your cloth of gold you will do exactly what England demands of you. You will withdraw all Scottish aid to French armies, and you will stop any plundering along the border between our two countries.'

I was impressed. How precocious he was, and how cynical, as were all the Beaufort clan. I could not look away as he stood, hands fisted on hips, outlining the future of English relations with Scotland. Edmund grinned, spreading his hands, long fingered and elegant. 'The cloth of gold is the last payment England will have to make for you. You'll be home in no time after the New Year. And we will send you off in good spirits, will we not, my lady?' He had spun round. Again, before I could prepare for it, that red-brown gaze was devouring my face and I felt myself flushing almost as rosily as Joan.

'What do you say, my lady?' he whispered, as if it were some intimate invitation.

And all I could do was swallow the breath caught fast in my throat.

'As for that, if you'll have us,' James interrupted, as he gestured to encompass his friends, 'we're in mind to stay here with you for Christmas and the New Year.'

'And the possibility of spending it with your newly affianced wife...' I managed to chide, pleased to have the attention drawn away from me.

'...has nothing to do with it.' But James's hand sought Joan's again.

'And you, Lord Edmund? Do your family expect you?' I held my breath, not quite knowing why. Or perhaps not willing to admit to it.

'No, my lady. I am here at your disposal.' His face was a miracle of deference.

'There are no festivities planned,' I warned. 'We live quietly.' I thought I sounded ungracious and tried to make amends. 'That is to say that usually we see no need to feast and...' This was no better. Windsor sounded much like a convent of aging nuns.

'Quietly?' Edmund interrupted, grinning. 'It's no better than a damned tomb. It's a dismal place. Old King Edward, who feasted and frolicked at every opportunity, must be turning in his grave. I think we should celebrate.'

'Celebrate what?' James asked warily, which gave me pause. It made me think that he might have had experience of some of Beaufort's wilder schemes. I could imagine Edmund Beaufort being wild.

'Your release, man. Let's make it a Christmas and Twelfth

Night to remember.' And Edmund Beaufort actually grasped my hand, linking his fingers with mine before I could react. 'What do you say, Queen Kat? Shall we shake Windsor back into life? Shall we make the old rooms echo with our play?'

Edmund Beaufort was irrepressible. *Queen Kat?* No one had ever called me that. But my heart was lighter. For the first time in many weeks my spirits had risen, and my room was full of noise and laughter. I did not know whether to laugh or rebuke him for his lack of respect. I did neither, for he gave me no time.

'Do you object to games and dancing, Majesty? I do hope not.' Releasing me as fast as he had seized hold of me, he swept me another magnificent bow, as full of mockery as it was possible to be, following it with a dozen agile dance steps that took him to plant a kiss on Beatrice's cheek. 'We'll celebrate around you if you've no taste for it—and you can sit on your dignity and let us get on with it.'

I laughed at the irreverent picture, and at Beatrice's astonished discomfiture. But there he was, waiting for my reply.

'Well, Cousin Queen? Do we celebrate with you or around you? Or do we leave you to your misery and take ourselves off to Westminster instead?'

I was struck by an overwhelming longing to be part of this youthful group.

'Let me arrange the festivities for you,' Edmund Beaufort pleaded in false anxiety. 'I will die of boredom if you refuse. Let me loose to bring this place back to life again.'

And you too. I heard the implication that was not spoken.

Entirely baffled, I felt the prickle of tears at his concern.

'I'd let him if I were you,' James remarked. 'He'll only badger you into insensibility if you don't.'

'Please let us dance, my lady,' Joan added.

'And even play games. We are not too old for games,' Meg observed.

'I would like it too,' Beatrice added solemnly.

I raised my palms, helpless before all the expectant faces. 'It seems that we celebrate,' I managed.

Edmund crowed at his success. 'Then we will. I'm at your feet, my lady. Your wish is my command.' True to his statement, he flung himself to his knees and raised the hem of my gown to his lips. When he looked up his face was all vivid life and expectation. 'We will turn night into day. We will transmute shadows into brightest sunlight.'

That was what I wanted.

The years fell away from me.

8

EDMUND BEAUFORT TOOK control with a snap of his impertinent fingers. I had never met anyone with so much inexhaustible energy. Or such a charmingly insolent denial of authority, such wanton disregard for my enforced cold respectability as Queen Dowager and Queen Mother. Or such wilful casting aside of court etiquette. Unleashed on the quiet Court at Windsor, Edmund Beaufort blew the cobwebs from the tapestries and stirred the old rooms into joyful activity, breathing life into rooms that had not seen occupation for years. I found myself at the centre of a whirlwind.

Our staid court became a place of ragingly youthful high spirits, the young courtiers who elected to remain with James and my damsels in no manner reluctant to be drawn into Edmund's plans. It was as if they were awakened from a long sleep, and I too. I was drawn in whether I wished it or no. And I did. I came alive, my despondency and desolation vanishing like mist under early morning sun. There was no lying abed in those frosty December mornings when the sound of the hunting horn beneath my window blasted me into activity. Neither was I allowed to cry off. We hunted through the days, come fair weather or foul.

Some days, seeing my wariness around horses, Edmund arranged that we take the hawks out into the marshes on foot.

There was little sport to be had, nothing but wet feet and icy fingers and shivering limbs by the time that the noon hour approached, but Edmund, in his role of Overseer of Inordinate Pleasure, had all arranged with my Master of Household. As the pale sun reached its zenith, wagons pulled by oxen trundled towards us along the track.

'What is this?' I squinted against the hazy sun.

'Everything for your comfort, of course, my lady.'

I watched with astonishment.

'When did he arrange this?' I asked James, who stood with his arm openly around Joan's shoulders.

'Lord knows. He's a past master. Give him an inch…'

And he would take a dozen miles. As he had. Hot braziers, the air shimmering around them, were manhandled onto the ground in our midst. Heaped platters of bread and meat and cheese, bowls of steaming pottage, flagons of warm spiced ale were all unloaded and a group of minstrels produced their instruments, blowing on their cold fingers. Soon the marshes echoed to music and song.

It was magical.

'Do you approve, Majesty?' Edmund asked with a bold stare.

'It's too late to ask that,' I replied in mock reproof.

He sank to his knees, head bent. 'I asked no permission. Am I in disgrace?'

'Would you care?' I thought he would not.

'I would care if I caused you to frown on me, lady.' Suddenly he was grave, looking up through his dark lashes, all light mockery abandoned, making me recognise that I must consider my choice of words. And so I kept them light as I borrowed a fiddle bow from one of the nearby minstrels and struck Edmund lightly on both shoulders.

'Arise, Lord Edmund. I forgive you everything. A hot brazier and a bowl of onion pottage on a freezing day can worm your way into any woman's favour. Even mine.'

He leapt to his feet. 'Come and be warm.'

Handing over the raptors to the waiting falconers, we ate, then danced on the frosted grass by the river, until the bitter wind dispelled even the heat of the fires and drove us in. I laughed at the irresistible impulsiveness of it all when we joined hands and circled like any peasant gathering, and my hand was clasped hard in Edmund Beaufort's as we hopped and leapt. As if he felt that I might run away if he released me for even a moment.

I felt like a young girl again. I had no intention of running.

Ah, but some days I felt old, older than my years, unable to respond to the simple magic of pleasure. A vicious cold snap found us skating on the solid stretch of river, silvered and beautiful in the frosty air, the grass seed heads coated in hoar.

'I cannot,' I said, when my damsels donned skates and proved their prowess. It looked dangerously uneven to me, the ice ridged and perilous to those who had no balance.

'Have you never skated?' Edmund was skimming fast across the frozen ripples, already at my side in an elegant slide and spurt of ice that drew all eyes, while I shivered miserably on the riverbank, reluctant even to try. I had a vision of me, sprawled and helpless and horribly exposed.

'No.'

'You can learn.'

'I doubt it.'

What's wrong with you? Why can you not just try? What will it matter if you fall over?

I am afraid. I think I have been afraid all my life.

And there was the familiar gloom lurking on the edge of my sight, waiting for me to allow it to approach closer and overwhelm me.

'You can, Queen Kat. There is nothing that you cannot do.' Edmund's certainty cut through my self-imposed misery. 'You will be an expert by tonight. I guarantee it.'

Still I sought for an excuse. 'I have no skates.'

He produced a pair, shaking them by their leather straps over my head. 'Sit there and I will remedy your lack.'

I sat on a folded cloak on the bank.

'Permit me, my lady.'

Without waiting for permission, he pushed back my skirt and lifted one foot, beginning to strap on the skate. I discovered that I was holding my breath, watching his bent head as he huffed at the stubbornness of the frozen leather. He wore a magnificently swathed velvet hood, his hair curling beneath it against his cheek; his fingers were sure and clever, even in the cold.

I took in a quick breath as they slid over my ankle, then round my instep. It was an intimate task but not once did he stray beyond what was acceptable. Quick and efficient, he was as impersonal as any servant. Not once did he look up into my face. Until it was done.

And then he did, holding my gaze, his own bright with knowing. 'There, my lady. It's done. You may breathe again.' His eyes outshone the jewels anchoring the velvet folds. He knew I had been holding my breath. My heart jolted against my ribs.

And then there was no time to think. Edmund braced himself to lift me, and drew me onto the ice. I clung to his arm as if he were my last resort in preserving my life, but I skated and my pride knew no bounds.

'A prize! A prize for Queen Kat, who has learned a hard lesson.'

He left me standing at the edge, to skate off to the far side, returning with a feather fallen from the wing of one of the swans that we had driven off in high dudgeon. It was perfect, shining white, and he tucked it into my hood.

'You are a pearl beyond price, Queen Kat.'

'Indeed, you must not...' Despite the cold, my body felt infused with heat, but a voice of sense whispered in my mind. Enchantment could be a dangerous thing.

And then before I could say more he was off with a whoop to swing Joan away from James and drag her along the curve in the river at high speed. And then even Alice, who had brought Young Henry down to see the jollity. He did not single me out again, for which I was glad.

I sat on the bank and watched, Young Henry tucked against my side. And when I shivered, my Master of Household strode across, shaking out a length of heavy woollen weave to wrap around the pair of us, anchoring it against the breeze with much efficient tucking. When I murmured my thanks, he bowed gravely in acknowledgement, sternly unsmiling, returning to his position.

As the wagons were repacked and we prepared to return to the castle, whose towers beckoned with promises of warmth and comfort, I retained enough presence to thank those who had added to our festivities—the minstrels, the servants, the long-suffering pages, who had been at our beck and call all day. I did not think Edmund would necessarily remember them, and it was my household after all.

'Master Tudor.' I summoned the young man who had stood, silent and watchful throughout. 'Do you have any coins?'

'I have, my lady.' Searching in the purse at his belt, he dropped into my outstretched hand a stream of silver.

I dispensed them with my thanks.

'You must tell me what I owe you,' I said.

'There is no need. I will note it in the accounts, my lady.'

His eyes were as dark as obsidian, his voice a slide of pleasurable vowels and consonants, but brusquely impersonal.

'Thank you,' I said hesitantly.

'There is no need, my lady,' he said again. 'It is my duty to see to your comfort.'

The winter evening's twilight was falling fast and I could see his face only obscurely, the planes of his face thrown into harsh dips and soft shadows. It seemed to me that the corners of his mouth were severely indented, almost disapproving— or perhaps it was a trick of the light.

A voice reached me, calling out to my left.

'Come and give me your opinion on this important matter, Queen Kat!'

I went joyfully where I was summoned.

I looked in my reflecting glass when we returned. My cheeks were flushed, my eyes bright, and not from the exercise. My thoughts were capricious, and all centred on Edmund Beaufort. I had wished he would not single me out, but was irritated when he did not. His wit, his outrageous compliments set fire to my blood, but then I found them too personal, too over-familiar.

I was swept with an urgency, a longing: I could barely wait to rise from my bed to experience a new day at the wilful hands of this man who had erupted into my life.

And then came the long evenings and nights, the days when it did not grow light and the twelve days of festivity drew close. The day before Our Lord's birth dawned, and the castle was shivering with anticipation. Perhaps I was the one to shiver, uncertain of what awaited me but exhilarated in equal measure.

I had had one Christmas with Henry, in Rouen, a rather sombre, religious affair, heavy with tradition and formal feasting and celebration of High Mass. And then I had spent Christmas alone at Windsor after my son's birth. We had made no merriment that year for I had not yet been churched. Neither did I recall any moments of festive joy as a child. This year would be different. This year Edmund Beaufort was at court. There was a distinct air of danger when we met together before supper on Christmas Eve. Not menace, but a waiting, a standing on tiptoe.

'We need a Lord of Misrule,' Joan announced. With James at her side she had blossomed like a winter rose. 'We cannot celebrate without a Lord of Misrule.'

We were standing in the Great Hall around the roaring fire, still in furs and heavy mantles after a foray along the riverbank. It was a tradition I knew of, such cunning and malice-laden creatures who turned the world upside down.

'I will be the Lord of Misrule,' Edmund announced, posturing in a fur-lined cloak of brightest hue. He looked like some malign being from the nether world.

'You can't,' Joan responded promptly. 'Tradition says he must be a servant, to make mockery of all things. You don't qualify.'

'I change tradition.' Edmund stared around the group. 'Who can stir us all to a frenzy of delight better than I?'

'I thought you had to be chosen,' James observed as he breathed on his fingers. 'A heathenish practice…' he grinned '…but one I've learnt to live with.'

'Chosen? I choose myself.' Edmund's brows rose, as if he was daring anyone to defy his decision, and then his stare fixed on my face. 'What do you say, Queen Kat? Am I your Lord of Misrule, from this day on?'

'Not allowed.' I shook my head solemnly, caught up in the game, but I thought there was more than a hint of petulance in the set of his mouth when his heart's desire was denied him.

There was no laughter in him. His scheming was not going as he wished, and I felt a mischievous urge to thwart him, whatever his intended plot. 'You know how it works,' I stated.

'And you will hold me to it?' he demanded, as if force of will could change my mind.

'I will. No cheating. We will all abide by the rules.'

I sent a page running to the kitchens while we retired to a parlour, casting aside cloaks and gloves, where Thomas, my page, bearing a flat cake of dried fruit, discovered us and placed it on a table in our midst with a wide grin. There was an immediate rustle of interest, of comment. Of excitement. The outcome would affect the whole tenor of our celebrations.

'Behold the Bean Cake.' Edmund brandished his sword as if he would cleave it in two. 'Do I slice it?'

I smiled graciously with a shake of my head. 'I choose the King of Scotland to cut it.'

And James responded promptly: 'And I give the honour to my affianced bride. She'll do it with more elegance than you, Edmund. And with more skill. You don't need a sword to cut a cake.'

Edmund tilted his chin, eyes gleaming dangerously. For a moment I thought he would resist. Then he laughed.

'Go to it, Queen Joan!'

James slid his dagger from his belt, passing it to Joan, who wielded it with sure expertise and cut the cake into wedges. The pieces were passed around. We ate carefully, looking from one to the other. Within one piece lurked the bean that would confer the honour on the Lord of Misrule.

'Not I.'

'Or I.'

There was much shaking of heads, some in palpable relief. James shrugged in disappointment. I said nothing. I waited.

I knew what would happen. He kept us waiting, for what a master of timing he was. And then:

'There! What did I say?' Edmund fished a bean from between his teeth and held it up. 'I am Lord of Misrule after all.'

'Now, there's a coincidence!' Beatrice observed.

'Do you call me a cheat?' Edmund swung round, his expression as fierce as if he would attack any who dare point the finger.

'I wouldn't dare.'

Neither would I, though I knew he was. Edmund had come prepared with a bean of his own, trusting to the force of his own will to impose silence on the true winner. It was a risky venture that could have ended in his discomfiture. But I held my peace.

My piece of cake had held the bean.

'I am the Bean King. I am the Lord of Misrule.' Full of wild satisfaction, Edmund leapt onto a chair, sword in hand. 'And my first command will be…'

'Who will be your Queen?' someone asked.

There was not a moment's hesitation. Again I knew what he would do before he did it. As I drew in my breath, because I did not know what I wanted, Edmund circled the point of his sword towards me. He stared along its length.

'You. I choose you.'

A sigh ran through the group.

I swallowed against a moment of panic. My habitual response. 'I cannot.'

'Why not?'

Because I could not romp and cavort and play the fool. 'Because I do not know how.'

'Then I'll teach you, Queen Kat. My golden queen. We will reign together.' Colour rushed to my face and I think he saw it, for he immediately turned to the practical to draw all eyes back to him.

'My first decree, my miserable subjects, as Master of Misrule. We'll take the Old Year out with mirth and jollity. We'll dance and sing and break all rules. We'll make these old walls resound and shiver.' He leapt down from the chair, whirling the sword around his head. 'And I know where there's treasure to be had.'

With a key obtained from Alice, who looked askance as if we were no more than a bunch of irresponsible children, Edmund, taking my hand in his and pulling me along in his wake, led us down increasingly dusty passages until we came to what had once been an antechamber. As he opened the door, we saw that it was now used for storing the detritus of lives past. We crowded in, the women lifting their skirts and stepping away from the dust-ridden coffers and tapestries. Edmund was oblivious, entirely wrapped up in his own intent.

'Let's see.' He took stock of the boxes and bundles. 'I command you to open up the chests, because unless I am ill-advised...'

We did as we were bidden, soon forgetful of the dust, exclaiming with admiration and astonishment, much as children might. Packed into the chests were layer upon layer of costumes intended for some long-distant royal procession or a mummers' play.

'Whose are these?' I asked, holding a pheasant's mask to my face, which muffled my question, feathers nodding over my head.

'King Edward, the third of that name. We have him to thank. They're old. But by God they will make us splendid this year.'

We pulled the costumes out, shaking them free of dust and cobweb and the odd spider. They were in remarkable condition, such a bounty of cloaks and masks and wings to adorn and transform. Soon the whole party was draped and garbed in starred and gilded splendour.

'And what would you be, Queen Kat?' Edmund asked, when I stood, still undisguised—for what would I choose?— but with a vast length of red and black velvet in my hands and draped over one shoulder. Edmund was already clad in a cloak painted with stars as if he were a magician, his face covered with a lion's mask so that his voice echoed strangely and his eyes glittered through the leonine stare.

'What on earth is this?' I asked, lifting the heavy cloth. I could not make out its shape.

Edmund growled with lion-like ferocity. 'I'll not tell you. Not yet. But you'll see on Twelfth Night. Now—for you.'

'I don't know.' I admitted forlornly, surrounded by so much glamour.

'This, I think.' Relieving me of the red and black, he cast a silver cloak over my shoulders and fastened a silver-faced angel mask with silver ribbons over my face. 'Turn round.' I did so, and I felt him fastening something to my shoulders.

'What are you doing?' I tried to turn my head, but could only see, and that indistinctly through the mask, some gossamer material stretched over a wooden frame.

'Giving you wings,' he replied. 'Angels need wings.' And he whispered in my ear. 'How would you fly without? And I need you to fly, my silver Queen.'

He came to stand before me again and bowed low, hand on heart. I curtsied. We were King and Queen.

How I was re-created, remoulded by Edmund Beaufort, an acolyte in the hands of a master.

★ ★ ★

By Edmund's decree—and because we discovered enough for all—we spent the festivities draped in green velvet robes, each embroidered from head to foot in peacock feathers, as if we were devotees of some strange mystic sect.

And thus clad, the days merged into one breathless intoxication of pleasure. We played disguising games, St George slaying the reluctant dragon, King Arthur discovering his magic sword. How was it that Edmund was so often St George or King Arthur? Young Henry, my astonished son, joined in with eyes as big as silver coins, a dragon's head perched on top of his curls, wings askew on his shoulders—until he fell asleep in my lap and the music went on around him.

We danced endlessly, and sang, arms linked, carolling the chorus as Edmund laid down the verses in a bright, true tenor. We wove our paths between an intricate pattern of cushions laid out on the floor, the penalty for disturbing any one of them being to obey some dire command of our misruling lord.

I was dispatched to the kitchens to fetch wine and ale, instructed to carry it myself in true reversal of roles, a queen serving her subjects. Which I could have done, except that Edmund accompanied me and carried the platters himself, ordering me to follow, bearing my steward's staff of office and also the grace cup, which I presented to everyone present with a maidservant's curtsey.

Nothing existed without his hand to it. Jokes and pranks and laughter. He wooed, seduced and charmed through an unending storm of activity. We ate and drank as we stood, not stopping for formal meals, and on a day when dark clouds lowered and might have driven us to the fireside, our young men fought out a Twelfth Night *mêlée*, the red and black velvet swathing their armour and that of their horses to a backdrop of a verdant green forest created from twelve ells of canvas, the whole painted with flowers and trilling finches.

Amidst the sword thrusts and trampling hooves, Edmund capered in the feathered costume of a vast golden bird, his vivid features hidden behind a golden beak and crimson crest as he tripped the unwary with his golden stave. A ridiculous prank that reduced everyone to helpless laughter.

We were exhausted, but who could not admire him? Who could not worship at his feet?

'I must sit down.' I sank to the cushions on the floor, my own feet aching after a tempestuous leaping and stamping, as far from a dignified court procession as it was possible to be. My shoes had rubbed against my heel.

'We will dance till dawn,' Edmund decreed.

'You might. But I—'

'We are young. You are no elderly widow, destined for prayer and endless stitchery, whatever Gloucester might tell you. It's a sin for you to hide yourself away.' I looked up, immediately unsure at the very personal nature of the jibe. 'Tell me you are not enjoying yourself. I swear you are, even if you deny it. You were going to deny it, weren't you?'

I frowned, thoroughly ruffled, but he would have none of it.

'When did you last laugh, Queen Kat? Dance? Play the fool without thinking who might be watching and commenting on your behaviour or decency?'

'Not since I was a child,' I admitted ruefully, 'when I cavorted recklessly with my sister, without constraint.' Not since then. Since then it had been as if my life had been shackled into good behaviour and moral rectitude. To my horror, tears stung my eyelids. 'I have forgotten how to play. And now my sister is dead.'

My loss of Michelle, the space she had left in my heart, took me unawares and caused the tears to overflow and slide down my cheeks as I mourned her anew. And there was Edmund, crouching beside me, drying them with the edge of my sleeve.

'You must not weep, lady. I should be whipped from your presence for causing you such grief.'

'You did not,' I denied, sniffing, pushing his hand away.

'I say that I did. And I ask pardon.' For a moment he remained at my side, silent. Then audaciously tilted my chin with his hand. 'You are too solemn, too circumspect for a beautiful woman of…I wager it's no more than four and twenty years.'

Still emotional, I ignored the question. 'I am not allowed to be other than solemn and circumspect.'

'But today you are allowed.' He let his thumb stroke slowly, heart-touchingly slowly, along the edge of my jaw, before taking my hand between both of his. 'And tomorrow. And the day after that—every day until you call a halt. Are you not Queen? Do you not make your own rules?'

I was too astonished to reply when Edmund placed a kiss in the centre of my palm.

'You are my queen,' he said before he left me. 'The fairest of queens. And I will serve you well.'

We wore masks through most of those days. We were enchanted beings, woven about with invisible threads so that we were made subject to Edmund's clever sorcery. Some mimicked lions, some pheasants, some adopted the gilded features of god-like humans. I kept my silvered angel face, and the wings when the foolish mood took me.

Beware masks. How much freedom they allow us when we are anonymous behind the painted expressions. My features were hidden, and therefore I acted as if no one knew who I might be. Of course everyone knew, but still I acted on impulse, abandoning Gloucester's strictures. And how strange, my sight narrowed and restricted to the two angelic apertures.

How often did Edmund fill that narrow view? Too often, some would say. For me it was a true enchantment.

But there was a time, at last, to take off the masks. It was agreed that, at midnight on Twelfth Night, we would gather for the unmasking in my Painted Chamber. I expect it was a truly festive moment—but I was not there. Waylaid by Edmund, I was effortlessly lured onto the battlements where the frost silvered the stonework and my companion wrapped me and my angel wings in the furred heat of his cloak.

It was there that Edmund stripped the hood from my hair and untied the silver strings.

'My golden queen,' he murmured against my cheek as his fingers loosened the ties, at the same time loosing the braids of my hair.

'You are still a large bird!' I accused, fighting to keep my breathing steady.

'That can be remedied.'

He pulled off the golden mask, with its cruel beak. And I raised my hand to smooth his tousled hair. Except that he caught it and pressed it to the rich damask above his heart. It beat hard and steady and alluring against my palm.

I froze, a cry catching in my throat.

'Well?' he asked. 'What are you thinking?'

'I am afraid to think.'

And he kissed me on my mouth.

'Do you love me?' he demanded.

I shook my head, a breath of fear crawling across my skin.

'Do you want to know if I love you?' he demanded, his eyes bright in the moonlight.

'No,' I whispered.

'I say you lie.' His lips stroked over my cheek. 'Do you want to know if I love you?'

'Yes.'

'Well, I do. Now you must kiss me.'

So I did.

'So do you love me, Queen Kat?'

'I do. God help me, I do.'

Edmund had opened his clever, fine-fingered hands and I had fallen into them.

Edmund Beaufort loved me. Tentatively, reluctantly at first, then step by glorious step, I loved Edmund Beaufort. I wanted to experience all I had never known about love, all I had failed to experience with Henry, knowing that I would not be rebuffed. Edmund loved me and made no secret of it. I absorbed every moment of delight. I was truly selfish.

By Twelfth Night I had lost my heart, seduced by his skilful antics and his single-minded assault on my emotions. I had not sought to submit to such an overwhelming longing, but Edmund Beaufort had stolen my heart from me and tucked it away so that I was without power to retrieve it.

When I returned to my room, and Guille removed my wings for the final time, she exclaimed that they were bent and frayed, beyond mending. But what did it matter? I was loved, and I loved in return. I could not sleep for the turmoil in my breast, and dawn brought me no respite from its thrall.

The end of the festivities should have brought with it the end of the magic. Yet Twelfth Night was merely the prologue to a feast for all the senses. I was consumed by love. I fell willingly into its flames, disregarding the lick of pain when he flirted elsewhere, tolerating the searing heat of his proximity, because I would have it no other way. My eyes were filled with him, my mouth tingling with his sweetness as if I had sipped from a comb of honey.

Edmund Beaufort ordered the whole panorama of my sol-

itary existence, and I willingly invited him in, keeping step
with him as he made my lonely world a thing of beauty and
desire. He had spun a silver web around me, but I was never
seduced against my will. I was a joyful participant as he made
himself lord of all my senses.

How bold we were. How shockingly daring in our pursuit
of passion as the New Year bloomed. When his breath stirred
my hair and his lips brushed against my nape, I cast aside my
much-vaunted reputation. I was as wanton in my desire as any
court whore, for his kisses were as intoxicating as fine wine,
as heady as Young Henry's favourite marchpane. The slide of
his fingertips along my jaw to the sensitive hollow beneath
my ear awoke desire in my belly.

How was it possible to conduct an affair of the heart under
the eyes of the whole Court, in the midst of a royal palace
where courtiers and servants, pages and bodyguards, scullions
and royal nurses abounded? How was it possible for a sequestered woman, ordered to live out a life of nun-like chastity
and respectability, to meet in secret a vital, dynamic man who
stirred her cold heart to flame?

How was it possible to keep vulgar tongues from wagging, or for a determined man to seek out the company of the
woman he desired when she was hedged about by the role she
was forced to play? For Edmund Beaufort desired me. He left
me in no doubt when his eyes smiled down into mine and our
fingers dovetailed together.

How was it possible? It was not very difficult at all when
James and his friends left us in the New Year. Did we not prove
its simplicity? When a King's household was no royal court
at all but a close, muffled establishment tuned to the necessi-
ties of a young child, where there was no ceremony, no public appearance, no visits from foreign ambassadors, but rather
a quiet nurturing atmosphere, it was so very easy.

No one looked for scandal or for gossip in so retired an existence. It was like looking to find a dangerous predator infiltrating a perfectly constructed nest, designed for the comfort and sustenance of only one precious chick. I was the perfect Queen Mother, steeped in respectability, Henry was the Young King who thrived and learned his lessons, and Edmund, the well-loved royal cousin, had every right to visit the Young King's household as he wished, bringing gifts and a breath of the outside world from Westminster and beyond.

Young Henry looked for his coming with innocent pleasure, delirious when Edmund lifted him high, swinging him round until he shrieked in excitement. The gift of a silver ship, magnificently in full sail and usefully mobile on four wheels, proved the perfect toy. Young Henry adored his cousin Edmund.

And so did I.

So Edmund became a frequent visitor to Windsor, and we sought each other out with no words that could be misinterpreted by a casual observer. Merely a glance of eye, the touch of fingertips as he gave me a goblet of wine, or a carefully contrived brush of tunic against houppelande. We made no extravagant promises that could not be kept. Our love was conducted entirely in the present. All I wished for was to be with him, and he with me.

'You are me and I am you,' he murmured in my ear.

He chased the shadows from my mind with expert, knowing hands and mouth.

So I was older than he by a handful of years. Yet Edmund's experience was so much greater than mine that I felt I was the younger. He was a true Beaufort, confident and ambitious, raised to see his strengths and develop them by every means possible. The royal blood, no longer denied but recognised by law, ran strong through his veins. And yet how subtle he could be for so young a man, when I might have thought that self-control would be overswept by pure, vibrant love of life.

His outrageous Twelfth Night schemes made me wary of my reputation, but I found there was no need. True, he carried me along, a leaf in a stream, refusing to allow me to linger in the eddy at the brook's side, refusing to allow me to hold back and think, yet never did he put my reputation into harm's way before inquisitive and prurient eyes.

Pouring out all the love in my arid existence, I thanked him silently, from the bottom of my newly awoken heart, for his ineffable compassion for my position. When his arms banded round me, shielding me against the world, I clung to him.

'Don't think,' he said more than once. 'Don't worry that the world will condemn. Dance with me, Queen Kat. Laugh and enjoy all that life can offer.'

But in public he never overstepped the mark of decency. He danced with my damsels too. He never showed a need to push me beyond the inexperienced limit of my own desires. Or not yet.

Sometimes, in my lonely bed, I questioned the vital happiness that gripped me. Did I deserve it? Perhaps I should step more slowly, perhaps it was wrong for me to allow Edmund to dictate my will and order my days. Perhaps I should worry about the world's condemnation. I had seen the results of cruel gossip in my mother's life. Perhaps I should know better than to follow in her dangerous footsteps.

And then, when I heard his voice raised in laughter or needle-quick response, my resolution to be sensible and abstemious was all destroyed.

Fleetingly I wished that James was still close, a valuable confidant for a troubled mind, but James had achieved his heart's desire. He and Joan, now wed, were deliriously ensconced in Scotland. I rejoiced for him—but I did not need him. My mind was not troubled, my feet were light with joy.

How many secret places were there to discover in a royal palace, for two lovers bent on a snatched moment of solitude? In Windsor I could map them all. I could trace our steps over that year and point to every single blessed spot on the paving stones where our love grew stronger, more intense. I could catch my breath as I recalled Edmund's seduction of my senses beneath every arch and carved rafter. How carefully, how cleverly those assignations were selected.

My guilt, if guilt it must be, was as great as his for I was a willing accomplice, lured by a wealth of poetry that tripped from his lips. My pale soul blazed with light, made vibrant and alive by a fanfare of colour.

Yours is the clasp
That holds my loyalty,
You dismiss all my heart's sorrow

There—exactly there at the turn in the stair in the great Round Tower, where we climbed from first to second floor. Where the light from the narrow window did not quite illuminate us, and the echo of approaching footsteps in either direction would alert us.

Your love and my love
keep each other company

Behind the carved screen in the Chapel of St George, such a sacred place to celebrate un-sacred love with passion-heated kisses. There we stood, I trembling in his arms, hidden by the rigid form of leaves and flowers created by a master craftsman who had had no idea that his artifice would hide the flushed cheeks of a Queen of England and her lover.

That your love is constant
in its love for mine
is a solace beyond compare

Yet not always so enclosed. In the calm solemnity of the King's Cloister, when the canons and clerks were busy about their affairs with no time to enjoy leisure, there we walked hand in hand. I had no recollection of what we said, only of the slide of his hand against mine, his fingers weaving with mine, his palm hard and calloused from swordplay and reins. And, satiated with each other, we progressed to the Little Cloister when the noisy choristers were absent, intent on their choral duties, their voices raised in miraculous polyphony as a plangent accompaniment to our sighs.

Adam lay bounden,
Bounden in a bond,
Four thousand winter
Thought he not too long.

A bitter-sweet backdrop. I too was bounden in a bond from which I had no desire to break free. The words, the minor harmonies, were almost too beautiful for me to bear.

And all was for an apple,
An apple that he took.
As clerkes finden,
Written in their book.

And Edmund, master of all miraculous sleight of hand, when passion became too much, our breathing too roused, calmed my desire. As if he had conjured it all—as perhaps he had, for I thought nothing beyond him—he produced an apple from his sleeve, smoothly russet, that he presented to me as if it were a precious gem, and we shared it, piece by piece as he wielded his knife. He licked the juice of it from my fingers—until desire built and built again, and I thought I could not exist without him.

Back within enclosing walls, the Old Hall, converted years ago into a chamber for personal use of the king but now unused until Young Henry would be of age to occupy it, provided us with a vast expanse of space. Here, where we might be seen, we were discreetly adroit, a brush of fingertips our only recognition. With its twenty windows, greedy eyes for the world, there were no kisses exchanged here.

Ah, but within the privacy of the Rose Chamber, now that was a different matter. Our garments merging with the blue, green and vermillion paint and the gleam of gold leaf, camouflaging us like a butterfly on a bright flower, our bodies were free to meet and cling, one chrysalis.

Your love and my love
Shall be steadfast in their loyalty
And never drift apart…

Perhaps we became bold as the months passed. Queen Philippa's chamber was hung with mirrors on all four sides. Here we dared fate, our two forms, melded into one in a passionate kiss, Edmund's hands taking possession over the damask folds, smoothing down over the dip of waist, the swell of breast and hip, multiplied again and again from every side.

And all the other moments, the sweet taste, the scent of him kept me from sleep, when the excitement engulfed me and the recall of his touch made my belly clench and turned my blood to molten gold. The dancing chamber where in an impromptu revel, ordered up by Edmund for no reason at all but that he considered the court a dull place, we danced and touched because it was allowed.

A breathless, laughing dash up the stairs of the Round Tower to where King Edward's weight-driven clock told the hours, its hands moving slowly, the gears clicking and groaning as we sighed and kissed and caressed. An audience chamber, deserted of all but us. The Spicerie Gatehouse, a dangerously thronged place as the main entrance to the palace, could still afford us the chance of a gaze of such longing that my fair skin was suffused with colour. Or the covered walkway between Great Hall and kitchens, busy with maidservants and pages, but not so busy that we could not linger...

And then, when the weather was clement, the private garden with its low hedges and herbs, where we were caught up in the deep shadow of the massive bulk of Salisbury Tower. Edmund's kisses became more possessive with tongue and teeth until my senses were awash with him.

Who could blame me for falling headlong into delicious love? Edmund Beaufort was the sorcerer who magicked my sad heart into joy. My winter melancholy, instead of returning at the turn of the year, vanished into oblivion, like smoke dispersed in a light breeze. A gesture as simple as the stroke of Edmund's tongue across my palm banished it entirely until I no longer recalled the depths of misery into which I had once fallen.

In that year I lived in a world apart, anticipating the next moment when I would see him, and the next and the next. My skin tingling, breath short, appetite destroyed, I lived for each moment we were together, mourning him through his enforced absences. A feverish pleasure gripped me, for was it not a fever? If it was, I embraced it. I danced through those days.

When Young Henry was knighted, John of Bedford's sword touching his four-year-old shoulder lightly, I could not contain my pride and delight. No doubt radiant with it, I smiled across the crowd to Edmund, deliriously happy to share my triumph with such a man as he. He was a Beaufort, a man of rank, of consequence. A man of potential in the English Court. He was truly worthy of my love.

Secrecy could not last. Intimate affairs must of necessity be discovered and come into the public domain. Endless discretion was not on the plate of a young man of barely twenty summers, or on the platter of a restless, widowed Queen, and so we ran the gauntlet of the Court and were eventually discovered. The rumours began, a whisper, an arch glance in our direction, then the soft hush of words that died away as I entered a room.

'It's not wise, my lady.' Alice, the first to voice her disapproval, was severe.

'It is glorious,' I replied, standing at the window in my chamber, tucking an autumn rose, a gift, into the knot of my girdle, humming the verse that Edmund had sung, wallowing in the soft sentiments.

> *Take thou this rose, O Rose,*
> *Since Love's own flower it is,*
> *And by that rose*
> *Thy lover captive is*

'No good will come of it.' Alice's features remained reproachful, her tone uncompromisingly censorious.

'How can you know that?' I turned away, my loving eye following Edmund below in the courtyard where he had mounted his horse prior to leaving for London.

'You must end it, my lady.'

'But why?' I could see no reason why I should. No reason at all.

'I foresee unhappiness.'

'But I am happy now.'

'My lady, it is a mistake!'

I ignored her.

My Master of Household, habitually taciturn, seemed to my mind more sombre than usual when supervising the taking down of tapestries in the gallery for cleaning.

'Is there a problem, Master Owen?' I asked. Neither the efforts of the servants under his authority nor the state of the sylvan scene with ladies and gentlemen engaged in music and song should merit his scowl.

'No, my lady.'

He bowed, then his hands were once more fisted on hips.

'Do you foresee a difficulty in removing the dust?'

'No, my lady.'

'Or is it the moth?' I walked closer to inspect for any tell-tale holes.

'No, my lady. And if I might advise, perhaps you should stand clear.'

I left. What was biting Master Owen, I could not imagine. Or perhaps I could.

Edmund returned.

'They are talking.' I met him on the stairs, and I warned him as we paced side by side, a careful arm's length between us, along the gallery. For a moment there was an arrested expression in his face, but then he smiled, and a glint of what I could only interpret as Beaufort arrogance.

'Let them talk. I care not. Neither will you, my love.'

The sparkling desire in his eyes, the heat of his mouth against my fingers, the admiration when he led me to my seat at supper ensured indeed that neither did I. I could foresee no danger for us.

Until…

'Come to my bed, Queen Kat,' he whispered when the minstrels withdrew and my household rose from the supper table, leaving us for a moment in a little space. 'Let me prove my love for you—if you doubt it to any degree. Let me worship you with my body.'

The invitation, with all it implied, loosed a bolt of desire from crown to soles, setting me aflame. Staring at him, I drew in a ragged breath.

'I cannot.'

'Then I must come to yours.'

I shook my head, aware of Alice's frowning scrutiny from where she lingered in the doorway, Young Henry's hand clutched in hers.

'Invite me!' he demanded. 'I will come to you when the palace sleeps. And I promise you that you will not regret this one step. Are we two not made for love?'

I sought wildly for a reply, managing only, 'I will not. You would not.'

'I would.' He took my hand, lightly innocuous, in his to help me to step down from the dais. 'I cannot continue this cat and mouse play longer.'

Too much. Too soon. Panic doused the flames. I tried to smile so that no one would suspect the content of his words, or mine. 'I cannot. You must see that I cannot. What revenge would Gloucester take if my reputation was besmirched?'

His grip on my hand tightened so much that I winced.

'You refuse me?' Extravagantly, his brows winged upwards. 'How can you, when we were meant to be together?'

'Yes. Yes, I do refuse. Forgive me.'

'I warn you—I will not give up.' His voice was low, but he kissed my fingers with an intensity that left me in no doubt of his passion or the hint of quick anger I had seen in his face. 'You have set me a hard task. As challenging as a quest set for one of King Arthur's knights. But I will not give up. I will win you, my lady. I will lay siege to the Castle Impregnable—and I will win. I will never admit defeat, for I cannot live without you.'

Releasing my hand, stepping back in one fluid movement, Edmund bowed. I watched him walk away. When he reached the door, he looked back, and bowed again. The light of battle was in his eye.

When I attended Mass next day, it was to be informed by an impassive-faced Master of Household that Lord Edmund had left Windsor at daybreak. He had given no indication that he would return.

So he had left me. He had left me because I would not go to his bed or invite him to come to mine. He had been furious, taking himself off to London—or anywhere else as far as I knew—simply to punish me, because he had been thwarted.

Had Edmund Beaufort ever been thwarted in his whole life?

I doubted it, but I would not be pushed into a commitment that left me so uncertain. Why would I not sleep with him? I pondered. I was no virgin, but I could not commit myself to so momentous a step. I was not totally lost to good sense, and reason told me that to lay my reputation bare to accusations of lewd scandal would throw me into the hands of Gloucester and the Royal Council. Who knew what measures they might take against me if they thought my actions discredited the Young King in any way? I had done the right thing.

Oh, but I missed him. I longed to feel his arms around me

again, his soft words against my throat. Perhaps I had just destroyed my only chance of happiness, a glittering gift offered on Edmund's outstretched palms. Yet I knew that I had not. I knew that I had not seen the last of Edmund Beaufort. I had become the Holy Grail for him, and I knew he would not give up until I lay in his arms.

Edmund's unheralded departure had given my damsels much food for speculation and Alice an exhalation of relief. After two days of my being the object of their interest, watched to see if I was languishing from unrequited passion, I informed my household that I planned to visit my dower property at Leeds Castle, once Madam Joanna's place of imprisonment. I found that the idea of the secluded retreat suited my mood, sequestered as it was, cushioned against the world, a place with no court and no damsels for they would not accompany me.

And if Edmund Beaufort discovered my absence and wished to see me, I knew in my heart that he would follow me.

I gave my orders to Master Tudor, who received them without expression. My small entourage was under way the following day, with my Master of Household and a handful of soldiers providing a stiff-backed and silent escort. Ensconced at Leeds with only Guille to serve my needs I wrapped my solitude around me. Every morning I climbed to the battlement walk and looked north towards London, my heart bright with hope. I was quite as capable of throwing down a challenge as my lover. We would see how strong his love was for me.

'You left me!' I accused as he strode with purpose into the entrance hall. I knew the role I would play. I had not had too long to wait—less than a se'ennight, in fact—for Edmund followed, gratifyingly quickly, but it pleased me to be less than conciliatory. It pleased me to see his steps hesitate momentarily as I addressed him with what might have been interpreted as temper. 'You walked away from me and made me the subject of common gossip,' I added, in case he did not realise the effect of his rapid departure.

'You were cruel. You refused my invitation. You rejected my love,' Edmund responded through gritted teeth. He was hot and sweaty from a fast ride, eyes fierce, russet hair mussed as he pulled off his hood. He was entirely appealing.

'I could not take the step you asked of me.' I was adamant.

'Do you not love me enough? You are happy enough to enjoy my kisses. Is there a limit to your love, my lady?'

Oh, his words were accusatory.

'There is no limit,' I responded. 'You know that I love you, but I no longer know if you love me. I think to reject me so openly was cruel.'

I was astonished at how cool and confident my voice sounded. I knew that I was in the right in my refusal. The thought of Gloucester passing judgement on my moral state still horrified me, so I met Edmund's furious stare with a steady regard.

'You are very cold,' he observed.

'I am hurt.'

He held out his hand in demand. I thrust my hands behind my back.

And, taking me aback, instead of the frustration or even anger I had expected, his face was illuminated with a smile that made my blood sing. 'Are you sending me away?' he asked.

'Yes.' But my heart quaked.

'Do you expect me to make an apology?' he demanded.

I suspected that he did not know the meaning of the word. 'Do you think you should?' I deliberately allowed a little edge to colour my tone. 'How could you inflict such hurt on me, Edmund? And so thoughtlessly, if you see no need to ask pardon.'

'Love is not love without hurt.'

'I don't believe you.'

Edmund swooped, and captured one of my hands, since I allowed it, falling smoothly into the verse:

'Love without anxiety and without fear
Is fire without flames and without warmth,
Day without sunlight, hive without honey
Summer without flower, winter without frost'

'What does that mean?' I asked, lifting my chin, as if I were in no mood for such complex sentiments. In fact, they thrilled me, but I held firm in my resolve.

'It means that love must have pain to make the joy more intense.' Edmund pressed my fingers against his mouth. 'Come to my bed, my golden one.'

'I will not.'

'Must I go away again?'

I lifted a negligent shoulder. 'I will not be browbeaten, my lord.'

'I beg of you, my glorious Queen Kat. Have mercy.'

I shook my head. Neither would I be cajoled, though I could not contemplate the thought of never seeing him again, not touching him, not savouring his mouth on mine. But I knew he would not leave me again.

'Speak to me.' Edmund pressed his lips to the soft skin of my wrist where my blood beat heavily. 'Come to my bed, my obstinate love. Who's to know here?'

'I will not.'

'Your mouth provoked me,
Kiss me, kiss sweet!
Every time I see you so it seems to me…'

'I don't provoke you.'

'But you do. Your refusal provokes me to madness.

'Give me a sweet, sweet kiss, or two or three!'

Edmund, still clasping my hand, in all his travel-stained boots and hose, sank to one knee, head bent.

'Don't ask me again,' I urged, trying to step away. 'For I will not.' And yet I felt that the mood in him had changed, the flirtation a thing of the past. Slowly his gaze lifted to mine.

'Katherine.'

There was no mockery in his use of my name, neither was there any residue of light in his eyes. I had never seen him so serious. Had he indeed given up on me? Perhaps he would ask forgiveness for his presumption and explain that he had been mistaken after all, that his regard for me had proved to be a finite thing. My hand tensed in his but I regarded him steadily to cover the flutter of nerves in my belly.

'Will you wed me, Katherine?'

It took my breath. 'Marriage?'

'Why not? We love each other. There is no one I would rather wed.' His brows flattened. 'Unless you have another man in mind?'

'No, no.'

'Then will you?'

I struggled to put my thoughts into words. 'I must think, Edmund.'

'Then think of this too.'

He stood, pulled me into his arms and kissed me long and thoroughly. I did not resist. He was mine, and I was his.

That night, alone in my room, curled on the cushions in the window embrasure with a single candle and the lap dog for company, I thought about what it would be like to be married to Edmund Beaufort. There would never be a dull moment, I decided with an unexpected wide smile that was reflected back at me cruelly refracted by the fault lines in the glass. It would be a highly respectable marriage, with a man at the forefront of politics and national events. Edmund would be a man I could be proud of and admire.

And it would be reciprocal. Did he not tell me that he admired me? I was his golden queen. I trembled at the thought of learning physical love in Edmund's masterful arms.

But would our life continue at this madcap rate? Would he continue to shower me with poetry and extravagant compliments, luring me into breath-stopping kisses in secluded corners? Real life is not like that, I informed my reflection seriously. You cannot be breathless for ever.

But why not? He loved me. He turned my limbs to water.

'Well? Will you wed me, Queen Kat?'

Edmund was waiting outside my chamber next morning, shoulders propped against the wall. How long he had been waiting I knew not, but of course it would have been no difficulty to discover the pattern of my days at Leeds Castle. He was dressed to perfection, linen pristine, boots polished, thigh-length tunic impressive in its richness, as he had intended. He bowed low, as I knew he would. The peacock feathers in his cap swept the floor.

'I beg you to put me out of my misery. Wed me and I will be the most attentive husband you could ever desire.' He cocked his head, his hair gleaming in the morning light. 'Must I kneel again?'

'No,' I replied slowly, all my thoughts of the previous night crystallising in my mind. 'Don't kneel.' I took a little breath. 'Yes, Edmund. I will. I will wed you.'

His mouth curved in a smile, his eyes glowed, and from the purse at his belt he took out a gold and enamelled brooch, which he pinned to my bodice, where it glittered in blue and red and gold on my breast. Not a jewelled confection such as a man might give to the woman he loved but a coat of arms, a badge of ownership. I did not recognise it.

'What is it?' I asked.

'It is a family piece—a livery badge. The Beaufort escutcheon.' He traced with his fingertip the portcullis and the lion rampant. 'I thought I would like you to wear something so personal to me.'

'It is beautiful. I will gladly wear it.' And I turned his hand and kissed his palm.

'I adore you, my beautiful Katherine.'

As we knelt together to hear Mass in the chapel, and my priest, Father Benedict, elevated the host, my blood ran hot with joy. The man at my side adored me. That was what he had said. And what a particular piece of jewellery he had given me, marking me as a Beaufort possession. Wearing it as I did that morning made a very clear statement of my intent. When Mass was complete, Edmund whispered:

'Can I ask you to be discreet in your wearing of the brooch?'

I looked my surprise.

'Just for a little time. Until I can announce to the whole world that you will be my wife.'

I agreed. Why would I not? Edmund would need to inform his family. When we returned to Windsor I would be free to wear the Beaufort portcullis and lion as openly as I pleased.

9

'WHY SHOULD WE not declare our love?' I was eager, wanting to shout it aloud to the whole world.

We had returned to Windsor, Edmund travelling openly with me as one of my escort, my preferred companion. Why should he not? His protection, as cousin to my son, was quite unexceptional. It was impossible not to watch his lithe figure astride his burnished mount as he paced beside my litter. I was so full of exuberance that it was hard to pretend that there was nothing between us but family ties, friendship and formal courtesy.

This was the man I would marry. Why should we not be seen to love and be loved? Was it not now more than a year since Edmund had wooed me at Windsor in a frenzy of evergreens and old traditions made new, cloaked in velvet and winged in silver?

'What need for secrecy?' I demanded. 'Who would possibly object?'

Edmund was well born. His blood could be no better, the slur of illegitimacy having long since been laid to rest. Who could take exception to his wooing of the Queen Dowager?

'Wait a little, my love,' he murmured against my temple, his lips a fleeting caress when he tucked me into my litter for the return journey.

But I gripped the front of his tunic. 'I don't understand why.'

Carefully he detached my hands, folding them one upon the other in my lap. 'Because it wouldn't do to cause political tongues to wag,' he stated, smiling down into my eyes, willing me to see the future as he saw it. 'Not yet. You must trust me.' Even though his voice remained unemotionally cool, as if we were discussing the arrangements for the journey, Edmund remained implacable. No one would suspect the heated tenor of his reply as he leaned over me, arranging the cushions for my comfort.

'One day you will be mine. I will take you to my bed as my wife, and there I will open the windows into heaven for you. You must be patient, my loved one. First I must make my intentions known to Gloucester and Bishop Henry. To the Royal Council. You are Queen Dowager and I am a Beaufort. Ours will be a political alliance, as well as one grounded in true love. It will not be done in secret.'

Which made good sense.

He reached up to untie the curtains, to shield me from the sharp wind. 'Exercise patience, Queen Kat, and hold on to the fact that my love for you is infinite.' And the curtain was dropped into place.

But how difficult it was to be patient. What possible obstacle would there be for the marriage of a widowed queen and a young man of royal blood? It would harm no one. Young Henry liked Edmund. And I was tossed in a sea of longing, to be with him and know the happiness of fulfilment.

I will take you to my bed and open the windows into heaven.

I could not wait.

But wait, Edmund had advised. Wait for a little time. So that was what I must do. I settled back against my cushions. I was too happy to be concerned, too secure in his love, anticipating the day when we would be together.

Back at Windsor, leaving Edmund to stable his horse and a tight-lipped Master of Household to organise the dispatch of my litter and escort, I went straight to the royal accommodations. And there was Young Henry in a creased tunic and hose, his fingers sticky with some sweetmeat, his hair clearly not having seen a comb for some hours. He ran to me and I lifted him into my arms. He was growing heavy at almost five years.

'Have you brought me a gift, *maman*?'

'I have.'

'Can I eat it?'

I enclosed his hand in mine to prevent him smearing honey on my bodice. 'I don't think you can.' A creak of the hinge on the door and a soft hush of skirts caught my notice. 'Look who's come to find you, Henry. What do you think, Alice? I think he has grown in even a short few weeks.' I turned my head, smiling my welcome. 'Do you?'

It was not Alice who had entered. In the doorway I saw that the woman had not Alice's upright carriage or robust figure; rather my visitor was fragile and moved with care over each separate step. And then she moved forward into a stripe of sunlight and my visitor was plain to see. Letting my son slide to the floor, I walked to meet her as I smiled, my heart warming, silently admitting that the blame was mine for the distance that remained between us.

'Madam Joanna!'

It had been too long—Henry's funeral, in fact—since I had last found time to sit and talk to her.

Young Henry ran to her, but, seeing her involuntarily drawing back, I caught him before he could hang on her skirts. The lines gouged beside eye and mouth, more cruel than I recalled, told their own tale.

'Will you sit? You are right welcome.' Keeping Henry at bay I took her hand and led her to a settle that was not too low, where I helped her to sink slowly back against the upright support.

Joanna sighed, a sound that was almost a groan.

'Thank you, dear child.' She managed to summon a smile. 'Now you can kiss me.'

I did, shocked by the quality of her skin at close quarters for it was dry and as thin and yellow as old parchment. The pain in her limbs was clearly great, the malaise gaining strength with each month's passing. Acknowledging that she would not wish me to talk of it, I merely kissed her cheek again.

'When did you arrive?' I asked.

'Yesterday. I came up in easy stages from King's Langley.'

'To see me? Then it is my fortune that I returned today.' I enfolded her gnarled fingers with their swollen joints very carefully in mine.

'They said you were at Leeds.'

'Yes.' I whispered in a restless Young Henry's ear and sent him off at a run to bring wine for our guest, nodding to my page Thomas, who would follow him, while I sat at Joanna's side. She shuffled in discomfort and I could not but ask, 'Madam Joanna, are you quite well? Should you have travelled so far?'

'My joints ache, but I expect no less.' The movement of her lips was spare. 'I thought I had to come.'

'Well, of course.' Not quite understanding. 'Why should you not visit me? Although it would have been more thoughtful of me to come to King's Langley. Forgive me, madam. Will you stay? If only for a few days? Henry will enjoy showing you his new skills with a wooden sword. As long as you stay well out of reach, of course.'

But Madam Joanna no longer smiled, rather withdrawing her hands from mine. In that brief gesture I had the impression that if she had been able to do it easily she would have stood and walked away to put some distance between us.

'What is it?' I asked. 'Has something happened to upset you?'

Madam Joanna's eyes were old, full of knowledge, full of past grief, but her gaze was uncomfortably direct. 'I have come for a purpose. When you have heard me out, you may not wish me to stay long.'

It was a disturbing disclosure, but still I did not follow. 'I'm sorry, why ever would I not wish you to stay?'

'Is Edmund Beaufort here?'

'Why, yes. Yes, he is.'

'Was he with you at Leeds Castle?'

Now I saw the direction of her questioning. 'Yes.' I raised my chin at the first trickle of apprehension that tightened just a little round my heart. But I was not perturbed. Perhaps she did not truly understand, and when she did—for surely Edmund would have no compunction about my telling Madam Joanna—why, then, she would wish me well for she had nothing but my happiness at heart. 'Yes,' I repeated, 'he was at Leeds.'

Startling me, she raised her hands to cup my cheeks as if I were a child to be cosseted, shielded from some unpleasantness. Then let them fall into her lap and her words drove straight through all my new-found happiness.

'Oh, Katherine! Will you take some advice from an old woman who has seen much and suffered grievously at the hands of ambitious men?' And for the first time I saw that her lack of ease was more than swollen and aching joints. She was sick to her soul, and my suspicions were grave. 'I am not your mother to give you advice, but I'm the nearest you've got. I think you should be wary of too close a friendship with Edmund Beaufort.'

I kept my reply even, though my heart quaked. 'Do you not like him?'

'Liking him or otherwise is not the issue. It is a dangerous liaison, Katherine.' How gentle her voice, how compassionate her eyes, but how ominous her choice of words.

'You do not approve of our friendship.'

'It is not wise.'

'How can it not be wise?' My replies were becoming more and more icy. 'He is cousin to my son.'

'If friendship is all it is, then I must ask your pardon.' She tilted her chin, as if she could read my mind. 'But I suspect it to be more than that, my dear girl.'

I looked away, quick to dissemble, fearing her displeasure, as I had always feared the displeasure of those around me. 'I don't understand.'

'Be honest with me, Katherine. How much is between you?'

I looked down at my clasped fingers, white with tension.

'He makes me happy.'

'Happy?'

Abruptly I stood and walked across the room until I came to a halt in the centre, keeping my back to her. I could not bear to see the reproof in her face. I concentrated on the leaping flames in the hearth as I chose my words to express all that I thought and felt from this miracle that was Edmund Beaufort.

'Yes, Edmund makes me happy. Is that a sin, Madam Joanna? I think it is not. Do you know? He makes me smile and laugh and enjoy all that life can offer. He makes my heart sing for joy. He has lifted a weight from my shoulders so that I feel young again. No one has ever done that for me. No one ever cared enough about me. Before I knew him, after Henry's death I was dragged down by loneliness and misery. I felt so old and superfluous. I was wretched indeed. Perhaps I should be despised for lack of will, of character. But so it was.'

I drew in a breath. Joanna waited, sensing that I still had things I needed to say.

'Then Edmund Beaufort came into my life with such energy, such immeasurable elation. Such skill in forcing me to see what I might be if I was brave enough to take the steps. I have never known anyone like him. He has saved me from my black humours, he has dragged me back into life. Can you understand that?'

'I too know what it is to be lonely, Katherine.'

And guilt flooded through me. Spinning round, I flung back to kneel at her feet, searching her face for some understanding.

'Forgive me. Forgive me. Of course you do—but then you must know how much I value...'

'Katherine! How much is between you?' she repeated.

'He loves me,' I replied simply.

'He has told you this, has he?'

'Yes. And I love him.'

'Damn the boy! He would, of course.' She touched my hair, tucking a wayward strand beneath my veil, and her question was soft but I heard the bite. 'I hear he seduced you in the heat of Twelfth Night revels.'

'Who told you that?' I demanded, displeased.

'It doesn't matter. James should have warned you, but I expect he was too taken up with his freedom and his new bride.' She eyed me. 'How unfortunate that he has gone back to Scotland. He's an astute young man and you might listen to his advice before you listen to mine.'

'But they are friends,' I objected. 'Why would he warn me against Edmund?'

'So they might be friends. But James has a keen nose for self-preservation and power-brokering.' For a moment she paused. 'Have you been foolish enough to be intimate with him?'

I flushed to the roots of my hair.

'Have you?'

'No. I have not.'

'Did he try to persuade you? I wager he did.'

I shook my head, turning my face away. 'I would not,' I whispered.

'Then you are fortunate. The Beauforts have more charm than is good for them, and Edmund more than most, while you are beautiful and lonely and...vulnerable.'

'Am I vulnerable? You make it sound as if Edmund tried to persuade me against my will. He did not. When I refused, he did not pressure me. He understood my reticence.' My voice became sharp as anger flamed. 'And you have no right to take me to task.'

'Is that what I was doing?' Her lips curved into what might have been a smile but there was a weight of sadness over her. 'Perhaps so. But I must speak out before you become even more entangled in this relationship. It will bring you nothing but grief. Has he asked you to wed him yet?'

'Yes.'

'What did you say?'

I smiled from the pure delight of it. This would surely make her understand. That Edmund was serious in his intent. 'I said I would.'

'My child, it cannot be.'

'I love him,' I said. Could she not see how right it was?

'As if love makes all right with the world. And you have been starved of it for so long. I am so very sorry.' She leaned awkwardly to place a kiss between my brows. 'They'll not let you wed, you know. They'll move heaven and earth to prevent it.'

Was I not Queen Dowager? I would not accept such interference. 'I cannot believe that anyone would deny me my right to choose the man I wish to wed.'

'Then you are a fool, Katherine,' she announced. 'You have not thought this through at all. And what Edmund Beaufort is planning! Gloucester will object, for sure. Bedford too when he returns from France. Even Warwick. Bishop Henry might be persuaded to give some lukewarm support if he sees an interest for himself in your union, but even he might have qualms.'

'They cannot stop me.'

Joanna sighed. 'Tell me this, Katherine,' she ordered, stern at my wilful intransigence, and leaned forward, willing me to listen and accept. 'Has he asked you to keep his proposal secret?'

'Yes, but only for a short time until—'

'Until when?'

'I don't know.' I sounded sullen even to my own ears, because it echoed my own fears.

'Use your wits, my dear.' She looked frustrated rather than angry. 'I'm the last woman to condemn you to a sterile widowhood. Do I not know better than most? And God knows you had little pleasure in your marriage to my stepson. He would have tried the patience of a saint. But Edmund Beaufort cannot be the man for you. Even he does not quite see his way forward, so he orders you not to speak of it.' She took a painful breath. 'You can't rely on this proposal, Katherine.'

'But why not?' I asked, suddenly thinking that Joanna's reasoning might be political. 'Am I wrong in my understanding of this very English situation? Has Edmund's family not been fully legitimised?'

'Yes, yes.' Joanna brushed aside my question with an impatient gesture. 'But have you thought about the possible repercussions from your marriage to this boy? Haven't you thought at all beyond Edmund's ability to seduce your senses? If you wed—what then?' Her brows drew together in a sharp winging angle. 'If you carried a legitimate child of your union, such a child—particularly if a boy—would have a volatile mix of Valois and Plantagenet blood in his veins. Anyone with an eye for mischief might consider his claim to the English throne to be as good as Young Henry's.'

'No!' My thoughts whirled. 'That cannot be. Young Henry is his father's heir.'

'And children die young, far too many of them.'

'It will not happen. Henry is strong and well cared for.'

'Still, a child borne by you from Beaufort's loins would be a risky proposition for the stability of this country. Any man with rebellion in mind might consider such a child a useful pawn in a very dangerous political game.'

I thought about this. Then shook my head. 'No!'

'Very well. Then consider this as a reason for your match being anathema to many: how much power would it give Edmund Beaufort, to wed you and become stepfather to the King?'

Horror washed over me. I felt as if I were sinking into a quagmire. My breathing was difficult, a constriction tightening around my lungs. Were there so many obstacles in my way that I, in my innocence and ignorance, had never considered? But then, knowing what I did of Edmund, I pushed them aside.

'He would wish no harm to my son,' I stated firmly. 'How could you suggest that?'

'Of course he would not. That was not my meaning. But such a position would allow him to make a bid to control the reins of power. Could he not demand to be made Regent in the Young King's name, with you at his side as Queen Mother? Could he not demand to be appointed the child's Governor in Warwick's place? Of course he could. And how much power would that invest in Edmund Beaufort, a young man not yet into his third decade, if I read it right. And don't, Katherine...'

Her lips almost curled. 'Don't tell me that that young man is not ambitious.'

The accusations drove deep, but I drew on all my self-possession.

'I know he is ambitious. I expect he might demand a role in Young Henry's upbringing. But would that necessarily be a bad thing? Is not Gloucester too ambitious?'

'Yes—and therein lies the danger for you. Gloucester wishes he had been born the eldest son. He resents having to share power with Bedford. For sure he will not willingly hand over even an inch of his power to Edmund Beaufort!' I sat at Joanna's feet, eyes wide, absorbing all that she said, as she stroked my hand. 'It is not good for you to be seen in a liaison with a young man who has so vast an amount of power in his own right.'

My thoughts were awry.

'Think about it, my child. The Beauforts have thrust themselves into every nook and cranny of state and church. Who would have thought it possible, descended as they are from an illicit liaison between John of Lancaster and the Swynford woman? And yet it is so. Now they are legitimate: they are gifted, with a distinct presence at court. But they will never be satisfied and their ambition is a force to be reckoned with. It means that they are not to be trusted.'

'I don't know that.' It was a cry that came from my heart. 'I can trust Edmund. I am certain of it.'

Madam Joanna struggled to her feet, as if delivering her final thrust at my happiness had robbed her of all her energy. At the door she stopped to look back over her shoulder to where I still sat.

'You are a very desirable woman, Katherine. And not only for your looks. You cannot put too high a price on your connection with both the English and the French crowns. Your

Valois bloodline and your position with the Young King are inestimable. Never forget that. Not that you will ever be allowed to. They will beat you about the head with it for the rest of your days, I'm afraid. As for Edmund...'

She lifted her shoulders in a painful little shrug.

'You don't like him.' I sounded like a child.

And at the last a smile lit her face, giving life to the beauty she had once had. 'Actually, I do. He's difficult to dislike, and he knows how to get into the good graces of an elderly woman. But I'd still be wary of him.' She lifted the latch of the door. 'Before you pin all your hopes on him, ask yourself this. Are you so certain that he...?'

Footsteps approached. Young Henry, I thought, at last bearing the wine that we no longer needed.

But it was Edmund who appeared in the doorway.

'Madam Joanna.'

He bowed as she turned, and saluted her hand. They exchanged smiles, greetings, both excruciatingly polite, before Joanna made her excuses. 'Think about what I said.' And she was gone.

Edmund grimaced, having read all that had not been said. 'So she knows.'

'Yes. I told her, but she already suspected.'

'Has she been warning you about me?' For a moment he frowned after her departing figure.

'Yes.' I could not lie when my very soul cried out for reassurance in the face of such a deluge of warnings. 'She warned me about the difficulties of our marriage. About Gloucester and Warwick and...' I felt tears of weakness, of disappointment, prickle behind my lids.

'You must not weep, my golden Queen.' Immediately he was across the chamber to my side, lifting me with strong hands so that I stood within the circle of his arms.

'She implied that you do not love me,' I remarked flatly.

Madam Joanna's final unfinished question remained in my mind. *Are you so certain that he…?* And I knew what she would have asked. *Are you so certain that Edmund wants you more than he wants power? Are you sure he loves you, or does he have an eye to the door you can open for him, to allow him a supreme position in the kingdom?*

'How would she know?'

'She does not.'

'Did she tell you that I seduced you so that your rank would enhance my own status?'

'Yes.'

'Do you believe her?'

I looked into his eyes, so full of understanding, of light and love for me.

'Have I not sworn that my devotion to you outranks all earthly power? How can power weigh in the balance with the overwhelming love that I feel for you?'

And there was all the reassurance I desired. Madam Joanna did not understand. His love for me was true. Nothing could undermine my certainty. As if he read it in my face, Edmund pressed his lips tenderly to my brow, and when he spoke, his words held the reverence of a vow.

'I know you have faith in me. As I have in you. We will win this battle. I will bring happiness and fulfilment into your life, such as you have never known.' The strength of his arms, the vibrant assurance in his face, the shower of kisses across my cheeks chased away my fears. 'I'll speak with my uncle.' Edmund's smile lit all the dark corners of my heart; delight bloomed as the reverence vanished and his lively humour returned. 'Bishop Henry will enjoy putting a spoke in Gloucester's wheel, if nothing else. Have I convinced you?'

'Yes.' I sighed. 'Forgive me my lack of faith.'

'It is not easy for you,' he murmured against my lips. 'But always remember. I worship at your feet, my dearest love.'

And there was Young Henry, carrying a flagon of wine with fierce concentration. While Edmund accepted his enthusiastic greeting and poured the wine, Madam Joanna's warnings dissipated as matters of no moment. Happiness settled on my shoulders and my mind quietened.

My conversation with Warwick was far shorter and more to the point than that with Madam Joanna. He did not mince his words. He did not even make an excuse for seeking me out, merely drawing me away from my damsels in the interest of privacy.

'I don't like to see Edmund Beaufort prowling around Windsor like a cat on heat.'

'Edmund does not prowl,' I replied, stiffening at the implication.

'A matter of opinion. He has a predatory air, Katherine. And a possessive one, so I'm told.'

He bent his stern gaze on me. He was Warwick today, not Richard. I drew myself up to my full height so that our eyes were on a level. 'He is here at my invitation.'

'I know.' The lines on Warwick's face, instead of being amiable and smiling, resembled the carvings achieved by a stonemason's chisel.

'We cannot forbid him to visit his cousin. My son enjoys his company.'

'I know that too,' Warwick snapped. 'And I don't like that either.'

'Edmund Beaufort is welcome in my household, and will continue to be so,' I stated.

'And I cannot stop you. But take some advice.' Warwick was

as brusque as I had ever heard him. 'Don't become embroiled in a predicament that will bring you more pain than pleasure.'

I raised my chin. I would not listen.

'I am going to Westminster,' Edmund announced the next day.

'Don't go,' I pleaded.

'You know I must.' Although he smiled, I read raw impatience in his eyes, in the set of his jaw. 'The sooner I see Bishop Henry, the sooner we can be wed.'

He kissed my hand with admirably restrained courtesy since we were in my solar under the eagle eye of Beatrice. All my fears were smoothed out, like a length of faultless silk, and I accompanied him down to the main door, where my Master of Household waited with Edmund's outer garments.

'Look for me within the week,' Edmund promised me, shrugging into his coat and drawing on his gloves, before leaping down the steps two at a time to where his groom held his horse.

'Thank you, Master Owen,' I said, as Edmund in his hunger to be gone had not.

'My pleasure, my lady,' he replied, watching Edmund ride from the courtyard with a jaunty gesture, hat in hand. But Master Tudor's tone caused me to glance up at him, and the dark reproach—or perhaps even contempt—in the gaze that followed Edmund startled me. Then it was gone, a mere shadow, as the Master bowed to me. 'Do you require anything, my lady?'

I shook my head. Only that Edmund return soon with a date for our marriage.

'Are you entirely witless, woman?'

It was not Edmund but Gloucester.

How I wished that Edmund stood beside me. As it was,

I was forced to face the battering ram of Gloucester's wrath alone. He arrived within two days of Edmund's departure, a virulent tempest, raining invective down on my unprotected head when he marched into my private chamber as if about to do battle. At his side came Bishop Henry in clerical splendour, stolid and smiling despite the uneasy flicker of his eye away from mine when I raised my brows. At least Edmund's uncle bowed, kissed my hand and asked after my health. All Gloucester could do was glower and fume as he launched his first tirade.

'Have you not even the sense you were born with?'

I gasped at his discourtesy, standing slowly, letting my embroidery slide to the floor.

'I won't ask you if the rumours are true. I'm quite certain they are.' He gestured at my damsels. 'Dismiss them!'

So I did, quivering with nerves.

'All of them!'

'No. Alice remains.' I needed some support, and since I was fortunate to have her company I would keep her with me.

'I suppose I should have expected nothing less from a daughter of Isabeau of France. A woman raised in the dissolute stews of the French court!' Gloucester's fury reverberated from the walls, hammering in my head. Never had I heard him address anyone with such ferocity. Usually icily polite in my presence, this was hot temper, and lethally personal. 'What are you thinking of?' he continued, flinging out his arms as if to encompass the length and breadth of my sins. 'To allow yourself to be drawn into this farce—'

'A farce? I don't take your meaning, sir.'

My anxiety was swept away by resentment quite as strong as Gloucester's ire. I walked forward to reduce the space between us, clenching my fists and pressing my lips together against his slight on my birth and my parentage, for I knew it would do no good to rant and return insult for insult. My blood and birth were as good as Gloucester's. I was Valois, daughter of King Charles VI. I would not bow before this man, however much he might be a royal prince. I would play the Queen Dowager with all the skill I had acquired in recent years.

'I deplore your accusation, my lord,' I announced, before Gloucester could tell me exactly what he meant. 'I think you should consider well how you address me.' Oh, I was haughty. And Edmund's love had given me a confidence I had previously lacked. My words were well chosen, my manner a perfection of regal disdain. 'You have no right to address me in such a manner.'

Not expecting such retaliation, Gloucester's face became suffused with blood, veins red on his cheeks as if he had been riding for long hours into a high wind. His next words bit hard. 'Are you really so empty-headed,' he accused, 'that you think you'll be allowed to wed Edmund Beaufort?'

'I think the choice is entirely my own. If I wish to wed him, I will. I am not under your dominion, my lord.'

'So it is true. You are considering an alliance with Edmund Beaufort. Ha!' Gloucester stalked to the coffer and flung his gloves and sword there, so furiously that they slid to the floor, causing my dog to skitter out of his path. For a little while Gloucester stood with his back to me, as if marshalling his plan of campaign, and I waited. I would not conduct an examination of my private life at a distance.

'Well?' He swung round and marched to within a sword's length of me. 'What have you to say about this mess?'

I refused to retreat, even though he used his height and breadth, and his fury, to intimidate. 'Edmund has asked me and I have agreed,' I stated. 'We plan to marry.'

'It will not be. You will break any agreement you have made.'

'Will I?' I looked towards Bishop Henry. 'What do you say, my lord? Do I wed your nephew?'

The cleric's wily eye again slid from mine, under pretext of focusing on his rings. 'I have to agree that it is a matter of concern, my dear Katherine.'

'A matter of concern, by God!' Gloucester's hands clenched into fists. 'How can you be so mealy-mouthed? It will not happen.'

'I will do it,' I reiterated, as if expressing a simple desire to travel to Westminster. Although sharp fear was beginning to undermine my composure, I braced my knees and spine.

Gloucester huffed out a breath. 'It is unheard of. An English Queen, crowned and anointed, taking a second husband on the death of the King…'

I allowed myself a little laugh. Was this the best he could do? A matter of precedent, and it seemed to me not a strong one. Why should a widowed queen not remarry? I was nervous no longer.

'Has there never, in hundreds of years of kingship in this country, been a royal widow who has chosen to remarry?' I asked. It sounded beyond my comprehension.

'No. There has never been such—and there will not. The Council will not permit it.'

Bishop Henry cleared his throat. 'Well—yes—in fact, there has.' He smiled self-deprecatingly, as if he was enjoying himself. 'Adeliza of Louvain remarried.'

'Who?' Gloucester demanded, momentarily baffled.

'Adeliza. Wife of King Henry the First.' The bishop's smile remained fixed when Gloucester flung up his hands in disgust. 'It pays to be a reader of history, does it not? Although it has to be said that Adeliza was Henry's second wife and was not the mother of the heir to the throne. Still, if we are speaking of precedents…'

'Before God! If she had no connection to the royal descent, she has no importance. This is an irrelevance, Henry. If you're thinking of supporting your damned nephew in this nonsense...'

I raised my hand to stop yet another diatribe against Edmund, even as horror returned to drench me from head to foot. 'Are you saying that I must never remarry?'

'Not exactly,' Bishop Henry offered.

'There is no precedent for it,' glowered Gloucester.

'I understand.' A bleak landscape, terrible in its vastness, opened up before me. 'So I must remain alone.'

When Gloucester nodded, I sensed relief in him that he had won his argument, and his voice became appallingly unctuous. 'Many would envy your position, Katherine. You have your dower lands in England, your son, an assured place at court. It is all eminently suitable for a royal widow.'

Eminently suitable. But, in my mind, lacking one essential perquisite. I knew in my heart at that moment that it was a lost cause, that I would never rouse sympathy from Gloucester, but still I asked.

'So I have every comfort, every show of respect, but I am not allowed to love?'

'Love!' Gloucester's lips curled as if such an emotion were a matter for distaste. 'Private amours are for foolish women of no standing. If you were not the Queen Dowager, then why not, if that is what you would seek? Why not find some innocuous nobleman to wed you and take you off to his country estate where you can devote yourself to raising children and good works? But you are not free to make that choice.'

'It is not right,' I said, clinging desperately to the last vestiges of hope as Gloucester stripped away all chance of happiness in marriage.

'Madam Joanna has found no difficulty in remaining a respectable widow.'

'Madam Joanna is fifty-seven years old. I am only twenty-five and—'

'And quite obviously incapable of ruling your carnal passions.'

So harsh a judgement! I could barely believe that he had used those words against me, and I froze.

Gloucester's eyes raked me from head to foot. 'You are too much your mother's daughter.'

It gripped me by the throat. Was my mother's reputation to be resurrected again and again, to be used in evidence against me? And by what right had Gloucester of all men to accuse me of carnal passions? Anger rolled in my belly, dark and intense, until it boiled up to spill over in hot words, scalding the space between us.

'What right have you? What right have you to accuse me of lack of self-control? I say that you have no right at all to besmirch my mother's name, as you have no cause to castigate me. Have I not played my part perfectly, in every degree that has been demanded of me? I have accompanied my son, I have stood by his side, I have carried him into Parliament when he was too small to walk. I have never acted with less than dignity and grace, in public and in private. Will I do any less, will I destroy the sanctity of my son's kingship if I am wed? No, I will not.'

All my resentment surged again, and my will to make my own choice. 'I do not accept your decision. I will wed Edmund Beaufort. There is no law that says I cannot.'

Gloucester's ungloved hands closed into fists at his sides. 'Why the temper? This should come as no surprise to you. Did I not explain what was expected of you when you returned to England?'

'Oh, you did.' Fury still bubbled hotly. 'I remember. Your timing was impeccable. In the week that I had stood beside Henry's body in Westminster Abbey, you told me of your wide-ranging plans for me that could only be altered by death.'

'It needed to be said. Your importance in upholding the status of a child king is vital to all of us. Of preserving the claim of Young Henry to be King of England and France. I cannot stress enough how important your role is to England.'

'And I will do nothing to damage that. Have I not said so? How would I do anything to harm my son's position as King?'

'You must remain untouched, inviolable.'

'I know, I know. A sacred vessel. Untouched until the day I am sewn into my shroud.' Against my will, my voice broke.

'Listen to me, Katherine.' Gloucester exhaled loudly, rolling out a new argument with fulsome confidence. 'Have you not thought of how this marriage would be seen? By the curious and the prurient? Our saintly Queen suddenly wed to a new husband, younger than she, whose social status is inferior to that of her own? The whole of Christendom will say that you took the first man you set your eyes on to your bed simply to satisfy your physical lust.'

'Lust?'

'It would prejudice your honour and your judgement,' he pressed on. 'It would defile your reputation. It would undermine the sanctity of the Crown itself.'

I was struck dumb by the enormity of this judgement.

'His social status is not so inferior,' Bishop Henry murmured, picking one comment out of the many. His voice seemed to come from a great distance. 'Edmund is not some peasant discovered by Katherine in the palace gutter. He has, after all, the same royal blood in his veins as you, my dear Humphrey.'

'I'll not argue against it,' Gloucester snarled, swinging round to face Bishop Henry, face livid with rage returned. 'That's the point, isn't it? Your nephew has too much royal blood. And I'll not allow a Beaufort marriage with the Queen Dowager.'

And there it was, Gloucester's determination to stand in the way of any Beaufort aggrandisement. No Beaufort would be allowed to rise to power clinging to my silk damask skirts. Gloucester turned back to me, now giving no thought to his words, or to the degree of offence he would give to his uncle the bishop.

'What role do you intend to give him, your new husband? Regent? Protector of the Realm? To replace me? Is that where the pair of you have set your sights? Oh, I'm sure Beaufort has. He would like nothing better than to lord it over the kingdom in your son's name.'

'Gloucester—' But Bishop Henry's intervention fell on stony ground.

'Your marriage to Beaufort could destroy all we have achieved to preserve a kingdom with a minority rule. Do you not see how vulnerable we are with a King not yet five years old? We must do all that we can to preserve the strength of my brother Henry's legacy, to strengthen the people's respect and loyalty to the child king. Nothing must be allowed to undermine the God-given sanctity of kingship. And your selfish behaviour threatens to undermine all we have done. A liaison with a man known for little but low buffoonery and high ambition! Is this the man you would choose to stand beside you, as stepfather to your son? It is an entirely inappropriate match.' He came to a halt, his breathing ragged.

And I, smarting from every criticism he had made of my character, my judgement and of the man I loved, summoned up a smile. Falsely demure, I asked, 'An inappropriate marriage? If we are to speak of inappropriate marriages and relationships, my lord…'

And I let my gentle-sounding words hang in the still air, conscious of Bishop Henry stiffening in awe at my side.

'How dare you!' Gloucester blustered.

'I think, my lord, that there is an English saying: about the relative blackness of pots and kettles. Am I not correct?'

Storm clouds raced across his face. The bigamous union between Gloucester and Jacqueline of Hainault had provided a short-lived attraction. And while he had set in motion an annulment, he had taken Eleanor Cobham to his bed, lady in waiting to the rejected Jacqueline. Oh, it was well known, but perhaps not tactful to mention here. I did so with a *frisson* of triumph as Gloucester's narrow features became rigid with rage.

'Your marriage has been far more inappropriate than any I might contemplate, Humphrey. Neither Edmund Beaufort nor I would engage in a bigamous relationship. Neither, I swear, would Edmund consider taking one of my damsels to his bed.'

Gloucester was beyond mere fury. 'You will not discuss my private affairs,' he snapped through closed teeth.

'Yet you are free to shred mine to pieces.' How bold I was.

'You will not wed Edmund Beaufort.'

'I don't accept that. You cannot prevent us.'

'Can I not? We'll see about that.'

And, scooping up gloves and sword, Gloucester stalked out, his brow blacker than ever. I heard his voice harsh, intemperate, echoing through the antechamber as he summoned his servants and horses. I pitied his retinue on the journey back to London.

'I suppose there is little purpose in my trying to make amends and asking Lord Humphrey to dine with us,' I remarked to Bishop Henry, who still lingered, thoughtfully, at my side.

His regard was quizzical. 'That was not wise, Katherine. What did you hope to achieve? Antagonising the man, however satisfying, as I know from my own experience, will not help your cause.'

But I shrugged, unregretful. 'It was eminently satisfying. I enjoyed the expression on his face. Nothing I say will win him round, so I have destroyed nothing that could be made to work in my favour.'

But Bishop Henry frowned. 'Be discreet. Compromising behaviour will bring you to the public eye, and who's to know the result.' Surprising me, he seized my hand. 'I beg of you, Katherine. It's not too late. Draw back from this.'

But I tugged my hand free. So he was not my friend either.

'I have no intention of flaunting my love in public as if it were some deplorable scandal. It is not. I have brought no ill repute to my son or the English Crown.' I eyed him. 'Have you spoken with your nephew yet?'

'No.' Head bent in thought, as if he would see the answer in the extravagantly floriferous tiles beneath his episcopal boots, the bishop was already making his way to the door, although I doubted it was to catch up with Gloucester. 'I'll try and get to him before Gloucester does, and beat some sense into him.'

'Sense? Do you think to persuade him to withdraw?' All the energy that had driven me into defiance against Glouces-ter began to fade in the face of this new opposition. It hurt that Bishop Henry should stand against me too. 'So you agree with Gloucester,' I said sadly. 'You would advise me against it.'

'I don't know.' At the door he paused, with troubled eyes. 'All I know is that Gloucester will stop at nothing to destroy the rise of the Beaufort star in the Heavens.' His smile was dry and brittle. 'It is my wish, of course, to see our star rise. And until I see my way to it, my advice to you, my dear Kather-ine, is that you remain…' he hovered over the word '…cir-cumspect.'

A word that could mean anything or nothing.

'And unwed,' I added despondently.

He shrugged. 'Don't give up hope, my dear.'

Alice, silent throughout, walked at last to stand beside me as the bishop departed and placed her hand on my arm, which now trembled. 'Madam Joanna did warn you, my lady.'

'So she did. And Warwick, in his way.'

What would Edmund say in the wake of this denunciation?

10

I FRETTED, SHAKING with anxieties, and with fears that built like a thundercloud. Not knowing where Edmund was, I wasted no time in struggling with a pen but sent a courier to Westminster with a verbal message. I must see him.

The days passed, with no word forthcoming from Gloucester or either of the Beauforts. My courier returned empty-handed with no news other than Edmund was not at Westminster. All I could do was wait, and worry, the final clash in my verbal bout with Gloucester resounding in my mind.

You cannot prevent us.

Can I not? We'll see about that.

And so we would. Caught up in the vicious battle with Bishop Henry for power over the Royal Council, Gloucester was set on bringing the Beauforts down. That much I now saw. Perhaps it had not been politic of me to challenge him with his own salacious dabblings in marriage, but it was a wound too late to remedy. I prayed that the desirable Mistress Cobham, commoner though she might be, would sweeten her lover's temper.

'I'll go to Westminster myself,' I announced, when I could bear the silence no longer, when my feet had all but worn a path to the high vantage point of the Winchester Tower. Madam Joanna had left Windsor for her favoured residence of Havering-atte-Bower even before Gloucester's arrival, so there was no solace to be had from her calm view of the world.

'I wouldn't advise it,' Alice replied gruffly, when I expressed my intention. 'Keep a low profile and it might all be swept onto the midden.' *And, with luck, Edmund Beaufort too.* I could read her unspoken thoughts but refused to respond. But we both knew it would not happen. The conflict between Gloucester and Bishop Henry had gone far beyond tolerance sealed with a handshake, reaching a climax when Beaufort troops had refused Gloucester access to the Tower of London. The outrage of the royal duke knew no bounds.

'A pity you could not see your way to be enamoured with a man without name or ambition,' Alice remarked caustically. 'If you had, the Council might just leave you alone to be happy.'

I knew that to be a falsehood too. 'If I had demanded to wed a man without consequence, the Council would object that he was not sufficiently well connected,' I remarked tartly, weary of it all. 'Marriage to a commoner would damage my integrity as Queen Dowager. They will not allow me to wed a nobody.' I frowned. 'Besides, it's Edmund I love.'

Alice opened her mouth to reply, then shut it.

'I do,' I insisted. 'I love him and he loves me.'

'As your ladyship says.'

'I know what you are thinking. Madam Joanna thinks the same,' I interrupted the unspoken slight on our love. 'Edmund's regard for me is genuine. I am convinced of it. He would not ask me to marry him if he did not love me.'

Alice's lips tightened, as they did when she reprimanded Young Henry for some lack of courtesy. 'You might ask yourself, my lady, what he would gain from such a union.'

I strode from the room. No one wished me well in this. How could they not see Edmund's love for me? How could they not appreciate the array of his gifts, of his skills, as bright as jewels, that he tumbled at my feet for my delectation?

I needed to see him. I needed to be reassured.

To my delight, Edmund returned to Windsor before I could sink into a bad humour. My heart lifted and I sprang to my feet, opening my arms to him as he lifted his to enclose me in their warmth. My lips rose to meet his in urgent welcome. For a little while we simply stood and savoured the closeness.

'Now, there's a welcome that no man could resist!' he remarked as he surveyed me at last, his hands caressing my shoulders.

'I have missed you.'

'And I you, so I am come. But what's this?' His gaze travelled over my face. 'You look as if you have been beset,' he observed, running a finger over my brow. 'What's happened to make you frown? Nothing must be allowed to distress my love.'

'Gloucester has been here. And your uncle,' I said.

'I know,' he growled. 'You don't need to tell me about it. I've had an earful from Gloucester already.' He strode away from me to pour two cups of ale. He presented one to me then downed his own in one gulp, wiping his mouth with the back of his hand. 'The great lord was brutal in his choice of words.'

'He says we cannot wed. He says they will stop us.'

'And he has a whole fistful of arguments why we cannot,' Edmund agreed. 'Chief amongst them the one he didn't see fit to list on his power-grabbing fingers, but the one that everyone sees, signalling like a beacon on a hilltop. That Gloucester would abandon his claim to the throne before he'd acknowledge any more power for the Beauforts. Except that he wouldn't do that, would he? How he wishes the crown was his!'

He glowered, the expression marring features that were

made for laughter. 'He'll not let me near the Young King, certainly not as your husband, for fear I lead him into the worst habits. Or try to influence his decisions to benefit the Beauforts as he grows.'

'Edmund—' I tried to draw his attention.

'Let me think,' he interrupted. 'I can't quite see my way around this.'

Edmund frowned into the middle distance, thoughts busy, tossing the empty cup in his hand. Fingering the little brooch pinned to the inner fold of my bodice, his introspection brought me close to despair. I had seen Edmund as my strength. Pray God that he and his uncle would be a match for Gloucester.

'Have you seen Bishop Henry?' I asked.

Edmund grimaced. 'No. He's sent for me—so I can't put it off. I don't see what he can do.'

'I thought Bishop Henry was not entirely unsympathetic to us,' I suggested. And when that merited no reply, 'Can the Council truly stop us?'

'I have no idea. Gloucester says so—so why not? They can always consign you to a convent and force you to take the veil. That would solve the problem of a marriageable royal widow for good. And they could send me to join Bedford in France. That would settle the issue.' His quick grin might be feral, but his eyes were bleak. 'Particularly if I happened to be cut down in battle. That would give Gloucester something to crow about.'

His tone was violent, the picture he painted monstrous, but not, I knew, without veracity. I did not know how to deal with this. I did not know what to say, so I stood and waited, all dreams for the future fading before my eyes. If Edmund saw no way forward, what was left for us but to obey Gloucester's commands?

At last, perhaps becoming aware of my silence, he looked at me, and his features softened as with a sigh he tossed the cup carelessly onto the coffer and crossed the chamber to hug me close. With the tenderness I had grown to lean on, he smiled ruefully, resting his chin on my hair.

'What a brute you must think me. Forgive me, Kat. Of course they won't pack you off to a nunnery. Or me to France. I'll wager my best horse it's all bluster and hot air from Gloucester.'

'He was very angry.'

'I know. And not complimentary to me or to my uncle. He accused me of being a power-grabbing upstart with tainted blood. I don't recall him being quite so savage before, but things are bad between him and Bishop Henry.' His eyes narrowed, as he read the dismay I could not hide and at last drew me against him, into his arms. 'I can't stay—but I thought I should come to reassure you. I'll talk to Bishop Henry. It will all come right, you know.' His mouth was warm, tracing a delicate path from brow to lips.

'Can I be with you, when you see him?' I asked. Surely if we were both there to plead our cause, the Beaufort cleric must listen.

'Not necessary,' he murmured, preoccupied as his teeth nipped lightly along my jaw, sending tremors of pleasure down to my feet.

'But I wish to.'

Edmund stopped kissing me, and instead framed my face with his hands. His eyes sparkled and his face lit with some deviousness.

'Then so you shall, Queen Kat. We will beard Uncle Henry in his den, and you will weep piteously and beautifully over his feet. And then, with my esteemed uncle unable to refuse you your heart's desire, we will cry failure to Protector Gloucester. It will all come to pass, my lovely girl, all your hopes and dreams fulfilled.'

My heart was still as I leaned on Edmund's reassurance.

'You took your time, boy. How long does it take to get your-self to Westminster?'

'Forgive me, sir. I regret the delay, but now I am here, to answer for my sins.'

Bishop Henry, seated behind a vast desk, was not in a good mood, but master of diplomacy as he was, after this first brisk exchange, he welcomed me urbanely and waved us to take softly cushioned seats, which we did. A servant poured wine and was dismissed.

Upon which the urbanity vanished.

'This marriage, Edmund. You've stirred up a damned pot of eels, by God.'

Hands clenched into fists on his thighs, Edmund still kept his reply as smooth as new-churned butter. 'I don't see the difficulty, sir. What matter if we wed? Katherine is free to do so, as am I. There can be no church ban, as we are not related to any degree.'

'Don't be obtuse, boy,' Bishop Henry drawled. 'You know the reasons as well as I.'

'What are you saying?' High colour crept along Edmund's cheekbones. 'So do you suggest I withdraw? That I break my vow to Katherine, that I reject her as my wife?'

My breath caught in my throat.

But Bishop Henry smiled. There was something unnerv-ingly reptilian about it. 'Did I say that?'

'To be frank, sir, I don't know what you're saying.'

'You have much to learn about political manoeuvring, my boy. I am saying that there are ways and means.'

I did not understand where this was leading, but Bishop

Henry's assurance stirred a nugget of hope where there had been none. 'Are you saying, my lord, that Gloucester can be persuaded to withdraw his objection?' I asked. I could not see how.

'No, my lady.' His smile became broader. 'He will definitely try to stop you attempting to wed. But I know of a way to bring a halt to his ambitions. It will please me immeasurably to chop the rungs of the ladder from under Gloucester's feet.'

So I did not need to weep over his feet after all. Bishop Henry was suddenly all politician, and out for blood.

'I don't see how,' Edmund interjected.

'Of course you don't. But I will show you. Am I not Lord Chancellor? I am not without powers, whatever Gloucester might like to think. My associates in the Council, always eager to snap at Gloucester's heels, will ensure that I have my way.'

'But Gloucester has a loud voice in the Royal Council.'

'I have Bedford's ear too. Bedford needs money to pursue the French wars. When the Council cannot raise enough gold, who is it that gets them out of difficulties and provides the loans?' He smiled serenely in answer to his own question. 'I do. The Council is very grateful to me.'

Edmund bowed his head, for the first time since we had arrived a smile lighting his countenance. 'I underestimated you, Uncle.'

'It is never wise to do so. You may get your lovely French wife yet.'

'You'll see. I'll make you my wife before the year's out,' Edmund said, all his enthusiasm restored as he escorted me to the door. He cradled my face so that he could kiss my lips in farewell. 'Gloucester's not a match for my wily uncle. I'll wed you and we'll prove Gloucester and the Council wrong. What a couple we will make.'

I left them to their plotting with their heads bent over a

manuscript. They were two of a Beaufort kind. Bishop Henry was on our side. What could go wrong?

There it was: a clever piece of sleight of hand, worthy of Bishop Henry at his most scheming. News of it reached Eltham, where Young Henry's court had moved on its annual progress from one royal palace to the next, by the usual convoluted route of gossip and legalistic assertion. I refused to rejoice until my Chancellor, John Wodehouse, could read the document and pronounce on it with certainty. He did so, with some bafflement as to its cause.

'I simply don't see the need,' he stated more than once.

For it transpired that when Parliament had met in Leicester, a member of the Commons had presented a petition, from the goodness of his heart and in the name of his fellow Commoners, all loyal subjects to a man. Would it not be an act of kindness to allow royal widows to marry again if they so wished? Upon payment of an appropriate fine, of course, to the royal coffers. Perhaps the Lord Chancellor would give the matter his expertise and consideration, based on his vast experience?

Bishop Henry, Lord Chancellor, had expressed his interest and his concern over the plight of royal widows in general, and would give the matter some thought.

'Does Madam Joanna intend to wed again?' my Chancellor asked of no one in particular. 'I would not have thought it.' He shrugged. 'Perhaps some aging knight has caught her eye, to give her companionship in her declining years—and she needs a legal blessing. Who's to know what ideas get into the heads of women when they reach a certain age?'

But I knew. The enterprising member of the Commons had doubtless had his palm oiled by a purse of gold from Bishop Henry. And the clever bishop would make the final decision.

How delightfully, pragmatically vague it was. How cunning. I admired the sympathetic wording.

And it was for me. Madam Joanna would never wed again— but I would.

I prayed for Bishop Henry's quick consideration and the Council's consent. Surely it was now only a matter of time before I stood with Edmund before a priest who would witness our union. Although I lived out those days in a storm of nervous tension, nothing could undermine my elation.

I looked daily for Edmund to ride to Eltham, bounding from horse to hall with triumphal energy, to deliver the good news. I got Bishop Henry instead, and I was surprised, for rumours had flown, darting like iridescent dragonflies over the surface of the sluggish river in recent weeks. Troops had appeared on the streets of London, outbreaks of violence had become the order of the day, and to my dismay Young Henry emerged as a valuable prize in the battle for power between Gloucester and Bishop Henry.

I heard this news with a kind of creeping terror. Beaufort or Plantagenet, sanctified bishop or noble duke—were either to be trusted when their own authority came into the balance? My little son had become a pawn in their deadly game. I buried my personal concerns deep as Young Henry's freedom came under threat, and prayed for Bedford's calming influence on his brother and uncle. But Bedford was still in France and the rumours became more disturbing as the armed retinues of Gloucester and Beaufort confronted each other on London Bridge, Gloucester threatening to descend on us and remove my son from Eltham into his custody, by physical force if necessary.

We sat and quaked at every noise, guards doubled, listening for the clash and clamour of approaching mailed knights. And here in the midst of the political upheavals was Bishop Henry, come to Eltham, to tell me—to tell me what?

'It is not good news, Katherine.'

As he entered the Great Hall and walked slowly across the worn paving slabs to where I waited for him, his doleful features confirmed my suspicions. Still suave, still impeccably dressed in clerical authority, Bishop Henry looked weary, as if he had indulged in a long battle of wits, and lost. I simply stood, unable to express my fears, my lips numb with anticipation of the worst.

But what was the worst Gloucester could do? I had swept aside the foolish thought that Edmund had mischievously planted, of being enclosed against my will in a convent. That could not be. It would not be! If it was mooted, I would simply return to the French court.

But if I returned to France, it would be without my son.

I willed myself to be sensible. It would not come to that. So what was it that gave Bishop Henry's features the aspect of a death's head? And, even more pertinent, where was Edmund?

'Tell me,' I ordered sharply, I who rarely ordered anyone sharply.

Bishop Henry replied without subtlety, his face expressionless. 'All is lost. My petition to the Commons on your behalf has been destroyed. Bedford has returned, and ordered a cessation of hostilities.' He lifted a shoulder in rueful acceptance. 'He is not best pleased. And in the aftermath Gloucester has taken pleasure in revenge on the Beaufort name. I am defeated.' I waited. There was more to come. Bishop Henry folded his hands and pronounced: 'There will be repercussions for you too.'

Ah, there it was. 'So I will not be allowed to wed Edmund.'

It was difficult to form the words. A fist of pure, raw emotion tightened in my chest, so strong that I could barely breathe, yet I firmed my shoulders and kept a level gaze, even as the bishop's eye slid from mine. I was right to fear the worst. His voice was rough as if he had argued himself into exhaustion.

'There are difficulties, Katherine. Gloucester is preparing to tie your situation into knots. And for me too there has been a high price to pay. I have been forced to resign my position as Lord Chancellor.' Even in my own pain I thought: how the years show on your face today. My heart was touched with compassion. I laid my hand softly on his sleeve, feeling the tension below the rich damask as he added, 'Gloucester is in the ascendant. It is a tragic outcome for you, I fear.'

He did not resist as I led him to my parlour, motioning for the damsels to depart. Once there, he sank wearily into my own chair with its carved back and arms, leaning back as if he needed its support, while I stuffed soft cushions behind him and sent for wine. And when we were alone I pulled up a low stool and prepared to listen to what had been done that was so tragic and that would have so great a bearing on my life.

'Gloucester intends to persuade the Commons in the next session to implement a statute. They will most assuredly comply.'

'And what is this statute?'

Bishop Henry drank deep. 'No man will be allowed to wed a Queen Dowager without the consent of the King and his Council.'

'Oh!'

I thought about this, studying my hands, my fingers interlocking. It did not seem so very bad. My remarriage had not exactly been forbidden. All I needed was permission.

'Is that all?' I asked, looking up into the bishop's weary eyes. It was bad, but not beyond redemption.

'Think about it, Katherine. Think about what he has done.'

And I did—and at last the simple statement spinning in my brain came to rest. I think I laughed at the enormity of it.

'Of course. The consent of the King.' I felt the rise of hysteria in my chest. 'And since my son is not of an age to give consent to anything...' How cleverly it had been done, how callously. He had not needed to name me—he would not wish to be accused of being vindictive—neither did he have to forbid me, merely make it an impossibility. 'Does Gloucester know what he was doing? Does he know that he will condemn me to widowhood?'

'I have no doubt he does.' Bishop Henry drained his cup, and refilled it. 'You will have to wait for at least a decade until Henry reaches his majority.'

I could wed Edmund, but not for a whole ten years, even supposing Young Henry could be persuaded. It stretched like an eternity before me. I could not even imagine so long a wait, seeing only that my thirtieth year would be well gone, my hair faded to grey, my face become marked and lined with the passage of time.

And Edmund—would he not look elsewhere, for a younger bride? Despair closed in on me as I looked up at the bishop again to see him watching me. His face was so full of pity I could not bear it. How could I expect Edmund to wait ten years to win my hand? I could not expect any man to wait a whole decade.

I looked away to hide the tears that slid down my cheeks, even as my thoughts wove a new pattern, seeking some way through Gloucester's cunningly worked maze. I was not entirely forbidden to enter into marriage, was I?

'What if I disobey?' I asked, astonished at how my thoughts had leapt from acceptance to defiance. Would I dare to go against the will of Parliament? I did not think so, yet with

Edmund by my side, what might I not dare to do? 'Will I be punished if I wed without Young Henry's consent?'

Bishop Henry put down his cup, the wine no longer of interest, and took my hands in his. 'Who can tell? There is one more consequence of Gloucester's revenge that you must know, Katherine. Arrangements have been made for you to live permanently in the Young King's household. You will not be allowed to visit your dower properties or travel as you choose. You will go where the Young King goes. Do you understand?'

I understood very well. I was a prisoner. Without bars, without lock and key, but still prisoner under my son's jurisdiction.

'It is intended to help you to withstand your carnal passions,' he continued gently.

And I flinched at the judgement that was becoming engraved on my soul. The image of my mother, painted and bejewelled, casting lascivious glances over the young courtiers, rose before me. What a terrible disservice, all unwittingly, she had done me. I dragged a breath of stifling air into my lungs as I felt my face grow hot from the humiliation.

'I regret what has been done,' Bishop Henry continued, when I could not find the words to reply. 'But it will not be so very bad, you know.'

And now the words spilled out, my voice broken. 'No? I think it might be. It is to keep me under permanent surveillance.'

'I'm afraid it is. Young Henry's claim on the French throne rests entirely on you, and so your reputation must be purer than the pearls in the Virgin's diadem.'

And at last I wept. For my trampled yearnings for a life with Edmund. For my soft incarceration in my son's household so that I might never again do anything to cause ripples in English politics. I would be tied fast under Henry's jurisdiction, anchored as irrevocably as mistletoe in the branch of an apple tree. My heart was broken, my spirit laid low.

'Don't weep. Katherine. You are still young.'

'What use is that? If I am young, I have even more years to live as a prisoner, encased in a shell of lonely respectability. There is no escape for me, is there?'

Would Edmund wed me out of the love he bore me, would he risk wedding me without permission? That was the question to which I needed an answer. The one question I dared not ask. But indeed I did not need to, for Bishop Henry delved into the recesses of his sleeve and drew out a single sheet of a folded document, sealed with the Beaufort crest.

'Edmund asked me to give you this, my dear. He will explain.'

I held it to my breast, tears bright in my eyes. I could see in the compassionate twist to Bishop Henry's mouth that he expected it to be Edmund's farewell to me and, with tears still threatening, I waited until he had tossed off the final dregs of his wine and made his departure—bound for Rome, he informed me, with a cardinal's hat in his sights since his ambitions in England had been so rudely curtailed—before I broke the seal and read it. I would not expose my broken heart further to the self-serving bishop. But as soon as I was alone I ripped the letter open. Better to know the worst. The lines were simple, the letter short, sufficient for my slow reading.

To Katherine, my one and only love.

How I miss you. It seems a lifetime since we shared the same breath. I long to hold you, to know that you are mine. Soon we will be together again, and I will see you smile.

As you will now know, Gloucester does his damnedest to keep us apart, but I swear he will not succeed. What will be the penalty if we wed, with or without the Young King's permis-

*sion? I think that there is no penalty that can be enforced against
a Queen of England and a Beaufort in such a case as ours. Is
my family so lacking in authority? What can they do to us? No
reprimand can keep me from you. No punishment can weigh in
the balance against our being together.*

*I know you will rejoice with me. As proof of my standing at
Court, I have been given the overlordship of Mortain. It is a
signal honour. How much more proof do I need that my feet are
firmly on the ladder to political ascendancy?*

*Hold fast to your belief in me, my love. I will be at West-
minster when you bring Young Henry to Court at the end of
the month. We will make our plans.*

Always know that I love you.
Your servant, now and always.
Edmund Beaufort

'Oh, Edmund!'

I cried out in my astonishment as I curled my hand around
the enamelled brooch with the Beaufort escutcheon, the lively
lion supporting the dominant portcullis, my talisman, that I
pinned to my bodice every morning. I was his, loved and valued beyond all others. And here, in his own words, he had
vowed to pursue our union. Had I not always known it? Edmund was bold enough, outrageous enough, confident enough
with his Beaufort breeding and Plantagenet blood to take a
stand against Gloucester and Parliament—against the whole
world if need be—to claim the woman he loved. To claim
me as his own.

He was Count of Mortain. Was he not in high favour?

As I crushed the letter in my hand it was as if he stood beside me. My mind was suddenly full of his laughter, my head
echoing with his murmured words of love. My lips could still
taste the quality of his desire as I pressed them to the parch-

ment where his words of love flowed from his pen to me. My body ached for him. We would be together again at Westminster. We would stand side by side, my courage bolstered by Edmund's love, and challenge the right of Parliament to keep us apart. If necessary we would defy Gloucester. Edmund would assuredly find some way for us to circumvent Gloucester's cunning maze.

He loves me and he will not desert me.

I held the words close in my heart, repeating them as if they were a nostrum, a witch's spell to bind us together, against all the odds, as I ran up the stairs to the very top of the great Round Tower, to look out towards London. I could not wait until I saw him again.

'Edmund!'

Young Henry, seeing a particular face that he recognised in the crowd, laughed aloud, before halting with an embarrassed little hunch of his shoulders beneath his new tunic. I placed a light hand on his arm, steering him forward, and smiled reassuringly when he looked nervously up at me.

'You can see him later,' I whispered.

With due formality, court etiquette as heavy on my shoulders as my ermine-lined cloak, I walked at Young Henry's side as the whole Court made its obeisance, straining for a view of the Young King. Another visit to Westminster, pre-empting the rapidly approaching moment when my son would be crowned King of England.

The days of his tantrums were over and he held himself with quaint dignity: face pale and still endearingly cherubic despite his growing limbs, fair hair brushed neatly beneath his cap, Henry smiled his pleasure, his eyes, round with astonishment, darting this way and that. Until they had come to rest on Edmund Beaufort, Count of Mortain.

'Can I speak with him now?' Young Henry whispered back. 'I have something to tell him.'

'Of course you have. But first you must greet your uncle of Gloucester,' I replied.

I too must exert patience. The days, a mere handful, since I had read his letter, had seemed like years in their extent. How many times had I reread it, absorbing the hope that shone through the words. Only a few minutes now before Edmund and I stood face to face, blatantly declaring our love. I smiled, conscious of happiness coating me like the gold leaf on a holy icon. We would be together.

Henry nodded solemnly and walked on, leaving me in his wake where all I could do was will my mind and my body into a semblance of perfect composure. I had seen Edmund even before my son's recognition, and I too could have cried out his name. My heart was beating so erratically I could barely swallow, my hands damp with longing.

There he was, to my right, bowing elegantly. I turned my head in anticipation. But our eyes did not meet, even when he straightened to his full height and smiled at my son's enthusiasm. Edmund Beaufort did not smile at me. My heart tripped in its normal rhythm, but I took myself to task. This was far too public for any passionate reunion. Of course we would not speak of love now. But soon, soon...

With confident grace I continued on my prescribed route, inclining my head to those who acknowledged me, taking up my position behind Henry when the necessary presentations were made. Greetings were exchanged, bows and promises of fealty. Gloucester, Warwick, the high blood of the land. And in their midst Edmund stepped up to be greeted by my son as a favoured cousin.

'We have missed you, Edmund.'

'Forgive me, Sire. I have been busy about your affairs in France,' Edmund replied solemnly, hand on heart.

'I know. You are Count of Mortain. I have a new horse,' my son announced with pride. 'He is not as handsome as yours.'

'I cannot believe that. If it was a gift from my lord of Warwick, it must be a fine animal.'

'Will you come to Windsor again? When it is cold you can teach me to skate, like you taught my lady mother.'

'It will be my pleasure, Sire.'

He stepped back, away, to let another approach.

How kind, I thought, as if from a distance. How thoughtful he was in his response to my little son. And how astonishingly cruel to me. Not once through the whole of that conversation, not once after a graceful inclination of his head in my general direction, had Edmund Beaufort looked at me. Instead, I'd had an impressive view of his noble profile, smiling and assured and so very arrogant.

Had I been mistaken? I could barely shuffle my thoughts into any sort of order. Had he deliberately ignored me? I tried to quell my rising panic. Perhaps he considered the need for discretion in our relationship. But to turn away, to address not one word to me was difficult to accept. Almost impossible to excuse.

Surely he could speak with me as the Queen Mother, as he was cousin to my son, without causing any ripples at court. The panic began to subside, my breathing to even out. Edmund would speak with me when the formalities were over. Of course he would.

'When you come to Windsor, will we unpack the masks and costumes again?' I heard Young Henry calling after Edmund, through the clamour in my head.

Then the presentations were over and the court was free to mingle and converse. *Now* he would come to me! Now he would walk through the little knots of courtiers, his gaze fixed only on me, alight with determination to let nothing and no one come between us.

But no. To my desolation, Edmund withdrew to the further side of the room. He had passed me by as if I were nothing to him. Once we had passed the hours in intimate dalliance, our blood running hot for each other. Now he did not even look at me as I stood in the group surrounding my son, exchanging greetings and general gossip with Warwick. He had told me that we could be together, that we would make our plans, that nothing could separate us. Conscious of his letter tucked in the bosom of my gown, I did not understand this studied rejection of what we were to each other.

The reception progressed through its habitual pattern, courtiers and aristocrats moving and mingling, making contacts, speaking with those with influence, being seen in the presence of those who could make or break a reputation. I played my allotted part, regal and decorous, but I was weary of it to my bones. Fear built in my breast as the minutes moved on and I tried to recall, word for word, exactly what Edmund Beaufort had written to me. *Always know that I love you. No reprimand can keep you from me.* Had he not made such declarations? Surely he must find a path to me, to spread his adoration once more at my feet.

He did not. Not once did he approach.

A pain settled in my chest, spreading out to my limbs, an agony that was well nigh physical as all became writ plain for me. This was no chance parting, caused by the demands of the court. This was a deliberate, intentional separation. And, drowning in misery, I fought for dignity. I turned my eyes from him. It crossed my mind, with harsh appreciation, that Henry, cold, superbly controlled Henry, would have been proud of my ability to mask my feelings that day.

But there was a limit to my self-control.

Although I had sworn to look anywhere but in my lover's direction, when the time came for Young Henry to withdraw, I sought the mass of faces for a last glimpse, as if to twist again the knife that Edmund had planted in my heart when he had so wantonly neglected me throughout the whole of that interminable reception. And there he was in sparkling conversation with a handsome young woman whom I knew well. Eleanor Beauchamp, Warwick's daughter, come to Court with her husband, Thomas de Ros.

But that did not stop Edmund Beaufort from flirting with her. Oh, I saw the careful attention he paid to her. I recognised the tilt of his head as he listened to what she had to say, I noted the set of his shoulders, the confidential manner in which he leaned a little towards her. All redolent of the manner in which he had once flirted with me. As he had once made love to me with honeyed words and playful gestures. And then, when he turned his head to respond to a passing friend, his handsome face, the sweep of his lashes on his cheek, the clean line of his profile drove the blade even deeper.

I stared. And as Lady Eleanor was escorted away by her husband, Edmund turned, so that as chance would have it he looked directly at me. Because I was looking at him, our eyes of necessity met and held. For the length of a heartbeat he paused. And then he made a full court obeisance, as he would honour the Queen Dowager, cold and distant and perfect in its execution.

My self-control snapped like a worn bowstring. He was my lover, the man who would wed me. There must be some terrible misapprehension that had taken hold of my mind, some mistake that Edmund could rectify and then all would be well again. All I needed to do was speak with him, to step to cross the space between us and demand... Demand what?

An explanation, I supposed. How could he not approach me, his professed love? How could he not smile and tell me of his heart's desire as he saluted my fingers with his lips? Throat dry, I determined that I must know.

'Don't.'

Barely had I taken a second step than a hand closed lightly around my wrist.

'Richard!'

It was Warwick, standing at my shoulder, his gaze following the line of my sight.

'But I must—'

'Don't go to him,' he responded gently. 'It is useless, Katherine. To cause a scene would be—'

'He said he would wed me and defy Parliament,' I interrupted, careless of any such scene yet still managing to keep my voice low.

'He won't do it. He won't wed you now.'

'How can you say that?' I resisted the gentle pull on my arm, but Warwick was intent on manoeuvring me out of the throng, towards the tapestry-hung wall.

'I know he will not. You have to know what has been done. Listen to me, Katherine.' In the little space he had created for us, Warwick gripped harder so that I must concentrate. 'There have been new moves. Gloucester has locked every door, barred every window against you.'

'But I know.' Still I remonstrated. How could it be so bad? 'I know the law says that I must ask my son's permission to marry but surely—'

'There's more. Another clause.' There was barely a pause. 'It will have serious consequences for your remarriage. To any man.'

'Oh.' Now I was afraid.

'Any man who risks the ban and takes you for his wife without royal consent will lose everything.' Warwick's face was stern, his words savage in the message they delivered, but his eyes were soft with infinite compassion. 'He will effectively be stripped of his lands and his possessions, his appointments in government.'

'Oh,' I said again, almost a whisper, absorbing the enormity of this.

'Such a man will forgo all promotions, all favour and patronage. All opportunity for his further advancement would be stripped away.'

'I see.'

'For any man to wed you—' Warwick was inexorable '—would be political and social suicide. Do you understand? If he took you as his wife, Edmund Beaufort would be ruined.'

'Yes,' I heard myself say. 'Yes, I do understand.'

My throat was full of tears as Warwick's bald statements, delivered one after the other, were like nails hammered into the coffin of my hopes and dreams. I stood for a while in silence, my hands still enfolded within the Earl's, as the pieces fell into place, finally driven to accept the impossibility of my union with any ambitious man by the neatest, most vindictive piece of legislation. No specific name had been mentioned, but the intent behind it as clear as the signatures written on the document. My heart was wrenched with hurt as I absorbed the inevitable in that one inexorable warning.

For any man to wed you it would be political and social suicide.

That was the end, was it not? Would Edmund Beaufort run head first into marriage with me, risking the loss of political and social advancement? Would he prejudice his ambitions for me?

Head raised, chin held high in a determination not to appear trampled beneath the weight of what I now knew, I looked to where I had last seen him. And there he stood, deep in conversation with the men who held power in the kingdom in my son's name, just as his uncle Bishop Henry would once have done. Gloucester, Hungerford, Westmorland, Exeter, Archbishop Chichele.

Edmund knew where his best interests lay, and as I took in his carefully selected, august company, so did I. The Beauforts were political animals through and through. Advancement would take precedent over all other interests. If I had still been of a mind to cling to any foolish hope, Edmund's present company confirmed all Warwick's warning.

'It is better if you do not approach him,' Warwick said gently.

'I understand. I understand perfectly.' I looked up into his face. 'How could he have been so cruel?'

'Did he not tell you?'

I shook my head, unable to put my sense of utter rejection into words.

'I am so sorry. He will not see it as cruelty but as political necessity. A pragmatic decision. All Beauforts would. They have been raised from the cradle to do so.'

'Even at the cost of breaking my heart?'

'Even at that.'

'He wrote that he would remain true to our love.'

'I am so very sorry, Katherine,' Warwick repeated.

'You did warn me.' My mouth twisted into what was not a smile.

'I know. But I would not have had you hurt in this manner.'

I looked across to where Edmund was laughing at something Gloucester had said, responding with a dramatic gesture with one arm I recognised so well. Oh, I was hurt. I floundered in desolation that all my visions of happiness were no more than straws in the wind, to be scattered, leaving me empty and broken.

That night I took anguish and tears with me to my bed. Bitter bedfellows indeed to keep me company through the sleepless hours. But I rose in quite a different mood.

'My lady. May we speak?'

His bow was the epitome of elegant respect, early sun making russet lights gleam in his hair as he flourished his velvet cap.

Anger beat softly in my head. He had found me of no value, and had rejected me as he would a crippled warhorse when no longer fit for purpose. And as he drew himself to his full height, his expression a winning combination of self-deprecation and rueful apology, I felt my simmering temper come dangerously close to the edge of boiling. I had not been aware that I could be possessed by such rage.

I was on my way to Mass, Guille accompanying me, crossing an anteroom where pages and servants scurried to and fro at the behest of their masters. There was no privacy to be had at Westminster, neither would I grant him that luxury. If he had wanted privacy with me, he should have come to Windsor.

'You will stay with me,' I ordered Guille as she slowed her step to drop back, at the precise moment that Edmund Beaufort made that bow with all his considerable charm, striking a dramatic pose.

And in that moment, beneath the green and gold panels of his knee-skimming tunic, the sleek hose and velvet-draped hood, I saw him for what he was: all picturesque pretence and show to win my regard, all driving ambition to play a vital role in England's politics. He was a Beaufort through and through. Yet he was still impressive enough to cause my silly heart to quake.

His stare, bright and confident, sought and held mine and he smiled, but then my heart quaked no more and I did not return it. I did not even consider a curtsey. I simply stood, straight-backed, hands folded neatly at my waist, and waited to see what he would say to redeem himself. Yesterday he had treated me as Queen Dowager. Today I would act as one, and ride the fury that was a burning weight in my belly.

'Queen Kat. You are as lovely as ever.'

How despicable he was. Did he consider me so shallow that I could be soothed by empty flattery?

'Why did you not tell me?' I demanded.

I had startled him with my directness, but he did not hesitate. 'I would tell you now. But I would still say that you are the most beautiful woman I have ever known.'

The conceit of the man. I could almost see his wily Beaufort brain working furiously behind his winning smile as he resorted to flattery. My temper leapt in little flames. I did not lower my voice: today I was in no mood for either compromise or discretion. 'You should have come to me and told me yourself that you could no longer wed me. You should have come to Windsor.'

'May we speak alone?' His brows rose with charming intimacy.

'No.'

His smile slid impressively into an expression of abject contrition. 'I should have come. It was wrong of me, entirely deplorable. I deserve your disdain, my lady, and I can only beg forgiveness. I thought you would understand.'

So he would try to win my sympathies. He held out his hand, expecting me to place mine there, as once I would have. I kept my fingers lightly laced.

'You are not making this easy for me,' he said.

'Nor will I,' I replied. 'And I would have liked to have been told of the circumstance that made you break your promise to me of undying love. I did not enjoy having to discover it from Warwick under the interested gaze of the entire court. Or to have you ignore me through the whole proceedings.'

And I was astonished. Where had this confidence, this impressive fluency, this desire to wound come from? Born out of irrepressible outrage at my lover's public rebuff, I was not subtle. I was not sensitive to the comings and goings around us. I wanted to hear it from his own lips, to see his discomfort as he explained that ambition made my love superfluous.

My tone attracting attention, bringing glances in our direction, Edmund's brow darkened and the contrition vanished, replaced by a flash of anger. He took a highly un-lover-like grip of my arm and pulled me out of the general flow of people into a window embrasure, waving Guille aside.

'There's no need to make public our personal differences.' I watched his struggle to contain his irritation and admired his success as his lively features became almost benign with compassion. How remarkably plausible he was. Why had I never suspected it when I had believed every word he had uttered? 'I understand your disappointment in me.'

'No, you do not,' I retorted smartly. 'And I was not aware that we had any personal differences. Our *differences*, as I understand it, are political.'

He sighed. An exhalation of deepest remorse. How well he was able to run through the gamut of emotions. 'You read it perfectly. But still—I thought you would understand.' He made a languid gesture with one elegant hand, which roused my temper to new proportions. There was nothing languid about Edmund Beaufort. This was all for effect, playing a role to relieve his conscience, if he possessed one.

'What is it that I would understand, Edmund?' I asked prosaically.

'I think it is obvious, Katherine.' At last an edge coloured his voice. 'I never thought you obtuse.'

His deliberate use of my name, which had once made me shiver with desire, left me unmoved. I found myself observing him, as Young Henry might sit for hours and watch the scurrying of ants beneath the painted tiles in the garden at Windsor. Without doubt he was a master of words and emotions, weaving them to his own purpose. My heart, which had once burned for him, felt as cold as ice in my chest.

'I think my appreciation of the situation is sound,' I informed him, without heat. 'My belief that you loved me was destroyed yesterday. By Warwick's kindness and your distance that was little short of insolent—'

'Katherine, never that! You must see.' His voice was softly seductive, urging me to be won over.

'I do see. I now see astonishingly well. I suppose I am honoured that you have taken the time to seek me out.'

Suddenly the charm was gone, temper returned. 'Then if you know the terms of the statute, what can I say that you do not know for yourself?'

'What indeed. But I think you should have had the honesty to tell me that you have placed politics before love.' For the first time in my life I felt in control of my emotions as I provoked the man I had once loved. 'I am sorry you were not able to explain for yourself that your desire for office and promotion must take precedence over my hand in marriage.'

Edmund's face paled, a little muscle tightening at the side of his mouth. 'They made it impossible for me to do otherwise,' he responded curtly. He was angry, but so was I.

'So they did. Love, it seems, even after such splendid promises of life-long fidelity, appears to be finite, my lord of Mortain.' I noted that his compressed lips paled further under my blow. 'Such an honour as the lordship of Mortain could not be thrown away, could it? You would have lost it before you had even set your foot on the territory if you had held out to marry me.' My mouth curled. 'I have been put very firmly in my place, have I not?'

And Edmund's features, once pale as wax, became engulfed in an unflattering tide of red that rose to his hairline, and his response was vicious as he admitted to everything I knew of him.

'Are you a fool, Kat? You know the terms of the statute. To wed you would cripple me. Would you expect me to give up my land, my titles? My ambitions as a soldier? I am a Beaufort. It is my right to hold office in this realm. Would you really expect me to jettison my ambitions for marriage?'

'No. What I would expect is that you would have the grace to tell me.' He shrugged a little. I considered it a crude gesture, and drove on. 'You have taught me a hard lesson, Edmund, but I have learnt it well: to trust no man who might be forced to choose between power and high politics on the one side and matters of the heart on the other. It is too painful a decision to expect any man to make.'

I tilted my chin as I watched his jaw tighten, my mind suddenly flooded with Madam Joanna's warnings. Had he indeed used me? Oh, yes, he most definitely had. My naïvety horrified me.

'Perhaps it was not such a painful decision for you. Perhaps you did not love me at all, except when I might have been your road to glory. Marriage to me would have given you such authority, wouldn't it, Edmund? There you would have been, standing at the right hand of the Young King. His cousin, his adviser, his counsellor, his superb friend. His father by marriage. Now, that would have been a coup indeed. I expect you thought that I could be tolerated as a wife if I brought you such a heady prize.

'I'm sorry your plan shattered into pieces at your feet. Gloucester had the right of it when he saw your promotion as no good thing.' And I hammered home the final nail. 'I expect he was right to suspect all Beauforts. They seek nothing but their own advancement.'

The flush had receded under my onslaught and Edmund was once more as pale as new-made whey.

'I did love you.' I noted the tense. 'I hurt you.'

'Yes.' I put a sneer into my voice without any difficulty. 'Yes, you hurt me. I think I could even say that you broke my heart. And don't say you're sorry for that,' I said as his mouth opened. 'I do not want your pity.'

'Forgive me.'

'No. I don't think I will. I am in no mood to forgive.' I lifted my hands and for a moment I struggled with the clasp of the brooch on my bodice. 'I would return this to you.' It tore the material, but I held it out on my palm.

He made no move to take it. 'I gave it to you as a gift,' he said stiffly.

'A gift when you promised to marry me. It's an elegant thing.' The portcullis gleamed in the rays of the sun and the eye of the lion glittered, giving it a louche, roguish air. Much like Edmund Beaufort, I decided. 'Now the promise is broken and the trinket is not mine to have. It is a family piece and should be given to your future wife.'

'I will not take it back. Keep it, my dear Kat,' he snapped, his tone bitter, words deliberately chosen to wound. 'Keep it in memory of my love for you.'

'Did you ever love me?'

'Yes. You are a desirable woman.' But his eyes could not quite keep contact. I did not believe him. 'No man could deny your beauty. How could I not feel the attraction between us?'

'Perhaps you did,' I compromised sadly. 'But simply not enough.'

'It was a truly pleasurable dalliance.'

'A dalliance?' I clenched my fist around the jewel to prevent me from striking him, dropping into French in my renewed fury. '*Mon Dieu!* How dare you dishonour my love, given freely and honestly, with the triviality of a dalliance? I *did* love you once, when I believed you to be a man of honour. Perhaps I should be thankful to Gloucester after all for sparing me from a disloyal and craven husband. I pity your future wife to the bottom of my heart.'

He stepped back as if I had indeed struck him.

'I can do no more than plead my cause,' he responded curtly. 'It would have been like nailing myself into my coffin before I was twenty years of age. You would ask too much of me.'

'I know. And that's the saddest part of the whole affair.' For it was all true, of course. It would have been cruel to have tied him to me, stripping away all hope of the life to which he had been born and raised. It would have been very wrong of me and, knowing it, I would have stepped aside. 'Take it.' I opened my palm again, the colours of the brooch springing to life. When he made no move to do so, merely regarding me with a strange mix of dismay and defiance in his face, I placed it on the stone window ledge at my side.

'I loved you, Edmund. I understand perfectly. I would have released you from your promises but you did not have the courage to face me. You are a man of straw. I did not realise.'

I walked round him and on, Guille following. I would not look back, even when my heart wept for what I had lost. Would he even now come after me, change his mind, tell me that his love was still strong and could not be denied? For a moment my heart beat loudly in my ears as I waited for his long stride to catch up with me and his command to stop.

Katherine—don't leave me!

Of course he did not so command me. When, at the door, I looked back—for how could I resist?—he had gone. I let my eye rest on the window ledge where the blue and red and gold should have made a bright smudge in the low sun. It was flat and grey and empty. He had taken the brooch too. Perhaps one day it would grace the bodice of the lady whom he, and the law, deemed suitable for a Beaufort bride.

Perhaps he had loved me. But what was such love if it was too weak to triumph against worldly considerations? Edmund's cold rejection of me had destroyed all my happiness. In that moment my love for him crumbled into dust beneath my feet. I thought he would not have been so very shallow.

Perhaps, I considered in that moment of blinding revelation, I had not fallen in love at all. Lonely and isolated, lured by the hand of an expert in the arts of love, I had simply fallen into the fatal trap of a glittering infatuation, only to be sacrificed on the altar of Beaufort aggrandisement.

I was infatuated no more.

11

WHEN HENRY DIED, I was beyond loneliness. Misery kept my spirit chained and I sank into unrelieved gloom, as if I were permanently shielded from the sun's warmth by a velvet cloak. Edmund's unchivalrous rejection of me—his deliberate choice of personal advancement over what might have passed for love in his cold heart—left me equally bereft.

But whereas in the aftermath of Henry's denial of me I had embraced despair, I now rejected any notion of melancholy. Anger blew through me like a cleansing wind, ridding me of any inclination to weep or mourn my seclusion or even to contemplate the pattern of my never-ending isolation. A fury hummed through my blood, instilling in me a vibrancy equal to that which I had experienced at the hands of Edmund Beaufort on that fatal Twelfth Night. Fury was a hot, raging emotion, and yet my heart was a hard thing, a block of granite, a shard of ice. Tears were frozen in my heart.

Neither was my anger turned solely on Beaufort. I lashed myself with hard words. How could I have allowed myself to be drawn in, won over? Could I not have seen his empty promises for what they had been? I should not need a man's love to live out my life in some degree of contentment. Obviously I was a woman incapable of attracting love: neither Henry nor Edmund had seen me as the object of their devotion. How could I have been so miserably weak as to be tempted into Edmund's arms, like a mouse to the cheese left temptingly in a vermin trap? Oh, I was beyond anger.

Holy Virgin, I prayed. *Grant me the strength to live out my life without the companionship of a man. Give me patience and inner contentment to spend every day until I die in the society of women. Let me not count the passing years in the lines on my face or mourn as my hair fades from gold to silver.*

The Virgin smiled serenely, her face as bland as a junket, so much so that it drove me from my knees, stalking from my chapel, to the astonishment of my chaplain, who was preparing to hear my confession, and my damsels, who must have seen more than religious fervour stamped on my features. My anger refused to dissipate.

'Love without anxiety and without fear
Is fire without flames and without warmth.'

Beatrice, fingers plucking the plangent chords, sang wistfully as we stitched in one of the light-filled chambers at Windsor. Detesting those melancholy sentiments, reminding me as they did of Edmund Beaufort's silver tongue, I stabbed furiously at the linen altar cloth with no regard for its fragile surface.

'Day without sunlight, hive without honey
Summer without flower, winter without frost.'

As her voice died away, there was a concerted sigh.

'I would not wish to live without the sweetness of honey,' Meg commented.

'But I would,' I announced. I was still careful around my English women, but I found the words on my lips spilling out before I could stop them. 'I reject all sweetness and honey, all fire with its hot flames. In fact, from today, I forswear all men.'

For the length of a heartbeat they regarded me as if I had taken leave of my wits, to be quickly followed by a slide of knowing glances. My estrangement from Edmund must have given them hours of pleasurable conjecture. And then they set themselves, as one, to persuade me of the value of what I had just rejected.

'Love brings a woman happiness, my lady.'

'A man's kisses puts colour into her cheeks.'

'And a man in her bed puts a child in her belly!'

Laughter stirred the echoes in the room.

'I will live without a man's kisses. I will live without a man in my bed,' I said, for once enjoying the quick cut and thrust. 'I will never succumb to the art of seduction. I will never give way to lust.'

Which silenced them, my damsels who gossiped from morn until night over past and present amours, causing them to look askance, as if it might be below the dignity of a Queen Dowager to admit to so base an emotion as lust.

I regarded their expressive brows as I acknowledged that today I wanted their companionship; today I would be part of their gossip and knowing innuendo. I had spent my life in England isolated from them, mostly through my own inability to be at ease within their midst, but no longer. A strange light-heartedness gripped me. Perhaps it was the cup of wine we had drunk or the unexpected camaraderie.

'I will show you.' I lifted a skein of embroidery silks from my coffer, deciding in a moment's foolishness to make a little drama out of it. 'Bring a candle here for me.'

They did, and, embroidery abandoned as Cecily brought the candle, they seated themselves on floor or stool.

'I will begin,' I said, enjoying their attention. 'I forswear my lord of Gloucester.' There was an immediate murmur of assent for consigning the arrogant royal duke to the flames. 'What colour do I choose for Gloucester?'

They caught the idea.

'Red. For power.'

'Red, for ambition.'

'Red for disloyalty to one wife, and a poor choice of a second.'

I had difficulty in being mannerly towards Gloucester, who had attacked my future with the legal equivalent of a hatchet. The Act of Parliament he had instigated would stand for all time. No man of ambition would consider me as a bride. I was assuredly doomed to eternal widowhood. And so with savage delight I lifted a length of blood-red silk, snipped a hand's breadth with my shears and held it over the candle so that it curled and shimmered into nothingness.

'There. Gloucester is gone, he is nothing to me.' I caught an anxious look from Beatrice as we watched the silk vanish. 'I can't believe you are a friend of Gloucester, Beatrice.'

'No, my lady.' She shuddered. 'But is this witchcraft. Perhaps in France…?'

'No such thing,' I assured her. 'Merely a signal of my intent. Gloucester will be hale and hearty for a good few years yet.' I looked round the expectant faces. 'Now Bishop Henry. He has been kind—but to my mind as self-interested as are all the Beauforts. Not to be trusted.'

'Rich purple,' from Beatrice. 'He likes money and self-importance.'

'And the lure of a Cardinal's hat,' Cecily added.

The purple silk went the way of its red sister.

Who next? I considered my father, who had instilled in me such fear—mad, untrustworthy, kind one moment, violent and cruel the next—but I knew that it had not been his choice to be so.

And then there was my brother Charles, who would be King Charles the Seventh if he could persuade enough Frenchmen to back him, and would thus usurp my son's claim to France.

But was it not his right, by birth and blood, to rule? I could not deny him his belief in his inheritance. This was no easy task, but the fascination of my damsels urged me on.

I chose a length of pure white silk.

'Who is that?'

'My husband. Henry. Sadly dead before his time.'

They became instantly solemn. 'Pure.'

'Revered.'

'Chivalrous. A great loss.'

'Yes,' I agreed, and said no more, knowing it would not be politic. Henry, as pure and cold as the coldest winter, as cruel through his neglect as the sharpest blade. I admired his talents but did not regret his absence, as the white silk flamed, and died as he had in the last throes of his terrible illness. 'He no longer has a place in my life.'

'He was a great king,' Meg stated.

'He was,' I agreed. 'The very best. In his pursuit of English power he had no rival.'

The memory of my immature infatuation, his heedless forsaking of me, flooded back and for a moment my hands fell unoccupied in my lap, the silks abandoned, and my women shuffled uncomfortably. The joy had gone out of it.

'What about Edmund Beaufort?' Beatrice asked, immediately looking aghast at her daring, for here was a sensitive issue. Would I lash out with anger at their presumption? Would I weep, despite all my denials of hurt? Would I embarrass myself and them?

And I thought momentarily of Edmund, how I had fallen into the fantasy of it, as a mayfly, at the end of its short existence, drops into the stream and is carried away. Edmund had woven a web to pinion me and take away my will. How I had enjoyed it, living from moment to moment, day to day, anticipating his next kiss, his next outrageous plot. How could any woman resist such a glorious seduction?

She could if she had any sense. He was as self-serving as the rest, and I had been a fool to be so compromised, with no one to blame but myself. In my folly I had trusted so blindly. I would not do so again. I would not be used by any man again. I would never again be seduced by a smooth tongue and clever assault. No man would command my allegiance, my loyalty. Certainly not my love.

'He is hard to resist,' Meg observed solemnly, as if she had read my thoughts.

Oh, my control was masterly, my sense of the dramatic superb. I lifted a glittering length of gold thread from my coffer and replied from my heart.

'Here he is. Edmund, who wooed me and could have won me if he had had the backbone. One of the glittering Beauforts. He was cruel in his rejection of me.' And I burnt the whole costly strand, not even snipping off a short length, as I smiled around the watchful faces. I think I had won their admiration, or at least their respect.

I left them, full of laughter as they considered the men of their acquaintance who failed to live up to their own high standards. I admired their light-heartedness, their assurance that one day they would marry and, if fortunate, know the meaning of love. I would always be lonely. I would remain isolated and unwed. I would never love again.

Anger kept me close companionship in those days.

Fired with my resolution to tread a solitary path, I embraced my new strength of spirit within the sharp confines created for me by his grace of Gloucester. I would be Queen Dowager, admirable and perfect in the role allotted to me.

I had grown up at last. And not before time, Michelle would have said.

'I wish to visit some of my dower properties,' I informed my little son. 'And you must come with me.'

Young Henry's glance slid from me to his beloved books. 'Do I have to, *maman*?'

'Yes, Henry. You do.' I would not be swayed.

'I would rather stay here. My lord of Warwick says that he will come and—'

I did not wait to hear what Richard might be planning. 'You will come with me, Henry. I am your mother and my wish takes precedence over that of my lord of Warwick on this occasion.'

'You could go, and I could stay here.'

'No, I could not.' No point in explaining why. I remained firm. 'It will be good for you to be seen by your people, Henry. It is your duty as King to be seen.'

Which did the trick. I informed Warwick and Gloucester by a slow-riding courier that the King would not be at Windsor but at the Queen Dowager's dower properties. I listed them, and we were on our way the following day, before either would hear of my decision. Not that they could complain. I simply took the King, servants, entourage and outriders—his household in effect—in full regal panoply, with me. We made a fine show as we visited Hertford, then on to Waltham and Wallingford.

And finally there was Leeds Castle, which Young Henry anticipated with joy and I with a residue of fear. Leeds, the beautiful scene of my abortive proposal of marriage, where I had been so full of joy for what the future might hold. All ground to dust beneath my feet. But this had to be done. I needed to make this visit to test the state of my heart.

I was cold with anxiety as we crossed the bridge, past the

gatehouse into the inner courtyard. My feelings for Edmund had seemed strong enough to last a lifetime. Would there not be some shimmer of memory here to assail me? I took a deep breath and prepared to have my confidence shattered.

Did Edmund tread on my hem of my gown? No, he did not. Did his voice echo in the corridors and audience chamber? Hardly at all. My heart continued to beat with a slow and steady purpose, and I laughed aloud.

I was cured. How cruel the heart, to lead a woman into thinking she loved a man when quite clearly she did not. I did not need love, I did not need marriage. I felt as if I had cast off an old, worn winter cloak to allow the summer breeze to refresh my skin. Oh, yes, I was cured.

We returned to Windsor where I acknowledged Warwick's caustic stare and consigned to the flames Gloucester's letter of admonition that I should have asked permission from the Lord Protector if I intended to jaunt about the country. I settled into a period of calm, soothing to mind and body, with nothing to disturb the serenity of the pool in which I existed. This was what I wanted, was it not? So why was it that the summer weeks dragged themselves past with wearisome slowness?

Distant voices, heavy in the humid air, snatched at our attention from the direction of the river. Male voices, loud, crude in tone, sliced through with laughter and groans and—I suspected from the words that carried to us—much rude blasphemy. Whatever the occasion, it was one of raucous enjoyment and nothing to instil fear into us. Besides, who would harm us, walking as we were within shouting distance of the castle?

With my damsels in close attendance, I continued along our chosen path to the bend in the Thames where it was pleasant to sit and catch a breeze, for we had settled into a period of intense heat. The voices became more distinct, more strident, so that I caught a grin passing between our two armed guards and a meeting of glances between Meg and Cecily.

'What is it?' I asked.

'Some of the servants, I expect, my lady.' Beatrice, fanning herself with a branch of leaves plucked from an over-hanging ash tree, was unmoved by the commotion. 'The men swim in the river when it is hot.' Her lip curled at the prospect of such wanton male behaviour. 'You'd think they had nothing better to do.'

Splashing and bellowing continued ahead.

'Perhaps we should turn back,' I heard, sotto voce.

'Perhaps we should go on!'

'It might not be seemly...'

I had seen the gleam in their eyes, and understood since there was little to entertain them at Windsor. Or—the thought struck me as a burst of invective assaulted my ears—were they truly trying to protect my royal dignity from the sight of naked servants cavorting in the Thames? I would not be so tender, and I continued to walk steadily.

'We will go on. I have seen a man unclothed before. I will not faint at the sight.'

We came to the riverbank, where it curved beside a willow with a vast spread of shallow roots, perfect for a shady resting place—and stopped.

'There! As I said. Nothing better to do with their time!' Beatrice looked down her elegant nose. 'I still think we should go back.'

'Not yet.' I raised my hand to still them.

A handful of the castle servants were making the most of their escape from palace duties, either sitting on the rough, close-cropped grass where it sloped into the water or immersed in the river itself. It was the most inviting of stretches, the bank worn away to create a deep pool, ideal for swimming in summer, equally good for skating, as I knew, when the water froze in a wide, flat expanse.

Some of the men I recognised: there was my cup-bearer and my carver. Quite unaware of their audience, they were stripped to the waist as they lounged and slaked their thirst from pottery ewers. Some were entirely naked.

We stood, motionless, and gazed our fill at a sight to entice, so much male flesh slick with sun and water. My damsels were engaged, eyes keen as if a platter of gilded almonds had just been presented for their delectation.

'So, if we are not to forswear all men, which one of these fine examples of manhood would we consider taking to our beds?' Meg asked, her solemnity belied by a catch in her breath.

I looked round, to smile and reply to her. And my words dried in my mouth as one figure with a flex of muscle in thigh and shoulder pushed himself to his feet, to stand for a moment on the riverbank, turning his head to laugh at some ribald comment, then dived into the water with barely a ripple, skin gleaming as he moved through the water with speed and agility of a salmon. Emerging some yards further into the gentle flow, he stood, drops of water bright as diamonds on his shoulders and in his hair.

I inhaled slowly to fill my lungs.

Owen Tudor. Master of the Queen's Household.

Water lapping around his waist, he raked his hair back from his face so that its black mass fell heavily onto his shoulders, the sparkling drops flung away into the sun in an arc of crystal. To my shame, I could not look away. I was enthralled, my gaze riveted, and I exhaled slowly as I had been holding my breath.

And all there was for me to do was to admire the physical attributes of a well-proportioned man, the flex of sinew and firm flesh, the definition of muscle that gave form to his chest and shoulders. And his face... Ah! I took another breath. His face was lit with such careless, unreserved joy, his eyes as dark as jet, his wet hair as polished as Venetian silk.

He was beautiful.

I realised that my loquacious damsels were silent around me.

'Well,' Lady Beatrice observed at last, breaking the spell.

But not for me. Not for me. For me, the spell had been irrevocably cast.

My Master of Household swam to the shallows, from where, unconscious of his lack of covering, he waded through the little wavelets. I discovered, dry-mouthed, that my eye, of its own volition, followed the line of black hair from chest to stomach and on. His belly was flat and taut, his thighs smooth with muscle. I was sorry when he scooped up and pulled on a pair of linen drawers to hide his masculinity—or perhaps it enhanced it, as the cloth clung damply. There was an exhalation around me.

This splendid man was so far from Master Owen Tudor who determined daily which dishes should be presented at my table. The dour, silent, stern Master Owen who ensured that the floors were swept and the candles replaced, who controlled the state of my finances and the quality of wine served in my parlour. How could clothing and a studied demeanour of cool discretion cover so much that was spectacularly attractive?

His smile struck a note in my chest, like the single toll of a bell.

'The Queen!'

We had been detected.

The little group, to a man, scrambled for clothing, all attempting something resembling a bow, incongruous given their state of undress, but their expressions were not hard to read. They resented my presence, my interference in a time that should have been their own, and free from surveillance. Owen Tudor pulled a shirt over his head as if clothing could restore his position, as perhaps it did for it brought home to me that although I might admire, I should not have been there. I should not have stayed. It was demeaning for me to be spying, and equally for them to be spied upon. A breath of conscience undermined my innocent appreciation.

'We will leave them to their leisure,' I said, turning my back on the river and the unsettling figure of Owen Tudor, black hair dense as satin in the sun. 'Their pleasures should not be a matter for our entertainment.'

'More pleasures for us if we had stayed, my lady!' Meg chuckled as we returned.

'Yes, for you,' I replied, surprised at the coldness of my tone. 'But it would not be correct for me to stay.'

'No, my lady, they would not want you there.'

It was a shock—although it should not have been. How could any Valois princess or English queen not be aware? But Meg's light-hearted remark and the rapid reclothing of my servants had proclaimed the unbridgeable chasm that existed between me and those with whom I lived more clearly than any sermon preached at me about female decorum or the sanctity of royal blood. My damsels could have stayed and enjoyed the scene; and the men, sensing their admiration, would have appreciated the audience. But to be watched by the Queen Dowager? That was not the order of things. They were servants and I was anointed by God and holy oil. I had shared the King's bed and now lived out my life in sacred chastity. It was not for me to peek and pry into their entertainments.

For men of rank, for Henry or Edmund Beaufort, it would have been accepted. They would have joined in, at sport or play. Men amongst men, the difference in status would have been swept aside in the competition or challenge of the moment. Even Young Henry, child as he was—they would have welcomed him, moderated their language and perhaps encouraged him to swim and play the man. But I was a woman, royally isolated, and my position sacrosanct, not far removed from that of the Virgin. I must be kept in a state of grace and innocence.

I retraced my steps, my damsels silent around me, striving to control an astonishing spurt of anger. Did they think I did not know the contours and specifics of a man's body? How did they think I had conceived a child? I was a woman and had the desires and needs of any woman. But that would not be accepted. If I had ever thought my royal status would not matter, that I was simply another woman amongst my damsels, I had been shown to be entirely wrong.

There had been no mistake: when Owen Tudor had bowed low, his body once more shielded from my stare by seemly linen, it had been as if a mask had fallen into place, all his earlier vivacity quenched. He thought I had no right to be there, perhaps he even despised me for admitting to the needs of mortal women.

For what had he seen in my face? I had no skill in the art of dissimulation. Had he seen my naked desire? I shuddered that I might have revealed far too much, and as I strode back to the castle, where I might hide my flushed cheeks, I could not banish the image of him from my imagination. The line of thigh and leg, the curve of buttock and calf, the shimmering moisture caught in the dusting of dark hair on his chest, and I knew exactly what it was that had intoxicated me most in that little display of male power.

Henry, always royal, always the king, had been conscious of the impression he must make, knowing that I could only pay homage before his superb majesty. Edmund had been wilfully, magnificently seductive, intent on sweeping me off my feet, energised when I could do nothing but respond to him.

And Owen Tudor? Owen Tudor, even when he had known

I was there, had had no desire at all to engage my emotions. But, by the Virgin, he had. My skin heated at the bright memory. And the horror, the shocking reality of it struck my breast with the force of a Welsh arrow.

No! No, no, no!

I would have covered my face with my hands if I had not been in the public eye. The words, repeated over and over again, beat in my head. I did not want this. I would not have it! Had I learned nothing from my experience with Henry? From my rapid falling in love with Edmund? Oh, I had learned, and learned bitterly. I would never again allow my heart and mind to be at the beck and call of any man. I would not have my will snatched from me by a futile desire to discover love.

This *lust* was no more than a physical attraction to a fine body and a well-moulded face. He was the Master of my Household, a man I had known for all the years of my widowhood. This was a wayward, immature emotion. Had I not proved that such superficial desire, however powerful in the moment, was quick to fade and die?

I marched back to the castle, furious with my own weakness. So much for my forswearing men. So much for my foolish drama with coloured silks. I had been hooked, like a carp from one of my own fish ponds, by the sight of a beautiful man rising from the waters of the Thames, a scene worthy of one of the romantic stories from the *Morte D'Arthur*, where women were invariable too silly for their own good and men too chivalrous to know when a woman desired more than a chaste kiss on her fingertips.

My women marched with me, uncomplaining, until, with a cry, Mary stumbled on the rough path and I moderated my speed. Flight was useless, since I could not escape my thoughts, or my sudden unfortunate obsession. Owen Tudor remained firmly implanted in my mind.

Was I really contemplating leaping into a liaison with Owen Tudor, my *servant*?

It is degrading. He is a servant. It is not a suitable liaison.

It might not be suitable, but I knew a craving to touch him, imagining what his arms might feel like around me. My cheeks were as hot as fire, my thighs liquid with longing, even as my heart ached with shame. Was this how I would spend my life? Lusting after servants because they were beautiful and young?

Returned to my parlour, I ordered Cecily to fetch wine and a lute. We would sing and read of true heroes. We would engage our minds in higher things. Perhaps even a page from my Book of Hours would direct my inappropriate thoughts into colder, more decorous channels. The Queen Dowager must be above earthly desires. She must be dull and unknowing of love and lust.

And if she was not?

Think of the gossip, I admonished myself, the words deliberately harsh to jolt myself into reality. If nothing else will drive Owen Tudor from your thoughts, think of the immediate repercussions. How could you withstand the talk of the Court with its vicious darts and sly innuendo? To succumb to my longings would brand me as a harlot more despicable than my mother. What was it that Gloucester had said of me? A woman unable to curb fully her carnal passions. A wanton child of Isabeau of Bavaria, the Queen of France, who everyone knew could not keep her hands and lips from seducing young men.

No, I could not bear the knowing looks from my damsels, the judgemental stares when I accompanied Young Henry to Court. My reputation, already tattered and shabby in some quarters, would be in rags. And would it not be so much worse if I looked at Owen? At least my mother, lascivious as she might well be, drew the line at seducing her servants.

Have you heard? The Queen Dowager has taken the Master of her Household to her bed. Do you suppose she persuades herself he is assessing the state of her bed linen?

I stifled a groan. How shaming. Gloucester would lock me in my bedchamber at Leeds Castle and drop the key into the river.

'Are you well, Lady?' Beatrice asked.

'I am perfectly well,' I croaked through dry lips.

'It is very hot,' she said, handing me a feather fan. 'It will be cooler when the sun goes down.'

'Yes. Yes, it will.'

I shivered uncomfortably in the heat, my cheeks flushed despite the breeze from the feverishly applied peacock feathers. If Beatrice knew what was in my mind, she would not be so compassionate.

'Perhaps you have a fever, my lady,' Meg suggested solicitously.

'Perhaps I do.'

Fever! For that was what it was, a passing heat of no importance, I decided. I was victim of an unfortunate attack of lust, of base physical longing for a handsome man, brought on by the hot weather and a lack of something better for my mind to focus on. Such obsession died. It must. If it did not die of its own accord, I would kill it.

Out of sight, out of mind. Was that not the best remedy? At Gloucester's command I travelled to Westminster with Young Henry, leaving my own household, and Owen Tudor, at Windsor. For a se'ennight I enjoyed the festivities, the bustle and noise of London. Every day I rejoiced in the sight of my little son growing more regal under Warwick's tuition. I gloried in the fine dresses and even finer jewels, something I had forgotten in my quiet, retired existence.

And every day I erected bulwarks against any encroaching thoughts of Owen Tudor. I would not think of him. I did not need him. I smiled and danced and sang, laughed at the antics of the Court Fool. I would prove the shallowness of my attraction to the man who had ordered the details of my daily life since Henry's death.

When I could exist a whole day in which he barely stepped into my mind, I sighed in relief at my achievements. My obsession was over. The wretched loneliness that fuelled my dreams was of no account. My infatuation was dead.

But we must, perforce, return to Windsor.

The hopeless futility of my plan was cast into bright relief not one hour after our return. My household met briefly for livery, the final mouthful of ale and bread at the end of the day and the giving out of candles. It was served under the eye of Master Tudor with the same precise and efficient self-containment that he showed in my company, whatever the task.

He handed me my candle. 'Goodnight, my lady.' The epitome of propriety and rectitude. 'It is good to have you back with us.'

For me the air between us burned. Every breath I took was fraught with a longing to touch his fingertips as they held the candlestick. To brush against him as I handed back my cup. My absence had done nothing to quench my thirst.

'May God and His Holy Saints watch over you, my lady,' he said, with a final inclination of his head.

Did he feel nothing for me? Obviously not. He regarded me simply in the light of Queen Dowager.

But I recalled, as I shielded my candle from the draughts on my way to my bedchamber, that our eyes had met very much on a level. And at night the Welsh Master of my Household crept into my mind, even when I denied him access. He stalked through my dreams. With the coming of dawn I wept at my frustration.

How could this be, that I desired him, when he showed no awareness of me as a woman? I railed at the unfairness of it, even as I despised my inability to deny him.

Dismiss him! a whisper flitted through my thoughts.

I could not contemplate it.

I tried not to watch Owen Tudor. I tried not to let my eyes track his progress across the Great Hall—much as Young Henry's gaze fixed on the approach of his favourite dish of thick honey and bread purée at the end of a feast. I tried not to be aware of the explicit contours of his body beneath his impeccable clothing.

It was impossible. Whether he was clad in dark damask and jewelled chain for a feast or his habitual plain wool and leather when we dined informally, I knew the slide of muscle beneath his skin, the whole line and form of him. Owen Tudor had taken up residence, a thorn in my heart.

I found myself searching through the little I knew of him. How long had he run my affairs now? Six years, I supposed, but since he had not been of my choice, I had paid little heed to him and knew nothing of his family or background. Recipient of the patronage of Sir Walter Hungerford, steward of Henry's own household, Master Tudor had been in France in Henry's entourage when I was first wed.

After Henry's death, when my entire household was composed of Henry's people, he had been appointed Master of Household. All I knew was that he undertook his role to perfection without any interference from me: he had learned his skills from a master of the art.

But what did I know of him as a man? Nothing. I knew nothing except that if I gave an order, it was carried out promptly and without fuss—and sometimes it seemed before I had even voiced my desire. I acknowledged that in all those years we had not exchanged more than a dozen words that did not deal with a request or the carrying out of it. I was mortified that I had so little knowledge of a man who had served me intimately.

Yet now I yearned for more than impeccable and aloof service from him.

How could I degrade myself so, following a servant with longing in my eyes, like a lovesick hound pining for its absent master? I turned away smartly, heading for the stair to my accommodations as he stretched to aid a young kitchen servant to replace candles in one of the sconces, laughing down at her when she fumbled and dropped one.

My throat was dry, as if parched by a long drought. Had I been dwelling in a desert all my life? Why had this fire been lit by something so basic as the deep note of male laughter that tripped along my skin?

This is no better than you being carried along into the embrace of Edmund Beaufort. Have you learned nothing, Katherine?

But this was not like my falling into love with Edmund Beaufort at all. Edmund had set out to charm me, to win me with gifts and extravagances, to lure me with conversation and ridiculous exhibitions of high spirits that had made me forget my age and my rank so that I had thought I was a young girl again and free to indulge my senses. I had been tempted and enticed, bewitched. I had been captivated so that I had been unable to see the dross of raw ambition beneath the gilded surface.

Owen Tudor did not set out to charm me at all. Rather it seemed to me that his prime desire was to repel me. Whatever I said, whenever I found the need to speak with him, never had he been so reserved, never had his conversations been so clipped and brief. He must have seen my interest, I decided, and was now intent on destroying it, for his sake and mine. I must presume that he was more discerning than I, for his ability to keep me at arm's length was truly comprehensive. Was every woman as driven to embrace misery as I, when faced with a man who had no desire for her?

And I knew in some strange manner, in a moment of blinding clarity one morning as I rose from my restless bed, what the fever was that persisted in tormenting me. Not physical desire with its raw urgency. Not a need for admiration and affection, or response to a courtly seduction. I had not wanted this, I had not sought this, but against all wisdom I had fallen disastrously in love. It was like falling down a shaft into a bottomless well.

How could I live like this? Loving but unloved for ever?

Dismiss him!

I shrank from it, from never seeing him again.

'Is there a remedy to quench a woman's ardour, Guille?' I asked, not caring when her brows rose.

'They do say that to rub an ointment of mouse droppings will do it.'

I turned my face away from her regard. I would live with the desire, unrequited as it would always be, and the pain of it. My rejection of men had been a sham, a mockery of the truth, for how could a woman of youth and hot blood think herself capable of living out her life without a man? I burned for him, but in the flames a tiny spark of rebellion was ignited.

I knew what I must do. My mother had given in to her lusts: her daughter would not. I would play out my role of Queen Dowager with all the sobriety and dignity expected of me. Master Tudor's dismissal was not necessary because I would never seek out Owen Tudor, even if in my heart I loved him. On my knees, I vowed that it would be so.

★ ★ ★

And then he touched me.

I had noticed that he never did. Not that a servant would touch a Queen without her invitation, but on that one occasion, neither of his making or mine, he held me.

It was one of those impromptu, merry moments when Warwick decided that it was well past time that Young Henry was introduced to the art of dancing. We used the large chamber after supper; the trestles cleared, the servants, the minstrels, pages and my damsels all commandeered to produce an opportunity for dancing. Simple stuff within the limited skills of the youngest and most inexperienced present: processions and round dances, their rustic naïvety guaranteed to appeal to the young.

My pages applied themselves with energy, and Young Henry loved it, but I swear there was never a more ill-co-ordinated child than my eight-year-old son. How could he wield a pen with such skill, how could he learn his texts, yet find it impossible to plant his feet with any degree of care or exactitude? His enthusiasm knew no bounds but his ability to follow a beat or a set of simple steps was woeful.

'He is very young,' Warwick observed. 'But he must learn.'

Young Henry leapt. He capered. He could not process with stately presence for more than three steps together. Warwick hid his despair manfully and withdrew from the affray. I adopted stalwart patience and took my place in the circling procession. My damsels and my pages adopted avoidance tactics.

Young Henry tried again with awkward diligence until, in a lively round dance, losing his balance and his hold on his partner, he fell against me, standing on my skirts so that I too stumbled. Young Henry sprawled on the floor with a crow of laughter, I floundered, struggling not to follow him, and a firm hand grasped my arm. I was held upright against a solid body.

I looked up, laughter catching me, about to offer my thanks. And any remaining breath I had was driven from my lungs. My whole body stiffened.

'You will not fall.'

No polite usage. Simply a statement of fact.

How close we were, our breath mingling, so close that I could see my reflection in his eyes. His hand slid down my arm to close round my fingers. And his voice, with all those soft and musical Welsh cadences, stroked over my skin like a fur mantle.

'You are quite safe, my lady,' Owen Tudor said, when I was struck dumb. 'And your son has taken no hurt.'

My thoughts were not on Young Henry. My thoughts were on his palm against mine, his fingers coolly wrapped around mine, his other hand solid on my waist to give me support against the drag of my skirts under Young Henry's weight. My thoughts were centred on the heat that leapt in my belly and spread to every inch of my skin.

Could he not feel it? Could he not sense the flames that licked over me? His hand was cool, but mine seemed to be as hot as the blood that beat heavily in my throat. Was he himself untouched by this urgent demand that pulsed through me like a stream in spate? Surely he could not mistake it? I felt my face flush from chin to hairline as embarrassment engulfed me, and, worst of all, my tongue refused to form any words to release the tension. My gaze was caught in his and I couldn't think of a single word to say...

My damsels swooped in like a flock of maternal chickens to rescue Young Henry. Warwick strolled forward to deliver some advice, but I was held fast in a fine net of pure desire.

'Can you stand, my lady?' Owen Tudor murmured.

'Yes,' I managed. And as I opened my mouth to attempt some formal gratitude for my rescue, he released me, his hands sliding away as if he had been caught in some misdemeanour. Immediately he turned from me to help to pick up my laughing son from the floor, and I was standing alone. The whole seemed to me to last a lifetime. In truth it was less than the time it took to snuff out the flame of a candle.

Had anyone noticed his act of chivalry? Had anyone noticed my reaction? I think they had not. It was decided that Young Henry had enjoyed enough activity that night, and he was escorted to his bed and his prayers. The rest of my household sank into exhaustion and gossip. It had been, all in all, a good evening.

But as I sipped a cup of wine and ate the evening bread, I shivered at the memory of Owen Tudor's hands holding me, preventing me from falling.

'You are tense tonight, my lady,' Guille observed as she removed my girdle and untied the laces of my houppelande.

'Yes.' I laughed softly. 'Weary, I think. My son is not a natural dancer.'

The thick damask slid to the floor and I stepped out of it, lifting my arms so that Guille could attack the side lacing of my under-tunic.

'You dance well, my lady,' she said, head bent over her task.

I would like to dance with Owen Tudor. The thought slid into my mind, followed fast by another. *He can never be for you. You will never dance together.*

I considered this. *He is a man who, for some reason I cannot define, speaks to my heart.*

I did not like the reply, which came in a style of forthright Alice. *You cannot wed such a man.*

Who speaks of marriage?

You would take your Master of Household as your lover? The denunciation rubbed my emotions raw.

How should I? He has no feelings for me.

So why bother thinking about him at all? He has touched your hand once…

And my waist! I added.

And dropped you like a hot pan. You are a fool, Katherine.

I scowled at the invisible Alice. So I was. I glanced down at Guille.

And don't even think about asking Guille what she thinks about the whole miserable affair. Unless you want your household marvelling at the antics of their queen, you will not say a single word.

I will if I wish.

I looked back over my shoulder to where Guille was still struggling with a knotted lace, huffing at her inability to loosen it. Her head was bent, her attention focused.

'Guille, in your opinion, would it be very wrong of a woman of rank to…?' This was more than difficult. 'To wish to speak alone with a servant?'

Guille looked up, brows as knotted as the lace, then lowered her regard to her task again.

'I'd say it depends, my lady.'

'On what does it depend?'

'On what this lady of rank wishes to say to her servant. And to which servant she wishes to say it. If it was to give instructions for a banquet or a journey…'

'And if it was more of a personal matter?' It was like wading through thick pottage, choosing the least guilt-ridden words. 'Would it ever be right?'

'No, my lady. I don't think it would.'

'So it would be wrong.'

There! I told you it would be.

'It might give rise to gossip, my lady.'

'Yes.' I sighed. 'It would be foolhardy in the extreme.'

'But still you wish to meet with Master Tudor?'

She stood, the knot untied, her question leaving me direc-
tionless. Had I been so obvious, when I had tried so hard to
preserve at least a modicum of dignity?

'Does everyone talk of it?' I whispered.

'No, my lady. But I know you well, and I see what you
would wish to remain hidden.'

'It is true,' I admitted. I would dance around it no more. 'I
join the ranks of many. How foolish women can be!' I plunged
the dagger further into my flesh, into my heart. 'Does he have
a special woman, Guille?'

'Not *one*, my lady.' Guille's mouth pursed but her eyes twinkled.

I laughed, picking up her implication. 'So many.'

'As many as he smiles on. He has great charm.'

But he did not use it with me. I was his royal mistress, he
was my minion. 'So you like him too?' I asked.

'I would not refuse if he invited me to share his kisses,'
Guille said, not at all abashed. 'It must be the Welshness in
him.'

'So it must.'

'Your rank stands in the way of such knowledge, my lady.'

'I know it does.'

But I could not leave it alone.

Oh, the excuses I made to hold conversation with him—for I
could not be direct. I was never a bold woman. How appalled I
was at my subterfuge when I found myself drawn to him, like
a rabbit to the cunning eyes of the hunting stoat. Yet Owen
Tudor was no predator. My desire was of my own creation.

'Master Tudor—I wish to ride out with my son the King.
Perhaps you would accompany us?'

'I will arrange for the horses, my lady. An armed escort

would be better,' he replied promptly, my judgement obviously found wanting in his eye. 'I will arrange that too.'

And he did, being there in the courtyard to see that all was as it should be. But when I needed a helping hand into the saddle—what woman did not, hampered with yards of heavy damask and fur?—he kept his distance, instructing one of the young grooms to come to my aid. When we returned, there was Master Tudor awaiting us, but the same groom helped me to dismount.

How to provoke a reaction—any reaction—from an unresponsive man?

'Master Tudor. My rooms are cold. Are we lacking in wood? Have you made no provision for this turn in the weather?' How unkind I was.

'There is no lack, my lady,' he replied, his tone as caustic as the east wind that gusted through the ill-fitting windows. 'I will remedy the matter immediately.' He bowed and stalked off, no doubt irritated that I had called his organisation into question. It was August, when fires were rarely lit. I refused to feel remorse.

And again. 'My son is old enough to own a falcon, Master Owen. Can we arrange that?' Surely he would show some interest in hunting birds. Did not every man?

'It shall be done, my lady. Your falconer will, I imagine, have a suitable raptor. I will speak with him immediately and send him to wait on you.'

Or even, with a smile and light request: 'Do you sing, Master Owen? I understand that Welshmen are possessed of excellent voices. Perhaps you would sing for us?'

'I do not sing, my lady. Your minstrels would make a better job of it. Do I send one to you?'

No response other than a denial. Always courteous, always efficient, always as distant as the moon and as unresponsive as a plank of wood. I failed to rouse any response other than that of an immaculate servant who knew his position and the courtesy due to his lady. I imagined that if I had said, 'Master Owen—would you care to share my bed for an hour of dalliance? Of even chivalrous discourse? Or perhaps an afternoon of blazing lust?' he would have replied: 'My thanks, my lady, but today is not possible. It is imperative that the sewers are flushed out before the winter frosts.'

Calm, cool, infinitely desirable—and utterly beyond my reach.

I tapped my fingers against the arm of my chair as we dined. It was like trying to lure a conversation out of the untouched stuffed pigeon in the dish in front of me. Bowing again, the Master turned to go. Not once had he raised his eyes to mine. They remained deferentially downcast, yet not, I thought, in acknowledgement of his status as one employed in my household. I did not think, after watching him for the past hour, that he gave even a passing nod to the fact that he held a servile position. I thought Master Tudor might have a surprising depth of arrogance beneath that thigh-skimming dark tunic. He carried out his tasks as a king in his own country, with ease and a certainty of his powers. He was... I sought for the word. Decorous. Yes, that was it: he owned a refined polish that overlaid all his actions.

I would discover what invisible currents moved beneath the courtly reserve.

'Master Tudor.'

'Yes, my lady?' He halted and turned.

A breath of irritation shivered over my nape. I would make him look at me, but what could I say that would not make me appear either foolish or too particular? 'I am thinking, Master Tudor, of making changes to my household.'

'Yes, my lady?' There he stood, infuriatingly straight and

numbingly deferential, as if I had asked him to summon my page.

'I have been thinking of making changes to those who serve me.'

His features remained unyielding as I rose from my chair and stepped down from the dais so that I stood before him.

'Are you quite content in your position here, Master Tudor?' I asked.

And at last, finally, Master Tudor's eyes looked directly into mine.

'Are you dissatisfied with my service to you, my lady?' he asked softly.

'No. That was not my meaning. I thought that perhaps you might choose to serve the Young King instead. Now that he is growing, he will need an extended household. It would be a promotion. It would allow more scope for a man of your talents.'

I stopped on a breath, awaiting his response. Still he held my gaze, and with no hint of self-abasement he replied: 'I am quite content with my present position, my lady.'

'But my household is small, and will remain so, with no opportunity for preferment for you.'

'I do not seek preferment. I am yours to command. I am content.'

I let him go, infuriated by his demeanour, angry at my own need.

'Give me your opinion of Master Tudor,' I said to Alice when she visited my rooms one morning with Young Henry, who was immediately occupied in turning the pages of the book he had brought with him.

'Owen Tudor? Why do you need my opinion, my lady?'

she asked, folding her hands neatly in her lap, and with something of a sharp look, as if settling herself for a good gossip.

'I think I have underestimated him,' I replied lightly. 'Is he
as efficient as he seems?'

'He is an excellent man of management,' Alice replied without hesitation, but her expression was disconcertingly bland.
'You could do no better.'

I considered what I wished to say next. What I ought, or
ought not, to say.

'And what do you think of him, as a man?'

Alice's smile acquired an edge. 'I'd say he knows too much
about flirtation than is good for any man. He could lure a bat
down from its roost with his singing.'

'He does not talk to me,' I admitted sadly. 'He does not
sing to me.'

I knew he was not always unapproachable. I had seen his
ease of manner, smiling when the maids passed a coy remark,
making light conversation with one or another of my household. Neither was he slow to come to the aid of even the clum-
siest of servants. I had seen him leap to rescue a subtlety—a
device of a tiger, accompanied by a mounted knight holding
the tiger's cub, all miraculously contrived from sugar—the
work of many hours and much skill in my kitchens—with
no remonstration other than a firm hand to a shoulder of the
page who had not paid sufficient attention. My cook would
have laid the lad out with a fist to the jaw if he had seen the
near-catastrophe, but Owen Tudor had made do with an arch
of brow and a firm stare.

As for the women... Once I saw him slide a hand over a
shapely hip as he passed, and the owner of the hip smile back
over her shoulder, eyes bright in anticipation, and I knew jealousy, however ill founded.

'Owen Tudor knows his place, my lady.'

I read the implication in the plain words. 'Do you think that I do not?'

And Alice reached forward to touch my hand with hers. 'It will not do, my lady.'

I thought of launching into a denial. Instead, I said, 'Am I so obvious?'

'Yes.'

'Oh.' And I thought I had been so clever. 'What if…?' But I could not say it. *What if I were not Queen Dowager?* In the end I did not need to—Alice knew me only too well.

'You are too far above him, my lady. Or he is too far below you. It comes to the same thing—and you must accept that.' She frowned at me, a little worried, a little censorious. 'And it would be wise if your thoughts were not quite so open.'

'I did not think I was…'

Alice sat back, refolding her hands. 'Then how is it that I can read your interest in this man, as clearly as the page your son is reading now?'

I gave up, and we turned our conversation into more innocuous channels. Until she left.

'He is a fine man. But he is not for you.'

Her wisdom was a knife with a honed edge.

'I never thought that he was.'

'There is a way, my lady,' Guille whispered in my ear as I dressed for Mass the next morning.

'To do what exactly?' Regretful of what I had revealed, ill grace sat heavily on my shoulders, exacerbated by the knowledge that I would have to make some confession to Father Benedict.

'To meet with Master Owen.'

'I have changed my mind.'

'Perhaps that's for the best, my lady.' She began to brush and coil my hair. I watched her face, waiting to see if she would say more. She didn't, but busied herself with the intricate mesh of my crispinettes and a length of veil lavishly decorated with silk rose petals.

'What would you suggest?'

'That you meet him in disguise, my lady.'

'And how would you suggest that I do that?' I asked. Had I not, in my fanciful meanderings in my dreams, already considered such a scenario—and discarded it as a plan that could only be composed by an idiot? Temper bubbled ominously.

'The only way I can see is for me to dress as a servant and waylay him—he talks to servants, does he not? But how would that be possible? He would recognise me. Do I have to meet him in a dark cupboard, my face swathed in veiling? Do I have to be mute? He would recognise my voice. And even if I did accost him as some swathed figure, what would I say to him? Kiss me, Master Owen, or I will fall into death from desire? And by the way, I am Queen Katherine!' I laughed but there was no humour in it.

'He would despise me for tricking him, for the shallow woman that I undoubtedly am, and that I could not bear. What's more, I would look nothing more than a wanton. Am I not already suspect, that I am too rapacious, too caught up in sins of the flesh?' I stood, too agitated to sit, and prowled, my petal-covered veils still half-pinned.

'I suppose my lord of Gloucester would say that.'

'Of course he would. And not only Gloucester. What would my damsels say? The Queen Dowager, clothing herself as a kitchen maid, to waylay a hapless servant who had no wish to be waylaid? It would be demeaning for me and for him. I'll not have trickery. I'll not lay myself open to ridicule and humiliation.'

'Forgive me, my lady.'

Instantly remorse shook me, so that I returned to where Guille stood and placed my fingers on her wrist. 'No. It is I who should ask forgiveness.' I tried a smile. 'I have no excuse for ill humour. I promise I will confess it.'

'Do you care what Lady Beatrice says, my lady?' Guille asked after a moment of uncomfortable reflection for both of us.

I thought about that. 'No, I don't think I do. But I would not court infamy.'

'Some would say better infamy than a cold, lonely bed. Try him, my lady.'

'I cannot.'

'I can arrange it. I can make an assignation for you.'

'It is not possible. We will forget this conversation, Guille. I am ashamed.'

'Why should a woman be ashamed that she desired a handsome man?'

'She should not—but when the handsome man has no feelings for her, and his birth and situation put him far beyond her grasp, then she must accept the inevitable.'

'His birth has no influence on her female longings.'

This offered no answer to my dilemma. *What do I do, Michelle?* I received no reply. I was alone to trace my uncertain path through an impossible maze.

Dismiss him!

Before God, I could not.

12

I STARED DOWN at the lengthy document in my hand. The official script of a Westminster scribe raced across the page, interspersed with red capitals and hung about with seals. At least I recognised those—they were newly created for Young Henry to mark his forthcoming coronation. As for the rest— the close-coupled lettering, the close alignment—resentment was my primary emotion, with a thorough lacing of self-pity and a good pinch of embarrassment. I was not proud of myself. I could make a guess at its strikingly official content but guessing was hardly sufficient for so wordy a communication, and so of necessity I would have to admit my need to someone.

'You look troubled, my lady.'

I started, like a doe in a thicket at the approach of baying hounds. Master Tudor had appeared, soft-footed, at my side. I had not heard his footfall, and I wished he was not there: I wished he had not seen whatever expression it was on my face that had alerted him. I did not want compassion. My own self-pity was hard enough to tolerate. Surely I could summon enough self-control to hide my discomfort. It was hardly a problem that was new to me.

I frowned at him, unfairly. 'No, Master Tudor,' I replied. His expression was dispassionate but his eyes were disconcertingly accommodating, inviting an unwary female to sink in and request help. 'Merely some news from Westminster.'

'Do you require my services…?' he asked.

I snatched at a sensible answer. 'No, no. That is…' And failed lamentably. He was so close to me that I could hear the creak of the leather of his boot soles as he moved from one foot to another. I could see the blue-black sheen, iridescent as a magpie's plumage, gleaming along the fall of his hair.

'Perhaps a cup of wine, my lady? Or do I send for a cloak for you? This room is too cold for lingering.'

I could imagine his unspoken thoughts well enough. *What in God's name are you doing, standing about to no purpose in this unheated place, when you could be comfortable in your own parlour?*

'No, no wine,' I managed at last. 'Or cloak. I will not stay.'

He was right, of course. I looked around and shivered as a current of cold air wrapped itself around my legs and feet. This was not a room—a vast and sparsely furnished audience chamber, in fact—to stand about in, without a fur-lined mantle. I was there only because I had just received an unnervingly official royal herald, complete with staff of office and heraldic tabard, dispatched to me by my lord of Gloucester. With all the formality that I had been instructed to employ when communicating with the outside world, attended by my damsels, clad impressively with regal splendour in silks and ermine, I had stood on the dais in this bleak chamber and accepted the document, before sending the messenger on his way and dismissing my women.

And now here was Owen Tudor, aware of my bafflement. I needed to escape, to hide my inadequacies. Taking in the fact that he was in outdoor garb, I seized my chance.

'I must not keep you, Master Owen, since you clearly have a task.'

'Was it bad news, my lady?' he interrupted abruptly.

I must indeed have looked distraught. I returned his stare, breathing slowly.

'No.'

My curt reply had the desired effect. 'I will send your chamber servant to you, my lady.' A brief bow and he turned away, abandoning me to my worries. Was that not what I wanted? I wondered what my lost, loving Michelle would have advised, what she would have done in similar circumstances.

'Master Tudor,'

He halted. 'Yes, my lady?'

'Can you read?' Of course he could. A Master of Household must read. 'Do you read with ease?'

'I do, my lady.'

'Then read this to me, if you please.'

Before I could change my mind, I thrust the bulky weight of it towards him. He could not think less of me than he already did. Without comment, Master Tudor's head bent over the script. Fearing to see his disdain, still I asked, held myself up for disparagement. 'Do you despise me, that I cannot decipher it for myself?'

'No, my lady.'

'Where did you learn?'

He looked up. 'In Sir Walter Hungerford's retinue, when I first came to court, my lady.' His eyes gleamed for a moment at some distant memory. 'Sir Walter insisted. A clip round the ear could be very persuasive. And before that I could read my own tongue, of course.'

'No one bothered whether I could read or not,' I found myself saying.

'The palace is full of people who will be pleased to do it for you, my lady,' he replied.

'I think they would be quick to condemn me for my ignorance.'

Owen Tudor shrugged mildly. 'Why would they?' And strode to the window where the light was good, and allowed his eye to run down it, whilst I breathed more easily. Perhaps I had been wrong in expecting censure.

'It is the best of news,' he reported. 'My lord Henry is considered old enough to be crowned as King at Westminster next month. And at some point in the following year—not yet decided—he will travel to France and be crowned as King of that country too.'

It was good news, was it not? Young Henry crowned and anointed. And he would travel to Paris, to sit, child that he was, on my father's throne and wear my father's crown. And suddenly I was tipped back into the past, to when I had last stepped ashore in my own country, when I had still been a wife, still hopeful for a reconciliation—except that Henry had died, and I had not known of it. All that had been left to me had been that I should accompany his body home, locked in stunned grief.

The cold anxieties of that journey, my own hopelessness, my abject misery and sense of abandonment, struck deep, astonishing me with the keenness of the remembered pain, so much so that my hands clenched involuntarily to crease the fragile weaving of my skirts. I had thought I had tucked away Henry's ultimate rejection of me, but it still lurked on the perimeter of my life, a wound that would not heal.

'You will accompany the Young King, will you not, my lady?'

I dragged myself back to the present, taking back the document. Master Tudor's question helped me to thrust Henry away.

'To London, yes.'

'And to Paris.'

Another worry to gnaw at me. 'I don't know,' I replied

honestly. It was no secret, not even from the servants. The restrictions on my life, and the reasons for them, must be the talk of kitchen and stable and undercroft, wherever they met to gossip. 'It will be at Gloucester's will whether I do or not. It might depend on my good behaviour. Or he might think I would choose to stay in France and refuse to return to England if he allows me to go. He would never risk that.'

I managed a smile but made no attempt to hide the bitterness. 'Although why that should matter, I know not. I no longer play any role in my son's life.' I bit down on my tongue as I heard my words. What had made me bare my soul so explicitly? Fearing to expose myself further, I walked a little distance away, turning my back to him.

'You will certainly go to Paris, my lady.' Master Owen addressed my shoulder blades.

'But Henry is considered old enough to stand on his own,' I observed bleakly. 'Once he is crowned King, then Warwick will give him all the guidance he needs. Valois guidance is not considered to have any value.'

'You are of the greatest value, my lady,' Owen Tudor responded. 'Even my lord of Gloucester knows that.'

I turned my head sharply, glancing back over my shoulder. 'You seem to be very well informed, Master Owen.'

'It is my duty to be well informed, my lady.' He was quite unperturbed. 'You will be with Lord Henry in Paris, proclaiming to all his royal Valois blood.'

'And I am beyond weary of being a vessel of royal Valois blood,' I snapped, my hands clenching on the document, to its detriment. My emotions were far too quick to escape my control this morning, so I must bring this conversation to an end. With a controlled breath and a tight smile, I swung round briskly to face him again.

'Thank you for your concern, Master Owen. You are probably right, of course. My Valois blood is of great significance. And as you said—it is far too cold to stand around in here, and you have your own duties.' I gestured towards his heavy cloak and outdoor boots.

'My duties are complete, my lady. I merely ensured that the herald had all he needed for his return to Westminster. Now my concern is for *you*.'

'There is no need.' I was already putting distance between us.

'I think there is every need, lady.'

'I have no needs.'

'You do, lady, if you will admit it.'

He did not move. It was I who came to a halt and looked back. Suddenly our exchange had taken an unsettling turn, everything around me leaping into sharp focus. The carved panelling, the intricate stonework, the tapestries, all glowed with brighter colour. It was as if the quality of the air itself had changed, taking on a chill far deeper than the cold rising from the floor tiles. My skin felt sensitive, tight-drawn over my cheekbones, the texture of the manuscript brittle beneath my fingertips.

Neither could I take my eyes from Owen Tudor's face, as if I might read something of significance in the flat planes and sculpted mouth that I had missed in the inflexion of his reply.

Without a word, Owen Tudor approached. He unfastened the brooch at his neck, swung the cloak from his shoulder and with a smooth gesture, without asking permission, he placed the heavy fall of fabric around me and fastened the simple pin at my throat. All very deft, thoroughly impersonal, but I knew it was not.

Only then, when it was done, did he say, 'Permit me, my lady. It will keep out the cold.'

He had—quite cleverly, I decided—not given me the opportunity to refuse.

The thick wool was warm with the heat of his own body, its folds settling around me, the over-wrap of its collar snug against my neck. But I shivered, for in the doing of it, the fastening of the pin, Owen Tudor's hands had brushed my shoulders and rested lightly at the base of my throat. I shivered even more when he readjusted the cloth against my neck, causing me to raise my eyes to his.

'You are very kind.' I said.

'It is my position, as Master of Household, to do all that I can to smooth your path in life, my lady. That is why you employ me.'

How formal he was, his voice as solemn as his face—but at the same time how generous. And I understood in that moment that his gentleness had nothing to do with the terms of his employment or the duty expected of him. It was far more personal than that. To my horror, tears gathered in my eyes, in my throat. And to my disquiet, he took a square of linen from the breast of his tunic and without more ado blotted the tears on my cheeks. At first I flinched, then stood unmoving to allow it. My heart was beating so hard I thought he must surely feel its vibration.

'I would do anything to spare you grief,' he murmured softly as he finished his task, using the edge of the linen to dry my lashes.

'Why would you? I am nothing to you.' When had anyone ever dried my tears, simply because they cared or wished to guard me from grief?

'I would because you are my mistress. My Queen.'

And I laughed, a little harshly, lifting my chin, refusing to acknowledge my disappointment at his denial of anything more particular. I had been mistaken in my reading of the tension between us: it existed only in my tortured mind. 'My thanks for your loyalty, Master Tudor. Wiping her tears away is only what any servant might be expected to do for his lady.'

'And because,' he continued as if I had not spoken, at the same time taking one of my hands lightly in his, 'because, my lady, you matter to me.'

My breath vanished.

'Master Tudor...'

'My lady?'

We stared at each other.

'I don't understand...'

'What is there not to understand? That I have a care for you? That your well-being is a concern to me? How could it be otherwise?'

I took an unsteady breath. 'This should not be,' I managed.

'No, of course it should not,' he replied, the lines that bracketed his mouth deepening, his voice unexpectedly raw. 'The Master of Household must never step beyond the line of what is proper in his dealings with his mistress, on pain of instant dismissal. He must be the epitome of discretion and prudence.'

What was this? I hesitated, considering so disquieting a statement, before falling without difficulty into the same role.

'Whereas the Queen Dowager must be aloof and reserved at all times,' I observed cautiously, not taking my regard from his face.

'The servant's role is to serve.' If I had been embittered over the value of my Valois blood, it was nothing to the scathing tone Owen Tudor applied to the word 'servant'. There was pride in him, I realised, and loathing of his servitude that I could never have guessed at.

'The Queen Dowager must ask only what is appropriate from her servant,' I replied. 'She must be just and fair and impersonal.'

Our eyes were locked. His fingers tightened around mine.

'The Master must feel no affection for his mistress.'

'The Queen Dowager must not encourage her servant to have any personal regard for her.'

'Neither must the servant ever allow it.'

'To do so would be quite wrong.'

'Yes.' For a moment I thought he would say no more. And then: 'It would, my lady. It would be unutterably wrong,' he said gently, the passion controlled.

How perturbing this conversation, how unsettling, and yet with a strange glamour that made me breathless. We had dropped into this observation of what was proper and improper, exchanging opinions in a carefully constructed distance from reality, as if it had no connection to us, to the world in which we lived. And indeed, as I realised, it had freed us to say some things we would never have spoken directly to each other. Had I been lured into this dangerous exchange? Owen Tudor had a way with words, it seemed, but I felt no lure. He was bound under the same intoxicating power as I. Imprisoned and helpless, mistress and servant, we were drawn together.

I must have moved involuntarily, for he let my hand slip from his and retreated one step. Then another. He no longer looked at me, but bowed low.

'You should return to your chamber, my lady.'

His voice had lost all its immediacy, but I could not leave it like that. I could not walk out of that chamber without another word being spoken between us, and not know...

'Master Tudor, it would be wrong in a perfect world...to have a personal regard, as we both agree. But...' I sought again for the words I wanted. 'In this imperfect world, what does this hapless servant feel for his mistress?'

And his reply was destructively abrupt. 'It would be unwise for him to tell her, my lady. Her blood is sacrosanct, whilst his is declared forfeit because of past misdemeanours of his race. It could be more than dangerous for the lady—and for him.'

Danger. It gave me pause, but we had come so far…

'And if the mistress orders her servant to speak out, danger or no?' I held out my hand, but he would not take it. 'If she commands him to tell her, Master Tudor?' I whispered.

And at last his eyes lifted again to mine, wide and dark. 'If she commands him, then he must, my lady, whatever the shame or disgrace. He is under her dominance, and so he must obey.'

Deep within me a well of such longing stirred. My scalp prickled with heightened awareness. It was as if the whole room held its breath, even the figures in the tapestries seeming to stand on tiptoe to watch and listen.

'So it shall be.' I spoke from the calm certainty of that centre of that turbulent longing. 'The mistress orders her servant to say what is in his mind.'

For a moment he turned, to look out at the grey skies and scudding clouds, the wheeling rooks beyond the walls of Windsor. I thought he would not reply.

'And would the lady wish to know what is in his heart also?' he asked.

What an astonishing question. Although the tension in that freezing room was wound as tight as a bowstring, I pursued what I must know.

'Yes, Master Tudor. Both in his mind and in his heart. The mistress would wish to know that.'

I saw him take a breath before speaking. 'The mistress has her servant's loyalty.'

'That is what she would expect.'

'And his service.'

'Because that is why she appointed him.' I held my breath.

He bowed, gravely. 'And she has his admiration.'

'That too could be acceptable for a servant to his mistress.' Breathing was suddenly so difficult, my chest constricted by an iron band. 'Is that all?'

'She has his adoration.'

I had no reply to that. 'Adoration.' I floundered helplessly, frowning. 'It makes the mistress sound like a holy relic.'

'So she might be to some. But the servant sees his mistress as a woman in the flesh, living and breathing, not as a marble statue or a phial of royal blood. His adoration is for her, body and soul. He worships her.'

'Stop!' Shocked, my reply, the single word, lifted up to the rafters, only to be absorbed and made nothing by the tapestries. 'I had no idea. This cannot be.'

'No, it cannot.'

'You should not have said those things to me.'

'Then the mistress should not have asked. She should have foreseen the consequences. She should not have ordered her servant to be honest.'

His face, still in profile, could have been carved from granite, the formidable brow, the exquisitely carved cheekbones, but I saw his jaw tighten at my denial of what he had offered me. The formality of servant and mistress dropped back between us, as heavy as one of those watchful tapestries, whilst I was still struggling in a mire of my own making. I had asked for the truth, and then had not discovered the courage to accept it. But I had been weak and timid for far too long. I spoke out.

'Yes. Yes, the mistress should have known. She should not have put her servant at a disadvantage.' I slid helplessly back into the previous heavy formality, because it was the only way in which I could express what was in my mind. 'And because she should have been considerate of her servant, it is imperative that the mistress be honest too.'

'No, my lady.' Owen Tudor took a step back from me, all

expression shuttered, but I followed, astonished at the audacity that directed my steps.

'But yes. The mistress values her servant. She is appreciative of his skills.' And before I could regret it, I went on, 'She wishes he would touch her. She wishes that he would show her that she is made of flesh and blood, not unyielding marble. She wishes he would show her the meaning of his adoration.'

And I held out my hand, a regal command, even as I knew that he could refuse it, and I could take no measure against him for disobedience. It would be the most sensible thing in the world for him to spurn my gesture.

I waited, my hand trembling slightly, almost touching the enamelled links of his chain of office, but not quite. It must be his decision. And then, when it seemed that he would not, he took my hand in his, to lift it to his lips in the briefest of courtly gestures. His lips were cool and fleeting on my fingers but I felt as if they had branded their image on my soul.

'The servant is wilfully bold,' he observed. The salute may have been perfunctory, but he had not let go.

I ran my tongue over dry lips. 'And what, in the circumstances,' I asked, 'would this bold servant desire most?'

The reply was immediate and harsh. 'To be alone, in a room of his choosing, with his mistress. The whole world shut out behind a locked door. For as long as he and the lady desired it.'

If breathing had been difficult before, now it was impossible. I stared at him, and he stared at me.

'That cannot be…' I repeated.

'No.' My hand was instantly released. 'It is not appropriate, as you say.'

'I should never have asked you.'

His eyes, blazing with impatience—or perhaps it was anger—were instantly hooded, his hands fallen to his sides, his reply ugly in its flatness. 'No. Neither should I have offered you what you thought you wished to know, but had not, after all, the courage to accept. Too much has been said here today, my lady, but who is to know? The stitched figures are silent witnesses, and you need fear no gossip from my tongue. Forgive me if I have discomfited you. It was not my intent, nor will I repeat what I have said today. I have to accept that being Welsh and in a position of dependence rob me of the power to make my own choices. If you will excuse me, my lady.'

Owen Tudor strode from the room, leaving me with all my senses compromised, trying to piece together the breathtaking conversation of the past minutes. What had been said here? That he wanted to be with me. That he adored and desired me. I had opened my heart and thoughts to him—and then, through my lamentable spinelessness, I had retreated and thrust him away. He had accused me of lacking courage, but I did have the courage. I would prove that I did.

I ran after him, out of the antechamber and into the gallery, where he must have been waylaid by one of the pages who was scurrying off as I approached. Even if he heard my footsteps, Owen Tudor continued on in the same direction, away from me.

'Master Tudor.'

He stopped abruptly, turning slowly to face me, because he must.

I ran the length of the gallery, queenly decorum abandoned, and stopped, but far enough from him to give him the space to accept or deny what I must say.

'But the mistress wishes it too,' I said clumsily. 'The room and the locked door.'

He looked stunned, as if I had struck him.

'You were right to tell me what was in your heart,' I urged. 'For it is in mine too.' He made no move, causing my heart to hammer unmercifully in my throat. 'Why do you not reply?'

'Because you are Queen Dowager. You were wed to King Henry in a marriage full of power and glamour. It is not appropriate that I, your servant—'

'Shall I tell you about my powerful and glamorous marriage?' I broke in.

So I told him. All the things I had never voiced to anyone before, only to myself, as I had come to understand them.

'I met him in a pavilion—and I was awestruck. Who wouldn't be? That he, this magnificent figure, wanted me, a younger daughter, for his wife. He wooed me with the sort of words a bride would wish to hear. He was kind and affectionate and chivalrous when we first met—and after, of course.' How difficult it was to explain. 'But it was all a facade, you see. He didn't need to woo me at all, but he did it because it was his duty to do so, because he wanted what I brought with me as a dower. Henry was very strong on duty. On appearances.' I laughed, with a touch of sadness.

'Did he treat you well, my lady?'

To my horror I could feel emotion gathering in my throat, but I did not hold back. 'Of course. Henry would never treat a woman with less courtesy than she deserved. But he did not love me. I thought he did when I was very young and naïve, but he didn't. He wanted my royal blood to unite the crowns and bring France under his control.'

'It is the price all high-born women have to pay, is it not, my lady?' He raised a hand, as if he would reach out to me across the space, the tenderness in his voice undermining my resolve to keep emotion in check. 'To be wed for status and power?'

'It is, of course. I was too ingenuous to believe it at first.' I returned in my mind to those biting sadnesses of my first marriage, putting them into words. 'Henry was never cruel, of course, unless neglect is cruelty. But he did not care. And do you know what hurt most? That when he was sinking fast in his final days, when he knew that death would claim him, he never thought of sending for me. He felt no need to say farewell, or even give me the chance to say goodbye to him. I don't know why I am telling you all of this.'

I frowned down at my interwoven fingers, white with strain. 'I thought I loved Henry, but it was an empty love, built on girlish dreams, and he destroyed it. Like a seed that withers and dies from lack of rain. He gave me nothing to help my love to grow—and so it died. I was very young.' I looked up at my imperturbable steward. 'I am not a very strong person, you see. I have had to grow into my strength.'

'I am so sorry, my lady,' he murmured, his eyes holding fast to mine. 'I did not know.'

'Nor should you. I hid it well, I hope. I am just telling you so that you know. There was no glamour in my marriage.' In the face of his compassion my eyes were momentarily blinded by tears, but I wiped them away with the heel of my hand, determined not to allow this moment to escape me. 'My courage tends to die when I feel unloved, unwanted, you see. When I cannot see a path for my feet to follow, when I feel that I am hedged in by thistles and thorn trees that sting and scratch. But today I have the courage to say this to you. What is in your heart is in mine too. What you desire, I too desire.'

Owen Tudor slowly retraced his steps to stand before me, reclaiming my hand, but not in the manner of a servant. I thought it was the way in which a man would approach a woman he desired, for, turning it within his, he pressed a kiss to my palm. His salute was no longer cold.

'It could be a wish that the mistress might regret for the rest of her life,' he stated.

'How would she know unless she allowed herself the means to savour it?'

'Perhaps the servant was wrong to accuse his lady of lacking courage.'

'I think he was.'

Slowly, he linked the fingers of one hand with mine, his regard intense, reflecting none of the bright light that flooded through the gallery windows to illuminate us.

'Have you enough bravery, Katherine,' he asked, 'to snatch at what you desire?'

He had called me by my name. If I would stop this, it must be now.

'Yes, Owen,' I said. 'I have enough.'

'Would you come to me? To that locked room?'

'Yes. Would you invite me?'

He lifted our joined hands to touch my cheek in reply, and his mouth curved in a vestige of a smile. 'What would be the punishment for a disenfranchised Welsh servant meeting privately with Queen Katherine?'

'I don't know.' Selfishly, I did not care.

'Do we risk the penalties? Will you come to me?'

'When?'

'Tonight.'

My heart thundered, but I would not step back. 'Where?'

'To my room.'

And pulling me close, so that my silks whispered against the wool of his tunic, he bent his head as if he would kiss me on the lips.

I froze. Footsteps at the end of the gallery were announcing the return of Thomas, my page, bearing a covered ewer and a cup. Before the lad had covered half the length of the room, Owen was no longer standing near me.

'It will be as you wish, my lady,' he said, as if some business between us had been completed. 'I will send your request to the Young King. And if you will consider my suggestion…?'

There was nothing here that was not proper. 'I have considered it, Master Tudor. I think it has merit and will act upon it.' I looked across at my page with a smile. 'Good morning, Thomas. Had you come to find me?'

'Master Owen sent me to fetch wine for you, my lady, in the audience chamber.'

So he had thought of me, even when he had been so angry.

'That was kind—but I have changed my mind. You can accompany me back to my chamber and you can tell me...'

Later I could not recall what small matter I had talked of with my page. I had done it. I had agreed to meet with Owen Tudor. There was a connection between us impossible to deny despite the unbridgeable rift between us. I had stepped over that rift and could find nothing but exquisite joy in the stepping.

At the door to my chamber I discovered that I was still wearing his cloak, redolent of the scent of him, of horses, and smoke from an applewood fire. Of maleness. I drank it in, before reluctantly I unfastened the pin, allowing the enveloping weight to slip from my shoulders as I examined the brooch. It was silver and of no great value, a little worn from long polishing and without gems, but when I looked closely I could see that its circular form was that of a creature I supposed was a dragon. Its wings were only half-furled as if it might take to flight at any moment, if its tail were not caught in its mouth. It had an aura of power, of mystical authority in the skilful carving of it. I thought it had no great value—how would a servant own jewels of any value?—but the little dragon had the essence of something old and treasured. Perhaps it had once belonged to his family, passed down through the generations. I traced the lines of the silver wings with my finger. It was a far cry from the Beaufort escutcheon with its enamelling and glittering stones, and yet...

'My lady?'

Thomas was standing, waiting for instruction.

I folded the cloak and handed it to him.

'Return this to Master Tudor,' I instructed. 'Express my thanks for his coming to my rescue.'

And the pin? I kept it. Just for a little while. It seemed to me that perhaps Owen Tudor had something of a dragon in him, in the display of brooding power I had just witnessed. I would not keep it long—just for a little while. To have something of him for myself.

I sat on his bed—for want of anywhere else. I had told no one of my intentions. Whom would I tell? Not even Madam Joanna could be a recipient of this wild step. My damsels were dismissed, Guille dispatched. I would put myself to bed, I stated. Was I not capable of it? When Guille showed some surprise, I claimed a need of solitude for prayer and private contemplation. Yet here I was, enclosed by dark shadows, alone in the room of the man I paid to supervise my household. An assignation with a servant. I swallowed convulsively, the nerves in my belly leaping like frogs in a pond on a summer's night.

I was dressed in the plainest clothes I possessed. Anyone noting me as I had made my way by antechamber and stair would not have looked twice at the woman wrapped about in sombre hues, her hair secured, its fairness hidden from sight in a hood. I was nothing more than one of the royal tirewomen out and about on her own affairs. And if it was with a man who had caught her eye, then good luck to her.

So here I sat on Owen Tudor's bed, my feet not touching the floor, and looked around. It was a surprise to me. Not the fact that it was small—Owen was fortunate to have a room of his own. It was barely large enough to contain the narrow bed, a plain stool, a coffer for small private items, a clothes press and a candle stand. If I had stood in the centre, with outstretched arms, I might almost have touched the opposite walls. The surprise was that it was as neat as a pin.

Owen Tudor took care of his possessions, making me realise again how little I knew of him. There were no garments strewn around, nothing where it should not have been. I slid my hand over the rough woven cover on the bed. Neither was there anything to indicate his status as the Master of Household. It could have been a monkish cell for all it might tell me of the man with whom I had made this liaison.

My eye travelled to the coffer and beside it the handsome slipware pottery bowl and ewer. And I smiled because I could not help it. Pottery cups and a flagon of what I suspected was wine stood there. A candlestick. And a book. Here was an item of value. He had left something for me to read to pass the time because he knew he might be late. How thoughtful! A book, a candle and a cup of wine. I laughed softly despite the stark beat of uncertainty in my mind. Had he known that I would be nervous, in spite of all my professed courage? Perhaps he had, and had done what he could to remedy it.

I opened the book—recognising it immediately as one of my own Books of Hours—how enterprising of him to give me comfort—and turning the pages, I discovered a well-loved illustration of the marriage feast at Cana, beautiful with its familiar depth of colour and lively participants. But I closed the book abruptly between my two hands. This was no sacred marriage I was contemplating. This was a sinful celebration of desire. And if Owen Tudor did not come soon, my much-vaunted courage would be naught but a puddle around my feet.

I heard his confident footsteps at the head of the stair. They drew nearer. Swift and purposeful, Owen Tudor sounded like a man spurred on by urgency. And I trembled.

This is a mistake…

When the door opened, I was on my feet, as if for flight. For a moment, there he stood in the doorway, blotting out the light from the corridor, as dark and solemn as always, as good to look at at the end of the day as he was at the beginning. If he saw my uncertainty, he gave no recognition, but smiled at me, and any thoughts of escape were thrust aside as the door was closed smoothly at his back.

'Forgive me, my lady,' he said, bowing as if we were meeting in public and our previous conversation had never happened. 'I am late. My mistress had tasks for me. My time is rarely my own.'

His lips curved and his eyes gleamed, and I thought that it was the first time that he had shown any humour in my company. His face was lit by his smile, the cheekbones softening, and although my hands were clasped tightly together, I found that I had relaxed enough to respond in kind.

'Does your mistress work you hard?'

'You have no idea.' He took two slow steps towards me. 'Have you had wine?'

'No.'

His actions were as neat and spare as his surroundings as he lit another candle and poured wine—just as if our meeting here was commonplace—whilst I stood unsure of what to do. I could not sit on his bed. I could not. He handed me a cup and raised his own.

'To your health, my lady.'

'To yours, Owen Tudor.'

I sipped, almost choking. I had no idea what to say. My awareness of him within these close walls traced a path over my skin from head to toe.

'I told you that I admired you,' he said softly. And when I looked blankly at him: 'I was right to do so. You had all the courage I expected of you.'

'I don't feel brave.'

'The door is not locked,' he stated.

'No.'

And I realised he was allowing me a choice, even at this late hour. Seeing my hands shaking, he took the cup from me and placed both on the coffer, so that his back was to me, inviting me to slide a hand over the fine material of the tunic he had worn for supper, to take cognisance of the firm shoulder beneath. But I couldn't touch him. I wouldn't touch him.

And as if aware of my difficulty, Owen took the decision out of my hands, for he approached, enclosed my hands in his and drew me towards him.

'Do I have permission to kiss the once Queen of England?'

'If you wish it.'

He filled my vision as he bent his head and placed his lips on mine. Gently. A promise rather than possession. And fleetingly. Barely had I registered the warmth of it than he had lifted his head and was looking down at me.

'I'll not ask permission again, Katherine. Is this what you want?'

I could not reply, unable to find the words to express the army of uncertainties that battered my mind, but I did not need to. Framing my face with his hands, his lips again claimed mine, and it was my undoing. How different this embrace! His mouth hot and hungry, body powerful, hands holding me so that he could take and take again, I was swept away with heat and the longing that built within me. He lifted his head again, hands still cradling me, his thumbs caressing my temples—until with a brusque movement he pushed back my hood so that it fell to the floor.

My hair free and released, it now tumbled over my shoulders to lie on my breast, and his, allowing him to curl his hand within it so that it wound round his wrist like a living shackle.

My breath shuddered out between my lips in a sound of pure wordless pleasure.

'Call me by my name. Call me Owen.' There was the urgency.

'Owen.' A breath of delight.

'You are the most beautiful woman I have ever seen. The most desirable. And I should know better than to have you here—but what man can stand aloof from a woman who fires his blood? I have wanted you for years. I can no longer resist you.'

His arms anchored me against him, and his fervent avowals slid through my blood like wine as he kissed me and I clung, my senses cast adrift, robbed of all will, all thought, only knowledge that here was a man who said he desired me and always had. An explosion of heady feeling swept through me. Owen Tudor wanted me, and I wanted him beyond all reason. I would let him take me. His hands moved to the lacing of my gown—

No!

Suddenly the desire was shot through with pure panic.

'No,' I said.

I pushed against his chest, and when he released me I buried my burning face in my hands. What was I doing? Horror bubbled through my blood, and a capering terror that tripped and hopped to its own rhythm. I looked at the man I would have taken as my lover, distraught, suddenly seeing Edmund's laughing face before me. Edmund had seduced me with laughter and song and carefree youth, making me think that I was a girl again without responsibilities, before abandoning me when he could not use me to climb his particular ladder of power.

This was no light-hearted seduction, but an explosion of passion that swept me along, dragging me down into a whirlpool of longing. I wanted it—but could not allow it, for it would bring nothing but humiliation for me, ignominy and dismissal for Owen. If Gloucester discovered...if the Council knew. A liaison with a servant? But I wanted him. I wanted him to touch me again. I wanted his mouth on mine.

Ah, no. It must not be!

And in that moment I was swamped by past hurts. Owen Tudor could never want me. Did I not have proof? No one else, neither Henry nor Edmund, had wanted me, except for what the Valois name or my position of Queen Dowager could bring them. Owen Tudor could not love me. Perhaps it was pity in his heart. Yes, that was it. All my confidence was undermined by terrible uncertainty...

I became aware that Owen was frowning as if trying, and failing, to read the morass of thoughts chasing through my mind. His hands fell away from my shoulders, yet he smoothed the backs of his fingers down my cheek, and my fears were almost overthrown.

'Are you afraid of me?' he asked.

'No.' I must not give in. I must not. 'It's not that. I should not be here.'

And I saw justifiable exasperation glitter in his eye as he sighed. 'It's a bit late for that.'

'It's all my fault.'

And I slid from his hands to flee. The door was unlocked. Two more steps and I would be there and out of this room that contained all I desired but all I could not have. I could be back in my chamber where I could wipe out my memory of what I had almost done. I could forget how I had almost fallen at his feet in longing—but before I had managed one step, Owen captured my wrist.

'Don't go like this.'

As his fingers closed, fear built irrationally. I pushed hard against him but to no avail.

'Katherine. Don't struggle. I'll do nothing that you don't wish.'

'I can't do this.' I was beyond sense, shot through with guilt that I might bring judgement against him. 'I have behaved outrageously. You should know that there is bad blood in my veins. My mother…no handsome man was safe with her. I have to ask your forgiveness.'

'No. No forgiveness is necessary between us.' He tried to gather me into his arms. I wanted it more than life itself and for a moment allowed myself to be drawn close, before self-reproach re-ignited in an agony of despair.

'I can't stay…' I struggled, overbalanced, so that he clamped me to his chest. 'Oh!' The sting of pain along my cheekbone shocked me into silence.

'What is it?'

I shook my head. 'Let me go!'

And now his voice was all ice, all understanding having fled. 'So you do despise me as a servant, too lowly for you to lie with. You can lust after my body but my birth isn't good enough for you.'

'No! That's not it.'

'That is what it looks like to me.'

'Please,' I begged. 'Please understand. You must let me go.'

'Then go if you wish, my lady. There is no compulsion. I would not endanger your mortal soul by forcing you to share a bed with a man who is not fit to remove your shoes.'

The heavy formality, the harsh judgement, was my undoing.

'You cannot possibly love me,' I cried out in my anguish. 'No man has ever loved me.'

And when Owen stood aside, I flung the door wide, hurrying down the corridors, through the rooms to my own, my hair loose, my face undisguised, praying helplessly that I would meet no one. I did not, but it was no relief. Despair drenched me from head to foot at what I had almost allowed myself to do.

And what I had thrown away.

Closing my door, I leaned back against it, willing my emotions to settle. Shame was a living entity, nasty and cruel, mocking my every breath with jeering contempt in every comment. Overcome with physical need, I had invited the intimacy. I had called him by his given name and agreed to the assignation, compromising my honour. I had drunk his wine, kissed him, and then I had fled for my life like a frightened child rather than a woman of almost thirty years. I had left my hood. I had run through the corridors like a court whore escaping from an importunate lover. Yet now, forced to accept my dishonour, I wished I was back in his room, sitting on his bed, allowing him to lead me in whatever path he chose.

You fool. You utter fool. You allowed desire to rule and look what happened. Have you learnt nothing from your life? How will you face him ever again?

And still my need for him would not release its hold on me. If he had come to my door at that moment, I would have opened it to him and bid him come in. I would have fallen at his feet in gratitude.

He won't come. He thinks you have damned him as inferior, unfit to consort with a queen.

I sobbed. Why? Why had I run away?

Because I was afraid. Afraid of putting my life into the hands of a man I barely knew, who might not have care with it. Afraid that the line between servant and mistress was impossibly blurred and, in the end, I had not been able to take my fortitude in both hands and leap over that line. What would Beatrice say if she knew that I contemplated removing my shift for Owen Tudor? Or Madam Joanna? I don't care, I had once said. But I did. I shivered at the thought of their reproof.

And what of Owen Tudor? I had denied him, rejected him, allowing him to believe that I thought him too far below me. A man of such self-esteem as he was would never forgive me for that. I was without honour: the blame was all mine.

Forcing myself to walk across the room, I picked up my reflecting glass. What would I see? Would I see the face of a slut? Would I recognise the woman who stared back at me? I looked, a quick glance. And was surprised. There was no imprint of the sin I had contemplated.

Then I looked again, carrying the glass to a candle. An unhappy woman stared back, a woman who had stood on the edge of grasping what she most wanted in life. There, enticingly before her, was the bridge over the chasm, there the helping hand stretched out, there the man who would give her her heart's desire—and she had stepped back. She had leapt away, destroying any chance of taking that step again. He would despise her, her lack of valour, her lack of courtesy. It was hopeless.

I relived the moments again in all their glory and all their pain. He had called me Katherine. He had kissed me and I had pushed him away, when all I had wanted was to say, 'Kiss me again!' and make use of the bed with the bright woven cover.

You can lust after my body but my birth isn't good enough for you…

Owen Tudor would despise me, but not as much as I despised myself.

I took a comb to my tangled hair, pulling on the knots as if the pain would dissolve my grief. I could not weep. The guilt was mine, choosing to go to the room of a passionate man then fleeing when he had kissed me.

I looked again, turning my head as I saw the abrasion on my cheek. It was red, with the slightest breaking of skin.

Of course. His chain of office had marked me. How appallingly apt.

A terrible memento of a disastrous evening.

Guille drew back the heavy bed-curtains that had been witness to my lack of sleep, and halted with a hiss of consternation.

'My lady!'

'What is it?' My reactions, both of mind and body, were slow.

'What have you done?' She disappeared, returned and held out my reflecting glass.

And I looked. The abrasion, a minor blemish the night before, was angry and red with the purple-blue of bruising flaring across my cheekbone.

'Who did this to you?'

I touched the tender spot, flinching at the pain. Here was truth I could not admit to.

'It was my own fault,' I managed smoothly. 'I fell against the bed foot. I had spent too long on my knees at my *prie-dieu*.' It was horribly noticeable. I closed my eyes: the last thing I needed was to draw attention to my reprehensible behaviour. 'Can we remedy it?' I asked.

'A day for some clever disguise, I think.' And Guille, rummaging, lifted a chest of cosmetics from the depths of my coffer.

I rarely used them. My skin was fashionably pale and close textured, but today I needed subterfuge. Guille and I knew enough from my mother, who had been expert in applying glamour to win the eye of a man. My need was to hide from him. Owen Tudor must not suspect that our meeting had left its mark on me.

We spent a useful hour opening packets and phials, finally applying powdered root of the Madonna lily to whiten my face and hide the abrasion. Ground leaves of angelica added a glow to my cheeks and drew the eye from the bruising.

'It's better,' Guille ventured, a frown between her brows. 'I suppose.'

'But not good.' I cast my looking glass on the bed in despair. 'We can't hide it completely.'

'No.' I sighed. It was the best we could do. I broke my fast in my chamber and absented myself from Mass, but I would have to join my household for dinner, or my empty chair would cause comment. I would have to scrape up what I could of my poor fortitude and pretend that nothing was amiss.

And I would have to face Owen Tudor.

When I took my place on the dais, with no thought of what was on my plate, and no ear for Father Benedict's blessings, all I could see in my mind was Owen Tudor's gaze sweep over me, then return, as I had first walked defiantly into the room. The gaze became a stare, his whole stance taut, until he remembered his duties and stalked away to summon the pages to bring in the serving platters. All I was left with was a memory of his stunned expression, for the much-vaunted cosmetics were not concealing the livid bruise to any degree.

I already knew this. My damsels, meeting with me in my solar, had been sympathetic with my plight and full of suggestions from their own remedies, but nothing could conceal the discolouring. Or my remorse when I saw Owen Tudor's reaction.

Not Master Owen. He would never be Master Owen again. How could I think of him as a man in a position of subservience to me when he had held me in his arms? When his kisses had turned my blood to molten gold? Unfortunately, such was my nature that the gold had turned to lead and I had dealt him the worst of blows. I had encouraged him, only to repulse him.

Throughout the whole length of that meal contrition stalked me, for what had I seen, for that one breath-stopping moment, before he had masked all thoughts? Shock certainly, for he would not have known. But then a sudden blaze of furious anger. It had made my blood run cold, and added to the muddle of my thoughts.

How dared he be angry with me?

And yet why should he not? I admitted as I picked at the plums in syrup and sweet pastry set before me. Did I not deserve it? I had given him to believe that I was willing, kissing him with a wanton fervour previously unknown to me. I had pressed my body to his in silent demand that he could not have misinterpreted. And then, when his embrace had grown too powerful, I had run away, when I should have had enough confidence to conduct an affair with a man with some self-possession.

If that was what I wanted. Even if he was a servant.

And if I did not want it, I should not have responded to him in the first place. Had he not given me the space to withdraw after my first foolish admission?

You need fear no gossip from my tongue.

The fault was undoubtedly mine, and I deserved his ire.

The meal proceeded. We ate, we drank. We gossiped— or my damsels did. The pages, well-born boys learning their tasks in a noble household under Owen's direction, served us with silent concentration. Owen's demeanour was exactly as it should be, a quiet, watchful competence. But he did not eat with us, taking his seat along the board as was his wont. Instead, he stood behind my chair in austere silence, a personal and reproachful statement to me, as if to broadcast the difference in our ranks.

I deserved that too.

I had no requests of him. My whole awareness was centred on the power of his stare between my shoulder blades. It was as if I was pierced by a knife.

I put my spoon down on the table. The pastry sat heavily in my belly, and I breathed a silent prayer that the meal would be soon over and I could escape back to my room. Except that when the puddings were finished and the board cleared, I had no choice but to walk past him since he had not moved. His eyes were rich with what I read as censure, when I risked a glance.

'Was the food not to your satisfaction, my lady?' he asked. He had noticed that I had eaten little.

'It was satisfactory. As always.' I made no excuse but my reply was brusque.

He bowed. I walked past him, my heart as sore and as wounded as my cheek.

'Master Owen is come to see you, my lady.' It was the hour after dinner and Guille entered my chamber where I sat, unseeing, my Book of Hours closed on my knee. 'To discuss the arrangements for the celebration of the Young King's birthday.'

'Tell Master Owen that I am indisposed,' I replied, concentrating on the page that I had suddenly seen a need to open. 'There is time and more to discuss the tournament. Tell him to see my Lord of Warwick if there are difficulties.'

My eyes looked with horror at the penitential psalm on the open page, expressing sorrow for sin.

Have mercy upon me, O God, according to thy loving kindness: according unto the multitude of thy tender mercies, blot out my transgressions.

Before God, I needed His mercy, and Owen Tudor's, for I had indeed sinned.

★ ★ ★

'Master Owen wishes to know if you will mark the day of St Winifred with a feast, my lady. He needs to make the funds available. It should be on the third day of November.' Guille again. Another hour had crawled by and my self-disgust was no less sharp. Neither was my self-immolation.

'Who is St Winifred?' I demanded crossly.

'A Welsh saint, Master Owen says.' Guille shrugged her lack of interest. 'He says that she was a woman who showed herself capable of integrity and fortitude under duress. He says that such qualities are rare in womankind.'

I stiffened at so pointed a comment from my Master of Household.

'Tell Master Owen that I am at prayer.'

'As you wish, my lady.'

How dared he? Did he think to discountenance me even more? Kneeling before my *prie-dieu*, I covered my face and ignored Guille's speculative stare.

The hour arrived, before we would all meet again for supper.

'Master Owen has returned this, my lady.' It was my hood, carefully folded. 'He says that you must have left it in the chapel.'

'Yes, I must have. Thank him, if you will, Guille.' Taking it from her, I buried my face in the soft velvet when she left the room. I could not face my own thoughts.

Our paths must of necessity cross at supper. I considered shutting myself in my room with some feeble excuse but was that not the way of the coward he thought me? I had played my part in this situation and thus I must see it through to the end. I must have the fortitude of the venerated St Winifred.

I took my seat, hands folded, appetite still impaired, and set myself to suffer.

And, oh, I did. Not once did he look at me. He stalked about the chamber as if he had the toothache, then became as before, a thunderous brooding presence behind my chair. If he was angry before, he was furious now. I ate as little as I had previously and at the end walked past him as if I had no knowledge of him.

That night I knelt once more at my *prie-dieu* but after the briefest acknowledgement of the Virgin's grace I turned my thoughts inward. I must make recompense, I must admit my fault, undertaking what I could to smooth out this tangled mess of fear and desire. After Mass next morning I would summon Owen Tudor and explain that. But what would I explain? I did not understand the turmoil in my heart and mind. But I would explain that the mistake had been mine, and accept that his attraction to me had died a fast death.

I would accept it, as I had accepted Henry's coldness and Edmund's betrayal in the face of ambition. It would be no worse. I had weathered those storms well enough. My marriage to Henry had brought me a much-loved son, and I rarely thought about my Beaufort suitor except to wish that I had been a little older and wiser. To lose Owen before I had even known him would be no worse.

Except that it would. However hard it was for me to acknowledge it, I did not think I could live without Owen Tudor. The fundamental aching need that had touched me when I had seen him stride from the river had not lessened with the passage of time. It had grown until I had no peace.

I lifted my face to the Virgin and promised that I would make my peace, with him and with myself.

13

I KEPT EARLY hours in the summer months when the sun drew me from my bed. The next morning, before we broke our fast, as was customary my whole household—damsels, pages and servants who were not immediately in employment—congregated in my private chapel to celebrate Mass. As the familiar words bathed the chapel in holy power, my fingers might trip over the beads of my rosary but my mind practised the words I would use to explain to Owen Tudor that I desired him but must reject him, that we must continue in the rigid path of mistress and servant.

At the end when I turned my thoughts to Father Benedict's blessing I had made at least one decision. I would meet with Owen in the Great Hall. I did not think my words would please him, but it would be public enough to preserve a remote politeness between us. I offered up a final prayer for strength and forgiveness, rose to my feet, preparing to hand my missal and my mantle—essential against the cold in the chapel—to Guille and—

He was waiting for me by the door, and there was no misreading the austere expression: his mood was as dark today as yesterday. Neither did he intend to allow me to escape, but I would pre-empt him, seizing the initiative despite trembling knees. The drawing of a line between us which neither of us would cross again would be on my terms.

'Our celebration for the Feast of St Winifred,' I said, a small, polite smile touching my lips. 'We must talk of it, Master Owen. Perhaps you will walk with me to the Great Hall.'

'Here will do, my lady.'

To order him away would draw too much attention. I waved my damsels through the door before me and shook my head at Guille that I did not need her. Then we were face to face. Father Benedict would be sufficient chaperone.

'Master Tudor—' I began.

'I bruised your face. And you would not receive me.' His eyes blazed in his white face, his voice a low growl.

'Well, I thought—' Unexpectedly under attack, I could not explain what I had thought.

'I marked you—and you refused to see me!'

'I was ashamed.' I would be honest, even though I quailed at his anger.

'*You* were ashamed!'

I took a step back from the venom, but I was no longer so sure where his fury was directed. I had thought it was at me. Still, I would say what I thought I must.

'I ask that you will understand—and pardon my thoughtlessness.'

'*I* pardon *you*? It is unforgivable that I should have despoiled your beauty.' He partially raised his hand as if he would touch my cheek, then, as Father Benedict shuffled about the sanctuary, let it fall to his side. 'I deserve that you dismiss me for my actions. And yet for you to bar me from your rooms, and refuse to see me—it is too much.'

'The blame does not lie with you,' I tried.

He inhaled slowly, regaining control, of himself and of his

voice. So he had a temper. I was right about the dragon in him. I feared it, yet at the same time it stirred my blood.

'I regret—'

'No. You have no need to regret.' Briskly he took my mantle from my hands, shaking out the folds and draping it round my shoulders, the second time he had felt a need to protect me from the elements. 'It is too cold without, my lady.' The control was back, the passion harnessed, but the words were harsh. 'I think the blame does lie with me in that I asked something of you that you were not capable of giving. I should have understood it, and not put you in that impossible position. My judgement was at fault. And because of that I harmed you.'

It hurt. It hurt that I had made him think me so weak.

'I was capable,' I retorted, but softly, conscious of Father Benedict still kneeling before the altar. 'I *am* capable.'

'Then why did you run from me?'

'I shouldn't have.'

His blood was running hot again, the dragon surfacing. 'What happened between us, Katherine? One moment I thought you were of a mind with me—and the next you fought me as if I were endangering your honour. You came to me willingly. You allowed me to touch you and kiss you. You called me Owen. Not Master Owen or Master Tudor, but Owen. You allowed me to call you Katherine. Can you deny it? Did you think I would hurt you?'

'Never that. But making a choice was too much to bear.'

'What choice? To seize happiness in each other's arms?' There was anger simmering beneath the bafflement. 'That was what I offered. I thought that was what you wanted too. And why did you accuse me of not being able to love you?'

'Because no one ever has!'

I covered my mouth with my hands, horrified at hearing my admission spoken aloud.

Was he angry? I dared not look at him. Contrition made me move to walk past him, to escape the inevitable accusations, but as I reached the door Owen took my wrist. I glanced towards Father Benedict but he was occupied before the altar. When I pulled hard for release, Owen simply tightened his grip and drew me back into the chapel.

'Katherine!' He huffed out a breath. 'Are all women so intransigent and intriguing? I swear it takes a brave man to take you on! I want to seize you and shake you for your indecision—and at the same time prostrate myself at your feet in sorrow for my savagery. You tear me apart. Two nights ago, for that brief moment, you burned with fire in my arms. Today you are as cold as ice. A man needs to know what his woman is thinking.'

It shocked me. 'I am not your woman,' I remarked. I was indeed as cold as ice.

'Tell me that you did not want me when you came to my room. If that is not being my woman, I don't know what is. Or do they have different standards at the royal court in France?'

Doubly wounded by an accusation that had some degree of truth in it, fury raced through me like a bolt of lightning. I felt like throwing my missal at his head. I gripped it, white-knuckled, and without thought, without respect, committing all the sins I had deplored, I replied, 'How dare you, a servant, judge me? You have no right!'

Gripping my missal hard, I instantly regretted my ungoverned words. Seeing what might be in my mind, Owen favoured me with an unequivocal stare and took the book from my hand.

'I think your words have done enough damage,' he observed, the soft cadence for once compromised. 'To resort to violence would be less than becoming, my lady.'

And I was stricken. It was as if I had actually struck him,

for how could I have spoken words so demeaning? Demeaning to both Owen Tudor and myself. What would he think of me now? First to play him fast and loose, and then to lash out in an anger that he would not have understood? How could I possibly explain to him that I feared beyond anything to be likened to my mother and her louche court where lust ruled and principle came a far second? I could not tell him, I could not explain…

'I am so sorry,' I breathed. 'I am even more ashamed…'

And how unforgiving was his reply. 'Well, my comment was ill advised, I suppose. What would a servant know of such high matters as behaviour between those of royal blood?'

'I should not have said that. It was unforgivable. Everything I say to try to put this right between us seems to be the wrong thing.'

And I covered my face at the impossibility of it, so that when Owen moved to pull me to sit on the settle he startled me, but I did not refuse, neither did I rebuff him when Father Benedict rose, genuflected, and withdrew into the sanctuary, and Owen took a seat beside me.

'Don't weep,' he said. 'What I said to you was intolerable for a man of honour. But I claim provocation.' His smile was wry. 'Your tears are sufficient condemnation of my actions towards you. Doubtless I should be dismissed from your service for it. I would do nothing to hurt you, my lady.'

'I'll not dismiss you. Do you not understand?' His return to formality overcame me, undermining all my intentions to remain aloof and distant, and the words poured as freely as my tears. 'I was responsible. I was too impulsive. I am ashamed that I came to your room, willingly kissed you and accepted your kisses, and then my courage gave out at the last moment. I could see no happiness, no future, for either of us. Do you not see? I am not allowed to have what would make me happy. My life is dictated by Gloucester and the Council. Yes, I wanted you. I would have lain in your arms if I had not had a fit of remorse for beginning what could not be ended. For Gloucester's anger at me would touch you also.'

He said nothing, merely leaned forward, forearms supported on his thighs, studying the tiles between his boots. I could not tell if he understood, or despised me as a weak woman who could not make up her own mind. I feared it might be the latter.

'I wish I had never seen you swimming in the river,' I sniffed.

He turned his head to look up at me. 'Why?'

'Because since then I am aware of you as I have been of no other man.'

'I didn't know you admired my prowess at swimming,' he said.

'I didn't. I lusted after your body,' I admitted.

He laughed softly, the sound not totally devoid of humour, as he returned my missal to me. 'So why refuse me?'

'Because I have to live as I am told to live, discreetly and circumspectly, to honour my son and the Crown.'

The dark brows drew together. 'You are not a child, to follow orders.'

'It is not as simple as that.'

'Why not?'

'Because I am alone. I have no one to encourage me, to give me strength. If I am to rebel against those who have power over me, I cannot do it alone. You were right. St Winifred had far more courage than I.'

'To Hell with St Winifred. I would give you strength.'

'But if we embarked on…that is to say…'

'If you allowed me to become your lover.'

'Yes. That is what I meant.' I kept my gaze on my fingers,

still clutching my ill-treated missal. 'When it was discovered it would bring Gloucester's wrath down on us. And that would mean dismissal for you, even punishment.'

'To Hell with Gloucester too. Do you not rule your own household? I could give you happiness.'

'And I could bring disaster down on your head.'

'Do we deny each other because of what others want for us?'

It all seemed so simple when he spoke it. But it wasn't simple at all. 'Yes,' I said. 'We must deny each other.'

His hand touched my arm. 'I say no. Where is your spirit?'

'I have none.' Self-pity washed over me like a wave. 'I don't believe myself to be worthy of love.'

'Look at me, Katherine.'

I did, wishing my face was not ravaged by tears, but still I looked, to discover all the anger and condemnation in his face had quite gone. I was caught up in such understanding, such compassion, such a tenderness of care that I could not look away.

'Use my name,' he said gently.

'Owen,' I said with a watery smile.

'Good. You have given me a hard task, have you not? To prove to you that my love is sure? Now, listen to me. Here is how I see it,' Owen stated solemnly. 'I see a woman of extraordinary courage. You came to a strange country as a young girl, to make a new life alone since your husband left you for the demands of war. You bore the loss of widowhood, and you have stood by your young son. Do you think I have not seen how you behave? Never has there been a Queen Dowager as gracious as Katherine of France. You have escaped from the toils of Edmund Beaufort, God rot his soul. And not before time—he was not the man for you. I say that you are a woman of spirit. And I say that you should not accept a life of solitude and loneliness because your brother-by-marriage thinks it would be good for the Crown. Do you not deserve a life of your own, on your own terms?'

There was a little silence.

'Look at me, Katherine. Answer me.'

'I...'

'My lady?'

Father Benedict, who had approached, was looking from me to Owen in some perturbation. 'Is there a difficulty?' His eyes were fixed on my tear-stained cheeks.

'No, Father.'

'Are you troubled, my daughter?' He was frowning.

'No, Father. Unless it's the troublesome matter of finance for St Winifred's festival. Master Owen was reminding me.'

'Money! Always a matter for discussion. Master Owen will solve it, I'm sure. He solves all our problems.' Reassured, with a smile he made the sign of the cross and blessed us both before leaving us.

'Is that an omen?' I asked, momentarily distracted. 'He blessed us both.'

'He would not have done it if he knew what was in my mind,' Owen replied, the unmistakable heat of desire like rich velvet in his eyes, making my heart bound. 'I have a longing for you. Even in sleep I know no respite.'

'And I long for you,' I said. I scrubbed at my cheeks, wincing at the abrasion. 'I wish I had not wept.'

'You are beautiful even when you weep.'

'You are beautiful too.'

Owen Tudor laughed and held out both hands. 'And practical, so your priest says. I can deal with St Winifred. I can handle the money. Will you allow me to solve your problems too? To give you happiness?'

He was smiling at me, and I knew that this was a moment of vast consequence. Whatever decision I made now would set my feet on a different road. Would Owen Tudor give me the strength, the audacity to take hold of the happiness he offered? If I took that step it would be irrevocable, but I would not be travelling along that road alone. I looked at the hands held out to me, broad-palmed, long-fingered, eminently persuasive.

I closed my eyes, allowing the silence to sink into my mind, my heart, bringing me its peace. And I made my decision.

'Yes. Oh, yes.' Abandoning the missal, I placed my hands in his. Warm and firm, they closed around mine as if they would never release me. 'I want to be with you, Owen Tudor,' I said.

'So it shall be,' he promised. 'We shall be together. You will be my love for all eternity. In this place I make it a sacred vow. I will never allow us to be parted, this side of the grave.'

And there in that holy place, the grace of Father Benedict's blessing lingering in the air, I had no qualms. I gripped his hands tightly as he drew me towards him and touched his lips to my damaged cheek.

'Forgive me, forgive me,' he murmured.

'I do,' I whispered back. 'I will go to the ends of the earth with you, Owen Tudor.'

'And I will guard you well.'

For a moment I leaned into his embrace, my head resting on his shoulder. 'But I have another sin to confess if I am to bare my soul.'

'Another one? How many sins can the beautiful Katherine have committed?'

His face was alight with laughter as I freed my hand from his and sought the recesses of my sleeve.

'I kept this.' And I lifted the silver dragon on my palm.

A strange expression crossed his face. 'There it is.' He took it from me, rubbing his thumb over the worn carving. 'I thought I had lost it—and regretted it.' He looked quizzically at me. 'Why did you keep it?'

'Because I wanted something of you, something that was yours and that you valued. I did not steal it,' I assured him. 'I would have returned it. I think you do value it.'

Still he held it in his palm, its dragon mouth swallowing its tail in whimsical beauty.

'I do value it. You have no idea.' Stern-faced, he pinned it to my bodice. 'There. The dragon looks very well.'

'But I must not.' I remembered another brooch, another time. I must not take it.

'It is what I wish. The Welsh dragon will guard you from all harm. There is no one I would rather have own it than you, the woman I love.'

And Owen Tudor kissed me, very gently, on my lips. It moved me to the depths of my soul.

We walked together from the chapel into the sun-barred enclosed area of the Horseshoe Cloisters, all that we had said and done and promised creating a wordless bond of delight between us. Until it was shattered. Usually a quiet place, the graceful arches stood witness to the scene of a fracas, causing us to halt to observe the group of young men who had joined the household to polish their knightly skills in the company of my son, under the tutelage of Warwick and the royal Master of Arms. They were invariably a boisterous fraternity, quarrelsome in the way of young men with too much unchannelled energy. Today raised voices echoed across the space, shouts, curses, some coarse laughter. A few punches would be thrown before the matter was settled.

But then came the dangerous rasp of steel as a sword was drawn from a scabbard. This was no formal passage of arms, controlled and supervised under Warwick's eagle eye, but rather an outburst of temper, the climax of an argument. In a blink of an eye the dispute spun from crude name-calling to a dangerous confrontation with the gleam of inexpertly wielded weapons. The two lads circled, swords at the ready, their comrades encouraging with cat-calling and jeering. A lunge, a grapple, a cry of pain. There was little skill—they were too impassioned—but they hacked at each other as if they had every intention of murder.

'They'll kill each other by pure mischance,' Owen growled, before he sprinted across the space to erupt into the rabble of an audience.

'Stop this!' His voice was commanding. The crowd fell instantly silent but the two combatants were too taken up with their quarrel to even hear.

'Damned young fools!' Owen addressed the watchers. 'Could you not stop it getting to this pitch? Fists would have done the job just as well and with less damage to everyone.'

As he was speaking, he seized the sword from the scabbard of the nearest squire and a dagger from another, and waded in, steel flashing.

'Put up your weapons,' he commanded.

He struck one sword down with his own, the other he parried with the knife. Then, when he sensed the belligerence had not quite drained, he dropped his sword and gripped the wrist of one, who turned on him in blind fury. A wrench on the wrist and a fist to the jaw brought it all to a rapid if ignominious end, while I, a silent watcher, was more than interested to see how Owen would handle this. I had seen him marshal my servants, but I had never seen him in the throes of an altercation such as this with young men of high blood.

Breathless, hair in disarray, face afire and to my mind magnificent, Owen stood between them, one lad spread-eagled in the dust, the other still clutching his sword but no longer with intent to use it. Rounding on the rest, who were already putting distance between them and the culprits, he issued his instructions.

'Go about your business. Unless you wish the Master or my lord of Warwick to hear about this disgraceful affair.' Then to the two dishevelled combatants, first offering a hand to pull one of them to his feet: 'You bring no credit to your families. Would you draw arms in the presence of the Queen?' He gestured in my direction. 'Make your bows!'

They did, shame-faced, one trying to brush the dust of the courtyard from his tunic. The rest of the conversation I did not hear. It proceeded for some time, low-voiced and mostly from Owen, monosyllabic and sullen from the lads. One such comment earned a cuff round the ear from Owen.

'Do it now.'

Although his order was soft-voiced, there was an immediate, if reluctant, clasp of hands. They were not friends now, but perhaps would be by tomorrow.

'There will be a penance for such stupidity,' Owen announced. 'You need to learn that the Queen's Household will not be disturbed by such ill-bred behaviour. Use your wits next time before you decide to settle a minor squabble with cold steel. And as you are both as much to blame as the other.'

He handed a sword back to one with a punch to the shoulder, gave a rough scrub to the hair of the other. 'A thorough cleaning out of the dovecote will give you pause for thought for the rest of the day.' A ripple of laughter touched me. He had chosen a noisome punishment, but there was no dissent from either. 'Now go. And show your belated respect to the Queen.'

They bowed again.

As I acknowledged them I saw Warwick, alerted by the raised voices, standing in the entrance from the Lower Ward. He had chosen not to intervene, but now walked forward stern-faced. The lads bowed rigidly and left through the same doorway at a run. Warwick grinned. The two men exchanged opinions, watching the squires disappear in the direction of the dovecote. I observed for a moment then left them to it.

The little scene stayed with me as I walked slowly back to join my damsels. It had piqued my interest: nothing out of the ordinary for a household of so many diverse souls, where conflict was frequent and often bloody in its outcome, but it had answered all my inner questions. Physical desire for a man could reduce a woman to terrible weakness, driving her to commit any number of irrational acts. But to desire and respect that same man? Owen Tudor had called to my soul in that moment of strict authority and grave compassion, as if he had known what it was to be the underdog, or the one unfairly accused, both injustices driving the boys to fight it out. Owen had meted out firm-handed but fair retribution.

Even more impressive, Owen Tudor had enough of a reputation in Young Henry's court to be obeyed instantly. Authority sat well on him. The lads had accepted his punishment, obeyed his commands, even though they might see the ultimate hand of judgement over them as Warwick's. They had vanished in the direction of the dovecote with alacrity, resigned to the rigours of the acrid, dusty toil apportioned to them.

Out of nowhere, I considered something I had never even thought about. My husband, Henry, had ignored his squires, young lads lifted out of their families and dropped into this strange world of the royal court where the demands on them were great. Sometimes they were lonely and homesick in the first years. Henry had barely noticed them, other than as young men to train up into knighthood. Edmund Beaufort had had no time for them, unless he had a need for their labours, co-opting them into some scheme for rough play or celebration. He had no patience when they did not obey instantly. Owen Tudor had known the lads by name. He had dealt with them with patience, with compassion. With a depth of understanding such as he had shown to me.

I had thought I did not know him well enough to share his bed. Now I was beginning to learn. And, yes, he was a man I could admire.

What path did we travel together, having reached this level of acknowledgement between us? *I will go to the ends of the earth with you, Owen Tudor,* I had vowed. *I will guard you well,* he had replied. It sounded well—but we travelled nowhere together for a considerable time, neither did I need guarding, for there was no occasion for us to be together in any real sense.

First St Winifred came between us. Young Henry was fascinated by the story of the virtuous lady, decapitated at the hands of the Welsh Prince Caradoc who had threatened her virtue, followed by her miraculous healing and restoration to life. Young Henry expressed a wish to visit the holy well in the northern fastnesses of Wales. I explained that it was too far.

'My father went on pilgrimage there. He went to pray before the battle of Agincourt,' Young Henry said. How had he known that? 'I wish to go. I wish to pray to the holy St Winifred before I am crowned King.'

'It is too far.'

'I will go. I insist. I will kneel at the spring on her special day.'

I left it to Warwick to explain that the saint's day on the third day of November and young Henry's coronation on the fifth day would not allow for a journey across the width of the country.

So we celebrated St Winifred at Windsor instead—earlier than her special day—but Owen's preparations filled Young Henry with the requisite excitement. We prayed for St Winifred's blessing, commending her bravery and vital spirit, and my coffers bought a silver bowl for Young Henry to present to her. Father Benedict had looked askance at making such a fuss of a Welsh saint—and a woman at that—but if King Henry, the victor at Agincourt, had seen fit to honour her, then so would we.

It was a magnificent occasion.

And then within the day all was packed up and we were heading to Westminster for the crowning of my son. Would Owen and I ever find the opportunity to do more than follow the demands of travel and Court life? It seemed that I would need all of Winifred's perseverance.

On the fifth day of November I stood beside Young Henry when he was crowned King of England. How ridiculously young he looked at eight years, far too small for the coronation throne. Instead they arranged a chair, set up on a step, with a fringed tester embroidered with Plantagenet lions and Valois fleurs-de-lys to proclaim his importance, and with a tasselled cushion for his feet. Kneeling before his slight figure, I was one of the first to make the act of fealty, wrought by maternal worries.

Pray God he manages to keep hold of the sceptre and orb.

His eyes were huge with untold anxieties when the crown of England was held over his head by two bishops. It was too large, too heavy for him to wear for any length of time, so a simple coronet placed on his brow made a show of sanctity. Henry would have been proud, even more so if his son had not taken off the coronet at the first opportunity during the ceremonial banquet to inspect the jewels in it, before handing it to me to hold, complaining that it made his head ache.

I saw Warwick sigh. My son was very young for so great an honour, but he received his subjects with a sweet smile and well-rehearsed words, before becoming absorbed in the glory of the boar's head enclosed in a gilded pastry castle.

Owen accompanied me to Westminster, but we may as well have been as far apart as the sun and moon.

And then home to Windsor to mark the ninth anniversary of Young Henry's birth on the sixth day of December with a High Mass and the feast and a tournament, with opportunities for the younger pages and squires to show off their skills. Henry did not shine, and became querulous when beaten at a contest with small swords.

'But I am King,' he stormed. 'Why do I not win?'

'You must show your worthiness to be King,' I reproved him gently. 'And when you do not, you must be gracious in defeat.'

'I will not!'

There was little grace in Young Henry and I sensed he would never be the warrior his father had been. Perhaps he would make his fame as a man of learning and holiness. Whatever the future held for my child, as the holy oil was smeared on his brow I felt I had done my duty by my husband, who had in some manner left me, simply by his death, to care for his son. Perhaps I was free now to follow my desire to be with Owen Tudor.

And then it was Christmas and the New Year gift-giving and Twelfth Night.

What of Owen and me?

There was no Owen and me.

After that kiss in the chapel, soft as a whisper on my mouth, we were forced back into the roles of mistress and servant. My cheek healed with no opportunity for a repetition of such an injury. The exigencies of travel, of endless celebrations, an influx of important guests who demanded my time and Owen's, and the resulting shortage of accommodation all worked against us. Neither of us was at leisure to contemplate even a stolen moment. There were no stolen moments. Edmund might have seduced me at the turn of the stair with hot kisses, but there was no seduction from Owen Tudor. In public Owen treated me with the same grave composure that he had always done.

So how did I survive? How were my nerves calmed when I was close to him, wanting nothing more than to step into his arms but knowing that it could not be until…? Until when? Sometimes I felt we would remain with this harsh distance separating us, like a stretch of impassable and turbulent water, for ever.

And yet there was a wooing, the most tender of wooings from a man who had nothing to give but the wage I paid him, and who could not pin his heart to his sleeve, even if he were of a mood to do so. I suspected that Owen was too solemn for the pinning of hearts.

There was a wooing in those months when we never exchanged a word in private, for I was the recipient of gifts. None of any value, but through them I knew that Owen Tudor courted me as if I were his love in some distant Welsh village and he a fervent suitor. The charm of it wrapped me around for I had no experience of it. Henry had had no need to woo me. I had come to his bed as the result of a signature on a document. Edmund had engaged me in a whirlwind seduction with no time for anything as gentle as courtship. From Owen, it was the small offerings, the simple thought of giving behind them, that took me by surprise and won my heart for ever.

How I treasured them. A dish of dates, plump and exotic, freshly delivered from beyond the seas, sent to me in my chamber. A handful of pippins, stored since the autumn harvest, but still firm and sweet. A fine carp, richly cooked in almond milk, served to me at my table—served only to me—by Thomas my page under orders from Owen. A cup of warm, spiced hippocras brought to my chamber by Guille on a cold morning when rime coated the windows. Had Henry or Edmund even noticed what I ate? Had they considered my likes and dislikes? Owen knew that I had a sweet tooth.

And not only that. My lute was newly and expertly strung by morning—one of the strings having snapped the previous evening—before I had even asked for it to be done. Would Henry have done that for me? I think he would have purchased a new lute. Edmund would not have noticed. When we suffered a plague of mice in the damsels' quarters, I was recipient of a striped kitten. The mice were safe enough, but its antics made us laugh. I knew where the gift had come from.

Nothing inappropriate. Nothing to cause comment or draw the eye. Except for that of Beatrice, who observed casually one morning when a basket of fragrant apple logs appeared in my parlour, 'Master Owen has been very attentive recently.'

'More than usual?' I queried with a fine show of insouciance.

'I think so.' Her eyes narrowed.

And the gestures continued. A rose, icily preserved and barely unfurled. Where had he found that in January? An intricate hood, the leather fashioned and stitched with a pretty tuft of feathers, for my new merlin. I knew whose capable fingers had executed the stitching. And for the New Year giftgiving, a crucifix carved with astonishing precision from that same applewood, polished and gleaming, left for me anonymously and without explanation on my *prie-dieu*.

And what did I give him? I knew I had not the freedom to give, as he had to me under the cover of the household, but the tradition of rewarding servants at Twelfth Night made it possible. I gave him a bolt of cloth, rich blue damask, as dark and sumptuous as indigo, to be made up into a tunic. I could imagine it becoming him very well.

Owen thanked me formally. I smiled and thanked him for

his services to me and my people. Our eyes caught for the merest of breaths then he bowed again and stood aside for others to approach.

My cheeks were aflame. Was no one else aware of the burning need that shimmered in the air between us? Beatrice was.

'I hope you know what you're about, my lady,' she remarked with a caustic glance.

Oh, I did. And after the weeks of thwarted love it could not come fast enough.

'When can I be with you?'

It was the question I had longed to hear from him.

'Come to my room,' I replied. 'Between Vespers and Compline.'

It was January, bleak and cold, and the court had slipped into its winter regime of survival: keeping warm; tolerating the endless dark when there was no light in the sky when we rose and it had vanished again by supper. But my blood raced hotly. The physical consummation of our love had to be. I wanted to be with him for I loved him with an outpouring of passion I knew not how to express. All I knew was that I loved him and he loved me.

And I had to take Guille into my confidence. She simply nodded as if she knew I could do no other, opening the door for him, closing it without a glance as she left us.

'I'll make sure you are not disturbed, my lady,' she had promised. She did not judge me too harshly.

And there he stood, Owen Tudor, illuminated by a shimmer of candles because, perhaps out of trepidation at the last, I had lit my room as if for a religious rite. Dark-clad, hair dense as the damask I had given him, face sternly glamorous, his presence overwhelmed my bedchamber, and me. But not quite. I knew what I would do.

'Will you run from me?' he asked softly, not moving from the door, giving me all the time in the world.

'Not this time.' The words rasped a little on an indrawn breath.

He raised his chin a little. 'I have nothing to give you but what you see.'

'It is enough.'

He walked slowly around my chamber, dousing the candles as if it were a final task as my servant, leaving the one beside the bed to flicker and paint shadows on the entwined flowers embroidered on my chamber robe. Drawing back the curtains of my bed, he held out his hand to me. 'My lady?' There was just the hint of a query, still allowing me the freedom to choose.

I did not move. I could not take that final step just yet.

'I have to say that I don't know...' I swallowed and tried again. 'It is just that...' And I raised my hands in despair. 'I have no idea how I should make love with a man. How I should make myself desirable to him.'

His expression showed no pity. Owen took the step towards me and laid his fingers on my lips. 'It is of no account. I will show you. I will lead and you will follow, as you will.'

And I did, allowing him dominion over me, following into undreamed-of paths of delight. It did not matter if my responses were clumsy and untutored. If he noted my ignorance, it made no difference. Between the caress of his two palms I came alive and learned what I did not know, that the physical bond between a man and a woman could be more than duty and necessity. It could be something dearly sought and much enjoyed. It could be blinding, blazing with a need that seared and consumed, then rekindled in driving passion. It could be a wordless bond of shared laughter and intimate caresses to enclose us in our own private world, a universe of two people. It could be as soft as a dove's breast, as tender as my kitten's paw. I could not have guessed at the half of it. I revelled in Owen Tudor's smooth skin and firm flesh, the experienced fingers and lips that stole my soul.

'My loved one. My brightest star of the firmament. Heart of my heart.'

Owen talked to me, even when his voice was ragged, his breathing under duress. His endearments shook me as the slide of his mouth from throat to breast awakened all the senses I had not known I possessed. Beyond control I cried out. And then again there was no need for words for we were flooded with the reality of what we had created between us.

His hair was a tangle of black silk against my breast and I wept with the wonder of it, and when it became too much for me to bear I buried my face against his shoulder that was wet with my tears.

'Sleep now,' he murmured against my mouth. 'You have travelled far and long, and you have travelled alone. You are no longer alone, my beautiful Katherine. You are at rest.'

My heart settled. I could not contemplate the superlative wonder of being together.

'What are you thinking?' I asked when sense and some semblance of control had returned to us. My eyes were dry at last, but I was thankful for the concealment provided by the bed hangings. Owen's eyes were closed, his face once more austere in repose, but then his mouth curved and his fingers linked with mine.

'That if I were a man of substance, I would carry you off from here, across Offa's Dyke.'

'What is Offa's Dyke?'

'The old border between Wales and England, marked by banks and ditches constructed by King Offa to keep the Welsh out of England.' His smile glimmered in the candlelight. 'Not that it worked. The Welsh have always had a habit of raiding across the border and enjoying the benefits of English live-stock.'

'Would I like it? Across Offa's Dyke?'

'Of course. It is my home. And once we were there I would wed you.'

I thought it was said carelessly, Owen tottering on the edge of sleep. 'No, you would not,' I murmured.

'Why would I not?'

'Because if you were a man of substance, you would lose everything you owned.'

Which woke him. Eyes open, dark with emotion, his lips tightened, thinned. 'And of course, as you well know, I have nothing to lose.'

I had not intended to spur so bitter a reaction, and did not fully understand it, but regretful of my thoughtlessness I sought for a less contentious issue. 'Tell me what it is like to be Welsh, living in England. Is it any different from being French and living here?'

But he would not say beyond 'I expect the English regard us all as foreigners out of the same disreputable bag'. I couldn't persuade him further.

'Then tell me about your family,' I said. 'You know all about mine. Tell me about your Welsh ancestors.'

It was a question destined to curtail even the mildest of confidences. He would not.

'It is like searching for meat in a Lenten pie!'

'Let it lie, Katherine,' he whispered. 'It is not important. It has no bearing on us.'

Nothing about his life before his arrival at Henry's Court could be squeezed out of him. I gave up and lived in the moment, sinking into the joy of it, except that there was one issue

I was compelled, against all sense, to raise. I placed my hand on his chest, where his heart beat.

'You did not like Edmund Beaufort, did you?'

It was a ghost between us, maliciously hovering, that I felt the need to exorcise, even if it resulted in Owen condemning me for my lack of judgement. I recalled the disdain that had clamped Owen's mouth on a former occasion when I had not understood. And as if he sensed my trepidation, Owen rolled, gathering me up into his arms so that he could look at me, his initial response surprising me by its even-handedness.

'He is a man of ability and wit with a powerful name and inheritance. I expect he will be a great politician and a first-rate soldier and an asset to England.' Then his arms tightened round me. 'I detested him. He saw your vulnerability and the chance for his personal gain, and he laid siege.'

Held tight against his chest, I turned my face into him. 'I am sorry.'

His arms tightened further. 'I don't blame you.'

'But I do. I should have seen what he was, what he wanted. I was warned often enough.'

'You were just a witless female.' He kissed me, stopping my words when I would have objected. 'How could you know? Beaufort could charm the carp out of the fish pond and onto the plate, complete with sauce and trimmings.' A little silence fell. 'He did not charm me. But *you* do, *ngoleuni fy mywyd*.'

'What does—?'

His mouth captured mine, his body demanded my obedience to his and I gave it willingly.

We never spoke of Edmund Beaufort again. He was no part of my life now, and never would be again.

'When did you first love me?' I asked, as any woman must when first deluged in emotion.

'When I first came to your household. I cannot recall a time when I did not love you.'

Drowsing, we knew our snatched moment together was rushing to a close. The daily routine at Windsor, the final service of Compline to end the day, claimed us back from our bright idyll.

'How did I not know?' I asked, trying to remember Owen in those days after Henry's death.

His lips were soft against my hair, my temple. 'Your thoughts were trapped in desolation. Why would you notice a servant?'

I pushed myself so that I could read his face. 'And yet you were content to serve me, knowing that I did not *see* you.'

Owen's smile was wry, so were his words. 'Content? Never that. Sometimes I felt the need to shout my love from the battlement walk, or announce it from the dais, along with the offering of the grace cup. But there was no future in it, or so I thought. I was simply there to obey your commands and—'

I stopped his words with my fingers. 'I am ashamed,' I whispered.

Owen's kiss melted the shame from my heart.

I glowed. I walked with a light step as my heart sang. Light of his life, he had called me. I could not imagine such happiness.

'He makes you content, my lady,' Beatrice observed carefully.

'Yes.' I did not pretend to misunderstand her. 'Is there gossip?'

'No.'

I thanked the Holy Mother for her inexplicable kindness as I lived every day for the time when Owen would blow out the candle and we would be enclosed in our world that was neither English nor French nor Welsh.

★ ★ ★

'What is our future?' I asked one morning when, in the light of a single candle and before the household was awake, Owen struggled, cursing mildly, into tunic and hose.

'I don't know. I have no gift for divination.' Applying himself to his belt in the near darkness, he looked across to where I still lay in tangled linens, and seeing the gleam of fear in my eyes, he abandoned the buckle and sat on the edge of the bed. 'We will live for the present. It is all we have, and it is enough.'

'Yes. It is enough.'

'I will come to you when I can.'

He took my lips with great sweetness. I loved him enough, trusted him enough, to put myself and our uncertain future into his care. How foolish we were to believe that we could control what fate determined.

14

AS SPRING BURST the buds on the oak trees, I became unwell. Not a fever or a poisoning, or even an ague that often struck inhabitants of Windsor with the onset of rains and vicious winds in April. Nothing that I could recognise, rather a strange other-worldliness that grew, until I felt wholly detached from the day-to-day demands of court life. It was as if I sat, quite isolated, with no necessity for me to speak or act but simply to watch what went on around me.

My damsels going about their normal duties, stitching, praying, singing, my household absorbed in its routines of rising at dawn and retiring with the onset of night. I participated, as insubstantial as a ghost, for it meant nothing to me. Those around me seemed to me as far distant as the stars that witnessed my sleepless dark hours. Voices echoed in my head. Did I hold conversations? I must have done, but I did not always recall what I had said. When I touched the cloth of my robes or the platter on which my bread was served, my fingertips did not always sense the surface, whether hard or soft, warm or cold. And the bright light became my bitter enemy, reflecting and refracting into shards that pierced my mind. I groaned with the pain, retching into the garderobe until my belly was raw, and then I was driven to my chamber with curtains pulled to douse me in darkness until I could withstand the light once more.

I covered my affliction from my damsels as best I could. Admitting it to no one, I explained my lack of appetite with recourse to the weather, the unusual heat that caused us all to swelter. Or to the foetid miasma from drains that were in need of thorough cleansing. Or a dish of oysters that had not sat well with me.

I was not fooled by these excuses. Fear shivered along the tender surface of my skin and my belly lurched as my mind flew in ever-tightening circles of incomprehension. Or perhaps I comprehended only too well. Had I not seen these symptoms before? The distancing, the isolation, the uncertainty of temper? Oh, I had. As a child I had seen it and fled from it.

'I am quite well,' I snapped, when Beatrice remarked that I looked pale.

'Perhaps some fresh air, a walk by the river,' Meg suggested.

'I don't want fresh air. I wish to be left alone. Leave me!'

My women became wary—as they should, for my temper had become unpredictable.

I could not sew. The stitches faded from my sight or crossed over each other in a fantasy of horror. I closed my eyes and thrust it aside, blocking out the sideways glances of concern from my women.

With terror in my belly, I made excuses that Owen should not come to my room, pleading the woman's curse, at the same time as I forced myself to believe that my affliction was some trivial disturbance that would pass with time.

Until I fell.

So public, so unexpected, one moment I was clutching the voluminous material of my houppelande, gracefully lifting it in one hand to allow me to descend the shallow flight of stairs into the Great Hall, and the next, halfway down, my balance became a thing of memory. My skirts slid from nerveless fingers, and I was stretching out a hand for someone, something, to hold on to. There was nothing. The painted tiles, suddenly seeming to be far too distant below me, swam, the patterns emerging and fading with nauseous rapidity.

My knees buckling, I fell.

It was, rather than a fall, an ignominious tumble from step to step, but it was no less painful or degrading. I felt every jar, every scrape and bump, until I reached the bottom in a heap of skirts and veiling. My breath had been punched from my lungs, and for a moment I simply lay there, vision distorted and black-edged, wishing the floor would open up and swallow me whole. After all these years as Princess and Queen, still I could not acknowledge being the centre of everyone's attention, for my household to witness my lack of dignity.

The floor did not oblige me, and my surroundings pushed back into my mind again, all sharp-edged with brittle sounds. Hands came to lift me, faces that I did not recognise—but I must have known them all—shimmered in my vision. Voices came in and out of my consciousness.

'I am not hurt,' I said, but no one took any notice. Perhaps the words did not even develop from thought to speech.

'Move aside.'

There was a voice I knew. My mind framed his name.

'Go and fetch wine. A bowl of water to Her Majesty's chamber. Fetch her physician. Now allow me to...'

The orders went on and on as arms supported me, lifted me and carried me back up the stairs. I knew who held me. He must have been in the Great Hall as I made my unfortunate entrance. I turned my face against his chest, breathing in the scent of him, but I did not speak, not even when he whispered against my hair.

'Katherine. My poor girl.'

His heart thudded beneath my cheek, far stronger than the flutter in my own breast. I felt a need to tell him that I was in no danger but I did not have the strength. All I knew was that I felt safe and that whatever ailed me could do me no harm. Fanciful, I decided. Did I not know how dangerous my symptoms could become?

Soon, too soon, I was in my chamber and had been laid down on my bed, and there was my physician, muttering distractedly, Guille wringing her hands, Beatrice demanding an explanation. Even Alice had heard and descended hotfoot. I felt comfort from them, their soft female voices, but then Owen's arms left me and I sensed his quiet withdrawal to the doorway. Then he was gone.

From sheer weakness, I turned my face into my pillow.

'A severe case of female hysteria. Her humours are all awry.'

My physician, after questioning Beatrice and Guille and peering at me, frowned at me as if it were all my doing.

'My lady is never ill,' stated Alice, as if the fault must lie with my physician.

'I know what I see,' he responded with a lively sneer that even I in my muddled mind could sense. 'A nervous complaint that has brought on trembling of the limbs—that's what it is. Or why is it that Her Majesty would fall?'

I was undressed and put to bed like a child, a dose of powdered valerian in wine administered with orders not to stir for the rest of the day. Nor did I, for I fell into sleep, heavy and dreamless. When I surfaced, it was evening and the room dim. Guille sat by my bed, nodding gently, her stitching forgotten in her lap. My headache had abated and my thoughts held more clarity.

Owen. My first thought, my only thought.

But Owen would not come to me. It would not be acceptable that he should enter my room when I was ill and my women with me. I plucked restlessly at the bed linen. What had they done with my dragon brooch, which I always wore? When I stirred in a futile attempt to discover it, Guille stood and approached.

'Where is it?' I whispered. 'The silver dragon?' It seemed to me to be the most important question in the world.

Guille hushed me, told me to drink again, and I did. But when she took the cup from me she folded my fingers over the magical creature, and I smiled.

'Sleep now,' she murmured with compassion.

I need you, Owen.

It was my last thought before I fell back into sleep.

With dawn I woke, refreshed but too lethargic to stir. I broke my fast with ale and bread, leaning back against my pillows, surprised to find my appetite restored.

'Your people are concerned, my lady,' Guille informed me as she placed on the bed beside me a book in gilded leather. 'From the Young King,' she announced, mightily impressed with the thickness of the gold embossing. 'He said I must tell you that he will pray for you when he has completed his lessons. But I have to say—I think you should not read yet awhile, my lady.'

And I laughed softly, for Young Henry's priorities were always predictable. At the same time, I wished the book had been from Owen—but, then, he would not send me a prayer book. He would send me a book of stories, probably of Welsh lovers. And I would read it, however long it took me.

There was a knock on my door and my heart leapt as Guille went to open it. But it was Alice who came purposefully towards my bed.

'May I speak with you, my lady?'

I stretched out my hand. 'Oh, Alice. Come and relieve my

boredom. I feel much stronger.' My vision was clearer and my whole body felt calm and sure. My only hurt from the previous day was the bruising where thigh and shoulder had made contact with the steps. Painful, but not fatal. My fears over my previous symptoms, which seemed to have vanished with the valerian-induced sleep, had also faded to a mere whisper of light-headedness. Perhaps I had been mistaken after all. Perhaps my fears were unfounded.

Alice pulled up a stool and waved Guille and her offer of wine away. She leaned forward, arms folded on my bed, eyes level with mine and her voice barely above a whisper.

'Let me look at you.' She narrowed her gaze, scanning my face.

'What do you see?'

'You look drawn and there's a transparency about you.'

'I will be better after I rest,' I assured her. 'My physician—'

'Your physician is a fool of a man who can't recognise what's at the end of his pointed nose. I have come to talk to you, my lady.'

'I am in no danger.'

'Danger? That's to be seen.'

My fears, which I had so light-heartedly cast off, promptly returned fourfold. If what I had suspected was indeed so, that the curse that had laid its hand on my father had touched me also, had Alice seen it too? Had she noticed that sometimes I was distraught?

'If what I suspect is true,' Alice remarked, 'you need some advice, my lady. And from someone who will not mince her words.'

'What do you fear?' I dreaded the answer. She must have seen my vagueness, heard my snap of temper, however hard I had tried to curb it. My women must have gossiped about my inconsistency so that it had reached even Alice. I found myself gripping her arm in my fear. 'What ails me, Alice?'

'I think you are carrying a child.'

Shock drove all thoughts from my mind: frozen, I sat and stared at Alice. A child. I was carrying a child. So perhaps it was not what I had most feared, the onset of a terrible fragility of mind from which I would never be free. Perhaps it was this unlooked-for child that had unsettled my mind and stirred my body to nausea and my mind to ill temper. But I recalled none of those symptoms when I had carried Young Henry. I had been full of health, calm and hopeful of a golden future, not the weak mewling, snappish thing that had fallen down the stairs. But, without doubt, this child, newly growing within me, was the cause of my sufferings.

In that moment of revelation I experienced relief so strong that I laughed aloud.

'I see nothing to laugh at,' Alice lectured. 'Well, my lady? Have you fallen for a child?'

'I don't know.'

She clicked her tongue as if addressing an ignorant maid-servant. 'Have your courses stopped?'

I thought about it. Perhaps they had, but they had never been regular to any degree and my recent mindlessness had impaired my memory. But, yes, it had been at least two months, perhaps three. I was carrying Owen's child. Owen's child... A little spurt of delight—but then of fear—began to lick along my arms, so that I shivered despite the heat in the room.

Alice took my hands in hers and squeezed as if she could make me concentrate. Not that her questions made any difference to my predicament.

'Did you not take precautions?'

'Yes. I did.'

'But not well enough, it seems.'

I blushed, hot blood rushing to colour my cheeks. I had been wantonly careless. In my brief marriage to Henry it had been necessary to be fertile and conceive as fast as possible, not prevent the possibility. With Owen, between my imprecise knowledge and Guille's flawed memory of drinking the seeds of Queen Anne's lace steeped in wine, I had fallen headlong into the net set to entrap all women who indulged in sinful union outside the blessing of Holy Mother Church.

'You should have come to me,' Alice said crossly.

'And admitted to you that I was steeped in sin?'

'Better to be steeped in sin and safe from conception than carrying the bastard child of a servant!'

I inhaled sharply at her hard judgement.

'What were you thinking? Do I need to ask who the father is? I don't think I do.' She shook her head, her fingers digging into my wrists, her voice anguished with what I could only think was distress. 'How could you do this, my lady? A liaison with a servant of your own household. A man who has no breeding, no income, no status. How could you even consider it? And now a child, out of wedlock! What will Gloucester say?' Her eyes widened. 'What will he do?'

'I don't care what Gloucester says.' I freed my hands from hers and inspected my palms, my fingers spread wide, as if I would see an answer written there. I carried Owen's child and I could see no future that was not shrouded in uncertainty, yet a strange happiness had me in its grip. I looked up, frowning a little: 'What do I do now, Alice?'

A significant pause. 'You would not consider ending—?'

My hand on hers stopped her. 'No. Never that.' It was the one certainty. Whatever difficulties this child brought to me, I would carry it to term. After Henry's death I had been forced to accept that I would never have another child. Now I carried a child by a man I adored. 'You must never speak of such things,' I said fiercely. 'I want this baby.'

Alice sighed but nodded. 'As I thought. It was a hard burden that Gloucester placed on you. It was not natural.'

'But what do I do? Advise me, Alice.'

She pursed her lips. 'You can hide it for a little time. Houppelandes have their uses, even if they are too cumbersome for words. But after that...' To my astonishment her eyes were moist with tears.

'What is it?'

'I don't know. I really don't. I see no happiness for you in this.'

No happiness? What was the worst Gloucester could do? Take my child from me at birth? Part me from Owen? It was not beyond the realms of belief.

'Gloucester will persist in preserving your immaculate reputation.' Alice's words echoed my thoughts.

'Rather than allowing me to be seen as a slut who allowed a servant to get a bastard child on her,' I added, fear making me unacceptably crude. I looked at her, at the tears on her cheeks, although I knew the answer before I asked the question. 'Do I tell him?'

'Yes. Tell him. You can't keep it secret long—not if you intend to continue to share his bed. Ah, my lady... Why did you do it?'

I replied without hesitation. 'Because I love him and I have no doubts of his love for me. It is given unconditionally. I have never known such joy.'

Alice sniffed and wiped away her tears. 'What if Gloucester insists that you dismiss him?'

The answer was there, before me. I had never fought for anything in my life, but I would fight for my right to be fulfilled at the side of the man I loved. For the first time in my life I felt a surge of power. In this one crucial battle I would not be dictated to or manipulated by the ambitions of another.

'I will not dismiss him,' I said quietly, startled to hear the pride in my voice. 'He is an exceptional man. I will not give him up. I am Queen Dowager. I am Queen Mother: how can Gloucester force me to dismiss servants from my own household? I will not. I will not live without him.'

Alice scowled, then smiled bleakly through the tears. 'If I were young again and unwed, neither would I.'

Not once had we mentioned his name between us, but it lay like a blessing in my heart.

Alone again, with Alice's words stark in my mind—*I see no happiness for you in this*—as was unfortunately my nature I was not so sanguine.

I am carrying your child.

I imagined saying it to Owen, and quailed.

'What will we do?' I had asked Alice before she had left me, but she had lifted her hands helplessly.

'I don't know. I have no advice to give.'

A liaison with a servant of your own household. A man who has no breeding, no income, no status...

My throat was dry with apprehension but I rose, dressed in a favourite emerald velvet with miniver cuffs, all worked with gold knot-work, and sent Thomas off to arrange a meeting with Owen in the audience chamber, the scene of our first charged acknowledgement of what we meant to each other.

With Guille in attendance to give me decorous company, I was there before he arrived, seated on one of the stools generally occupied by petitioners who came to ask for royal intervention, aware of the same watchful audience of stitched feral eyes. I stood as he entered and waved Guille to the far side of

the room to stand against the leafy forest. Even if she overheard, it would not matter. She would know soon enough.

I thought he looked more than a little severe, formally and
richly clad as he was, complete with chain of office, for Young
Henry was expected to dine with me. But when he saw me,
when he stood from his habitual show of courtesy, his mouth
was soft. I resisted blurting out my news but held my tongue,
heart thudding against my ribs. What would he say? What
would any man say, receiving this awkward confession? All
my inner certainty was in danger of leaching away.

'You have a request, my lady?'

'Merely to speak with you. Don't mind Guille,' as he glanced
in her direction. 'Her loyalty is not to be questioned.'

He moved to stand before me, not to touch me but to sur-
vey my face as if he might read all he wished to know there.
And he smiled at last, as if a weight had fallen from him.

'You look restored.'

His beautiful voice washed over me, calming me, restoring
my earlier knowledge of what I wanted, what was right. 'I am.'

'Before you fell I thought you looked strained and sad.' His
voice was suddenly ragged. 'Before God, Katherine, I have
been torn apart, not knowing, not being able to come to you.'

'I was sad, but no longer.' I touched his sleeve. 'I heard that
it was you who carried me to my room. I did not know what
was real and what was in my mind.'

He lifted my hand and kissed it. 'You fell at my feet.'

'Then that was fortunate.'

'I hope your maid is discreet. I can no longer be discreet.'

Before he could take me into his arms, for that was clearly
his intent, I stopped him, my hand pressed against his chest.

'Owen…' I arranged and rearranged the simple words. And
finally I stated them baldly. 'I am carrying your child. That
is why I fell.'

His face paled, eyes darkened, all movement suspended. And then he slowly allowed his arms to fall.

'Owen...' I whispered.

But he swung away from me, to stride to the windows that ran along one side, away from the vivid forest, the hunted and the huntsmen. He did not stare down into the Inner Ward, as I expected. Instead, he turned his back to the fast-scudding clouds that heralded an approaching storm and looked at me. Still silent, thoughts masked, emotions impossible to read, he simply stood. As I walked slowly forward I could see how shallow his breathing was, how rigid his chain of office lay on his chest so that the gems were dark and opaque. His hands were splayed against the stones of the wall at his back.

'Are you angry?' I asked.

'Yes.' And as if all his emotions had suddenly re-ignited, he spun from me to drive his fist into the carved window surround. Owen Tudor was no longer my impassive Master of Household. When I placed my hand on his shoulder, I could feel the vibration of his heart beating as hard as mine.

'Are you angry with me?' I asked.

'How could I be?'

But still he did not turn, so I stepped round so that I could witness his profile.

'You're scowling,' I said, hearing the tremble in my voice.

'I should be whipped for this. I should have known.' His expression was savage, his tone no less so. 'What was I thinking, to put my own physical gratification before your safety? Before your reputation?'

'I am in no danger.'

'Only from the filth that will be flung at you by the court scandalmongers.'

'They will fling it at both of us.'

'You don't deserve it.' Now he looked at me, eyes wide,

jaw hard clenched. 'Forgive me, Katherine. Forgive me, forgive me for my wretched selfishness. If I had loved you less, it would never have come to this. If I had loved you more, I would never have touched you.'

I had no difficulty in replying. 'But if you had never touched me, I would have died from longing.' I tried to smile as I leaned to kiss his cheek, but he stepped back, away, hands raised against me.

'How much I have hurt you.'

'But do you not want this child?' I asked. 'A child born out of our love?'

He inhaled sharply, so that now the gems deep set in his chain gleamed balefully in the stormy light.

'Can you ask me that? How would I not desire a child of your blood and mine? But this is no perfect world where we can choose. I have cast you into a maelstrom.' His gaze pierced mine, precise as a dagger. 'And do you know the worst thing?' he demanded. 'I don't know how to put it right for you.'

But I did. There it was, newborn in my mind, as clear and tempting as a sparkling pool for a thirsty traveller, sweeping away all my irresolution.

'I do,' I said. 'I *know*.' I was so certain, I who had never been certain in her life. 'I know how to put it right for both of us.'

'Nothing I can do will.'

I did not hesitate. 'Wed me, Owen.'

If the air had been charged before, now it screamed with tension.

'Wed me, Owen.' I repeated, my words crossing the divide.

'Wed you?'

'Is marriage so distasteful to you?' His thoughts were awry so I drove on, even if it would increase the pain of his refusal if he could not tolerate it. 'Or is it marriage to me that you balk at?'

And as he flung wide his arms, I saw the blood, along the knuckles of his right hand, beginning to drip to the floor, the skin scraped from flesh along the stonework. Showing me, if I was not already aware, just how close to the edge of control he was.

'Your hand,' I said in distress, reaching out to him.

'To Hell with my hand!' He took another step back from me. 'You consider that marriage to me would solve all your problems? To shackle a Valois princess to a penniless servant will make a bad situation even more sordid.'

'Sordid? I won't accept that. I do not consider my situation—as you describe it—to be sordid. Do I not love you? Your position in my household can be redeemed instantly.'

'But my race cannot. God's Blood! Do you know what it is like for a man to be branded *Welsh*?'

'No.' How would I? I was ignorant of all Welshmen, apart from Owen.

'Of course you don't. It is a monstrosity of injustice, of bloody vengeance that has wilfully brought about the destruction of Welsh pride, of all our heritage and tradition. Of our rights before the law.'

It still meant little to me. Why would this deter him from marriage? I could not understand the rage that lit his face with such rampant power. In spite of everything, all I could think was that he was magnificent in his anger.

'I have nothing to offer you, Katherine,' he continued. 'Nothing at all.'

'Why would you need to offer me anything? I don't need material things. I have my own properties—'

'Katherine!' He silenced me, one hand raised, his voice dropping to make a harsh, even statement. 'That's what makes it so much worse. You have a queen's dower, while I...' He scrubbed his hands over his face, leaving a smear of blood along his jaw. 'I have too much pride to take you with nothing to give in return.'

My heart wept for this proud man, but I summoned all my courage to reply as evenly as I could. 'Why is pride so important? Is it stronger than love?' I asked. 'I want to be with you. If we were wed, then there would be no impediment. Will you allow pride to stand in our way?' And I was astounded when my question rekindled the wrath.

'By God, I will. I am a servant under your command, and yet I have the blood of Llewellyn the Great in my veins. I lay claim to the same blood as the mighty Owain Glyn Dwr. Yes, I am a proud man.'

'Is that good? The blood of these men?' I had never heard of Llewellyn or of Owain Glyn Dwr. I could barely pronounce them.

'You don't even know!' His answering laugh was savage but he did not mock me. 'They are the best, the finest names. Princes of our people, leading the Welsh to glory in battle, until defeat at the hands of the damned English.'

His impassioned words puzzled me. 'If you are so well born, connected to this Llewellyn the Great, why do you serve me?'

'Because the law has robbed me of all hope of making anything other of my life. God forgive me, Katherine—but I should never have taken you to my bed so thoughtlessly.'

'I thank God that you did.' My mind was already racing along, abandoning this Welsh hero Glyn Dwr and my lover's pride. One thought—one thought alone—clung with sharp claws. 'You say that you are without any means at all.'

'Exactly that. Do you know what you pay me?'

'No.'

'Forty pounds a year. And the provision of clothing so that I might make a good impression on your guests. That would be the value of your husband, Katherine. It is not to be thought of.'

'I think it is perfect. The perfect choice for me.'

'It is a travesty.'

This time it was I who called a halt by the simple expedient of stepping forward two paces and placing my fingers across his lips.

'Any man who risks marriage with me will suffer the confiscation of everything he owns. No man of wealth or land will look at me. But you do.' I smiled at him, willing him to understand. 'You look at me and you have nothing to be stripped from you. You have nothing. You cannot be punished.' I held out my hands to him, my mind suddenly full of the possibilities. If only I could persuade this obstinate man. 'Do you not see, Owen? There will be no retribution, because you have nothing.'

He did not respond enough to take my hands, but I watched as he followed my line of argument.

'I cannot do it, Katherine.'

'Why not? I love you. We have made a child together. Here we have a chance of being together. The only reason I can see for you not wanting me is if you do not love me enough. And if that is so, then you must tell me now.'

I waited, my heart in my mouth. I had not considered that, faced with marriage, he might retract his words of commitment to me. Had I misread the depths of his love?

'If you wait before you tell me,' I warned him, 'it will break my heart so much more. Do you not love me, Owen? Was this idyll merely a product of lust on your part? I can accept that but I won't accept that your pride should stand between us.'

No, I could not accept it at all.

'Lust? By the Rood, Katherine! Is that what you think of me?'

'I might, unless you tell me otherwise.'

Still I waited. The decision was his and he must make it

alone. At last the air moved between us, and Owen took my hands lightly in his, breathing deeply to disperse his wrath.

'You know that I love you,' he stated, every contour of his face finely etched in the strange glimmering light. 'You are with me until I fall asleep. While I sleep you never leave me. And when I awake I see your face in my mind before even I see the light of day.' His lips curved a little. 'You are a surprisingly calculating woman, Katherine.'

'No, I am not,' I said seriously. 'But I have learned that I must fight for what I want. And I want this so much. If I have to be calculating and wilful and manipulative, then I will. Wed me, Owen. Give my child your name, as he deserves.'

'Gloucester might punish you. Have you thought about that?'

'I have. We might both be punished. But if we are wed in the sight of God, what can Gloucester and the Council do to us? I defy Gloucester to make scandal where the Queen Dowager is concerned, and I think if I appealed to Bedford, he would not stand against us.' Confidence blossomed as Owen finally drew me into his arms. He was still thinking, still stubborn, but I was now sure of my ground.

I spoke, my fingers spread wide on his breast. 'If you do not marry me, Owen, they will make me take the veil and my child—our child—will be taken from me.' And I used the last weapon in my armoury. 'I don't think I could forgive you if you allowed your pride to enclose me in a nunnery for the rest of my life and cause our child to be brought up without knowledge of either of us.'

His mouth twisted in bitter self-deprecation. 'Who am I but a disenfranchised Welshman, beaten and despised by his English victors? Who am I to wed a Queen?'

I did not understand 'disenfranchised' so ignored it. 'A

Queen who has never known love. If you love me, you will wed me.'

The planes of his face flattened in near despair. 'Oh, Katherine! Unfair!'

'I know. I'm fighting hard.'

'I don't like it,' he murmured, his breath stirring my hair. 'King's daughter weds landless servant.'

'But I do. Lonely widow weds the man she loves.'

'Beautiful widow of the victor of Agincourt weds disenfranchised commoner.'

'Abandoned widow weds the only man she has ever loved.' How assured I was.

Still he resisted. 'Queen Dowager weds the Master of her Household.'

I pressed my forehead against his chest. How many objections could he find?

'Katherine weds the man who owns her heart.' I sighed. And when he finally kissed me: 'If you will not,' I warned against his mouth, 'then I will remain alone, unloved and unwanted, for ever.'

'That must never be.' Still I waited. 'You are so very precious to me,' he whispered.

'Then, for God's sake, wed me!'

He laughed—and at last he said what I wanted to hear. 'We will do this as tradition dictates.' Sinking to one knee, head bent like a knight in some chivalrous tale of love for his lady, voice clear and low, Owen enclosed my hands in his. 'Wed me, Katherine. Take me as I am, a man without recognition, whose birth and honour stand for nought but a man who swears on the untarnished names of his ancestors that he will love you and honour you. Until death parts us—and beyond.'

Briefly, fleetingly, I recalled Edmund kneeling at my feet in an enchantment of flirtatious laughter, but in the end without honour, casting aside the heart he had entranced. Owen Tudor held that heart in his sure hands. He would never allow it to fall. Love for him filled my breast.

'Will you wed me, Katherine?'

'You know I will. Now stand up so that I might kiss you.'

Alice was waiting for me in my chamber, not exactly glowering but redolent of unease. She had been there for some time, judging by the empty platter and cup at her side. She glanced at Guille, reading who knew what in her lively stare, before she dispatched her. Then demanded, 'Have you told him?'

'Yes.'

'And?'

'We will marry.' I found that I was smiling. So simple a statement of intent. It held all I wanted and for a little time I could close my mind to the tempest that we would stir up, as black and threatening as the clouds that still hemmed Windsor about. 'Owen and I will marry.'

When her breath had returned, Alice said what I knew she would say. 'You cannot. It will break the statute. Your son is not old enough to give his consent, and the Royal Council won't do it. Gloucester will make sure they don't. The law is against you, my lady.'

I linked my hands, loosely, calmly. 'Then I will do it without Young Henry and the Council's consent. I will ignore the law. It is an unjust law and I will not abide by it.'

My lips were still warm from Owen's kisses. I felt that I could face the world, challenge any who stood before me. What strength love can endow.

'Gloucester might take steps to stop you.'

'Then I will not tell Gloucester.' How easy it seemed, yet a little ripple of worry teased at my mind. Was I being impossibly naïve? I neither knew nor cared. My feet were set on the path I had chosen, and I would not divert from it.

'If Gloucester did not chastise you,' Alice persisted, 'he might take his revenge on Owen Tudor.'

The ripple became an onslaught. Would I wilfully bring harm to the man I loved? No, I would not. But the alternative was to live without him, and that I could not do.

'Would you risk that?' Alice asked.

'I must,' I said, my vision clear. 'We have decided. We will stand together, against the whole world if we have to. And this child will be born in wedlock.'

'God bless you, my lady. I will pray for you.'

We decided what we would do, Owen and I. It did not take us long, no more than the time it took to share breath in one kiss. If we wed, we would do so in the full light of day and in the open knowledge of Young Henry's court at Windsor.

What use in hiding a scandalous marriage between the Queen Dowager and her Master of Household? What value to us in a clandestine ceremony if we wished to live openly as man and wife? And as the child grew in me, secrecy was not something to be considered. I might hide my condition beneath my skirts and high waists for a good few weeks but not for ever, and this child would be born without a slur on its name. We would wed now, and damn the consequences, as Owen put it.

'We'll do it in the face of God and man,' Owen declared. 'I'll not hide behind your skirts, Katherine. Neither will we participate in some undisclosed rite that can later be questioned for its legitimacy. We will be man and wife, with all the legal proof necessary.'

Had he thought I would choose a secret ceremony, at dead of night, with no witness but the priest? He did not yet know me well. Or at least not the new Katherine who seemed to have emerged fully fledged under his protective wings. Soon he would know me better.

'No man will ever have the right to label you Owen Tudor's whore,' he continued.

'They will not.'

'Do you think? Gloucester will discover every means possible to prove our marriage false. Forewarned is forearmed, so we'll give him no grounds. I'll take you as my wife under the eye of every man and woman in this damned palace, and be proud of it.'

'And so will I take you as my husband. I will not demean our love, or my position as your wife, by travelling the corridors in cloak and veil to spend a clandestine night with my husband as if I was a whore,' I replied.

My plain speaking surprised him into a laugh. 'It will not be popular.'

It did not need saying, so we did not speak of it again, and it was so simply done, so smoothly arranged, without fuss. Who was there to prevent us? As for my son's permission, I did not tell Young Henry of my plans. He would have done whatever Gloucester or the Council instructed him to do, so I did not burden him with it. As for the law of the land, manipulated by Gloucester—well, my desire to marry was far stronger than my respect for such a statute. I denied its binding on me.

'Do you love me enough to do this?' Owen asked finally when we stood before the door of the chapel. 'Are you truly prepared to face a nation's wrath?'

'Yes.'

'I'll stand with you, whatever happens.'

'And I with you.'

'Then let us do it.' He kissed me. 'When I kiss you again, you will be my wife.'

We exchanged our vows in the magnificence of St George's chapel in Windsor, in the choir built by King Edward III, the weight of past history bearing down on us. No high ceremony here, other than the celebration of love in our hearts. Owen wore a tunic of impressive indigo damask, my gift to him, but no chain of office. Today he was no servant, and would not be so again. Responding to female inclination, I wore a gown that best pleased me, with not one inch of cloth of gold or ermine to mark it as royal. Leopards and fleurs-de-lys were also absent, and I wore my hair loose beneath my veil as if I were a virgin bride.

I made no excuses for my choices, meeting Owen's eye boldly, admiring the figure he made, stern and sure, sword belted to his side, as we stood, face to face before Father Benedict, who twitched with more nerves than either bride or groom. Persuasion had been necessary.

'Your Majesty...' He wrung his hands anxiously. '...I cannot do this thing.'

'I wish it.'

'But my lord of Gloucester—'

'Her Majesty wishes you to wed us,' Owen stated. 'If you will not, there are other priests.'

'Master Tudor! How can you consider this ill-advised act?'

'Will you wed us or not, man?'

Father Benedict gave in with reluctance, but when the moment came the ponderous Latin gave sanctification to what we did, sweeping me back to my marriage with Henry in the church at Troyes with all its ostentation and military show; cloth of gold and leopards and French lilies. Then I had married a King. Now I was marrying a man who owned nothing but my heart.

And our witnesses?

We were not alone. 'We will wed in full public knowledge,'

Owen had vowed, and so we did. Guille carried my missal. My damsels, torn between the appalling scandal and the lure of romance, stood behind me. And every one of us had our senses alert for anyone who might intervene at the last moment and put a stop to this illicit act. Alice had not come, for which I was sorry. She had not been without compassion, but this liaison would be too much to swallow for many. I must resign myself to such disapproval from those I loved.

Father Benedict addressed Owen, his voice uncertain but resigned.

'*Owen Tudor vis accipere Katherine—*'

'No!'

There was an astounded surge of movement through our little congregation and a bolt of fear ripped through me. My breath caught in my throat, I looked at Owen in horror.

'No,' he repeated, but more gently this time, seeing my wide-eyed shock. 'I will wed the lady under my own name, not some bastardised form to allow the English to master it. I am Owain ap Maredudd ap Tudor.'

Father Benedict looked at me. 'Is that what you wish, my lady?'

'Yes, Father,' I said. 'That is what I wish.'

With commendable fortitude, Father Benedict began again, making as good a case of the Welsh syllables as he could.

'*Owain ap Maredudd ap Tudor, vis accipere Katherine, hic…?*'

And we stood hand in hand as I waited for Owen's reply. Would he? By now my nerves were entirely undone, jangling like an ill-tuned lute. Would the danger prove too great at the eleventh hour? But there was no hesitation. None at all. Owen's fingers laced with mine as if, palm to palm, the intimate pressure would seal our agreement.

'*Volo,*' Owen stated. 'I do.'

Father Benedict turned to me.

'*Katherine, vis*—'

Footsteps!

All froze, breath held. The noise of the door pushed open, creaking on its vast hinges, and the clap of shoes on the tiles echoed monstrously. More than one person was approaching. Father Benedict closed his mouth, swallowing the Latin as if it might preserve him from retribution, plucking nervously at his alb. All eyes were turned to the entrance to the choir. The tension could be tasted, the bitterness of aloes.

Not Gloucester, I decided, not a body of soldiers to put a stop to what we did. But if Father Benedict was ordered to halt the ceremony, would he obey? I glanced at him. He was sweating, his eyes glassy. His words hovered on his lips. Owen's right hand released mine and closed round the hilt of his sword.

Holy Mother, I prayed—and then smiled for the first time that day. For there in the doorway stood Alice, accompanied by Joan Asteley and a cluster of chamber women of Henry's personal household. They stepped in and joined my damsels, Alice with a nod of apology and severe demeanour, while I turned back to Father Benedict, the sweetness of relief in my veins, and Owen once more took my hand.

'Father,' I urged, as his eyes remained fixed on the doorway, as if he still expected Gloucester to march through it.

'Forgive me, my lady.' He cleared his throat and blinked, picking up the strands of this unorthodox marriage. '*Katherine, vis accípere Owen…?*'

'*Volo,*' I replied. 'I do.'

We exchanged rings. Owen gave me a battered gold circle. 'It is Welsh gold. A family piece. One of the few pieces of value left to us, and all I have.' I gave him Michelle's ring—because it was Valois, not Plantagenet, and mine to give freely—pushing it onto the smallest of his fingers. And there it was. We were wed. We were man and wife.

Owen bent his head and kissed me as he had promised. *'Rwy'n dy garu di. Fy nghariad, fy un annwyl.'* And he kissed me again. 'I would give you the world on a golden platter if I could. I have nothing to give you but the devotion of my heart and the protection of my body. They are yours for all eternity.'

My hand in his, where it now belonged, we walked from the choir.

No bride gifts, no procession, no feasts with extravagant subtleties. Only a hasty retiring to our chamber where Owen removed my gown, and then his own clothing, and we made our own celebration.

'What did you say?' I whispered, when I lay with my head on his shoulder, my hair in a tangle. 'When you spoke in Welsh and promised me the world?'

'I couldn't manage the world, if you recall.' I heard the smile in his voice as he pressed his mouth against my temple. 'My Welsh offerings were poor things: I love you. My dear one, my beloved.'

I sighed. 'I like that better than the world. Why do you not use your name?'

He hesitated a moment. 'Can you pronounce it?'

'No.'

'So there is your answer.' But I did not think that it was.

15

THE EFFECT ON my household in the Rose Tower was immediate, and in a manner that I had never considered. We gathered in my solar at noon before making our way in informal manner to eat in the inner hall. I walked to the table on the dais, as I had done a thousand times before, taking my seat at the centre of the board. The pages began to bring water in silver bowls and napkins, the servants bustling in with jugs of ale and platters of frumenty. I had not given even a moment's thought to the practicalities of our new situation. Now forced to consider the reality of it, I felt my face pale with irritation. How thoughtless I had been for Owen in his new status, how blindly insensitive.

And Owen? He had envisaged it all, of course. He had known exactly the problems we had created for ourselves, and had made his plans without consulting me. Perhaps he thought he would save me the burden, the heartache that it would bring me. Or else he knew I would object. I discovered on that day that I had acquired a husband of some perspicacity.

For the question that must be addressed was so simple a decision, so full of uneasy pitfalls. Where was Owen to sit? As my husband he had every right to sit at my side on the dais.

As I sat I looked to my left and right. The stools and benches were apportioned as they always were, and occupied. I raised my hand to draw the attention of a passing page, to set a place at the table beside me, ruffled at my lack of forethought. To have to set a new place now simply drew attention to the dramatic change in circumstances and caused unnecessary comment. I had been remiss not to have anticipated it.

And where was Owen Tudor?

I saw him. Oh, indeed I did. He stood by the screen between the kitchen passageway and the hall, and he was clothed as Master of Household, even to his chain of office. I was not the only one to see him, and the whispers, the covert glances, some with the shadow of a delicious malice, were obvious, as was the well-defined expression on Owen's face, so that I felt a little chill of recognition in my belly, nibbling at the edge of my happiness.

I had not expected to have to fight a battle with him over status quite so soon, or quite so publically. But I would. I was resolute. My husband would not act the servant in my household. And so I, who never willingly drew attention to herself, stood, drawing all eyes. I raised my voice. If he would force me to challenge him under the eye of every one of my household, then so be it.

'Master Tudor.' My voice held a ringing quality that day, born out of a heady mix of anger and fear.

Owen walked slowly towards me until he stood before me, of necessity looking up at me on the dais.

'My lady?'

His eyes met mine, his face a blank mask of defiance. I knew why he felt the need, but I would not accept it. Last night I had been wrapped in his arms, our love heating the air in my chamber. I would not tolerate this.

'What is this?' I asked, clearly.

His reply was equally as crisp. 'I have a duty to your household, my lady.'

'A duty? You are my husband.'

'That does not absolve me from the tasks for which I am employed. And for which I still draw a wage from you, my lady.'

The pride of the man was a blow to my heart, a pride that bordered on arrogance. But I did not flinch.

'My husband does not work for me as a servant.'

'We wed outside the restrictions of the law, my lady, without permission. Until we have stood together before his grace of Gloucester and the Royal Council and made our change of circumstances known, and it is recognised, I will continue to serve you.'

'You will not!' I was astonished, senses shattered by this reaction in him that I could never have anticipated. I would not allow him to demean himself, and yet I suspected his will was as strong as mine.

'And who else do you suggest will do it, my lady?'

'I will appoint your successor. You will not serve me and you will not stand behind my chair.'

'I will. I am still Master of the Queen's Household, my lady.'

'I don't approve.' I was losing this argument, but I could see no way to circumvent his obstinacy.

'You do not have to. This is how it will be. I will not sit at my wife's table when there is still doubt as to my status.'

At my side Father Benedict chose to intervene. 'Indeed, there is no doubt that your marriage is legal, Master Owen.'

But I waved him to silence. This was between Owen and I.

'There is no doubt,' I said.

'Not with you. Not with you, *annwyl*. But look around you.'

I did, refusing to be touched by him calling me his beloved in public, and I realised that we-—Owen and I—stood at the centre of a concerted holding of breath. I looked at those who sat at my table, at those who waited on me. At my damsels and my chaplain. We had a fascinated audience. I read prurient interest from those who hovered to see who would win this battle of wills: some pity for me in the conflict I had naïvely created for myself; more than a touch of rank disapproval for the whole undignified exchange between mistress and servant. Even envy in the eyes of my women who had not been untouched by Owen's charms. But all waited to hear what I would say next.

I looked back at Owen in horror.

'Well, my lady?'

His voice rasped but his eyes were so full of compassion that I was almost overcome. And I retreated from the battle, admitting defeat. His will had proved stronger than mine, and to exhibit our differences in public on the first day of our marriage was abhorrent.

'Very well. But I don't like it.'

Owen bowed, as rigidly formal as the perfect servant. 'Is it your pleasure that the food is now served, my lady?'

'Yes.' I sat down, my face aflame.

And Owen? He merely proceeded to beckon in the bread and meat as if it were an uneventful, commonplace breaking of our fast. A more silent meal I could not recall, with Owen, my husband of less than a day, standing behind my chair.

Never had the servants scurried as they did to serve that repast. Never had we been served with such efficiency or such speed. Never had the bread and ale been consumed so smartly. The usual chatter was almost silent, and what little there was in furtive whispers. Eyes glanced from me to Owen and back again. I tried to keep a flow of trivial comment with Beatrice and Father Benedict about something I cannot even recall.

When I could tolerate the atmosphere no longer, I stood and without excuse I marched from the room, Owen still ordering the dispensing of the remains to the poor.

★ ★ ★

I waited for him in my chamber, knowing that he would come. And if he did not, I would send for him. But things were not as they had been. By the time he opened the door with quiet precision, anger ruled.

'How could you do that to me?' Owen had barely closed the door on the hastily departing Guille. I was rarely roused to such passion but the very public audience to our difference of opinion had shaken me, and his inflexible intransigence had stirred up an unusual temper. I would tolerate neither my humiliation nor his. I would not! How could he have made me the object of such interest in the first meal we had shared together? 'How dare you put our marriage on display in that manner?' I demanded.

Owen stopped just within the door, arms folded, nothing of servitude in his stance, as I launched into my justifiable complaint.

'Have you nothing to say?' I noted with some surprise that my hands were clenched into fists. I squeezed them tighter. 'You had enough to say an hour ago. It will have set the tongues wagging from here to Westminster and beyond.'

He walked slowly across the room, his eyes never leaving my face.

'Is this our first quarrel, *annwyl*?' he asked mildly, but his eyes were not mild.

'Yes. And don't call me that! And certainly not in public.'

'So what do I call you? Is it to be *my lady*?'

I ignored that. I ignored the bitterness behind the innocuous question, as if I would so demean him after I had wed him. 'Do you intend to stand behind my chair at every meal?' I demanded.

'Yes. I do.'

'Is your pride so great? So great that you cannot accept your new status through marriage to me?'

'No,' he replied softly. 'My pride is not so great. But my care for you is.'

'Your care for me?' In my anger, my voice rose. 'How is it possible that this public exhibition of disagreement would denote a care for me? You drew every eye, and made an issue of something that should never have been an issue. I did not appreciate being centre of attention in that manner. And I will not—'

'Katherine.' He took a step closer so that he could clasp my shoulders and stop my words with his mouth, notwithstanding my automatic resistance. I was thoroughly kissed. And then when he released me: 'We'll not rouse Gloucester to more anger than we have already. If he found me lounging at your side in silks and jewels, ordering ale and venison with all the authority that you would undoubtedly give me, can you imagine what he would do?'

I shook my head, realising that I had not thought about it in quite such graphic terms.

'I doubt you thought about it at all,' he said gently, kissing me again. 'But I have. He would pull the sky down on both our heads. But on yours particularly. You need his blessing, Katherine, or as much of a blessing as is possible. You don't need him as your enemy. Gloucester is the power in the land whether we like it or not. So, much as I despise the man, I must not compromise your position further.'

He stepped back, releasing me.

'That is why I will continue to be Master of Household and stand behind your chair until we see how the land lies.'

I looked at him, all that was left of my anger draining away. It was me. It was me he cared about. I walked forward into his arms, sighing as they closed around me.

'You foresaw this, didn't you?' I whispered.

'I promised to shield and protect you. I will not encroach on your royal dignity. Or not until we have made our position clear before the Council.'

'I'm sorry I challenged you as I did.'

Owen gave a bark of laughter. '*Gan Dduw*, Katherine! The faces of your women. They'll have enough to pick over, and gossip about, to keep their tongues as busy as their needles as they stitch their never-ending altar cloths for the next twelve-month. Your sanctimonious chaplain nearly choked on his ale.' But beneath his apparent enjoyment I read the gleam of worry in his eyes, overlaid with sharp irritation.

'I don't think I can tolerate many more meals like that,' I admitted. 'Do you always use Welsh when you are angry?'

'Not invariably.' But at last the ghost of humour in his face was genuine. 'As for the meals—we had better hope Gloucester travels fast.'

'And when he does?'

'Then we inform him of some changes to your household.'

It was all we could do. And yet: 'Living like this is impossible.'

'So we move to one of your dower properties.'

'Will Gloucester forbid it?'

'Short of locking us up, how can he? And that is what you will tell him. You will live where you choose.'

So I would. I would call on all the respect and honour I had worked for in my role at Young Henry's side and I would challenge Gloucester. I would demand that Owen and I be left alone. How I wished I had never set eyes on Edmund Beaufort with all his worldly charm. But it was done and I must work with the consequences.

'Will you stay?' I asked him.

Owen lifted his chain over his head and cast it onto the

bed. 'I have no duties for the next hour, so pour me a cup of ale, woman.' But as I walked past him with a little laugh to do just that, he caught me by the wrist and pulled me close. 'And then I will kiss you,' he murmured, his mouth against mine, 'and I will unwrap for you the pleasures to be found in healing a disagreement between two lovers.'

And so he did. He turned to a new page, to a new bright illustration, that filled my mind with its beauty.

My son must be informed, I decided, and although Owen raised his brows, I took him with me from the Rose Tower to the royal apartments where Young Henry, at his lessons, smiled vaguely at Owen. He reluctantly took his attention from the book he held open on his lap, but he stood, laid the book down and bowed.

'Good morning, *maman*.' His manners were improving. He kissed my cheek.

'I have married this man,' I said without preamble. I had learned with Young Henry that to get straight to the point was good policy. He lost interest quickly.

'Have you?' he asked, looking at Owen. 'I know you. You are Master Owen. You are Welsh.'

'I am, my lord.'

'I have never been to Wales. I wished to go to St Winifred's well but they would not let me. Is Wales a wild place?' he asked. 'Have you ever lived there?'

'Yes. And it is, my lord,' Owen replied solemnly. 'A land of mountains and rivers.'

That did not interest my son. 'And do you speak Welsh?' he asked. 'I do not.'

'I do, my lord.'

'Say something to me in Welsh.'

Owen bowed very formally. *'Yr wyf yn eich was ffyddlon, eich mawrhydi.'*

Henry laughed in quick astonishment. 'What does that mean?'

'I am your loyal servant, Your Majesty.'

'I like it. I like your new husband, *maman.*' He turned back to his book. 'I don't think I will learn Welsh. I must know Latin and French. Perhaps I will send you a gift.'

We left him to his preoccupations. Henry was always generous with gifts.

'You charmed him!' I accused. 'Just like you charmed me with a few Welsh words!'

'Of course I did, *annwyl.*' But although he slid an arm around my waist, his face was grim. 'We might be in need of all the friends we can get. Even a nine-year-old boy, when he happens to be the boy-King.'

I sighed as Warwick eyed us with a disapproving air. It seemed that I would have to explain myself to every man at Court. Yes, I had known it would be like this but I felt that I must be constantly on the alert, quick with an answer. I was already weary of justifying myself and I had not been wed longer than a se'ennight. Warwick's observation was trenchant.

'Well, Katherine, this will stir up a hornet's nest.'

'Yes, Richard. I am aware of that.' I raised my chin. 'I do not regret it.'

'I suppose there's no point in me telling either of you that it would have been better not to do it.'

'No,' I replied.

'Better for whom, my lord?' Owen added. His patience was also wearing thin but his demeanour held all its old dignity.

'Richard.' I touched his arm when he shrugged his incomprehension. 'I know what I have done. I know that I must answer for it. Will you support me before the Council?'

'It's not my support you need.' His tone was bleak. 'It's Gloucester's. And I don't see you getting that.'

'Why would it matter so much?' I glanced at Owen. 'We would not draw attention to ourselves. It is my wish to live privately in one of my dower properties. I would not bring disgrace on the Crown or my son. I have little place in his life now.'

'Gloucester won't see it like that. You defied him, Katherine. He'll not brook defiance, not from anyone. You saw the battle royal that developed between him and Henry Beaufort. He'll not tolerate opposition to any degree.'

'He never did approve of me, did he?' I smiled a little sadly.

'No, he didn't. He acknowledged your usefulness, but he has no admiration for the Valois. But now you've made a bitter enemy of him.'

I thought about the three brothers. Henry, who tolerated me. Gloucester, who actively disliked me. And Bedford, the only one to show me and my plight any understanding.

'I wish Lord John were back in England. He would not be unsympathetic. He might sway the Council,' I hazarded.

'No chance of that.' Warwick grimaced. 'Affairs in France are too crucial and not in England's favour.'

So I was on my own.

But I was not. Owen was all the strength I needed. His arm was warm and strong around my shoulder. I needed it.

Gloucester arrived before the end of the week, travelling from Westminster in one of the royal barges, standing in the prow, hands braced on hips like a carved figurehead.

'His face is as red as a winter beet, my lady,' Guille remarked. We were watching from the old Norman gateway as he disembarked. 'Neither is he wasting any time.' He leapt from boat to landing like a scalded cat.

'I expect it will be even redder after he's said what he has come to say,' I replied. 'I'm tempted to refuse to see him if he demands that *I* wait on *him*. Which he will.'

Sure enough, as soon as he had marched from river landing to entrance hall, he had sent a page at a run to summon me to the main audience chamber. A summoning, not a request, forsooth. So it was to be a bitingly cold and formal confrontation.

I spent a little time over my appearance, considering the ermine and cloth of gold then rejecting it as it would do nothing to assuage Gloucester's fury. I did not run.

'I think I should go alone,' I said when I found Owen waiting for me at the foot of the staircase, neat and suave and authoritative in shin-length dark damask and chain of office. He was obviously, as Master of the Queen's Household, out to make a statement.

'Do you?' he replied mildly.

'As you said, it will only antagonise him. It might be worse if we see him together.'

Owen's hand closed on the sable edge of my sleeve as I walked past him. There was no longer anything mild in his response. 'And do you think I will allow you to face him alone?'

'It would be for the best.'

'But it will not happen. I will escort you.'

My relief was strong and for a brief moment I clasped his hand. 'He might see reason, of course,' I said consideringly, 'and accept that what is done cannot be undone.'

I chose not to react to Owen's jaundiced air.

It was a very brief meeting. There was no courtesy from Gloucester, no semblance of the good manners that he was so keen to see instilled into the Young King. He ignored Owen, addressing me as if he was not there, yet rampant hostility shimmered in the air between the two men.

'So it's true,' he said, his delivery no less threatening for its extreme softness.

'Yes.'

'Words are wasted on you. You—both of you…' now he glanced across with venom '…will present yourselves at Westminster. You are summoned to appear before the Royal Council to explain your aberrant behaviour.'

He looked me up and down, as if he could spy my thickening waist beneath the velvet pleating, yet there was no way of his knowing. I stood straight-backed, and kept my eyes fixed on Gloucester's inimical regard.

'I will agree to accompany you, of course,' I replied, refusing to acknowledge that it had been a command. 'I will explain to the Council. I know that I will be awarded a generous hearing.'

Gloucester left without further comment, enveloped in a cloud of ill humour.

'Well, that went well,' Owen observed, watching our guest stalk back to his river transport. 'I think he saw reason, don't you?'

How brave I had sounded, but in my heart was fear. I had always known that it would come to this.

Owen and I attended the Royal Council, as we were bidden. We were in no position to refuse, neither did we wish it. So there we were, with the proof of our marriage tucked in the breast of Owen's tunic—Father Benedict had witnessed it with a disapproving scrawl at the foot of the document—and my belly still effectively disguised by the width of my skirts. The faces of those who sat in judgement on us were familiar to me, lords temporal and ecclesiastical come to condemn the Queen Dowager and her inappropriate lover.

And what a range of emotion slammed against us as we were announced into the Council Chamber, much as I had witnessed in my own household. Outrage and lascivious interest were uppermost. But some compassion, enough for one of the bishops to provide me with a stool. As I moved to sit, I looked up at Owen where he stood by my side, features well schooled into frozen courtesy, but then he smiled down at me, a sign of our love and one that I returned. Whatever they did, they could not destroy our union.

I might smile at Owen but fear hummed through my blood, and I knew he was not at ease. If he had worn a sword, he would have had a hand firmly on the hilt. Who was to know what Gloucester might persuade his fellow councillors to do? What if, deeming me untouchable, they took out their frustrations at my intransigence on Owen? A term in a dungeon in the Tower of London would not seem beyond the realms of possibility. As he too knew. We had talked about it late into the night.

'What if they incarcerate you?' I had asked.

'They won't.'

I did not believe him, but I let it lie, and loved him for his need to pluck troubles from my mind, as a blackbird gobbled the berries from a winter hawthorn. Would my consequence be sufficient to save him? I did not think it would. I had no consequence. Now I steeled myself, grasping what courage I could muster with both hands, to withstand the onslaught. When Gloucester had descended on Windsor, driven there by a gust of fury, he had been beyond words. He found them that day.

'You have broken the terms of a legal statute, madam. You have defied the law of the land.'

I was barely seated, still disposing the folds of my skirts and removing my gloves.

'Yes, my lord,' I replied. 'I have.' Owen and I had discussed at length how we would manage this confrontation. Even though he did not touch me, I felt the tension in him, vibrating like a strummed lute string.

'You knew the terms of the law.'

'I did, my lord.' Nothing would shake me.

'And yet you were determined, wilfully determined, to flout it!'

I stood, handing my gloves to Owen. I would stand and face them. How could I argue for my greatest desire from a position of inferiority?

'Wilfully?' I said, strengthening my voice, but not too much. I had a role to play here, and I allowed my gaze to range over the ranks of those who would judge me. 'I did not fall in love by intent, my lords. Thus, it was not my intent to break the law. But when my emotions were engaged and I desired marriage—then yes. Perhaps I was wilful. Or perhaps I would say that I was pragmatic. My son is too young to give his consent—and will be so for at least another seven years.'

'Could you not wait? Could you not wait to indulge your physical needs until the King is of age?'

I felt my skin flush, cheeks and temple hot as fire. There was no mistaking this innuendo or Gloucester's displeasure as his eye swept over my figure. So the rumours had spread, suspicions ignited. Beside me I could feel Owen straining to hold his temper. We had known it would be like this, and that Owen's participation would do nothing but harm. The burden was on me. I prayed that he could keep a still tongue.

I drew myself up, and with all the pride of my Valois blood I marshalled the arguments that we had talked of.

'How long would you wish me to wait, my lords? I am

thirty years old. If I wait for the Young King's blessing, I may be beyond the age of childbearing.' I let my gaze move again, lightly, over the assembly. 'Would you condemn me to that, my lords? How many of you are wed and have an heir to inherit your title and lands? Is it not a woman's role to bear sons for her husband?'

I saw the nodding of some heads. Pray God they would listen and understand...

'You have a son.' Gloucester had his response at his fingertips to destroy any strength my words might have with the august gathering. 'A fine son, who is King of England. Is that not sufficient?'

'But my husband, Owen Tudor, has no son to follow and bear his name. He has no one to continue his line. Do I deprive him of children? And for what purpose I do not understand. My marriage to Owen Tudor does not, as I see it, detract from the King's authority. My son is now crowned. The ties of childbirth have been loosened and he is, as he should be, under the tuition of men. Why should the Queen Dowager not wed again?'

Once more I surveyed the faces.

'I am a woman, my lords. A weak woman, if you will, who has had the misfortune to fall in love. Would you condemn me for that? I did my duty by my husband, King Henry. I brought him the crown of France and an heir to wear it. I have been a vital part of my son's childhood years. Now I wish for a more private life as the wife of a commoner. Is it too much to grant me that, or do you compel me to live alone?'

I pushed on, repeating the salient points, finding no favour with what I had to say, but if I had to plead on my knees to achieve my heart's desire then I would do it.

'My son is now nine years of age. He has not needed his mother's constant care for many years. Those appointed to his education—by yourselves, sirs—are men of ability and good character, such as my lord of Warwick.' I inclined my head towards him. 'That is how it should be. But my womb has been empty for those years. Would you condemn me to a barren life? The Holy Mother herself would not. She bore other children after the Christ Child.'

How did I find the courage? I did not even look at Owen, not once, for I did not need to, conscious throughout of the strength of his love, urging me on. When I felt an almost overwhelming need to seek his hand with mine, I did not. I must stand alone and make my plea, for this attack was directed at me, not at Owen.

A new, harsh voice intervened. 'It is blasphemy for you to draw comparison with the Blessed Virgin.' I recognised the disparaging features of the Archbishop of Canterbury.

'It is no blasphemy, my lord,' I replied. 'The Blessed Virgin became a mother in a human sense. Her sons were brothers of Our Lord Jesus Christ and recognised by him. She would understand my need. Do not you, my lords?'

There was some murmuring.

'There might be something in what you say, madam.' Was this a possible ally in the smooth intervention of the Bishop of London? I thought he might be stating a position in opposition to the Archbishop rather than in support of me, but I would snatch at any vestige of hope.

'The Holy Mother is full of compassion, my lord,' I said, turning a smile of great sweetness on him. And on all the councillors.

'Amen to that,' the bishop intoned.

So what now? I shivered as a little silence fell on the proceedings, and again, astonished at my own temerity, I forced the issue.

'Well, my lord of Gloucester? I have stated my case. Are

we free to go? To live together, united by God, as we most assuredly are?'

And I sighed silently when Gloucester picked up my challenge without hesitation.

'We are not finished here. Any man who weds you without permission will forfeit his property. You transgressed the law, and so must pay the penalty.'

'But my husband has no property,' I said gently.

'Then he made a fine bargain, did he not?' Scorn all but dripped from the walls. 'Seducing a wife of wealth and influence!'

I dared not look at Owen. Every muscle in his body was taut with controlled outrage, straining for release.

'There was no seduction,' I said. 'You dishonour both myself and Owen Tudor, my lord. Do I not have the wit to make my own choices? Neither did my husband set himself to seduce me. He had been Master of my Household all the years since I was left a widow. It is only of late that we were touched by love. I was not seduced or forced against my will.'

It was a strong argument.

'It seems to me that it was not so great a bargain for him in taking me as his wife,' I continued. 'Why should a man have to appear before the King's Council over his choice of his bride? Yes, I am a wealthy woman, but as for influence— what influence do I have? None, I would suggest. Owen Tudor would not work his way up the ladder to greatness by marriage to me. And that is not our intent. We do not seek a life in the full light of the royal court. We would live privately.' I lifted my hands in appeal. 'My lords, that is all I ask of you. Your recognition of my married state and permission to live as and where I choose.'

But Gloucester was not finished. 'How could you choose a man in disgrace before the law?'

'I chose a man of pride. A man of honour and integrity, my lord.'

'A man of honour?' Oh, he was inordinately, savagely pleased. He had found a weak spot, and I knew immediately what it would be. 'And when is the bastard you carry due to be delivered?'

'My child will be no bastard,' I replied serenely. 'He will be born within holy wedlock, recognised by his father and by the Church.'

'He was conceived in sin.'

'But he will live in the light.' I stared at Gloucester, no longer dominated by him. How dared he speak so to me? 'I find you presumptuous, my lord. Do I deserve such calumny? If you have nothing more to say—'

'You are still to remain at Windsor in your son's household,' he ordered, grasping at straws, so it seemed to me.

'No.' I allowed a little smile even as anger beat in my head. 'I will not.'

'It is the law.'

'Then I will ignore the law. I will live in one of my dower houses. They are mine, given for my use by the late king in his wisdom. I will live in them with my husband.'

'And if we insist?'

'Will you insist, my lords? The only means to determine where we will live is by the use of force. And if you do…' once more I eyed Gloucester '…if you force me to live at Windsor, I will broadcast to the world the disgrace of your treatment of the once Queen of England, the Queen Mother, Princess of France. The wife of the hero of Agincourt. I think my royal state deserves respect. I think I will be given a hearing by the Commons, don't you?'

Gloucester flung himself down into his chair, denying any respect.

'God's Blood, woman! Was it not possible for you to embrace a chaste and honourable widowhood?'

'I could have. But I chose to be a lawfully wedded wife again.'

'To a palace minion, by God!'

And since Gloucester at last stared at Owen, my husband bowed and replied, 'I was not always a servant, my lord.'

'And Welsh too!'

'I consider that an honour, my lord, not a detriment. The law of England cannot dictate my pride in my birth.'

'Pride in your birth?' Gloucester's disgust grew to vast proportions as he turned his ire on me again. 'Could you not have let your eye fall on someone of your own status?'

'I tried that, my lord. You refused Edmund Beaufort because his status was equal to mine.'

I had him there, and he knew it. Oh, it was a direct challenge and my heart beat against my ribs. Gloucester, his face the hue of parchment, had thought I would bow before his dictates because I had in the past. He swung his attention from me to Owen.

'And what have you to say? We note that you have left your wife to plead your cause. That does not strike me as being the stand of a man of honour. Is your facility in speaking the English tongue not good enough?'

I sensed Owen inhale slowly. He held my gloves lightly in his hands and addressed himself to the Council rather than to Gloucester. How calm he looked, how impressively dignified. Not one man there saw the fire in him, the fury at his and my treatment.

'I have not spoken, my lords, because this is concerning the freedom of the lady who is my wife. It is her right to put her own case, and that is what she wished. I agreed that it should be so, although I found it hard to hold my tongue when she was subject to such crude accusations. My blood may be Welsh, but I was raised a gentleman and I know degradation when I witness it at first hand, as I have here today.

'No Welshman would ever address a nobly born lady in such a manner, certainly not a lady who has been nothing but a shining gem in England's crown. I feel her shame. And I feel her courage, as I am certain you do, my lords. She has all my admiration.'

Pausing, stepping to close the small space between us, Owen smiled at me, a smile of such brilliance that it steadied my heart, and now, at last, he took my hand in his.

'What can I add to a situation that is already plain? Katherine is my wife. She carries my child, as you are aware. We will live together and raise our children, imbuing them with integrity and loyalty to the English Crown. But we will not live at Windsor. Or anywhere that the Queen does not wish to live. She must have her freedom to live as she chooses. And now I think it is her wish that we leave. Her health is fragile and she should rest. I ask your permission for this Council session to end, for her sake.'

I held his hand as tightly as I could. It all hung in the balance.

It was not Gloucester who spoke. It was the Bishop of London.

'Let the lady rest. We will consider the situation in the light of our findings, sir.'

Incensed, Gloucester leapt to his feet: 'The law has been broken. We cannot overlook the fact that the Queen Dowager has brought England's government and King into disrepute by her selfish actions. This cannot go unpunished.'

But we walked from the Council Chamber, not stopping until we had escaped the confines of the buildings and could stand in the open, with sun and a light breeze and the caw of rooks in the elms by the river. And I drew in a breath, relief flooding through me. I had done it. I had done the best I could. What the outcome would be I had no notion, but for the moment we were free.

'I think that was the worst hour of my life.'

But beside me Owen exploded. 'God's Blood! How could I remain silent? How could I not answer word for every damned insolent word Gloucester directed at you? The law has been broken—yes, it has—but we are wed. Can they not accept that? What does it matter to the state of the realm? They were not even interested in the legality of our marriage. All they did was follow Gloucester's lead and harp on about the damned law. Have they no sense? No compassion? I despise them! I despise all the bloody English for their narrow-minded, opinionated—'

'And that is why we agreed that I should make our case,' I said, with a little laugh. 'Thank God you did not tell it to their narrow-minded, opinionated faces.'

Owen dragged in a breath, forcing himself to rein in his temper, but it still rumbled dangerously below the surface. 'We'll just have to wait.' He thrust my mangled gloves back into my hands. 'Take these before I destroy them!' But at last he looked at me with a softer expression. 'You were magnificent, you know.'

'I was terrified.'

'No one would have known it. How I didn't use my fist against Gloucester's smug face and his insinuations, I'll never know.'

'I couldn't have done it without you.'

'Oh, I think you could. You have hidden depths, *fy nghariad*.' He kissed my cheek. 'And that from a despised Welshman.'

'What does it mean?'

'My love. And, *fy nghariad*, we still have our freedom and no compulsion to live anywhere than as you choose. Let's go.'

'It wasn't very satisfactory, was it? Our marriage is recognised only in so far as they can do nothing to end it.'

'It's the best we can hope for.'

So it was. And perhaps it was enough. Yet I frowned.

'Is it enough to stop you from standing behind my chair at every meal?'

Owen thought about it.

'Yes, By God! It is enough.'

We decided to leave that very day, that very hour, Owen looking back over his shoulder as he was helping me into the litter, surveying the bulk of the Westminster palace that cast its shadow over us.

'I'll not be sorry to leave this place. Gloucester hovers over it like a bad smell. It smacks of English military aggression, not to mention dungeons and locked vaults where poor incarcerated fools never again see the light of day.' Sometimes Owen was very Welsh. He stared at me. 'Now, are you comfortable? Or do you wish to stay a night?'

'We leave immediately.' Suddenly my desire to depart was as strong as Owen's.

'Immediately, my lady.' And he grinned at what had been a very imperious tone.

'Master Tudor?'

A tall, lean man in clerical glory hailed us and approached from the wing of rooms behind us, and I smiled. It was the Bishop of London, who had spoken up for me, or at least not against me. Robert FitzHugh, a friendly face, all in all, and not one of Gloucester's coterie. He was followed by another cleric I knew, Bishop Morgan of Ely. They ranged up beside us and bowed to me. And, interestingly, to Owen. I remarked it, but Owen's face was implacable.

'We will not stay, my lords,' he said unequivocally.

'I understand,' FitzHugh replied. He looked across at Morgan, who nodded. 'But just a word, sir, my lady.'

Owen scowled, and I saw the direction of his thoughts. What would these clerics want with us? 'We'll hear you—but I wish to make good time, my lord,' Owen stated. 'It will not be a comfortable journey for my wife.'

'Where will you go?' Morgan, as rotund as FitzHugh was lean, asked.

'To Hertford. We'll stay there until the child is born.'

FitzHugh merely nodded with a thin smile. 'A suggestion, my lady. And an offer. To you and to your husband.'

Owen eyed him speculatively. 'Is it possible that you're of a mind to circumvent Gloucester's plans, my lord?'

'It might be. His ambitions gnaw at my conscience sometimes.' The smile grew a little. 'But here is my offer. Your marriage is legal, without any doubt. You have the proof of your priest and the Council can do nothing—neither do most of them wish to. Yet Gloucester still rails against you breaking the law. May I suggest that your child be born under the auspices of the church?'

'I don't see the need,' I replied, uncertain.

'May be there is none.' Morgan took up the ecclesiastical view. 'But if there should be—if the legitimate birth of the child is ever questioned…'

'My offer would circumvent it,' FitzHugh completed the thought. 'I suggest that you smother yourselves—and the child—in righteous legality.'

'I don't understand why…' I didn't want to be here, to be involved in plots and counterplots. I was weary beyond measure. All I wanted was to settle into my own property, away from prying eyes, but a hand suddenly enclosing mine stilled my tongue.

'My lord Bishop is right, my love.' Owen's voice was harsh with the acknowledgement of how the world might see our union. 'Do you want our children to be called bastards?'

'But they never will.'

'It is best to be sure,' Bishop FitzHugh advised, patient with my concerns. 'One of my properties—Much Hadham Palace, not too far from your castle in Hertfordshire—is at your disposal. You may travel there as you please.' He beamed. 'Your child will be born in the bosom of Holy Mother Church, hedged about with ecclesiastical favour. It may be that you—and your child—will need friends. I am privileged to count myself as one of them.' His eyes positively twinkled.

'And I,' added Bishop Morgan. 'We were both close to the policies of your husband—King Henry, that is. We feel it our duty to support you at this time.'

Owen's brows rose. 'Gloucester will be beyond rage.'

'Yes, he will, won't he?' FitzHugh smiled. 'Will you accept my offer?'

'Yes, my lord,' said Owen promptly, before I could open my mouth. 'We'll accept your offer. And with thanks.'

'Excellent. A man of sense.'

The three men shook hands on the agreement without even asking me, Bishop Morgan making one final observation.

'Are you aware, my lady, that the law, in fact, makes provision for you taking a new husband, with or without permission?'

No, I was not. My face must have registered shock, followed by bright anger.

'Any children born of your union...' he inclined his head to me and to Owen '...will be recognised as half-brothers to the King.'

'And Gloucester knew of this.'

'Of course.'

I despised Gloucester even more, and as if my hatred called up his presence, Gloucester himself appeared, striding down the steps and halfway across the courtyard in the wake of the bishops. I saw him lift a peremptory hand to Owen, and I watched, narrow-eyed, as Owen, now mounted, nudged his horse in Gloucester's direction, bending his head to hear the royal duke's clipped delivery.

What passed between them I could not hear, but it was no friendly well-wishing. Gloucester had his hand on his sword hilt. Owen shook his head, raising a hand as if in denial, before hauling on his reins to leave Gloucester standing, frowning after him.

As Owen's silence registered cold outrage I made no comment but, 'What did Gloucester have to say?' I asked at the first opportunity on the road to Much Hadham.

'Nothing to disturb you, *fy nghariad*.'

I did not believe him. There was still fire in Owen's eye and an obstinate set to his mouth but I had to admit defeat. His reticence was sometimes most infuriating.

Our son was born at Much Hadham without fuss, with only Guille and Alice in attendance. No withdrawal from society for me, no enforced isolation until I was churched. I was Owen's wife, not Queen of England, and I was sipping ale in our chamber with Owen, idly discussing whether we should eventually move our household to my castle at Hertford or whether we would perhaps prefer the beautiful but damp environs of Leeds, on the morning that our son entered the world with lungs like a blacksmith's bellows and a shock of dark hair.

Owen held him within the first hour of his life.

'What do we call him?' I asked, expecting a Welsh name.

'Something indisputably English,' Owen replied, much taken up with the tiny hands that waved and clutched. 'Will he always bawl like this?'

'Yes. Why English?' I asked.

'As the wily bishop said, we want no question of his legitimacy or his Englishness.' He slid a glance in my direction as Alice relieved him of our firstborn. 'We'll call him Edmund.'

'We will?' I blinked my astonishment. Why choose a name so uncomfortably reminiscent of my Beaufort indiscretion?

Owen's expression remained beautifully bland. 'Do you object? I think it a thoroughly suitable name for a royal half-brother. No one can possibly take exception to it.'

I could not argue against so shrewd a thought, and so Edmund he was. And the church remained our steadfast ally, for within the year our second child—another black-headed son—was born at Hatfield, one of the Bishop of Ely's estates. The church continued to smile on us, while Gloucester glowered ineffectually at Westminster.

'And this one will have a Welsh name,' I insisted, with all the rights of a new and exhausted mother. 'A family name—but a name I can pronounce.'

'We will call him Jasper,' Owen pronounced.

'I can say that. Is that Welsh?'

'No,' he said as cupped the baby's head in his hand. 'But it means bringer of treasure. Does he not bring untold blessings to us?'

The boys brought us joy and delight, and, unlike my firstborn, their father knew and loved them. I adored them, for their own sakes as well as for Owen's blood that ran strong and true. My sons would never say that they were not loved.

16

DANGER! DANGER RIPE with blood and terror. Bright as sunlight on a frozen pond, sharp as the taste of too-early pippins. I had not expected it. How would I, taken up as I was with my own concerns?

We were travelling back from France, in the depths of a frozen February, after the momentous occasion when the crown of France, my father's crown, had been lowered onto Young Henry's brow. The culmination of all Henry of Agincourt's ambitions. What power did the old prophecy have now on the life of my son?

Henry born at Windsor shall long reign and all lose.

None, I decided, even though Lord John was ill with the strain of war, and my brother Charles had claimed the French Crown for himself in Rheims Cathedral the previous year. My son's inheritance was secure. I knew I would never return to France, and Young Henry's future had passed into stronger hands than mine. My future was with Owen. I knew I carried another child for Owen.

And so I drowsed as we pushed on with a small escort to Hertford—for this was now where Owen and I had established our home—where Edmund and Jasper waited in Alice's care. It was cold enough to turn our breath to clouds of white and the ground was rock hard with frost. I travelled in a litter against the icy wind, the leather curtains drawn, with every frozen rut and puddle jarring my body. I longed to be home, and as if reading my mind, the curtain was twitched back, and Owen leaned down from his mount to peer in.

'Are you surviving?' His words were snatched away by the wind.

'Just about.' I grimaced, weary to my bones. 'The bits of me that are not frozen are battered into submission. How long?'

'Not long now.'

He reached out to grip my hand and was about to drop the curtain back into place when his head whipped round. And I too heard it. Approaching hooves from ahead and behind, shouts that seemed to come from the undergrowth beside the road to our right and a cry of warning from one of our escort.

'Footpads, by God!' Owen snarled. 'Sit tight!'

As my litter came to a juddering halt, he hauled on his reins, shouting orders to our escort—a little band of half a dozen men well armed with sword and bow. I pushed the curtain aside again to see a motley collection of riff-raff leap from their hiding places in the undergrowth, daggers and swords to hand, at the same time as armed assailants descended from front and rear. And then all was full-scale battle.

In the midst of it, I was aware of Owen. For a moment he sat motionless on his horse then spurred it forward towards a thief who, dagger drawn, was grappling with one of our men. And I realised. Owen had no weapon, neither sword nor dagger. He was helpless. Insanely, recklessly, he spurred his horse back into the fray.

'Owen!' My voice croaked soundlessly in my throat as Owen swung round, ducking to avoid a blow, yet still he caught a glance of a sword on his arm that made his breath hiss between his teeth. And I heard him call out above the mêlée...

'A sword. Give me a sword, man!'

Immediately one of our escort hefted his weapon in Owen's direction. Owen caught it and wielded it as if he had been born with a sword in his hand, so that his attacker was beaten back. And I forced myself to watch as, cutting to left and right, managing his horse with skill, he lunged and parried even as his sleeve darkened with blood. With every clash and scrape of metal, every grunt and groan, I held my breath and dug my fingers into the litter supports until my nails cracked and splintered.

And then the attack was over after a short skirmish, our own escort eventually proving more than a match for the attackers, and they were driven off, leaving two of them dead in the road. As our sergeant-at-arms ordered removal of the bodies, Owen dismounted and walked slowly back to me. His face was livid, his hair matted with sweat, but he was alive. Vibrantly alive. There was blood on his blade that was not his.

'You are wounded,' I said, all senses as frozen as the landscape, watching the blood drip from the fingers of his left arm.

'Yes.' Tight-lipped, wincing a little, he pulled at the material of his sleeve. 'A flesh wound. I was careless.'

'Can I help you, bind it up?'

'No.' He was as curt as he had ever been with me.

I said what was uppermost in my mind. 'Was that a deliberate attack against us?'

'No. A chance encounter by particularly enterprising robbers.' He did not look at me.

I did not believe him, but let it slide. 'Why were you not armed?' I demanded. Even I heard the accusatory note in my voice.

Now he looked up at me, anger bright in his face, his lips pale and thin, his words ungoverned.

'I was not armed because I have to live under the damnable restrictions that the English law puts on me.'

'But—'

'It's not a matter for discussion.' Oh, he was brusque. 'Close the curtains, Katherine, and we'll be off again.'

He left me, and I obeyed, but not before I saw him toss the sword back to its owner.

Back at Hertford within the hour, his face still set in stark lines, I kept a still tongue as I dispatched him to have Alice inspect his wounds. Giving him time, I visited Edmund and Jasper in the nursery, listened to their achievements and woes, but my mind was busy elsewhere. I was certain that the only time I had ever seen Owen wear a sword had been on the morning he had stood with me in St George's Chapel and taken me as his wife.

So he had a sword. He could indubitably use one, had been taught to wield one, and taught well. But—what was it that he had said? English law forbade him to wear one. What a morass of difficulties the law of England gave us. And how little of it I understood.

I kissed my sons and went in search of my husband.

For I knew that the ambush had not been the work of some chance vermin, some motley collection of riff-raff, as I had first surmised, but a well-mounted, well-armed, well-organised force. Furthermore, wearing no identifying livery, they had been waiting specifically for us. Owen might deny it, but it seemed to me that their focus had been set on Owen, not on our baggage wagons. In my heart I knew it with a cold certainty. They had been there to harm my husband.

I found Owen seated on a wooden settle in the kitchens, where Alice, muttering irritably about law and order in general and footpads in particular, was in the process of cutting away the ruined cloth of his tunic from arm and shoulder. His ill humour had been subsumed under the painful exigencies of the past half-hour. Taking a seat, I waited as Alice cleansed his forearm with white wine, ignoring his hiss of pain as she wound a length of linen around it and then applied herself to another sword slice through the flesh of his shoulder, the source of most of the blood.

'They say you fought well,' she observed, forming a tight knot. 'Why is it that brave men make such a fuss about a little scratch?'

Yet I saw her apply her ministrations more gently. It was an uncomfortable hour for all of us, but when Owen showed his teeth in a feral snarl, Alice patted his unharmed shoulder and pushed a cup of ale into his hand.

'You'll do,' she said. 'If you could manage not to put any strain on your shoulder for a day or two—but I expect you'll be back on horseback by tomorrow.'

As she left us, I slid along the bench I was occupying until I sat opposite him.

'Owen.' I held his gaze when it lifted to mine. His eyes were dulled with pain and whatever alleviating substance Alice had added to his ale. 'Why?'

'I know what you're going to ask,' he interrupted with a grimace as he tried to brace his shoulder. 'And the answer is this—just as I said when in danger of being hewn down by some lawless villain—I don't wear a sword because the law forbids it.'

'But you have one. I know you have. You wore it the day we stood before the altar.'

'And that was the damned foolish reaction of a man with too much pride for his own good.'

Which did not make sense. 'Why does the law forbid it?'

'A penalty of my being Welsh, and retaliation for the rebellion of Owain Glyn Dwr. A rebellion that threatened English sovereignty and thwarted the English king's desire to rule

Wales.' He winced again as he lifted the cup of ale to his lips. 'It was a pretty successful rebellion, all in all, until it was crushed with bloody and savage retribution. And so have we Welsh all been crushed ever since. The law discriminates against us.'

I had not thought about this to any degree, but I did now.

'Tell me what it means to be Welsh under English dominion,' I demanded. 'When I asked you before, you didn't tell me. I want to know now. How does the law discriminate against you?'

He leaned back on the settle, placing the cup beside him, weariness heavy in his eyes, resignation in his voice. 'You know that I own nothing of my own. Have you never considered why?'

'I think I presumed that your family had nothing for you to inherit.'

His smile was grim. 'My family had much to inherit. But after Glyn Dwr was overthrown, all who fought for him were stripped of their property. My father fought for Glyn Dwr.' He scrubbed his hands over his face as if he would obliterate some unpleasant memory. His voice quiet and measured, without inflection, with Alice bustling in the background and the faint chatter of servants, the heat of the ovens and the appetising scents of roasting meat, Owen told me about the restrictions he knew by heart as if they meant nothing to him, whereas I knew they were a wound on his soul.

'The law says that I can neither wear nor own weapons. I am forbidden to own land in England. I am forbidden to enter some towns. I am not allowed to assemble with other Welshmen, for fear we might hatch another vile plot against the English government. And many would, God help them. The law keeps us penurious and powerless. That is why I have worked for you all these years. That is why I had nothing to give you and nothing to forfeit.'

And he had never told me any of it. He had kept the shameful dishonour of it bound and shackled in his heart and belly. It almost moved me to tears, but I would not. Here was no time for weak sentiment. I listened silently, and when he had finished, we simply sat. After a little while I took his hand as I pondered what I now knew.

'No one has ever told me this.'

'Why would they? It matters to no one who is not Welsh.'

'It is unjust.'

'Many would say we earned it by spilling English blood. Rebels are not well thought of.' His brief smile was humourless. 'And before you ask—there's nothing that can be done about it. We have no rights before English law.'

'I would have asked that,' I replied. And then: 'Not wearing a sword means a lot to you, doesn't it?' He turned his face from me. 'You wore it when we were wed. You stood in your own name with a sword at your side.'

'So I did.'

'And what's more,' I observed as the memory of his part in the bloody fight surged back, 'you used the sword as if it was second nature to you. Who taught you?'

'My father,' he replied. 'When I was a boy at home.'

'So you have worn a sword.'

There was a flash of anger in his face, quickly masked. 'All men of my family are warriors. It would have been a dishonour for me not to have the skill.'

'Then if your father taught you, and you can use it well, why not wear—?'

He silenced me with a glance. 'I'll not wear Llewellyn's sword again until I can do so with honour. I will not speak of this, Katherine.'

I lifted my hands in exasperation and gave up. He would not admit it, but I could read all that he did not say in the dark bleakness of his eyes, the proud flare of nostril and edge of cheekbone. So his family had once been landowners. Was not a sword the symbol of a man of birth? It was so in France, and I saw no reason why England should be any different. An English or Welsh gentleman would feel the need to wear a sword at his side just as much as his French cousin. But what exactly was his family? Were they men of rank and social standing? I remembered that when I had asked him he had become marvellously reticent for a man so clever with words. There was still so much I did not know about Owen Tudor.

'What would happen if you were caught wearing a weapon?' I asked, ignoring, in true wifely fashion, Owen's decision.

'I don't know.' He hitched a shoulder, resulting in a grunt of discomfort at Alice's tight bandaging when he forgot. 'I might be fined. Clapped in prison perhaps?' Carefully he began to shrug himself back into what was left of his tunic, to cover the remnants of his shirt.

'No one would know, of course,' I suggested. 'If you did happen to wear one.'

He abandoned the attempt to dress. 'By God, that woman's ministrations are more incapacitating than the damned sword thrust!'

'Owen!'

He shook his head, but relented under my persistence. 'No one would know,' he replied gently, 'except those who make it their interest to watch what I do, and inform on me. The Council and Gloucester would be only too triumphant to find some excuse to move against me. And so I will not wear one. The last thing I want for you is to have you visiting me in the Tower of London. And because of that I'll abide by the damned law. You once asked me why I did not use my true name—'

'And you dissembled.'

'I did, and I regret the need. But, truth to tell, it does not do for a man to draw attention to his Welsh lineage.'

It was despicable, shameful. I watched the flattened planes of Owen's face with anguish, as some of his comments hit home in my heart.

'Are we watched?' I asked. 'Are we spied upon?' And when he shook his head, 'Owen, are we—are you—under surveillance?'

'Yes. There are those who would undo our marriage if they could. They will look for any contravention of the law to hold against us.'

My lips were dry, my throat raw. 'If you were not wed to me—' I pulled my hand away when he tried to silence me with his own. 'If you were not, would anyone care if you wore a sword?'

Owen forced his mouth into a smile of sorts. 'Probably not. But there's no point in us second-guessing. It may be that I'm constructing a Welsh mountain out of an English molehill here.' He pushed himself to his feet, signalling the end to his frank admissions.

'Now, let us leave Mistress Alice, who keeps frowning at me every time I move, and I will show my honourable wounds to Edmund and Jasper and bask in their admiration.' He stood slowly, placing his good arm around my waist when I stood too, kissing my cheek in what I recognised as a warning to leave the matter be.

But I knew, as did he, that this was no molehill. My mind refused to abandon the thought that our waylaying on the road had not been some unfortunate accident of time and place. Our attackers had not worn livery, but they had been a force assembled and paid by someone of note. Neither could I push aside from my own mind the terrible burden that Owen had to shoulder, day after day, simply because of his Welsh blood.

He had no protection before the law if he was attacked. Would my sons, with their Welsh blood, be equally compromised? I feared that they would.

'Come and praise my exploits to our sons,' Owen invited, and I did, knowing when to keep my counsel. Owen was not a man to accept sympathy lightly. His self-esteem would not allow it and so I did not raise the subject again, even when it added a sharp layer of anxiety to my life.

Until the following week. 'Where have you been?' I demanded.

I flinched at the shrewish note that rebounded off the walls of living quarters and stabling in the courtyard, but it was born of rampant fear. Owen was late. The short day was now thick with shadows and I had spent the hours since his departure that morning with my mind full of blood and grotesque images. How long did it take a man and a handful of servants to go into Hertford to collect supplies and a consignment of firewood? My imaginings, after the roadside attack, were lively and graphic.

'It is almost dark. I have been worried out of my mind!'

I tried to moderate the accusation in my tone, but then I saw the state of them, even of Owen, and was forced to absorb what had previously slid under my notice. Why had my husband gone the short distance into Hertford with quite so many henchmen at his back?

'What happened?' Without waiting for a reply, I was down the steps and into the chaos of the enclosed space.

Without doubt, there had been foul play. Immediately I was searching for any sign of serious hurt, of wounds as Owen began to organise the unloading of the two wagons, only allowing a breath of relief when I saw there was none, apart from Owen's shoulder, which still showed traces of stiffness. Yet all of them were the worse for wear, clothes ruined with mud and ill usage. I saw one bloody nose and a gashed forehead.

'A drunken brawl?' I observed with commendable calm to cover my thudding heart. And when Owen was taciturn, 'Are you hurt?' I asked.

'No.' He grimaced.

'Are you going to tell me what happened?'

'An incident in the market, my lady,' the sergeant-at-arms responded to my impatience. 'We restored the peace right enough, after it got a bit lively. More lively than usual, I'd say. They had weapons. But we put an end to it—with a little show of force.' He flexed his scuffed knuckles and stretched his shoulders. 'More than a little, if truth be told.'

I nodded, as if reassured, leaving them to their work, but pounced as soon as Owen stepped into his chamber to strip off his clothes. I was waiting for him, and knew that he wished I were not.

'Just give me a moment to get out of this gear, Katherine. I'll join you for supper in a little while.'

I saw the dull tangle of his hair, the thick smear of mud along his side. I thought there might be a graze along his jaw. I heard the anger and weariness in his voice, and I was at his side before he could even loosen his belt. I tilted his chin so that I could confirm my fear then my hands were fisted in urgency in the cloth of his sleeves.

'Tell me this was a plain market-day accident, Owen.' I made no attempt to hide the trepidation that beat through my blood. 'Tell me it was a just a parcel of drunken louts.'

'It was a drunken brawl over false weights,' he said briefly. 'It got out of hand.'

'As the attack on us last week was pure misfortune.'

He looked at me and I saw resignation grow in his eye, overlaying the glint of anger.

'Tell me the truth, Owen. Is this ill luck? Or is it a campaign against you?'

He exhaled slowly, and for a moment rubbed his hands over his face, through his hair. 'What can I say, that you do not already see?'

I released his sleeves, but framed his face with my hands.

'Will you tell me?'

'Yes. If you'll let me get rid of some of this filth.'

He kissed me, pushed me gently away, before proceeding to loosen his belt and drag his tunic over his head, dropping it on the floor. Then he sat to pull off his mired boots, where I knelt beside him. His face was drawn, pinched with a simmering fury, his movements brisk with heavy control. He would not look at me, but I would not be gainsaid.

'It was not ill luck, was it?' I nudged his arm.

'No.' He dropped a boot on the floor with a thud.

'Who is responsible? The robbers on the road wore no livery but someone paid them.'

'I know not,' Owen snapped, turning his anger on me.

'I say you do!'

And Owen took the second boot and hurled it at the wall, where it bounced off the stitched forms of a pack of hounds and a realistically bloodied boar, and fell with a thump beside the hearth.

Which outburst of temperament I ignored. 'You are in danger!' I accused. 'And you will not tell me!'

'Because I can do nothing about it,' he snarled with none of his usual grace. 'I have to accept that I am a marked man.' His words froze on his lips, his eyes lifted to mine for the first time for some minutes.

We stared at each other. My earlier fears leapt into life again, and bit hard.

'I didn't mean to say that.' Owen sighed a little, but the tension was still strong in every muscle of his body.

'A marked man? What do you mean by that?' I gripped his good arm as all my anxieties returned fourfold. 'What else have you not told me? And don't say that I must not worry. Who says that you are a marked man?'

I had to withstand a difficult pause.

'Tell me, Owen. You must. You cannot leave me in ignorance of something that affects you and me—and our children.'

And he did, in a flat tone and even flatter words, confirming all that I feared. 'It's Gloucester at the bottom of it. Our noble Plantagenet duke. His warning was vicious and intended as a threat. But probably with no real heat in it.'

Which, on present evidence, I did not believe for one minute. Neither, I warranted, did Owen. 'When we left the Council.' Now I recalled the incident. 'He spoke with you, didn't he? What did he say?'

'Just that. That I am a marked man.' Owen's brow snapped into a black line. 'No doubt to destroy any pleasure I might gain from successfully seducing the Queen Dowager to my own ends, and enjoying the fruits of her possessions. He said that he would have his revenge, despite the Council's weak acquiescence. It's a damnable thing, but there's nothing can be done to undo it.' The bitterness in his words increased, and with it the depths of my own grief. 'I am a Welsh bastard, he observed, and do not know my place. It is Gloucester's mission to teach me what that place is. With blood and fire if necessary.'

We sat in silence for a moment. The implications of Owen's confession pressed down on me, until I could do nothing but accept the truth that stared me in the face. I considered it as I rose, collected Owen's maligned boots and placed them neatly side by side. I stood before him.

'Are you saying that by marrying me you have put your life in danger?'

Looking up at me, his forearms resting on his thighs, Owen's brows drew down into an even straighter line. 'I doubt it's as extreme as that.'

'Has our marriage put your life in danger?' I demanded.

'Yes. It is possible. But it may be that he intends to teach me a lesson rather than take my life.'

Fear dried my mouth. The child kicked as if it could sense my perturbation.

'Is there nothing we can do?'

'Against Gloucester?' Owen's brows winged upwards.

'But the law should protect—'

'I have no rights before the law,' he replied gently. 'You must know that. I am Welsh.'

'Ah! I had forgotten.' I lifted my hands in helplessness. 'I am so sorry.'

Owen stood. As his arms closed around me, as he raised my face so that I must look up, I felt some of the tension in his body leach away at last. And because of that I spoke the one pertinent thought in my mind.

'When you married me, you opened yourself to danger. And I did not know it. But you knew, didn't you?'

'Yes.'

'And still you made me your wife.'

'I would do the same tomorrow. And the next day. And the next.' Releasing me, he moved to enmesh his fingers with mine. 'Would *you* have refused to make your vows, if you had seen the future?'

'I should have done.' I felt disturbed by the depth of my selfishness. When I had stood before the altar afraid of every creak and shuffle that someone would appear to put a halt to it all, I had not once considered that Owen might have a price to pay. Now I was rigid with inner fears.

'I would not have allowed you to run away from me. Once you did, when I frightened you. I would not let it happen again. But we must not forget.' Owen's kiss on my lips might be sweet with understanding, yet it held an underlying warning as firm as the imprint of his mouth. 'We must always be aware and take every precaution. We cannot afford to be careless with our safety. But we will not let Gloucester destroy our happiness. We won't allow it, will we?'

'No, we will not,' I agreed softly, for once mistress of the art of deception. 'We will take care.' But as I smoothed the tangles from his hair with my fingers, my heart leapt and bounded in sheer fright.

17

HOW CONTROLLED WAS my reply to Owen. How well I hid the terror that dogged my steps and troubled my dreams. How I wept in the privacy of my bedchamber. Or stormed at the monstrous turn of fate. What woman would not weep or call down curses, when the man she loved was forced to live with an invisible death sentence hanging over his head?

I am a marked man.

And when that woman herself had helped to place the weapon of execution into the hands of the enemy. Enemy. I could think of Gloucester in no other light. Twice Owen had been the target for his revenge. Twice it had failed. But one day, one day the dagger sent and paid for by Gloucester might find its mark.

Guilt stalked me, clawing at my mind, giving me no peace. If I had not carried Owen's child. If I had not offered myself in marriage to him. If I had not fallen so catastrophically in love with him. How heedless, how thoughtless I had been, swept along in the miracle of our love without consideration of the turbulence it might lead us into, of the blatant threat to Owen that was now unfolding!

Now I saw it all too clearly, pre-empted, so I thought, by Owen standing with me at the coronation of Young Henry in Paris. Nothing could have spoken more clearly to Gloucester that the Queen Dowager had taken an unsuitable man to her bed. It was like striking his cheek with a gauntlet. I had not realised.

There's nothing that can be done about it, Owen had said.

Was there not? I could not sit and allow Gloucester's revenge to unfold. My fears for Owen became a rock beneath my heart, yet what could I, a powerless woman, do in the face of royal power?

We must not let Gloucester destroy our happiness.

How could we possibly prevent it? Was it not out of our hands if he chose to send armed men to spill Owen's blood?

And it came to me, even though I shrank from it. The remedy was in my hands if I had the courage to apply it. My love for Owen was so strong. It held so great a power that it would enable me to step across any chasm, attack any well-defended fortress, challenge even the authority of Gloucester and the Council. I could destroy the threat. All that was required from me was that I make one simple decision.

My breath caught, my heart hammered. Not simple. Not simple at all.

Yet I hugged the knowledge close to me throughout the whole of that endless day. When I had wed Henry, the wilderness of my childhood had provided me with no guiding lines to measure love, to either give or receive it. Now I had travelled its path. I knew love's glory for myself, and I had my maps and charts to hand. When I closed my eyes, there was Owen in my mind. There in my thoughts was the interplay of two people who adored one another. Who were made for each other. There was the love that would last until death. It gave me the strength to see the truth of what I must do. Yet having seen it, it took me a day and a night of terrifying thought to step to the edge of the chasm, prepared to make the leap.

★ ★ ★

I found him in the entrance hall, just come in from the stables, handing gloves and hat and an unidentifiable package to one of the pages. His hair was ruffled, his face touched by sun and wind. There had been no attack today.

'Katherine.' Owen's smile, his eyes as they rested on me, spoke to me of joy in reunion. How long a matter of hours apart could seem. We were never apart for long.

I slowed my steps before he could reach me. I must not weaken. No preamble. No warning. I must say it now. I had opened the gates to this marriage with all its rapture, and its unforeseen menace. Now I would close them.

'I set you free,' I said. 'Go home. Go back to Wales.'

Owen stopped as if hit by a battle mace.

'Katherine?'

Shock flattened his features. His face registering utter incomprehension, he took another step forward, but I retreated.

'I have arranged for money. A horse. Take an escort.' I dared not touch him. I dared not let him touch me or I would shred all my resolution and fall at his feet. 'If you died because of me, how could I live knowing that you were dead? I don't want you here.' The words fell from my lips without restraint. 'I will not see you done to death. I will not carry the guilt of harm coming to you. I relieve you of any obligation to me.'

'What are you saying?'

I firmed my shoulders as if addressing the Royal Council. 'I wish to end our marriage, Owen. I wish you to leave Hertford and find refuge in Wales. I will not allow you to remain here with your life open to constant danger.' In spite of an anguish that was tearing me apart, never had I spoken so firmly. Never had I sounded so much the Queen Dowager. 'I command you to leave.'

It was as if Owen had turned to ice. His hands fell loosely to his sides. His face as pale as wax, his eyes glittered like obsidian. His voice, when he finally spoke, was as emotionless as mine.

'You would send me away? Am I still your servant, to be dismissed at your whim?' It was like the lash of a whip. 'Does our love mean nothing to you?'

I would not bow before his retaliation. 'It means everything. For your sake, you must leave. And for mine. I cannot contemplate the possibility that we will not breathe the same air, feel the heat of the same sun on our skins. Do you not understand? Do you not agree that it must be so?'

'I hear what you say. By God, woman! Will you take the decision out of my hands?' I could hear the rumble of temper in the ominous quiet.

'Yes,' I responded, before I could be swayed.

'And if I do not agree?'

'You must. We will not be together in body, but we will in spirit, and I know that you will be alive, and safe, to live your life to its allotted time.' How well I had learned my words, even though my heart shuddered. I missed him between our rising and sitting down to break our fast. How could I contemplate a lifetime apart? Knowing that I had come to the end of my control and that Owen's temper was about to explode like a hunting cat after its prey, I turned my face from him. 'I have made my decision. Go back to Wales, where you will find peace and safety.'

And I walked away, climbing the stairs, closing the door of my chamber quietly behind me, because to do otherwise would be to slam it shut so that the sound reverberated through the whole castle.

Owen did not follow. He did not see the tears that washed ceaselessly down my cheeks to mark the velvet of my bodice. He did not see me stand with my back to the door, my palms pressed there as if I needed support. He did not see me dry my tears and determine not to weep again because tears would solve nothing, then fall to my knees and hide my face against the coverlet of my bed.

What had I done? How could I have sliced my heart in two? Even worse, how could I have condemned Owen to the same wretched misery that made every breath I took without him a separate agony? I was beyond thought, beyond reason.

But reason returned, as it must, and with it all my previous conviction. I would live alone. I would send Owen away if it would save his life. I would live alone for ever if it meant he, my love, my life, would be free from Gloucester's anger. I would do it. I would step away from Owen out of pure love.

It was the right thing to do.

So why did it hurt so much?

That night I slept alone. I barred my door to him, which I had never done before. And I waited, when my household settled for the night, until I heard his approaching footsteps. I swear I would recognise them in the turbulence of a winter storm. Breath held, I heard them pause outside, and placed my palm against the wood, leaned my forehead against the panels, as if I could sense him there. He did not knock or try the latch. I listened, but could hear no words. Not even his breathing. How long did we stand there? Time had no measure in my distraught mind. Then his footsteps passed on.

Tomorrow we would be separated for ever.

Exhaustion laid its hand on me but I did not sleep. I kept a solitary vigil for the death of our marriage.

'Where is my lord?' I asked Guille next morning. I rose late. Very late. I had not heard Owen and his escort leave, but there were the usual sounds of castle life reaching my windows from courtyard and stables. He would have seen the sense of it and gone at dawn, without my presence. I could not bear to watch him ride away. Neither would I wish to burden him with my volatile emotions.

'I'm not sure, my lady.' Guille was carefully not noticing my wan cheeks, her fingers busy as she pinned my hair beneath a simple veil. My temples were too sore to support close padding.

'Has he left the castle?'

She took a breath. 'I think he might have.'

'Did you see him?'

She affixed a pin with deliberation. 'No, my lady.'

I inhaled against the blow. However much I had anticipated his leaving, nothing could have prepared me for the force of it. Owen had gone. He had left me. I knew he must have because, unless away from the castle, his routines always brought him back to me at mid-morning. But not today. It felt as if he had taken my heart with him, leaving a space of pain and loss in my chest. And I would accept it because Owen would live.

Now I must begin the impossible task of living my life without him. I inspected my face in my mirror. I straightened the hang of my sleeves, the fall of my girdle, checked the safety and position of the chain that Guille had clasped around my neck. Little details of my existence that I attended to every day.

I stepped outside my door.

'What time is this to rise from your bed? Your sons are asking for you.'

The question, soft-voiced, slammed into my mind as if it were a roll on a military drum. Collecting my thoughts was almost beyond me. I stared at him, unable to trust my reactions.

'Guille told me that you were gone.'

What a facile reply, when he was clearly not. When everything I wanted in life was there before me. Within touching distance. Within kissing distance. Owen should not be here.

'I ordered her to,' Owen said.

'Why?'

'To catch you off guard. So that I could talk some sense into you before you could resurrect the fortifications against me.'

'I told you to go, Owen.' To my horror my voice wavered.

'And I choose not to.'

I could see that he had slept as little as I. Now he pushed himself to his feet, from where he had been sitting on the floor, his back against the wall with his arms resting on his bent knees, outside my chamber. It might have seemed the demeanour of a servant outside his mistress's chamber, but there was nothing servile in Owen's stance, as he drew himself to his full height and stretched cramped limbs, or in his expression. It was thunderous. He was wearing, I decided, the same clothes as he had worn when I had delivered my royal command.

'How long have you been there?' I asked, inconsequentially. I suspected he had been there all night. He should not be there at all.

'Long enough.' His hands were clamped around the broad leather belt that rested on his hips. How easy it was for me to recognise the strength of will in that posture. Far stronger than mine, I feared.

'You must not make it harder for me than it is,' I said as I raised my chin.

'It is my intent to make it impossible for you!' Yesterday his anger had been cold with shock: today it had the heat of a sleepless night behind it. And I braced myself. 'I will not go. I will not run off to Wales like a whipped cur. Neither will I let you make a martyr of me, or of yourself, for that matter. Are we made to live apart? I love you. God help me, I love you in all ways known to man and angels.'

'Owen—' All my carefully built ramparts were crumbling under the onslaught.

'You are my soul, Katherine. And I defy you to tell me that

your feelings for me have died. Unless you have indeed suffered an aversion to me. Have you? For that is the only reason that would drive me from your door. Is that true?'

'No.'

Owen drove on. 'Do we sacrifice everything that binds us, for the sake of what might—or might not—happen?'

'I cannot bear that you should die because of me. I will willingly bear the pain of our parting if—'

'But I will not. Better to live a day with you, dear heart, than a lifetime with the breadth of the country separating us.'

Dear heart. His voice might lash at me, but the endearment undermined me completely and I covered my face with my hands, for all my carefully reasoned argument lay in pieces at my feet. Then he was there, in front of me, holding my wrists.

'Don't weep, my dear love.'

'I am not weeping. I vowed I would not.' I looked up, dry-eyed, furious that he could reach me so easily. 'Why will you not see the sense of us living apart?'

'There is no sense. Are we not two halves of one entity? You might be prepared to spend your life in abject regret, but I will not.' He placed a fierce kiss on my brow. 'Hear me, Katherine. I will not live a day apart from you or from my sons.'

My hands, clenching into fists, beat in despair on his chest. Without any noticeable effect. Then all it took was the warm enclosing of his hands around mine, the smoothing out of my fingers within his clasp, and I was still. I knew I had lost.

'I am not the enemy here, Katherine.'

'I know.'

'You will not bar your door to me again.'

I felt my skin flush in shame at what I had done. 'I am so sorry, Owen.'

'There is no need. I understand.' And I was drawn into his arms. The anger had gone, and the tenderness had returned, to soothe and restore. 'You were faced with something too great for you to bear alone, and I should have seen it coming.' His lips were warm on my face. 'Together we will face it. Together we will rejoice at our fortitude.'

Owen took me to bed, unpinning my carefully pinned hair, removing the girdle and jewelled chain, casting the embroidered sleeves to the floor. Considerate of my state, he allowed me my shift, holding my body close. This was no time for passion but for a renewal of a closeness that was more of mind and soul than of body. It was healing, of a wound of my making, and in that healing I had no regrets. Whispered words, tender kisses, heartfelt promises, all made me see that my decision had been untenable. I was not made to live apart from Owen. We slept in each other's arms.

Then, as the afternoon moved on into evening, I awoke and lay to take cognisance of the serenity on my lover's face. The softly moulded mouth, the relaxed planes of cheek and brow, the untidy fall of black hair. Yet I did not think that he was in any manner serene when I noticed that even in sleep a groove was dug between his brows.

We had solved nothing, except that we could not be separated. Owen had decreed that we could not with a fervency that defied disobedience. How willingly I handed over my will to him because, in the end, it was too monstrous to contemplate. I smiled. Until a little cloud passed over the sun, and I shuddered at the brush of shadow over my skin, but when I looked up through the window I could see no cloud. Perhaps nothing more than a flight of doves from the dovecote beyond the wall. Shaking my head, I leaned over Owen and kissed his brow.

And as I did so, a wave of pure, bright anger swept through me, scouring away every doubt that had led me to sever our union. I had been wrong. We could overcome this together. And, driven by a conviction so urgent that my head was light with it, I made a silent promise. I would fight. I would fight and I would not rest until Owen and my children were free of the stigma brought by their Welsh blood, and free of Gloucester's long arm. I would restore Owen's pride and rank before the law, and I would destroy Gloucester's power to harm him without redress.

I would not rest until it was done. And I had a thought on how it might be accomplished by a determined woman and a clever man, if the woman could be persuasive enough. Why had I thought that the only solution was to admit defeat and send my love away? I would never do that again.

Shouts from the courtyard rising sharply to infiltrate my room, Owen opened his eyes. And smiled ruefully at me.

'I think neither of us slept last night.' And when I shook my head he added, rubbing my brow with his thumb, 'You look thoughtful.' He grinned. 'It is always a danger sign when a woman looks thoughtful.'

What a measureless thing it was to me to see him smile again. 'Perhaps I am.' I turned my face into his hair so that he might not see my expression. 'I am content. I am beyond happiness. And I have just made the most important decision of my life.'

'As long as it does not entail you living in Hertford and me in Wales,' he growled, his mouth against my throat.

'No,' I said softly. 'Not that. I was wrong. I cannot live apart from you.'

My mind shrank from what it had decided. My heart trembled with it. But I must do it, and Owen must be at my side when I did.

Since Owen's obstinacy in matters appertaining to his Welsh heritage and his masculine pride could not be shifted, I needed information. Where best to get it? I considered travelling to pay a much-delayed visit to Madam Joanna at Havering-atte-Bower but my pregnancy was progressing apace. Neither did I think she would have the knowledge I needed to draw on. So who would know? Lord John would, of course, but he was, as far as I knew, still in France. That left Warwick.

I sent a courier to ask him to come to Hertford when he next rode north. I used no pretext, merely that there was a matter of some importance to me that I must discuss.

'You look as if life at Hertford suits you,' Warwick observed, saluting my hand and my cheek, when he arrived within the week and I caught a private moment with him.

'It might if Owen were not threatened.'

'Threatened?'

'There have been attacks. But it is my intent to put a stop to them. Before Owen arrives, Richard, I need you to tell me what you know about two men. Their names are Llewellyn the Great. And Owain Glyn Dwr.' I mangled them beautifully.

Warwick's brows twitched together. 'Who?'

I tried again and we made progress.

'Should you not ask your husband? Since they are Welsh?'

'But my husband will not talk about them, even under strong persuasion. And you, dear Richard, will.'

It was a thoroughly illuminating half-hour.

'And how is Young Henry?' I asked, my inquisitiveness finally slaked.

'Driving his tutor to tear out his hair,' Warwick observed. 'He has developed a keen sense of his own importance since he acquired two crowns.' He eyed me quizzically. 'Does your husband know what you are about?'

'No.'

'It may be that he will object.'

I was sure that he would, but I would not allow that to

stop me. 'I don't think he will be in a position to do so,' I replied, with more confidence than I felt. I had the information I needed, and now that I had it, I knew that I must use it to right a wrong. I was determined on it.

'I wish to address the Council,' I told Warwick. 'I would like to think I had your support, Richard.' I would call in all old friendships. 'I would like to think that you would give me a hearing, even when Gloucester refuses.'

'Tell me what you have in mind,' he invited.

All my life I had been shifted here, made to hop there, allowed—or forced—to linger in this place rather than that one. I had been raised to expect nothing else, neither had I desired it in my girlhood days, expecting to live out my life in the glory of King Henry's love, surrounded by our children. Maturity and disappointment had brought me foresight. Now this late-flowering love with Owen Tudor had brought me a single-minded sense of purpose, which the threats against his life had honed into a blade of steel.

Despite my increasing clumsiness, I was driven with an energy that shook me to the core. It sang in my blood, the righteous justice of it, and I knew what it was I must set out to accomplish. I would do it for Owen, for my children. What was I not capable of, with Owen at my side?

'I am going to Westminster,' I said, easing myself into a chair in the parlour where Owen sat with a pile of financial ledgers before him.

Owen's response was succinct, after he had clapped his pen onto the table in disbelief. 'You will not. I'll tie you to your chair if I have to.' We were still ensconced at Hertford. I swear his denial could be heard all the way to the stables. 'Look at you. You are within a month of the child being delivered, and you would go off to Westminster on some wild-goose chase. Have you no sense?'

'No wild goose, Owen.' I smiled fondly at the stunned expression that darkened his eyes to black and sharpened the line of his jaw. 'Only the future of a stubborn Welshman and the future of our children. I want my sons to have the right to carry a sword. And any daughter of ours too, if she is of a mind to do it.'

'Your foolishness does not persuade me one inch,' he replied, entirely unmoved. 'Surely you can see it's dangerous for you to travel at this time.'

Which I wafted aside with a list of figures from one of the rent rolls, continuing to develop my argument, which I knew was unexceptionable. If only I could persuade this difficult, argumentative man—whom I loved more than was good for me—to accept.

'I have no objection, my love, to our children having your Welsh blood. But what I will not do is sit back and allow the law to make examples of them. This unborn child is the best argument we've got.' I spread my fingers over the formidable swell of my houppelande. 'The greater my belly, the more persuasive I can be.'

'You'll have to be carried into the Council Chamber at this rate.' I was pleased to see that he had calmed a little.

'I will not. I will walk. You will walk with me. And we take the children with us.'

'Why in God's name would you drag them all the way to Westminster?' The volume climbed again.

'Because I wish it.'

'I forbid it, Katherine.'

I loved him for it. 'But I insist, Owen. Listen to me. I want this child to be born to a man who is free to act as he wishes. To carry a weapon. To have his birth recognised. To own land on this side of this remarkable Offa's Dyke.' I ignored the gleam of Owen's eye at my reference to this inexplicable place that seemed to mean so much to him.

'They must be recognised as English, before the law. I will go to the Royal Council and get it. And,' I added, placing my hand on his, 'I go with or without you.'

He didn't believe me for a minute, of course.

'Not without me.' He scowled at me. 'Neither will I stand silent this time.'

'Neither will I ask it of you. It's time they gave you the status due to you as my husband. Since we've been wed more than two years now, and they've found no cause to part us, then they must accept the rightness of it. How ridiculous that the Dowager Queen is wed to a man against whom the law discriminates!'

His scowl did not abate, but at least he thought about it, his fingers shredding his quill.

'Are you sure about this?'

'As sure as I have ever been in my whole life.' The child kicked lustily beneath my hand. 'This child will be born to a free man. You will have redress before the law for any action taken against you. You will be English in all but name. And I will argue no more about it.'

'Yes, Your Majesty.' The scowl vanished into a twist of a smile.

'Are you mocking me?'

'Yes.'

'You won't in a minute, when I tell you what I need you to do.'

He eyed me speculatively. Since my attempt to banish him to the fastness of Wales, he had been wary. 'And what would that be?'

'I want to talk to you about Llewellyn the Great.' I was becoming proud of my pronunciation.

'You know I will not.' The smile fled again.

I leaned to kiss his cheek. 'But you must.'

'It will serve no purpose to resurrect memories of the Welsh spilling English blood.'

The ruined quill snapped in his fingers. I ignored it. And the tightness of his mouth. Instead I stood and moved towards the door.

'Is our love dead after all, if my kisses cannot soften you?' I looked back over my shoulder, unforgivably arch.

'Leave it be, Katherine.'

I simply raised my brows.

Owen stood. 'Will you give me no peace?' Relenting at last and wrapping his arms around me as well as he was able, he planted a kiss on the soft spot below my ear. 'And, no, our love is not dead.'

Which I knew anyway. But after Owen had proved to my satisfaction that his love for me was as intense and powerful as it had ever been, I nudged him.

'Here we have pen—or what is left of one—and parchment. And here is Father Benedict, come to act as scribe.'

It was a risky plan—for me, for my unborn child, for Owen to put himself so firmly in the public eye when we had spent our energies since our forbidden marriage into preserving anonymity. But I got my way. A woman in an advanced stage of pregnancy could, I found, be very persuasive. And so, once again, after a brief diversion to visit Young Henry, I addressed the august gathering of the Royal Council in the magnificent surroundings of Westminster.

'We have requested this interview, my lords,' I announced, 'to put right a great wrong.'

On my right Owen stood, hat and gloves in hand, all emotion tight reined. Father Benedict trembled on my left, clutching the document. The King's Council regarded us with a flat stare, and I shivered.

It was little different from when we had last stood there: the same faces, some with signs of advancing age but much the same, like viewing a tapestry, well known but faded with time and ravages of the sun. Gloucester, Warwick, a clutch of bishops. They were thoughtful of my condition, and this time I took the stool offered. My child was too near its time for me to make a gesture by standing throughout. Neither was I allowed much choice in the matter. Now that I had announced our purpose for being there, Owen's hand was heavy on my shoulder.

'I will make the case, Katherine, because it is my honour that is at stake,' he had insisted again, at the very door to the chamber.

'I know—'

'No, you don't. You should not even be here.'

'We'll not argue through that again.'

'No, we won't, but you'll do as you're told.'

So I sat as Owen bearded the dragon in its den. Standing tall and straight, his shoulders braced, the chain he wore not one of servitude but of status; the sapphires, which gleamed with sullen power, were the size and hue of ripe sloes. Owen had sneered at my intent, but I would spare no expense, and he wore it with panache as he allowed his considering gaze to travel over the ranks who held his future in their hands. What was going on behind that superbly disciplined facade? I wondered. Would he be able to impress and persuade them against their better judgement? He looked magnificent. All I could do was listen, and pray.

Then he began. His voice was quiet and respectful but confident in its presentation. Our planning had been extraordinarily thorough.

'We came here two years ago, my lords, at your request, when we provided proof that Queen Katherine and I were legally wed. You have seen the evidence. We have two children legally born, under the powerful protection of the Church.' He bowed towards Bishops FitzHugh and Morgan. 'The birth of our third child is imminent. Yet because of my Welsh ancestry and my people's demand for autonomy under Owain Glyn Dwr, I am not a free man. I ask for a ruling and a judgement from you.

'Are the heirs of my body also to face the same discrimination? Would you condemn the children of the Queen Dowager to penalties before the law, as descendents of a man who is proud of his Welsh blood? I say this, my lords. I say that, for the dignity of Queen Katherine and her children, I should be granted the rights and freedoms enjoyed by every Englishman here in this chamber.'

As he took a breath, I surveyed the faces. They were listening. But that did not mean that they would concur. Everything hung on the outcome. The weaving of the strands of our future together lay in the balance. Rejection, and we would always live with the fear of attack and betrayal. Of untimely death. Success and—

I would not think of it. I reached out to Owen with my thoughts, opening my mind with all its love and encouragement, and when he tensed a little then glanced in my direction, I knew that he sensed it.

'It is not dignified that the Queen Dowager be wed to a man who is condemned to live under the force of penal statute, for a crime that he has not committed. That her sons, the brothers of the King of England, must accept that their father is subject to the law as an enemy of the state. I have committed no crime. I have done no wrong. I have served in Sir Walter Hungerford's household, under our valorous King Henry in France. Yet still I am punished for a rebellion in which I played no part.'

Gloucester, predictably, stood.

'Are you expecting us to believe that you would not have backed Glyn Dwr's rising, and wielded a sword against us?'

I held my breath. It was a moot point and we had seen it coming. There was a flash of temper in Owen's eyes.

Don't! Don't retaliate!

It was quickly masked, and I exhaled softly. He would not be shaken from his purpose.

'No, my lord. I would not have you believe that. I expect, if I had been of an age to fight and hot-headed enough, I would have marched with Glyn Dwr against English forces. But times have changed. The Welsh are at peace. I have a wife and young family to consider. I am no danger to England. Would my wife as Queen Dowager have wed me if I intended to plot and rebel against her son, the Young King? I think she would not. Any man here who would argue the point does not appreciate the utmost respect and loyalty that Queen Katherine maintains towards this kingdom not of her birth.'

A waiting silence fell on the chamber, so strong that it deafened the clamour in my own head. This was for me to fill. From where I sat, I dropped my own words into it.

'I consider, my lords, that my husband should have the right to own land. And also to own weapons—as does any other man in this kingdom—to protect his family from those who would break the law and attack us. For you should know that twice in recent weeks we have come under duress from armed men. Twice his life has been put at risk.'

'No!' Gloucester's expression was inimical.

'It is a point to consider.' In comparison Warwick was courteously bland. 'But some would say that, even if we are willing to discuss the rescinding of the law in this particular case, it is not appropriate for us to single out this man for so great an honour. A man of less than noble birth—'

It was beautifully done. I thanked Richard with all my heart.

And Owen replied on cue, 'If my birth is something that you cavil at, my lords—'

'Your birth, by God.' Gloucester sprawled in his chair again, glowering across at Warwick, who stared back complacently. How I despised his ill-judged disdain against a man of whom he knew nothing. 'The Queen Dowager's dignity. Have we not heard enough, my lords? What dignity did she show when she chose to marry a man no better than a servant from her own household?'

'It is true I was a servant in the lady's household,' Owen replied evenly. 'It is no secret. But as for my birth, it is as good as any man's here.' He paused a little, before addressing Gloucester directly. 'Even yours, my lord.'

'Have you gone mad?' Gloucester responded, leaning forward, hand fisted on his knee.

'No, my lord, I am not. My descent is a long and honourable one. And I have proof.'

He gestured to Father Benedict, who might be trembling like a reed in a gale but who walked forward to place his document in Gloucester's hands.

'As you can trace, my lords,' Owen advised, while Gloucester unrolled it but barely scanned the contents, 'my family is high enough to be connected with Owain Glyn Dwr himself. Glyn Dwr was first cousin to my own father, Maredudd ap Tudur.'

'It is no advantage to be linked with a traitor to the English Crown,' Gloucester replied.

'All Welshmen have fought for their freedom through the ages,' Owen observed carefully. 'But my ancestry cannot be questioned. My grandmother Margaret came of direct line of descent from Angharad, daughter of Llewellyn the Great, Prince of Gwynedd. His blood is in me, and in my children. I think there is no higher rank that any man could desire. I am honoured to call the Prince of Gwynedd my ancestor. He was defeated by King Edward the First of England but that does not detract from his birth or his legitimate wielding of power over the kingdom of Gwynedd.'

Would it work? Would the argument of Owen's descent sway them? Unable to remain still, I struggled to my feet to step to Owen's side, although I did not touch him. We would retain our dignity here.

Warwick, as if it were all new to him, twitched the scroll of genealogy from Gloucester's hand and observed, 'It is an impressive argument.'

'I wish to say one thing, my lords.'

I braced myself at a twinge of discomfort in my belly, but forced myself to speak calmly and surely of a matter I considered very pertinent.

'The King, whom I have visited, has no difficulty in recognising my sons as his brothers. They are with him now. He has been generous in his gifts to them.' My heart warmed as I recalled, only a few hours before, Young Henry, kneeling on the floor of his chamber, for once careless of his dignity, graciously donating the little silver ship, which no longer took his interest, to a loudly appreciative Edmund and Jasper.

'Will they, as sons of their father, continue to be punished as they grow to manhood?' I held my breath at another inconvenient knotting of my muscles and, abandoning my own dignity, gripped Owen's arm. 'Will the brothers of the King be held up before the law as less than English citizens? Will they find no protection from English law? This, my lord, will open them to persecution, as it has my husband, by those who would wish them ill.' I looked up at Owen. 'I cannot believe that such an injustice—such a ridiculous travesty—should be allowed to stand.'

We had said all we could.

'We will give our opinion.' Gloucester gave nothing away.

And how long would it take them? A lifetime? I did not think I could wait that long.

18

'WHERE DO WE go now?' I fretted, nerves jumping at every footfall, every shadow. 'I need to be here. I need to know what they are doing.'

We were standing outside the Council Chamber, in the courtyard that seemed to attract every blast of cold air. I shivered, thinking that, despite my reluctance, we would have to go to my old rooms in Westminster after all. Edmund was almost asleep on his feet. Jasper had already succumbed in Joan Asteley's arms, head heavy on her shoulder. I smoothed Edmund's hair as he clung to my hand.

'It's wicked,' Alice muttered, as anxious as I, 'that a good man's freedom should be so circumscribed. I say we should go.' I could feel her eyes on my face. 'But we must find shelter soon.'

'And it won't make any difference to the Lords' decision-making whether we are here or not.' On the surface Owen was far more sanguine than I as he lifted Edmund up into his arms. 'They'll do what they will in their own good time, but you can't travel, Katherine. We stay at Westminster.' I did not think he was sanguine at all, simply more intent on soothing me. I would not be soothed, for my mind was full of Gloucester's outrage. At every stir in the icy air I expected to see a group of armed men in Gloucester's livery appear, sent to lay hands on Owen with some trumped-up charge that would put him in a cell.

The decision was taken out of our hands.

'Owen!' I clutched his arm, clinging with one hand as I spread the other across my belly. I felt him stiffen, brace himself against my weight, but before he could ask me if I was in pain, my waters broke, splattering on the paving. I clutched harder as the familiar pains gripped me, almost forcing me to my knees.

Passing Edmund to Alice, Owen was supporting me. 'Well, *fy nghariad*. It's decided. We're staying at Westminster.' His arm was around my waist, holding me firmly against him. When I tried to concentrate on his face it was stern and set, but he managed not to say 'I told you so'. 'We'll make use of the chambers you used to occupy.'

'Too far,' I gasped, the wave of pain refusing to release me. I knew this rabbit warren of a palace well, knew how long it would take us to reach my accommodations. The pains ebbed, giving me respite, but I tensed for their renewed onset. Edmund and Jasper had taken their time in sliding into the world but now— Another wave gripped me. 'This child is in a hurry.'

Still holding Edmund, Alice was there, clasping my other hand, searching my face where perspiration was already gathering on temple and upper lip. I groaned as the familiar agony washed over me. 'She's right, sir. There's no time. Somewhere close.'

Owen held me upright with what might have been the ghost of a laugh. 'There is one possibility, which could solve all our problems. Can you walk?' When I nodded, with his arm clamped firmly around my waist he led me up steps, over cold paving, through one doorway after another until it seemed that I was surrounded by arches. When I looked up I could glimpse the early glimmer of stars in the winter sky but I was sheltered from the wind. Our slow footsteps echoed hollowly.

'Where are we?' The pain was intense again.

'The Abbey cloisters.' Owen settled me on the stone ledge that ran round the edge, where monks would sit to read and study. 'It may be the answer—even if it does put the fear of Almighty God into the holy brothers!' He turned to Father Benedict. 'Go and—' He saw the dazed look in my chaplain's eyes. 'I'll go myself. Wait here.' He pressed down on my shoulder, as if I could do any other.

'Don't go.' It was too much to let him out of my sight. What if Gloucester's men snatched him up and I did not know?

'I'll come to no harm.'

'How can you say that?' I panted.

'I have an idea. I don't know why I did not think of this earlier. Look after her,' he ordered Alice, and strode off.

'Where is he going?' I was beyond ideas, feeling panic rise as his footsteps faded into the distance. Suddenly, although I had Alice and Joan and Guille and even Father Benedict fussing in the background, I felt very alone.

'I don't know.' Alice patted my hand, helpless in this situation. 'Hold this child,' she ordered Father Benedict, handing Edmund over, and turned back to me. 'Don't fret. It will be some time yet.'

'I don't think so,' I cried out in renewed distress.

The clip of footsteps crept back into my consciousness as I clung hard to Alice's hands.

'Thank God,' Father Benedict muttered.

When I opened my eyes, there was Owen, flanked by two black-robed men. Old monks, dry as dust, cautious in their words, but compassionate in their way as they peered at me in the light of a lantern that one carried and held above my head.

'My lady. You need our charity.'

'This is Brother Michael,' Owen murmured, touching his fingers to my cheek, bringing me back to reality.

The all-consuming pain receded momentarily. 'I do indeed, Brother Michael. I think I am in desperate need unless I wish this child to be born here in your cloister.'

'We can help. If you will follow me.'

But I saw Owen grip Brother Michael's arm. 'I need more than that, Brother Michael. I need to claim sanctuary. For me and for my family.'

The old eyes travelled over us. 'Are you in danger, sir?'

'It may be so.'

He smiled and nodded his head. 'Then you are safe in God's house. We will give you and your people sanctuary. Bring the lady.'

'Thank God!' Alice sighed.

I was beyond relief.

'Can you walk?' Owen asked again.

'No.' The pains were almost constant.

Owen swept me up into his arms and carried me after the two Benedictine brothers, eventually, when I thought I could no longer stop myself from screaming, entering into a long room lined with beds, some flat and empty, others occupied by the ancient and infirm. The infirmary, I acknowledged hazily. The infirmary of the monks of Westminster Abbey. Ignoring this strange influx of visitors, busy with their own tasks, were a handful of black-robed Benedictines and lay brothers who nursed the sick and needy.

'In here.' Brother Michael gestured. 'We will pray to St Catherine for you and the child.'

'And I will call her Catherine.'

I was carried into a small chamber, spare and narrow, furnished with one bed and a crucifix on the wall. Perhaps, I thought with a tremor beneath my heart, it was used for the dying. Owen did not hesitate. Shouldering his way in, he sat me on the edge of the bed.

'We'll put the boys to bed in the infirmary, my lady,' Joan said.

I was past caring. The pangs of imminent childbirth were wrenching me asunder. Shadows closed around me as my belly was riven with hot pain, as if talons gripped me.

'You should not be here, sir,' I heard Alice admonishing Owen as she and Guille set themselves to the difficult task, given the constraints of space, of removing my outer garments.

'Tell her that,' Owen muttered. I was clutching his arm, nails digging through his sleeve as the pain seared through me. My whole world was nothing more than this room and the monster that had me in its maw.

'Holy Mother, save me,' I whispered.

'Amen to that,' Alice added.

It was a memorable hour. No seemly seclusion. No community of women to give support and succour. No luxurious cushioning against the outside world with tapestries and fine linen and warm water. Just a bare room without heat, the narrowest of beds and the distant monkish voices raised to sing the office of Compline. Just an hour of agonising travail, then a squalling child, red-faced and vigorous, was delivered onto the coarse linen, Owen catching the baby as it slithered from my body.

'Not Catherine,' he said as he placed the mewling child in my arms.

'Another son.' I looked down, bewildered at the speed of it all, at the furious face with its no longer surprising thatch of black hair.

And then we were surrounded, the old monks drawn from their beds in the infirmary by the new life in their midst and the now dying whimpers as my child slept. There they stood, black cowled around my bed, giving me their silent blessing.

'Give him to us,' one said, his seamed cheeks wet with tears. 'He's ours, I reckon. I don't recall ever having a child born here before. We'll make a fine monk of him, won't we?' He looked round his fellow brethren, who nodded solemnly. 'Has the little one a name?'

'Owen,' I said. 'He is called Owen.'

And I fell into exhausted sleep. At least it had taken my mind off my worries over Gloucester and the Council.

It was a strange time, suspended between the reality of my new son, the incongruous setting of sanctuary that had been forced upon us, all overlaid with the constant fear that Glouces-ter might still be biding his time. I stayed for two days in my makeshift chamber in the infirmary before being allowed to walk slowly round the cloisters when the monks were engaged elsewhere, granting my newly extended household and myself some privacy. I would have travelled home sooner, but Owen and Alice were at one and I bowed before their joint will. The Council was ominously silent. As long as we stayed as guests of the monks, we were safe.

But we could not remain there for ever. What would it matter if the Council did not judge in our favour? I tossed the thoughts, catching them as they spun and returned in a con-stant circling. It would not change the pattern of my life with Owen. We would live out our days far from policies and laws and Gloucester's hostility. It could not come between us. Our love was strong, stronger than any outside influence.

Now that we had laid our case before the Council, surely not even Gloucester would dare to impugn justice. Surely not?

'They will decide in their own good time,' the Prior said, come to admire the babe. 'And if they decide against you, it is the will of God.' He made the sign of the cross on my infant's forehead.

'The will of Gloucester,' I responded bitterly, then regretted my lack of courtesy to this kind man.

He bowed. 'And sometimes they are not the same,' he conceded.

After two days I had had enough of the smothering kindness and the Council's continuing silence. I wanted to go home, urgently, and Owen relented. He knew as well as I that we had used all the weapons in our armoury, so we would go home. As our coffers were packed, Alice took my swaddled baby into the infirmary, where the old monks bade him a final farewell. They gave him a blanket woven of the finest wool.

'Are we ready?' Owen asked, returning from overseeing that our carriages and horses were made ready, impatience a shimmer around him. This was the moment I had been waiting for, its outcome uncertain.

'Not quite.'

One coffer still stood, unpacked, at my feet. Stooping, I lifted out an item wrapped in cloth. At Hertford, adopting a degree of guile, I had taken it from Owen's personal chest, without his knowledge, without his permission and with no conscience at all. It had travelled to Westminster, deep in one of my own chests: it would not, if I had my way, travel back again in the same manner, no matter what decision the Council saw fit to make.

And Owen knew what it was, still draped as it was, the moment I held it out. His eyes darkened, his face taking on the rigidity of a mask, and I read there the pride of ownership, rapidly displaced by rejection in the name of what he saw as good sense. Would he listen to me? Would he listen to the voice of inheritance and family honour that I was sure beat in his mind, against every denial he made?

I held it out like a holy offering.

He did not take it. 'Where did you get that?' he demanded.

'From our chamber at Hertford.'

'And you brought it with you?'

'Yes.'

Still I held it out, offering it on the palms of my hands.

'Wear it,' I said.

I knew his argument against it. I knew his pride in Llewellyn, his magnificent ancestor, just as I understood that, discriminated against by law and rank, he felt himself a man without honour, reluctant to don the weapon of so great a man. But I also knew the fire that burned in his blood.

'I care not what the Council says,' I told him. 'We did what we could. We know your lineage to be as noble as that of any one of those men sitting in judgement against you. You have nothing to prove to me. Wear it, because it belonged to a great warrior and does not deserve to be packed away in a chest at Hertford. Wear it for me, because without it you put yourself into danger. I cannot bear that, even now, Gloucester might be sending men against you, and you not be armed.'

How long I seemed to wait. The low winter sun emerged, slanting coldly through the high windows, then dipped behind a cloud again. I let the cloth slip partially from the blade so that its lethal edges glowered.

'Wear it, Owen.' I put my whole heart into that plea. 'Wear it for me because I cannot live with fear that you cannot defend yourself.'

And at last he took it from me, allowed the cloth to slip wholly to the floor. He held the sword up so that the pale sunshine, well timed in its reappearance, glimmered along its length and played on the furled wings of the dragon hilt. Running his hand reverently along the chased blade, he pressed his lips to the cross of the hilt.

'I have brought the sword belt too.' I smiled. 'You have no excuse, you know. You have a new son. You cannot lay yourself open to Gloucester's vengeance. You can't refuse me.'

'No,' he said softly. 'No, I cannot.'

And taking it, Owen strapped the belt around his hips.

Light-headed with relief but still hesitant, I touched his arm. 'I thought you would refuse.'

His gaze lifted to mine. I could not mistake the emotion in the glitter of defiance. 'I will not refuse,' he said. 'As you say—I have a new son to protect. And a wife who is very precious to me.' And he gently wiped my tears away with the pad of his thumb. 'I'll fight against Gloucester and the whole world to protect you.'

My tears became a torrent. The monks, a silent audience through all of this, not realising the drama of it, nodded and smiled.

'We have enjoyed your stay, with the children.'

'We have not seen such events since the celebrations for Agincourt.'

'And a new birth.'

'Thank you,' I said to them, holding out my hands to them, thinking that they might enjoy the return to their previous tranquillity. Edmund and Jasper had filled the rooms with their laughter. And to Owen I said, 'Now I am ready. Now we will go. And I think I will never return here.'

'Then it is good that I have caught you—'

I turned at the brisk voice, dread flooding back.

'No!'

Was this what I had feared, an escort of armed men, a document of intent, some makeshift infringement of the law that Owen could not answer? Owen had already spun round, shoulders braced, his hand sliding to his sword hilt as he stepped by instinct to stand between me and any danger. I heard the rasp of the steel as he loosed it in its scabbard in the quiet room, then I laughed on a little sigh for our fears were unnecessary. It was Warwick, and there was no force at his back. No Gloucester, crowing with sour delight.

'I see you've been busy here.' He grinned as he surveyed Alice with our new son, but his attention was on Owen. 'I have something for you, Tudor.' But his eye had followed Owen's instinctive movement. 'It seems my news is too late,' he added. 'You have pre-empted the issue.' In his right hand he held a sword with a fine jewelled hilt. 'I brought this for you. You have the right to it.'

'They have decided?' But Owen knew the answer, and I saw the light grow in his eye.

'In their wisdom,' Warwick replied dryly. 'It should have been done long ago, if they had had any compassion for you.'

I closed my eyes. 'Thank God.' Then opened them as Warwick's words sank in. 'Are you certain about this?' I asked, needing confirmation to destroy the anxiety that had lived with me for so long.

'Your argument drove it home. The Council has instructed the next Parliament—a matter of weeks now—to recognise your rights, Tudor, and your status as an Englishman.' Warwick produced a scroll from his tunic with the flourish of a royal herald. 'This is more important than the sword. Here are your letters of denizenship.'

'So I have you to thank for it?' Owen asked.

'A little. And others. You have friends at Court, however difficult it might be sometimes to believe.'

They clasped hands, and Owen took the gift from Warwick, tucking the document into the coffer at our feet. His features might be controlled but I saw the strain, the struggle to command every response against the news that had stunned him to the core.

I placed my hand on his arm. 'We have done it.'

'So we have.' Owen covered my fingers with his own, his eyes searching my face. 'I would not have done it if it had not been for you.'

I shook my head in denial. To shield me from a renewed onset of emotion, Owen addressed Warwick. 'My thanks for the sword, my lord. Once I was forbidden to own one. Now I have a surfeit.'

'Give it to your son.' Warwick nodded to indicate Edmund, who had escaped supervision to come and investigate the delay.

'He is young yet.' Owen hoisted him into his arms.

'But one day...' Warwick smoothed the untidy thicket of my son's hair. 'Edmund Tudor. Who knows what you will be?'

Edmund grasped the costly jewelled hilt, making the stones glint and catching my attention. My little son, the high blood of both France and Wales running strong in his veins. A little presentiment touched me, but not of fear, rather one of power, of rank. The gems glittered in my son's clasp, and my son was a man with fire in his eye and determination in the set of his mouth. And then the moment was gone. He was a child again, and a weary one, close to fretting.

'You are a free man, Edmund Tudor,' I heard Warwick say. 'Your father's heir. Free to own land and bear arms. And to marry as you choose.'

'I want a horse,' Edmund announced, unimpressed.

Owen looked across at me and smiled. What would be the future for our son, with the law of England on his side and the King, his half-brother, well disposed towards him? I wept again in a flood of emotion, part joy, part exhaustion—tears seemed so close in my weariness—prompting the Benedictine brothers to pat my shoulder and offer me a linen sheet to dry my cheeks.

'Don't forget. The little lad. We'll make a fine monk of him.'

And I laughed through my tears. 'I'll send him to you. Unless he has the inclination to be a military man, I will send him to you when he is grown.'

I took the baby in my arms, smiling round at them. Then I looked at Owen, who was looking at me.

'Let us go home, my husband.'

'It is my wish, *annwyl*.'

Owen was restless, a difficult disquiet that took hold of him. I saw it, building day after day, even though he tried for my sake to hide it. Were we not happy? Had we not made for ourselves the life we wished for, when to spend time in each other's company was ultimate fulfilment, to be apart bleak wilderness?

The death of my mother, Queen Isabeau, touched us not at all, and although we mourned the passing of Lord John with real grief for so great a man, the happenings in London and in France no longer had any bearing on our tranquil existence. But I saw Owen's frustrations at the end of the day, when we sat alone in our private chamber or relaxed with company after a more formal meal, replete with food and wine, a minstrel singing languorously of times past.

Owen's gaze turned inward as the plangent notes and tales of heroes and battles wove their glamorous mystery in the chamber, and I knew he was thinking of the days when his forebears had had wealth and status and land. When glory had shone on them and they had fought and won.

Owen, although free, had nothing of his own.

The family lands in Wales had not been restored to him with his recognition under English law: how it rankled with

Owen that he had no property in his name, to administer and nurture. No house, no land, nothing to pass down to his heirs with hopes and pride for future generations. How degrading for a man of his birth. Neither was it a good thing for a man's esteem that he be dependent on his wife.

Oh, he masked it well. He was a master of dissimulation, born of the long years in servitude, but sometimes it rubbed him raw and his eyes were dark with a depth of yearning that I could not plumb.

'Tell me what eats away at you,' I begged.

'It is nothing, my love,' he invariably replied, the crease between his brows denying his reassurance. 'Unless you mean our second son's determination to throw himself under the hooves of every animal in the stables.'

And I smiled, because that was what he wanted me to do. Our son's obsession with horseflesh had its dangers.

'Or it may be that I regret my wife not having found the time to favour me with even one kiss this morning.'

So I kissed his mouth, because it pleased him and me.

I might lure him into my bed. I might put before him a plan to drain the lower terrace and build a new course of rooms at Hertford to improve the kitchens and buttery. He would always respond, but his heart was not in it. It was not his own.

Well, it could be put right. I should have seen to it years ago.

I summoned a man of law from Westminster, and consulted with him. And when he saw no difficulty, I had the necessary documents drawn up and delivered into Owen's hands. I made sure that I was there when they arrived and Owen opened the leather pouch. I watched his face as he read the first of them. As he looked up.

'Katherine?' His face was expressionless.

'These are for you,' I stated.

I was very uncertain. Would his independence be too great

to receive such a gift from a woman, a gift of such value? And yet it was given with all my heart. I wished I could read something in the sombreness of his eyes, in the firmness of mouth and jaw, but I could not, not even after four years of marriage.

'It is to commemorate the day that we were wed,' I said, as if it had been a light decision to make the gift. As if it were no more than a pair of gloves or a book of French poetry.

'It was a bold move, for you to wed me,' he said. His eyes were on mine, the first documents of ownership still in his hand, the rest yet to be removed from their pouch. 'To choose a penniless rebel was foolhardy, and yet you did it.' He smoothed the deed with his hand. 'Some would say that this is a bold move too.'

I still did not know if he would refuse or accept it with the grace it was given. 'I consider it a decision showing remarkable business acumen on my part,' I responded lightly.

And his mouth curved a little. 'I did not see business dealings as one of your strengths when I wed you, *annwyl*.'

'Neither did I.' I paused. 'But now I have considered. These are mine. It is my desire that you have them. They need a master to oversee them and ensure their good governance. It would please me.' I thumped my jewel casket down onto the table—for I had been engaged in selecting a chain of amethysts to wear with a new gown. 'Stop staring at me and put me out of my misery. Will you accept?'

'Yes. I will.' In the end there was no hesitation. 'Did you think me too arrogant?'

'It had crossed my mind—yes.'

'I'll not refuse so great a gift.' The smile widened, encompassing me in its warmth. 'I am honoured.'

And removing the companion documents, he sank to the settle to read through them all. The custody of all my dower

lands in Flintshire. I sat beside him. Waited until he had finished and replaced them in their pouch.

'Well?'

'I will administer them well.'

'I know you will.'

'Now I have a dowry to provide for a daughter. As well as
three fine sons.'

I had carried a girl. Tacinda. A Welsh child with a Welsh
name, all dark hair and dark eyes like Owen. Another confirmation of our love.

'You are a gracious and generous woman, Katherine.'

His kiss was all I could ask for.

I had another motive for giving Owen overlordship of my
Welsh dower lands. Our idyll was magnificent—but with a
lowering cloud of ominous destruction gathering force on my
horizon. Like a sweet peach, full of juice and perfume, but
with a grub at the heart that would bring rot and foul decay.
How fate laughs at us when we think we have grasped all the
happiness that life can offer us.

I was afflicted.

I denied my symptoms at first, hiding them as much from
myself as from Owen for they were fleeting moments, soon
passed, merely a growing unease, I told myself, brought on by
a dose of ill humours as winter approached with its cold grey
days and bitter winds. Had I not been so afflicted in the past?
I need not concern myself.

Some days, on waking, my mind scrabbled to grip the reality of where I was, what was expected of me. Some days
I found myself just sitting, unseeing, without thoughts, not
knowing how long I had been so engrossed in nothingness
except for the movement of sun and shadow on the floor.

I felt a tension tightening in my chest, like a fist drawing in the slack on a rope, until I feared for my breathing.

And then such feelings receded, my mind snapping back into the present, and I forgot that I had ever been troubled, except for the faint, familiar flutter of pain behind my eyes that laid its hand on me with more frequency. I forgot and pretended that nothing was amiss. Owen and I loved and rode and danced, enjoying the unfettered freedom that had become, miraculously, ours. Had I not experienced such symptoms in the days following Edmund's conception? Although I had been afraid then, fearing the worst, they had vanished. Would they not do so again?

Our children ran and thrived in the grass beside the river and I watched them.

But then the darkness closed in again. Minutes? Hours? How long it engulfed me I could not tell. I saw it approaching and, leaving my children in the care of Joan or Alice, I took to my room, my bed, pleading weariness or some female complaint as I had done once before to ensure no questions were asked. Only Guille was aware, and she kept her own counsel.

I managed it well.

And what was it that I hid? A space widening in my mind, a vast crater that filled to the brim with dark mist. I did not know what happened around me in those hours. It could be a black billowing cloud, all-encompassing, or a creeping dread, like river water rising, higher and higher, after a downpour. My hands and fingers no longer seemed to be mine. They did not obey my dictates. My lips felt like ice, clear speech beyond me. My servants, my family were as insubstantial as ghosts emerging from an impenetrable mist. I must have eaten, slept, dressed. Did I speak? Did I leave my room? I did not know.

Was Owen aware of my travails? He suspected, even though he was often away, busy now with his own affairs. How could he not know, when I became increasingly detached from him and our world? He said nothing, and neither did I, but I knew he watched me. And perhaps he told Guille to have a care for me, for she was never far from my side.

'Are you well?' he asked whenever we met. A harmless enquiry but I saw the concern in his sombre gaze.

I smiled at Owen and touched his hand, the mists quite gone. 'I am well, my dear love.'

When he took me to his bed, I forgot the whole world except for the loving, secret one we were able to create when I was in his arms. I denied my inner terrors, for what good would it do to bow my head before them? They would engulf me soon enough.

Alice knew, but apportioned the blame for my waywardness, my increased awkwardness to my pregnancy with Tacinda. When I dropped a precious drinking goblet, the painted shards of glass spreading over the floor, splinters lodging in my skirts and my shoes, she merely patted my hand and swept up the debris when I wept helplessly.

Four children in as many years, she lectured. Why was I surprised that sometimes I felt weary, my body not as strong as it might be, my reactions slow? She dosed me on her cure-all, wood betony, in all its forms—powdered root or a decoction of its pink flowers or mixed with pennyroyal in wine—until I could barely tolerate its bitter taste.

'It's good for you,' Alice lectured. 'For digestion. For every ache and pain under the sun. And for the falling sickness too.'

My minutes of dissociation concerned her, but it was not the falling sickness. I took the doses, and wished that wood betony might indeed cure all, but my mind went back to my father and his delusional existence. My father, who had sometimes recalled neither his own name nor the faces of his wife and children, who could be violent, running amok as he once

had with a lance, killing those unfortunates who had stood in
his way and tried to restrain him for his own good.

I tried to shut out the memories but I failed. They muscled
their way into my consciousness, forcing me to acknowledge
my father's constant attendants, more gaolers than servants.
His guards: to protect him and others from him, as he became more and more divorced from reality and in the end
had to be restrained.

'Drink this,' Alice insisted. And I did. I clutched at every
hope.

Sometimes my father had believed that his body was constructed of glass that would shatter if he was touched. Then he
would withdraw into the corner of the room, holding everyone at bay with pitiful cries. Was that the future for me? Was
it possible for the miraculous wood betony to cure that? I did
want to think so. And I prayed that the frailty of my father's
stricken mind would not come upon me.

I did not tell Owen the full substance of my fears. Did he
guess? I could not tell. He permitted me my times alone, treating me with great care. Perhaps he hid his own dread—and
I allowed him to do so because if he admitted to it, then it
would be all too real.

And what when I could pretend no longer? I considered it
as I lay, my cheek in the soft hollow below Owen's shoulder,
while his chest rose and fell in sleep. The day would come
when I could dissemble no longer. What then?

I recalled my sister and I, mocking and fearing my father
in equal measure. Would my children mock me, fleeing from
me in terror?

God help me. I prayed that this madness would not come
to me.

EPILOGUE

THE DAY IS HERE.

I am well and lucid but I know it will not last. I *know* it, with every breath.

'We are pleased to see you restored, my lady,' my new steward says, the man who replaced Owen as Master of my much-reduced household. 'We have been concerned.'

My steward is perhaps less careful with his words than he might be, for no one else speaks of it, as if to ignore it will deny its existence, but I am grateful for his well-wishing. It reminds me that I am becoming an object of interest to those around me, and I vow that I will not be a burden. I will not be an embarrassment. I will not drag Owen to the depths of despair, where he cannot reach me, and I cannot reach him. It is time for me to take the step I have had in my mind for some months.

Owen reads it in my mind.

'Don't leave me, Katherine,' he whispers against my throat when we lie together on that final morning as the sun rises, as if he can read my intent. 'We have had so little time together. Six years out of a whole lifetime.'

'My love.' I kiss his lips. 'Enough time for me to bear you three fine sons.'

I catch my breath as I do not speak Tacinda's name. She died, leaving us within the first year of her fragile life. It is a pain in my heart that cannot be healed, but with my lover's arms around me I smile, my face turned into his hair. How handsome he is. How I love him. This man who has taught me what love can be like between a man and a woman who trust each other infinitely.

I run my hands softly over the fine bones of his face, smoothing the dark brows, combing my fingers through his magnificent hair. I trace the well-moulded lips, the flare of his straight nose; I press my mouth against his. I need to fix his beloved features in my mind so that they will not fade.

'Stay, Katherine. I will be with you.'

There is more urgency in his voice now, and his arms band tighter round me. So he knows.

'I am afraid,' I say.

'No need. I love you more than life. I'll let no harm come to you.'

'But you cannot stop it. How can you stand before the approaching storm and will it to disperse, my dear love? How can you scatter the winds that will destroy all we have together?'

'Stay with me,' he insists, lips warm and persuasive. 'With our children.'

And I allow myself, for that one brief day, to be persuaded. His love is as potent as strong wine. Of course he will keep me safe.

'I will stay,' I promise.

His mouth demands, his body possesses with all the old energy and he enfolds me in love.

'We will live for ever, Katherine. We will grow old and see our children grow strong and wed.' And then the softest of whispers. 'I cannot live without you.'

I hear the desperation in his voice.

'Or I you,' I reply. How will I exist without him?

Next morning he is gone, on some weighty errand of business, and my thoughts run clear again.

'I will return by noon,' he says, his hand on mine. 'I will return as soon as I can.'

'Yes,' I reply. I fashion a smile and return his clasp.

As soon as he is gone, my eyes blind with tears, I order up my litter. I will need no belongings so I pack nothing. While I have my wits, I will determine my future: I will impose no unnecessary grief on those I love. My mind skitters back to that terrible time when I took the decision to set Owen free because I could not contemplate the anguish of his death, only to return to him when we found a way out together, a solution that our minds could fathom and apply.

But now there is no solution for me. Madness strips away all solutions. Death cancels all loyalties. I know I must free Owen to live his own life without the burden of my slow disintegration. There is no going back for me this time.

And yet, when the litter arrives at the door, for a moment still I hesitate. Will this be the greatest mistake of my life? I feel well, strong, in control of my actions. Perhaps I am misled after all. I should dismiss the litter and wait at the door to welcome him home, take his hands and kiss his dear face.

How will you tolerate the pity in his eyes? How will you tolerate it when passion dies and he cares for you out of duty? When he sits beside your bed, rather than carrying you to his own, when you no longer even recognise him and he turns from you in grief that is too great to bear?

I dress as a widow in sombre state, my still golden hair hidden, my still beautiful face veiled. I leave no written note. What to say? He will know. We said all that was needed without words when his body loved mine and my responses were of my own volition. I will remember that final moment until I can remember no more.

One final task. I visit the nursery and kiss my children: Edmund and Jasper and Owen. They do not understand. I hold them close and kiss them.

'Be good. Be brave and strong. Obey your father and remember your mother.'

I touch Alice's hand. She is weeping.

I am ready.

I leave my ring and the dragon brooch on the coffer beside his bed. The ring he gave me when we flouted all law and decency and wed, the brooch I took when I first loved him. I leave them for him, and I step into my litter.

I stand at the door of the great Abbey at Bermondsey. How cold my hands are. The door swings open because they expect me—I have sent word. They will take me in for my own sake with as much compassion as my money can buy for me. I will bear Owen's final child here, in the care of the nuns.

I take one step forward.

If I go in, I will never step back into the world.

No, I cannot! Owen, my love, my love.

His promise, made to me in the chapel at Windsor, slams into my mind. *I will never allow us to be parted, this side of the grave.*

But it cannot be. My heart is breaking, my face is wet with tears that I cannot stop. Almost I step back, to be with him until I have no more breath in my body. Then my father stands before me. The capering halfwit, the vague, gibbering remnant of the king he had once been. The pain sets up a flutter in my head, behind my eyes. I know that soon it will become intense.

Goodbye, Owen. Goodbye. God keep you. Always know that I love you. Know that I have given you your freedom because I love you too much to tie you to a mindless ghost.

I take a breath.

One day I know that Owen and I will be reunited, in God's grace. There will be no more grief, no more tears to overshadow our love. It will last for all eternity.

I step over the threshold.

★ ★ ★ ★ ★

ACKNOWLEDGEMENTS

ALL MY THANKS to my agent, Jane Judd, whose support for me and the courageous women of the Middle Ages continues to be invaluable.

To Jenny Hutton and all the staff at MIRA, without whose guidance and commitment the real Katherine de Valois would never have emerged from the mists of the past.

To Helen Bowden and all at Orphans Press without whom my website would not exist, and who come to my rescue to create professional masterpieces out of my genealogy and maps.

AUTHOR'S NOTE

KATHERINE DE VALOIS is an enigma.

History books make little comment on her, the underlying thought being that there is very little to say, other than that she was daughter of Charles VI of France, wife of Henry V, and died at a comparatively early age, perhaps afflicted by the instability that affected her father. As Queen of England and Queen-Dowager, she played no role in English government and in fact very little in the raising of her son. The same could be said, of course, for many medieval women from aristocratic or royal families. Their main importance was as a marriageable commodity for the transference of property—'an animated title deed' in effect. Thus Henry's desire to marry Katherine.

Katherine de Valois merely fits into this pattern of medieval land transference, as a woman silent and generally unimpressive.

Nor have historians been complimentary to Katherine. We receive the notion of a young woman who was beautiful and gracious but lacking in more than basic intelligence and with a very limited education. The archetypal 'dumb blond' in fact, who had little to say and no opinion to give.

Was this all that could be said for Katherine?

Solid evidence for much of her life is lacking, but what it lacks in hard fact, it gains in rumour, myth and legend, particularly in her falling in love with Owen Tudor. The blatant romance of it has been open to wide speculation.

In writing *The Forbidden Queen* I have made use of the outline of Katherine's history as far as we know it. I have placed her firmly in the centre of English politics, as she undoubtedly was, making sense of what is not recorded. As for the romantic myths, I have made use of them, and make no excuses for doing so.

By the time I wrote my final sentence, I had decided that Katherine, rather than a rather dim but lovely creature, must have been a remarkable woman.

I am always delighted to keep in touch with my readers who are interested in my writing, both the process and the content. I enjoy receiving feedback and readers' thoughts and insights into my heroines.

You can keep up to date with events and signings on my website, and contact me through my website, www.anneobrienbooks.com, on my Facebook page, www.facebook.com/anneobrienbooks, or follow me on Twitter @anne_obrien.

I also have my own blog where I write about history in general, and what I am investigating in particular. Or anything historical that takes my interest...

www.anneobrienbooks.com/blog/2012/11/katherine-swynford/

DISCUSSION QUESTIONS

1. What do you think of Katherine? What appeals to you about her, and what doesn't?

2. Apart from Katherine, who is your favorite character in the book and why?

3. What influence did Katherine's childhood have on her as a young adult? To what extent do you consider our adult characters to be formed in these earliest years?

4. Katherine was described as 'tall, fair and beautiful.' Yet history has written her off as the archetypal 'dumb blond.' Do you, from the decisions she made and the way she responded to influences at the English court, think this does justice to Katherine?

5. After Henry's death, Katherine is left with no role to play, her part in the childhood of her son is restricted by those placed in authority over him and her. How does Katherine react? What would you have done in a similar situation?

6. Shakespeare wrote a wonderful love scene for Katherine with King Henry. Do you think that the evidence merits

it? If not, why did he do it? Can we forgive authors for writing their own version of history?

7. What is your feeling about Henry V's relationship with Katherine? Could she have done anything to improve it?

8. Katherine lived though a period of bloody warfare, and yet seems untouched by it. Can we excuse her for this, even when the war is between the two sides of her family, English against French? Would we expect her to have more sympathy with her disinherited brother?

9. Katherine's relationship with Edmund Beaufort was at best foolhardy, at worst politically dangerous. Can we have any compassion for her? Is her falling in love with Owen Tudor just as foolish and lacking in judgement?

10. Do you consider that Katherine deserved the punishment and restrictions inflicted on her by the Duke of Gloucester and the Royal Council?

11. In what manner does Katherine's character develop when she falls in love with Owen Tudor? Is she a better or worse person? Does your reaction to her change throughout the novel?

12. What do you think of Owen Tudor? Is he hero or villain? Did he fall irrevocably in love with Katherine, or merely use her to improve his own lot in life?

13. At the end, faced with impossible pressures, Katherine retires to Bermondsey Abbey. Could you have done the same in similar circumstances?